the deep end

KRISTEN ASHLEY

NEW YORK TIMES BESTSELLING AUTHOR

PRAISE FOR KRISTEN ASHLEY

"I adore Kristen Ashley's books. Her stories grab you by the throat from page one and . . . continue to dwell in your mind days after you've finished the story." —Maya Banks, *New York Times* bestselling author

"Kristen Ashley's books are addicting!" —Jill Shalvis, *New York Times* bestselling author

"Kristen Ashley captivates." —*Publishers Weekly*

"There is something about Ashley's books that I find crackalicious." —Kati Brown, *Dear Author*

"When you pick up an Ashley book, you know you're in for plenty of gut-punching emotion, elaborate family drama, and sizzling sex." —*RT Book Reviews*

"Reading a Kristen Ashley book, it's a journey, an adventure, a non-stop romantic thrill ride that is absolutely unparalleled in the romance world." —*Aestas Book Blog*

"Nobody starts a book off better than Kristen Ashley. And while I'm on it, nobody ends a book like Kristen Ashley, either. Precious. Poetic. Perfect." —*Maryse's Book Blog*

"Kristen Ashley books should really have a separate rating scale as they truly stand in a book universe of their own." —*Natasha is a Book Junkie*

"Any hopeless romantic would devour everything Kristen Ashley has to offer!" —*Fresh Fiction*

the
deep end

KRISTEN ASHLEY

ST. MARTIN'S GRIFFIN ✷ NEW YORK

THE DEEP END. Copyright © 2017 by Kristen Ashley. All rights reserved. Printed in the United States of America. For information, address St. Martin's Press, 175 Fifth Avenue, New York, N.Y. 10010.

www.stmartins.com

The Library of Congress Cataloging-in-Publication Data is available upon request.

ISBN 978-1-250-12111-0 (trade paperback)
ISBN 978-1-250-12112-7 (e-book)

Our books may be purchased in bulk for promotional, educational, or business use. Please contact your local bookseller or the Macmillan Corporate and Premium Sales Department at 1-800-221-7945, extension 5442, or by e-mail at MacmillanSpecialMarkets@macmillan.com.

First Edition: March 2017

10 9 8 7 6 5

This book is dedicated to Natasha Tomic,
due to her gracious input into the writing of it,
but mostly because of her friendship.

It's also dedicated to Joey W. Hill,
because she opened a cage I had long since been locked behind,
freeing me to fly,
and then she became my friend.

Acknowledgments

They say the only ones who like change are wet babies. That may be the truth, but the death of any creativity is not taking chances and doing something new.

Writing, for me, is a very singular process and one that I love. I fall into the world of a book and rail against any time I have to tear myself away to do something like eat or sleep. These worlds I build are precious to me, and the process of creating one through to unleashing it is a process I fall into with abandoned glee and mourn its loss when the time has come to type *The End*.

But even if my process of writing a book is a singular one, it's not singular in the slightest after that. I cage my beautiful bird and nurture it to the point I feel it's strong enough to fly on its own and then I set it free.

Doing something new, taking a chance—the kind of chance I took in stepping out of the genres I'd been reveling in and into the bold new world that is embodied by this book—is frightening. Even if I've been wanting to write a book like this for years (and years), the idea of writing it, and opening that cage and letting my beautiful bird free for all to see, was terrifying.

So I cannot say how meaningful it was when Natasha Tomic

offered to read this manuscript after its first draft. And I cannot say how magnificent it was to have someone with such intellect, grace, and thoughtfulness share her insights into this novel. And I cannot say how wonderful an experience it was to have someone who understands what I try to achieve with my writing feed into the process, making something usually singular into something collaborative in a way that I feel made this particular bird sing beautifully. And last, I cannot say what her support for this work meant in emboldening me to open that cage and let fly.

I would also like to thank Rose Hilliard for her excitement and enthusiasm for this book and the series it heralds. And as ever, many thanks and a great deal of love should be sent the way of Emily Sylvan Kim, my agent, who is the most graceful and diligent tag team partner a girl can have in her corner.

I very much hope my readers embrace the risks I took with this book, opening paths for me to continue to take chances and try new things when I let my beautiful birds fly free.

the
deep end

one

There Could Only Be One

AMÉLIE

Amélie sat in the semicircle booth at the back of the club, her lips to the rim of her champagne glass, her eyes to the bodies moving through the large space in front of her, her mind wondering when it had happened.

Seven years.

For seven years, as a day passed that she knew at the end of it she would be going to the club, she felt a mild but persistent anticipation.

This, as she'd make her preparations to go, she'd allow to build into excitement.

But right then, as Amélie took a sip of her drink, she observed the bodies shifting around her in the early throes of the game as if she were in a mall, seated on a bench, taking a break from shopping to sip coffee and regard the mundanity of human existence, which was curiously watchable at the same time it was unreservedly boring.

She put her drink down and continued to inspect the specimens on display.

This was not a difficult task. From the moment she'd sat down half an hour ago, they'd peacocked in front of her table, the males, definitely, and even some females.

She found this annoying. It smacked of desperation, something that most assuredly didn't stir her—unless she was the one who painstakingly roused that emotion through hours of play.

As for the females, that caused deeper irritation.

She'd been a member of the club for seven years. In that time, she'd seen many come and many go.

Amélie had remained.

She was known.

Even if the member was new, they could (and should) talk to their equals.

If they did, they'd get more than an earful.

Further, they could go to the small room behind the luxuriously welcoming and highly secured foyer. A room that held the computer (a computer that was attached to no network, not even a modem, thus it couldn't be hacked). A computer that would provide them the information they needed.

Of the many strict, absolutely unbreakable rules that one must sign upon membership being granted to the club known as the Bee's Honey, keeping this information up to date was one of them.

This also wasn't a difficult task.

If you were trained and experienced, a true member from skin to blood to bones to soul of the decadent world these fabulously appointed walls contained, none of the rules was a difficult task. They were as natural to you as the knowledge of how to pick up a fork. How to swallow a bite of food that had been chewed. Indeed, how to just *chew*.

Therefore, Amélie kept her information up to date, checking it on occasion out of respect for her culture as well as out of respect for Aryas, the club's owner and her dear friend.

Although up to date, that information gave very little away. If she were to interact with one in any meaningful way, her superior class of membership would share the essential traits in their nature with their inferiors in far more personal ways than a profile on a computer.

However, the fact that she did not—*ever*—choose female toys was part of her profile.

This information was provided with the aim to focus the hunt, offering details to the prey of who might wish to flush them out.

That was the kind way Amélie chose to look at it.

The purpose was more integral to the world in which they lived.

You did not waste the time or attention of your superior. It was disrespectful and it was intolerable.

Amélie assumed the females continued to strut with the dim and useless hope that she'd feel moved to teach them a lesson.

She never was.

If they listened to their peers, they would know this too.

When a lesson needed to be learned, Amélie was very willing to teach it.

But she had a certain way she preferred to play. She was known for that. *Well known* for that.

Kinder.

Gentler.

Not exactly a stickler for the rules, though there were some she enjoyed enforcing.

It was simply that Amélie liked to play.

She had no interest in slaves.

No, she was searching for toys.

This being well known, it continued the vicious cycle of why the females' maneuvers were so very irritating.

Or perhaps, she thought, taking another sip of her drink as she looked through a beautiful woman who had been a member for over a year (in other words, she should absolutely know better), the scene had become irritating.

In fact, the aimlessness with which the entirety of her life seemed to flow was irritating.

She felt her spine straighten as this thought broke through with naked honesty for the first time since the inklings of it started months ago (inklings that she'd denied).

A thought that shocked her.

But more, it dismayed her.

Regardless, sitting there experiencing those emotions, she could no longer deny the simple fact that that feeling had been creeping up for some time. And not just here at the Honey. Aryas owned seven exclusive clubs west of the Rockies. Amélie paid bundled membership, which meant she could go to any of them. As she traveled frequently, she availed herself of this.

And although she might find a toy to while away a few hours, as weeks turned to months and those months turned to *more* months, it was coming clear she was giving more than she was receiving. She was assuaging a need and not having her own needs assuaged.

No.

That wasn't it.

She wasn't finding what she needed.

In play *or* in life.

She licked her lips to hide discomfiture, something that was unusual for her, and looked down to her champagne glass, understanding with a strange sensation of a fist squeezing her heart, that wasn't it either.

She wasn't finding *who* she needed.

At the Honey and not at the Honey, Amélie was Mistress Amélie. A Dominatrix. A very good one. A respected one. A coveted one. Even a craved one. Her affectionate style of play, coupled with her experience and skill, made her highly sought after.

As that, she could easily find toys to play with.

She'd done that.

And she felt very real fear that she was becoming bored with it.

It wasn't the lifestyle that bored her, for Amélie didn't consider it a lifestyle. A choice. Something she could have or lose. Something she could move on from. Something she could grow out of. A curiosity she could satisfy and leave behind.

It was what she considered a *Life*style, capitalized with appropriate emphasis. As essential as oxygen. And if she were not to have it, she fancied it would feel like climbing nearly to the peak of Everest. Every next step a struggle. Every breath a blow, for you were doing what came naturally, but it didn't fully provide the essential element that would allow you to continue existing. Every second a mental battle as to what level of insanity you'd breached that you'd even consider going on.

The problem was, Amélie had been born with champagne tastes. Tastes bred imperatively through her line for generations as to weave right through her DNA.

There were many ways she could find toys: other clubs, ads, parties, conferences, personally hosted weekends.

The Honey, however, was the only place that truly offered champagne. Aryas had a certain philosophy that even if an individual had the means to be a member, this didn't mean they would be accepted. In fact, he gave "scholarships" to those in both membership classes who could in no way afford to be a member at regular rates, but who would provide services to the club that were invaluable.

It wasn't about how someone looked. It was about how they played, their experience and training, their personalities. At the Honey, there were no boundaries, anything went as long as it was consensual.

That said, there were vagaries in their world, genuinely troubled souls who used the *Life*style to work out issues that should be communicated in a certain kind of doctor's office.

This, along with the majority's resilient inclination to judge that which they didn't understand, cast a shroud of depravity on her world.

This, with his lengthy and highly invasive application policy, Aryas kept out of his clubs. His members were safe in every aspect they could be.

The people there not only practiced the *Life*style, they embraced it.

She lifted her gaze and instantly saw Bryan. It wasn't difficult. He'd been around some time and she'd had him so he knew not to peacock. But he also knew to put himself directly in her line of sight.

Seeing Bryan, another realization came to her, hitting her with a cruel blow to the solar plexus that made her struggle with not appearing winded.

There were not many like Bryan.

When Bryan's membership had been approved and he'd started moving through the viewing floor of the club (the large space in the middle that had some high, narrow bar tables with plushly upholstered stools, all this surrounded by booths Doms could sit in to evaluate and make their choices), Amélie had felt a powerful curl of excitement gather in the pit of her belly the likes of which she hadn't experienced in years.

This was because Bryan's type was not often found, not only in D/s clubs, but also out in the world.

Darkly handsome with the air of an alpha vibrating around him like a visible aura, he was a large man, tall, six foot four, and very well developed. Indeed, when she'd had him strip naked, Amélie had found he'd pushed it right to the edge where he could be considered unappealingly overdeveloped. Fortunately, the appearance of his genitalia did not support her quick assessment that he was aided in the endeavor of bulking out his frame with certain substances.

This, of course, made him all the more appealing.

Amélie was five foot ten. Not only in the club but out in the world she easily dominated nearly everyone in sheer size, both men and women obviously intimidated by her. This was not helped by the fact that she was curvy yet lean, exclusively wore heels, high ones, and she was filthy rich and looked it.

Therefore, with men whom she was eye-to-eye to, or looking down on, who were slighter or leaner than her, part of the challenge, the fun of the game, was removed at the starting gate.

Playing with a six-foot-four, 240-pound toy would be a challenge, even to Aryas (who did not do men but that didn't negate the point), who was six foot six and not a small man by any means, and not simply because of his height.

However, Amélie had broken Bryan within fifteen minutes.

Not a true break. This was the heart of the disappointment in the loss of the promise of him.

But the façade of the alpha melted away to expose the pleaser, making him less of a challenge than many subs who read as recalcitrant and wanted (in other words, *needed*) a firm guiding hand to take them where they needed to be.

Nevertheless, as he physically was her type from the top of his dark head to the tips of his large feet, she'd tried him again.

It was not overexcitement during that first session that brought him to his knees.

It was the sub he was.

And that was not the kind of sub she needed.

Watching him sip his drink, though, doing his best to pretend he didn't know she was looking at him, Amélie moved her study from Bryan to his drink.

Whisky.

Not whiskey.

Whisky. The pure kind that didn't need another letter of the alphabet. Others had learned the art and mastered it, but there could only be one.

Yes.

Whisky.

She'd been mistaken in her taste in toys.

It was not champagne she was looking for.

It was that coveted, priceless, smooth, deep, incomparable burn of the finest scotch whisky.

Bryan might be sipping that.

But Bryan was not that.

In all her years playing, Amélie had not encountered that.

And to her increasing distress, it occurred to her that, even as it was with the actual liquid, there might be one bottle existing in the entire world, owned by another and never to be on offer.

Not even for a sip.

"Jesus, Amélie, are you on Mars?"

Startled, Amélie's eyes moved up to Mirabelle.

Mistress Mirabelle, a Domme at the club, her tenure there a little more than three years, her prevailing penchant exhibitionism, her indisputable talent restraint, her most important role being one of Amélie's closest friends and her co-conspirator in starting their Domme-exclusive book club.

"*Chérie*, you're right. I was in another world," Amélie murmured in reply.

She lifted her chin for Mirabelle to touch her, even in Phoenix, doing this European—cheek to cheek and the switch to do the same to the other cheek, as Amélie's mother had taught her to expect, to teach those around her that she did and anything else was intolerable.

Mirabelle moved out of the way and Amélie was startled again, this time she hid it, when she saw Trey coasting behind her friend.

This was a surprise.

Amélie hadn't been to the club for more than a month.

The first two weeks this was at her choice, the beginnings of unease about what was on offer, the hope that when she returned, there would be something fresh to play with.

The second two weeks she'd been traveling, the first week to France, a duty visit for a cousin's wedding, the second on business.

She'd been home for several days and put off going to the club, hoping her long absence would bear fruit.

From what she'd seen, this had not occurred.

What she witnessed now, as Mirabelle slid into the curve of the booth opposite her, was that she'd left with her friend breaking in Trey, a tall (*ish*, a man had to be *tall* for Amélie to consider him tall) lean man who was very pretty. When he'd made his debut over a year ago, they'd both clocked him, seeing as he was an alpha-sub. However, they both were drawn to more rugged types.

Mirabelle experimented more in a variety of ways so she'd given him a try.

By the time Amélie had left for France, Mirabelle had had three sessions with him. She'd also declared she was besotted.

Mirabelle could get besotted. Then her attention would wander.

It hadn't wandered.

It wasn't as if Mirabelle wouldn't return repeatedly to a certain specimen. But it appeared she'd actually arrived with him or at the very least ordered his arrival time to coincide with hers so she could strut into the hunting ground with him at her heels.

A communication of ownership.

Mirabelle settled in and Amélie looked to Trey as he moved to stand at his Mistress's side in the booth.

Unlike many clubs, the bar/social area just inside the front doors of the Honey, known affectionately by all the members as the "hunting ground," was circumspect.

Another of Aryas's rules.

There was a generous variety of choices of places to play beyond the hunting ground, privately, publicly, on display, and socially.

But in the hunting ground, members came dressed well. They behaved well. There were things you could do, things that *were* done, more than likely nightly, that were not flaunted. But Aryas had a definitive feel he wished to nurture in his establishments. You couldn't even see any of the back playrooms from the hunting ground. There were no suggestive paintings or sculptures. And no one was wearing traditional BDSM or role-playing attire.

The walls were paneled in gleaming wood with beautifully designed light fixtures dripping with unpretentious crystals that sat over the booths and hung from the ceilings. At the back wall, there was a showstopper of a bar with beveled mirrors. And lining the other walls, semicircle booths upholstered in the deepest burgundy velvet.

It was an opulent but nevertheless relaxed and comfortable atmosphere where Doms could scrutinize and select which specimen suited their fancy.

Now, behind the doors leading off the hunting ground, the experience Aryas wished to provide (and succeeded in doing so) was a different story entirely.

Therefore, Trey was in a nice pair of dark slacks and a tailored shirt in light blue. His shock of thick ginger-blond hair was tamed. Amélie couldn't see his shoes, but they were no doubt polished to perfection . . . and not by Trey.

He looked, as did Mirabelle and Amélie, as if they were out on the town at a fashionable watering hole having a cocktail before they were going to go out and drop five hundred dollars on a meal.

Regardless if the rules of circumspection in the hunting ground where adhered to, even there the rules of play were never to be ignored.

In this vein, when Trey felt Amélie's attention, he did not lift his eyes to hers as he said, "Good evening, Mistress Amélie."

"Trey," she murmured, her gaze moving to her friend.

"Mistress Mirabelle, it would be my pleasure to get you a drink," she heard Trey say.

"Vodka, rocks, my lovely," Mirabelle replied, her eyes on Amélie. She tipped her head to the side. "Would you like Trey to get you a fresh drink?"

"Thank you, darling, I'm fine."

Mirabelle nodded to Amélie. Given his unspoken order, Trey moved toward the bar.

He shifted away walking backward for a few steps so as not to show his Mistress disrespect by giving her his back, but as Mira's attention was on Amélie, he eventually turned toward the bar.

When he was well away, Mirabelle's attention turned to her toy.

Part of Amélie's allure to a sub being that it was known widely in their circles that she'd gone above and beyond the traditional training, including painstaking hours manipulating devices, flogs, paddles, cats, switches, crops, straps, and so on, Amélie had also perfected the art that was, in her opinion, the single most crucial skill a Mistress or Master could hold.

Observation.

This being so, she easily saw that Mirabelle's eyes were on Trey's backside.

"Did you come with him or order him to meet you here?" she asked, and Mirabelle looked to Amélie.

"He's been waiting for me in the foyer for twenty minutes," she answered.

Amélie allowed her lips to curve in a small smile as she again lifted her drink.

Mirabelle, a large-chested, slim-hipped, dark-headed goddess with the dauntingly effusive and equally well tended beauty of a professional football team cheerleader, leaned forward and her eyes flashed with exhilaration, even in the subdued light.

"He's exceptional," she whispered.

Amélie felt something stir in the pit of her belly.

As mentioned, in the past, Mirabelle had fallen for many a sub, however one of those subs had gone very wrong. She'd come to the Honey in order to avoid him at the other clubs, only able to afford the membership at a pinch.

But regardless of this failed relationship, Mira had not lost hope.

It was certainly not unheard of that a Master or Mistress would enter in a lasting relationship with subs that would lead to them becoming spouses or life partners, including the minivan and the kids. In fact, it happened regularly.

Mirabelle wanted this.

As did Amélie.

Unlike her earlier reaction to understanding she was growing jaded in regards to pretty much all aspects of her life, the acknowledgment that she wished for a lasting union was not a shock to Amélie. She'd known it since she was a little girl. It had grown alongside her understanding of the side of her nature she would begin to research in her late teens. Find opportunities to observe. Form relationships where she would be afforded opportunities to train and gather experience.

Through this, she knew all along she held that delicate, pulsating hope many women nurtured that there was someone out there.

Someone you'd know you wanted to go to sleep next to every night. Argue with about whiskers in the sink. Plan vacations with. Have everything feel better when something terrible happened and his arms closed around you. Watch his features soften with delight when you told him you were carrying his child.

Someone you could tie to a bed and make perform for you, forcing mind-scrambling orgasm after orgasm, him needing that in all the forms you could imagine, unashamedly gifting you with the trust you'd give them to him.

And then the memory of each and every single one of those precious moments when time wore on and age made this no longer something you both could share.

Until you both quit breathing.

This was what Amélie was beginning to face with a sense a grief.

Grief for the loss of something she wanted desperately but was coming to terms with the fact that she would never have.

Grief for something she saw as hope that was budding that she'd found in Mirabelle's eyes.

The sub who had shattered her heart wanted Mirabelle to force mind-scrambling orgasms from his ringed cock and strapped balls.

What he didn't want, and shared with her with some revulsion, was to spend his life and make children with a woman who could do that to him.

Trey, Amélie could not read for certain. She'd not played with him. He'd also not accepted even club ownership from a Mistress in his tenure at the Honey. He wasn't a submissive whore (not that there was anything wrong with that), bouncing without any real connection from Master to Mistress thoughtlessly. But what he wanted, Amélie couldn't fathom.

She just hoped it was what Mirabelle could offer.

But more, if he wanted that, he could offer exactly what Mirabelle wanted in return.

"Mistress Romy had shared he was unusually enjoyable," Amélie noted cautiously in response to Mirabelle's assertion of Trey's talent.

She watched her friend's face carefully.

What she expected to see, she saw.

The slight tightening of her perfectly lined and filled lips.

Jealousy.

This happened.

Most checked it at the door. It was their world.

In play, subs were frequently shared, borrowed, ordered to serve another, and Doms, as was their nature, partook of whatever they fancied (if a toy was owned, for the night or longer, they did this with the Master's or Mistress's permission, of course).

Mirabelle's reaction was thus telling.

If this happened for her and Trey, she would not share. It was even doubtful she'd do so in social play. Exhibiting him, undoubtedly. Allowing touch or further, not a chance.

This, too, happened.

And this, too, was something Amélie craved to call her own.

It was, in fact, already part of her repertoire.

Not jealousy. Alas, she'd never felt that.

But she visited the social playroom on occasion, and when she did, she brought along a toy. She did this to show off that toy. She very rarely allowed touch or others to play. If she did, there was a point. Not for those who she allowed such privileges. A lesson that needed to be learned or an experience that she could gift to her sub that she knew he desired.

"Mirabelle," she called when her friend had no response.

Mirabelle continued to regard her but she said nothing.

"I just want you to be careful," she explained.

"Once burned . . ." Mirabelle stated.

Amélie nodded and grinned. ". . . twice shy. I get it. But I urge you to be three times shy. Or four. Or allow me to have a few quiet words."

It went without saying that confidentiality at the club was paramount.

In reality, the fourteen-page contract she'd had to sign that she'd given her attorney for his perusal (something he'd done and two months after, his application had been accepted at the club) had elicited him saying, "Memorize this, Amélie. If you don't and you breach even a sub-clause to a sub-clause, if you were a man, Aryas Weathers would have your balls in a vise, and not the way this type of club plays that. As you're a woman, you'll be homeless and cleaning his toilets with a toothbrush for the scraps his dog won't eat."

She didn't need to memorize the contract.

Even so, she'd read it three times.

So outside these walls, talk was forbidden. If you saw a member in public that was not a good acquaintance, if given the signal, you proceeded cautiously. Normally, you ignored them altogether.

On the other hand, as was human nature, inside the club, talk, and even gossip among members, was rampant, and for their play, essential. Who liked what. Who'd done who. The ones who'd left the blinds open on the playrooms you needed to be sure to take the opportunity to watch.

The ones who lived the life and left it at the club's door.

Amélie did not fancy Trey so she hadn't been paying close attention. She knew no Master had had him. She also knew, outside Mirabelle and Romy, he'd serviced Mistresses Felicia and Pasquel.

All of them repeatedly.

And all of them both Mirabelle and Amélie were friendly with for more than the book club they all belonged to.

"Let me think about that, okay?" Mirabelle answered Amélie's offer. "He showed no hesitation when I required him to wait for me in the foyer." She grinned a calendar girl grin. "Of course, he'd just ejaculated a parcel that would make a horse feel envy, but he knows what that means. He knows a note will be put in his file. And he could have balked, talked to me outside, or not shown up."

This was all true.

"If he doesn't broach it, ask me out, meet me in the humdrum, maybe I'll get you to snoop around before I ask him," she finished.

"I approve of your plan," Amélie remarked.

"I don't need your approval, Mistress," Mirabelle returned, still grinning.

Without taking her attention from her friend, she noted, "He's returning."

"Caught that, but thanks," Mirabelle murmured, her gaze shifting to the hunting ground.

Trey returned and set her drink in front of her, taking his position standing outside the booth like he was her bodyguard, saying in a deep, pleasing, quiet voice, "I hope your drink pleases you, Mistress."

"My gratitude, slave, I'm sure it will," Mirabelle replied just as quietly, taking up the drink, her eyes still wandering, but not to Trey.

He settled in, leaning his ass against the side of the booth, her protector, her servant.

Amélie had had that, subs she'd decided to own for a spell in the club. Subs who had waited for her in the foyer and entered with her. Subs that stood sentry while she sat with her friends, sipping and chatting. Subs that, in their profile, staff made notes that they were not to be approached unless she gave permission.

"Slim pickins for you, dearest heart," Mira, who knew her well, noted after she'd done her sweep. "Though, Mistress Delia is here and I know that not only because I've seen her but because from the minute I walked in, my flesh felt like it was crawling."

Amélie searched for and found the Domme in question.

Delia, like Amélie, was in her early thirties. Unlike Amélie, she had a beautiful but cold face, an icy, black-haired beauty, and mean in her eyes.

She'd moved from New York City to Phoenix, coming to the club with the requisite for Masters or Mistresses—four references, two from Dominants, two from subs. Aryas had shared with Amélie that he knew the Master and Mistress who'd made the references. They were lukewarm, and as was his policy, he'd followed up on them. He then had, in a rare move, decided to accept her regardless of his tendency toward safety.

He'd shared his reasoning for this too.

There were no real reasons the New York Dominants could give for the fact that their references were unenthusiastic. She was a known player. There had been no incidents they knew of that would mark her as unwelcome.

They just didn't like her.

Amélie understood that.

In a world that was roundly judged, Aryas or any of them were not fans of judging one of their own.

Even with all of that, he'd regretted his decision immediately.

"Just a feeling, my sweet," he'd muttered, sitting with her, sipping his Hennessy and watching Delia work the room.

She was being given her head. If she overstepped any boundaries, it would be reported.

But Amélie knew he was hoping for any small infraction so he could bounce her. Even if she left a tuna sandwich unattended in her locker in the Dominant lounge, he'd get rid of her.

Amélie had this information because they were very close and she was Aryas's top Domme. He knew her discretion.

He also knew she'd keep an eye.

And that she did right then, seeing Delia move in front of the bar with the pretty, young sub named Tiffany dogging her steps.

It was Tiffany Amélie studied.

In her mid-twenties, Tiffany was the daughter of friends of Amélie's family. As any Dominant would do with any submissive, toys were looked after, even if they weren't yours.

But knowing Tiffany in the outside world before she'd entered

Amélie's domain, knowing her parents would excommunicate her with extreme prejudice if they knew about this part of her life, she'd kept a closer eye.

And now Tiffany looked pale even in the dim light.

And afraid.

This could be for a variety of reasons, most of them acceptable.

It could be something far darker.

The entire club had tight security and even playrooms were monitored. Cameras caught everything. This served many purposes, including a means to assure confidentiality, a threat Aryas had rarely used and wouldn't unless given no alternative.

It also kept the subs safe.

Delia's ministrations would be watched, likely with Aryas's concerns, closely.

"We all must have a care," Amélie said to Mirabelle.

"Always," Mirabelle replied.

Taking a sip of her drink, Mirabelle's attention focused on Bryan.

As did Amélie's.

When it did, he swiftly lowered his gaze and turned his head away.

He'd been watching her.

"You could give that a go again," Mirabelle suggested.

"He called Mistress Marisol 'Mommy.'"

The smooth, sultry voice came from behind Amélie and she turned to see Mistress Talia there, her lips curved in a cat's smile, her brown eyes lit with their usual good humor, her wild, wide orb of soft-curled, café-au-lait-with-bronzed-tips Afro adding to an overall exotic look of exquisite African-American beauty.

Her slender neck, Amélie noted not for the first time, was a tempting vulnerability. A vulnerability that Amélie knew Aryas found tremendously tempting. So much so, he'd agreed for the first time in what Amélie thought was at least three years to mentor her into the Dominant role personally.

Her training had been long and thorough.

He'd let her loose two months ago.

She was unsurprisingly very popular.

What she was not was a submissive. A capable, if rookie, Domme. Amélie had observed her in training and had observed her when she was set free to go it alone—and it was clear she had one bent.

Which meant Aryas would not go there for he had the same bent, and in that case, outside some interaction during social play, the twain didn't meet.

Trey making a noise that could be taken as amused disgust (or disgusted amusement) took Amélie out of her contemplation of the new Domme. Trey doing this was something not surprising from an alpha-sub.

"Seriously?" Mirabelle asked as Talia leaned the side of a hip against the side of the booth by where Amélie was sitting.

"Yep," Talia answered, still grinning wickedly.

Mirabelle looked to Amélie. "Is Mari into that?"

"Nope," Talia answered for Amélie. "Pretty sure that Latino lovely isn't gonna go for seconds."

Amélie wasn't surprised this had slipped from Bryan. However, it did mean he was forevermore out of the question for her.

"What a waste," Mirabelle murmured, her head turned, her eyes trained on Bryan.

But Amélie looked to Trey.

Mirabelle's comment was not meant to be insulting. Her words were meant for Amélie, who she knew would no longer have interest in Bryan for she didn't share the inclination he clearly had in order to give him what he needed.

Trey obviously did not know this.

He'd been leaning hips to the side of the booth, unlike Talia, facing the room straight on. His pose had been relaxed.

He was now tensed.

She observed his jaw.

It was tight.

Her lips curved.

Trey did not like his Mistress thinking Bryan was a waste.

Interesting.

She turned her regard to Bryan, and as if he felt her eyes, he looked to their booth.

His expression took on surprise as his focus shifted up over Amélie's shoulder.

"Okay, girl, serious? Are you gonna go there?" Mirabelle asked, causing Amélie to turn and look up to Talia.

She had one slim arm up, one long, slender finger pointed Bryan's way. She casually shifted it to the side, indicating one of the doors to the playrooms.

Very cool, and not the cool of the frosty variety.

She'd learned well from Aryas.

Amélie looked back to Bryan to see him up, his big body in its dark suit moving toward the door.

"Big, naughty boy stretched over my knees, getting his spanking, fuck yeah," Talia answered Mirabelle's question and Amélie again turned her gaze. "And I'll spank that fine, firm white ass until he vows he'll never utter that word again." The cat's smile came back. "As Ary taught me, there's *infinitesimal* ways to skin a cat. Give that baby what he needs in a way that doesn't make me feel skeevy."

There was the green.

Daddy and Mommy play was not frowned upon. Amélie didn't get off on it but she'd seen daddies do wondrous things with their babies, and the same with mommies, and she knew it had absolutely nothing to do with a psychological complex a vanilla needed to use to shove that square peg into their desperately round hole.

It was not okay in any sense to cast aspersions on any type of play.

Express surprise someone did something, went somewhere with a sub, coaxed something out, went to a place that was unexpected, most definitely.

Pronouncing it as "skeevy," no.

It was a novice mistake and Amélie knew either she, or Mirabelle, would be having a word with Talia about it in the future.

Aryas would be livid.

Therefore, he could not know.

Now, though, Trey was there and you didn't speak to a Mistress that way in front of a sub.

"Best go top that," Talia murmured and looked down to them, doing this looking through Trey and finishing on Mirabelle. "Enjoy your night." She turned to Amélie. "Happy hunting, honey."

"Have fun," Amélie replied.

Talia moved away.

Amélie watched her, wondering if her slim neck or her round ass was the key to Aryas's infatuation with the rookie Domme.

She'd never know and understanding that, she lost interest and was about to turn away when Talia switched directions, heading to the booth where Stellan sat.

Stellan was a Master who had been a member of the club nearly as long as Amélie.

And in some ways, Stellan was Amélie's Talia.

Not that she'd trained him.

That she'd always wanted him.

Physically her type, perhaps a little shorter than she'd like (but not much), a little leaner, but nevertheless powerfully built with dark hair and strong features so excruciatingly handsome, in weaker moments, she had to quell the desire to look away.

He'd slipped in without her seeing him and hadn't come to offer her a greeting.

This would normally have annoyed Amélie.

At that moment, for the first time in years, she was paying no attention to Stellan.

This was because Talia's tall frame shifting out of the way offered an unhindered view of something else that had slipped in without her notice.

And gazing at him, Amélie went still.

As did her breath.

And her heartbeat.

Leaning a shoulder against the wall beyond the edge of the bar, six or seven feet from the door to the playrooms, he was surveying the scene as if he wasn't part of it.

Or as if it was *he* who was on the prowl.

But although a Dominant could mingle freely in the open space, this would be done with some intent.

If they were on the hunt, they'd be at a booth.

Subs were not allowed to sit in a booth unless the invitation was extended. They populated the floor, on display, it was requisite.

In the mesh of bodies, a sub could be identified in a variety of ways. The cast of their gaze. Their bearing. Jewelry that declared their status.

And their position in the hunting ground.

No Dominant would linger there like he was, partially for that reason. Clear communication and transparent messages were key in their world. No Dom would give the impression of being a sub.

This was explained at length during membership orientation.

That magnificent beast was a sub.

An alpha-sub, assuredly.

It came from his sheer size, like a cloak stitched to his skin he had no hope of shrugging off (not that he'd wish to).

He had to be six five, perhaps taller. His dark suit and monochromatic shirt necessarily tailored for his physique for there were very few men on this earth that had it. His shoulders as wide as a log. His chest a veritable wall. The muscles Amélie had no doubt were hidden under his clothing apparent in the exposed line of his throat. It wasn't that he had no neck. But that lethal shank of corded, sinewy muscle could not be established and maintained if the rest of him didn't match precisely.

She knew he was alpha beyond that. His stance at the wall, casual and self-assured, it was openly cocky. He knew his allure. He knew his beauty. He knew even if he wasn't exactly your type, every being would understand with base instinct his attraction.

He also knew how to use this. All of it. It was his art as sure as reading it on him was Amélie's.

From what she could tell, his hair was dark blond, the thickness of it, how it was longer at the top, clipped short at neck and ears was so appealing, she was willing to make that single allowance for she preferred her toys to have dark hair.

She made that allowance, but if she had her way, and she often did, he'd grow it longer so there'd be more of it to fist her fingers into as a means to use to make him serve her will.

His facial features only heightened his appeal that already, with the rest of him, defied belief.

A strong brow over eyes she couldn't see the color of from her distance. Hollowed cheeks under high cheekbones and over a firm, cut, clean-shaven jaw. And a large nose that was openly pugilistic, the dent at the top of the bridge not created by God but by a break that he didn't deem important enough to have set properly.

Staring at him, utterly incapable of not doing it openly, she felt the insides of her thighs tingle. And her nipples were hard buds, the restriction of the lace of her bra suddenly excruciating.

That . . .

Now *that* was whisky.

"Oh my, Leigh, are you seeing what I'm seeing?" Mirabelle asked. And before she could answer, her friend went on, "It's like he was made for you."

It was, indeed.

She watched in fascination as something caught his attention, shifting the half-amused, half-bored expression from his face and pulling him away from the wall.

His eyes focused on something a beat, two, three, then dropped.

That small movement, the respect of a sub given to a Dom, barely discernible from the distance, still convulsed the walls of her pussy.

"Trey, find a member of staff." Amélie heard Mirabelle order.

"At your pleasure, Mistress," Trey muttered in return.

Amélie didn't look away. Now not because she couldn't, but because what captured his attention was Mistress Delia.

"Fuck," Mirabelle hissed the word that flitted through Amélie's mind.

Stunned still again, Amélie watched as, within five seconds, words were exchanged. Words that made Delia toss her head, lift her hand, snap, and stomp toward the door to the playrooms, Tiffany following.

But that male sub did not.

Crash and burn.

The beast didn't even look over his shoulder to watch them leave. His expression settled into blankness again as his attention turned back to the gathering.

"You ladies wanted something?"

Before she was caught staring, feeling like a greenhorn Domme on her first prowl, Amélie tore her eyes from the beast and looked to Heather. She was a staff member of the club, none of whom had titles and all of whom were paid very handsomely because all of them had a variety of roles they could be called on to play—from server to someone who needed to mop a puddle of cum off the floor so a recently vacated room could be reused.

"That baby, against the wall, the one who looks in dire need of a lesson or seventy," Mirabelle stated, not pointing even to jerk her head his way. "He's new."

"O.H.," Heather stated, smiling big and giving them the code they needed. "He was approved two weeks ago. Not here every night, but as far as I know, he's been in three times. A number of takers gave it a shot. So far he hasn't felt up to playing. Think his profile is burned into the screens of pretty much every Dom who's seen him."

This was without a doubt, but even if it weren't, Mirabelle digging in her purse would have proved it.

"Thanks, *chérie*," Amélie kindly dismissed her.

Heather nodded, shot them another smile, and moved away.

Amélie attempted to unobtrusively deep breathe.

The system was set up as such that, if subs wanted to know about Doms, they went to the secure computer in the room behind the foyer. They could not access data anywhere else.

Hidden behind a site that you had to access through a username, a secure password with the requirement to change it monthly as well that it be twelve characters long, answering a security question and entering a captcha, Dominants could look up subs on their phones in the comfort of their booths.

These did not have full names or photos or anything of an identifying nature. In fact, the data provided was offered via code so if someone happened onto a hack, they wouldn't know what they were seeing.

It wasn't the enigma machine but it did offer another level of security.

What those profiles didn't have were the notes a member of staff or another Dominant could add to a sub profile. All notes were approved by management, namely Aryas's operating manager, Tina Marie, so catty, sulky or other inappropriate notes would not be communicated.

If there were notes, the profile would indicate this. And to get to this information, a Master or Mistress would have to go to another one of the computers on the premises (this in the Dom lounge) to read these notes that also weren't networked, even locally.

These notes in most cases included such things as toys who were owned, either literally (life partners or husbands and wives), or the agreement had been noted that a sub would serve only one Dominant at the Honey, a circumstance which Mirabelle and Trey communicated that very evening.

They also could provide information essential to a Dominant that a submissive would need to relinquish prior to being approved for membership. This could be anything from the sub being in counseling for a reason that a Master or Mistress would have to understand and appreciate before selecting them for play. It could be the brief description of a tragedy that could affect the scene, the loss of a loved one in an extreme way, a history of domestic abuse, a survivor of rape.

"Here you go, Leigh."

Mirabelle was extending her phone, which was good and bad.

Good because Amélie had not managed to unobtrusively deep breathe, her shallow breaths making her feel light-headed, and she needed something else to focus on.

Bad because what she was focusing on would be the profile of that beast.

She took Mirabelle's phone and turned it her way.

O.H.
Security: Kitten
Hobbies: Everything
Limitations: Nothing
Notes: None

Translated, this meant:

INITIALS OR OTHER IDENTIFIER
Safe word: Kitten
Inclinations: Into anything
Boundaries, Rules, Unacceptable Play: None

Even with those few words, it was a surprising profile. Experienced subs, the only ones allowed on the floor, knew their boundaries and most had them. In this club, the vast majority were extreme, such as branding, marking, scarring, strangling, sensory deprivation, and so on.

But they had them.

She hadn't seen a profile that open in a long time.

And the safe word "kitten" showed the beast had a sense of

humor. He had the look that just uttering that cute word, which would bring images of the adorable creatures, would make him violently ill.

"Go hit that, tigress," Mirabelle urged, and Amélie looked to her.

Before she could say a word, Mirabelle continued.

"Get in there. Three times here, he'll have heard of you. He'll be holding out in hopes you'll be extending the invitation to initiating him to our playrooms. I know it." She leaned across the table. "Rock his world, lovely."

She studied her friend, the open excitement, the budding love she was experiencing with her submissive, that time when life takes on clarity so pure and extraordinary, you want everyone to experience it with you.

She turned her head to the beast.

Years of experience only marred twice by two toys she'd had who held great promise, but who eventually fell short of the real thing, taught her that tonight, she would definitely enjoy herself.

But he might be champagne. He might be bourbon. He might, surprisingly, be cognac or port.

The bottom line was that she had to keep expectations low so she wouldn't be devastated when he didn't turn out to be top-shelf whisky.

two

Rainbow?

AMÉLIE

She slid out of the booth with murmurings of "good night" and "have fun," taking her stiletto-heeled-sandal-shod feet with the will of steel her mother had begun the process of instilling in her and her training as a Domme had completed.

She could not have her legs give out on her and she could not expose her nervous anticipation.

And she wouldn't.

But, God, she had not felt like this in years. That sub she'd spied or she'd had who was so promising or such a transcendent experience to play with that she could barely control her own reactions to exploring that promise or again feeling the wholeness, togetherness, *oneness* with another.

She moved in his direction, no game playing. She didn't even glance at Stellan in his booth.

Amélie didn't participate in those games, not ever. There was no reason for her to be coy with a sub.

And she moved with the gait and bearing that it was solely her mother who'd ingrained in her in the sporadic times they'd had together, doing it with an unrelenting fervor that it would take the threat of death to force her to move any other way.

Chin up. Shoulders straight and slightly back. A sway of her hips so subtle, it was elusive. Long, confident strides.

Amélie could walk a catwalk.

She could also make a specimen she was approaching get so hard his cock was aching by the time she made it to him.

She hadn't even gone halfway when he sensed her approach and she was gratified that his response was instantaneous.

He pushed from the wall. He turned fully to face her. And she felt his eyes drop, not with the respect a sub owed a Domme, but to take her in from sandals to hair.

Then his gaze locked on hers and he didn't look away.

He didn't look away.

He watched her approach not like he was taking the risky liberty he was taking but like it was his God-given right.

Amélie felt her clit quiver.

She arrived at him, stopping several feet away, knowing that the minute her body language made it clear she was going in for the capture, most eyes in the room, if not all, were on her.

She did not care about this. Not that she'd ever care about this (which she wouldn't), but because, now close to him, she found to her enchanted surprise, he was not big.

He was *colossal*.

A mighty beast.

A magnificent beast.

Exquisite.

He was not six foot five. He was at least six-six, more likely six-seven. A mountain of compacted muscle encased in a very fine, very expensive suit.

Taking him in, in proximity, she wanted him more than she'd already wanted him. She wanted no boundaries. She wanted everything. Her diverse skill set, experience, imagination, creativity, and if it came down to it, sheer determination and grit, she'd utilize it all to wring him dry in a way he'd contemplate murder in order to have the opportunity to come back for more.

She was on the verge of speaking when he did.

His direct gaze appreciative, an arrogant smile curving his full lips, he asked, "How you doin', sweetheart?"

She froze.

Full eye contact. Speaking without being spoken to. Using an unconsented and unearned endearment.

The already damp gusset of her panties soaked to the point her wet crept up the silk of her front and back sides.

But her brows snapped together, her censure clear, and her lips ordered, "Follow me."

She shifted on her sandal and strode toward the door to the play-rooms.

She did this and did not look back to see if he followed.

A feeling so foreign she almost didn't recognize it, that being fear of rejection, stole through her belly as she moved unerringly toward the door.

The feeling melted and elation replaced it as she felt him following.

She stopped at the door, moving slightly to the side, and he finally demonstrated his understanding of the game. He opened the door for her and held it as she moved through.

However, he did this with his eyes firmly planted on her breasts.

He was deliciously *unbelievable*.

He was not green, even though his actions might communicate that. Aryas didn't allow beginner subs to roam the hunting ground. He allowed membership to them and they were available for play to only a small cadre of Aryas-approved Dominants who would guide them through the submissive experience with unerring attention to detail.

Amélie was an approved Domme. Even so, she had long since stopped partaking. She had a wealth of patience, but she also had a wealth of practice.

If she could not find what her heart and pussy desired in a sea of practiced subs, putting the effort into training one would be an exercise in futility. A gesture of benevolence she simply no longer had any interest in offering.

So she didn't.

Knowing Aryas would not approve him for the hunt, or accept him without references from two Dominants who'd worked him, that gave light to three possibilities for his behavior.

The first, he liked punishment and from the get-go wanted her to know that.

The second, being aware of his uniqueness in any realm, definitely this one, and his attraction to the opposite sex, not to mention his natural alpha bent, he thought he could top from below (this, incidentally, would be in his profile as a note, something which would be shared by one or both of his previous Mistresses . . . or Masters).

The third, he'd thrown down the gauntlet. He felt he was unbreakable but he wanted to see her try.

She hoped like all hell it was the third. The first, she could do . . . and enjoy it. The second, she had no interest in (obviously).

The third would be nirvana.

She entered the darkened hall that led to the maze of playrooms. There were forty-five. Some small, almost closets. Some large, for group play. Most a uniform size but equipped for different types of scenes.

When Amélie came to the club and did not know which toy she'd be selecting, she always reserved two rooms.

One was utilitarian. Perfectly appointed for its purpose, it didn't offer anything special.

The second, Aryas actually had designed specifically for her. Even so, she rarely used it for she never took a new sub there and it was with disheartening infrequency a sub earned the reward of the wealth she could offer him there.

Not thinking about why she chose as she did, she made her decision of where she intended to take her beast. Only glancing into the floor-to-ceiling-windowed cube rooms that had their blinds raised for display of play, Amélie strode purposefully along the wide, plush burgundy-carpeted passageways that made up the cobweb of playrooms.

In one of her glances, she caught Talia with Bryan. He was naked, ass in the air, ball gag in his mouth, stretched over her legs getting his spanking.

The ball gag was a creative solution, one that almost made her smile.

She did not smile.

She led her brute to her special room.

There were two others appointed for its purpose.

This one might be used by others, but it was still hers.

The silhouette blinds were drawn. Through them, due to her reserving it, she saw the lights were on and this time, she did not wait for her selected specimen of the evening to open the door for her.

She opened it and took only a moment to flip the switch by the door that would tell the control room this space was now being used, a mandatory requirement of all Doms the instant they entered a playroom. This was so staff could turn on the cameras and open the other room she'd reserved.

That done, she walked right to the center of the room.

She turned to him and saw him automatically duck, as if the top of the frame of the door could not always be assumed would be one he wouldn't run right into.

It was a sight that made him even more alluring.

As he slowly closed the door behind him and moved his eyes to look through the room, taking it in, she watched them get wide.

They dropped to her and his amusement was clear. Not only radiating from his gaze but twitching at his lips.

Another unusual—and unacceptable—reaction.

He thought this was funny.

She hoped like fuck she had the opportunity to prove him wrong.

She crossed her arms on her chest and slightly put out a foot, like she was about to start tapping her toe. In the wrap dress she wore, she knew this opened the overlap, not exposing anything, but the promise for him was impossible to resist.

His attention dropped to her legs.

"In the playrooms," she began with a snap, and his gaze cut up to hers, "I want eye contact. Unless otherwise instructed, you should not only feel free to look me directly in the eyes, if I'm in your line of sight or I'm not giving you something that your body's natural reaction would make it difficult to meet my gaze, I require it."

She stood there staring as he did nothing but dip his chin in acknowledgment.

Cheeky.

Exceptionally cheeky.

Fabulous.

"Unless I've asked for their silence or for them to ask for leave to speak, I also require my toys to respond when they're spoken to. Even if it's only a 'yes, Mistress,' or 'no, Mistress.'"

His stance relaxed, like he was settling in at the beginning of a show he found vaguely intriguing, and his deep rumble of a voice bounced like boulders through the room. "Yes, Mistress."

Christ, even his voice declared his challenge.

"Excellent," she allowed. "Your name?"

"Olivier," he answered.

French.

Also unusual, at least in this country. And interesting.

She liked it a great deal.

She studied him.

He let her, holding her eyes.

"I'm Mistress Amélie," she eventually informed him.

"I know. You got a lotta fans out there . . . Mistress."

The hesitation over him saying "Mistress" gave less of the impression he was testing her and more of the *strange* impression the word was unpracticed when, with any experienced sub, it would slip right off their tongue.

She made no comment to that.

"There are things we should go over," she remarked.

"Right," he stated, his big body adjusting again, now like he was settling in further, intent on giving her the same attention he would a flight attendant who gave the safety address.

That being no more than a courtesy.

She fought the shiver his actions created but allowed the irritation.

"Your safe word is kitten," she stated.

"Yes, Mistress."

"You're open to any kind of play," she went on.

"Yes, Mistress."

"It's important and now's the time to share should there be anything you wish me to shy away from, Olivier. Especially as this is the first time I've played with you."

Something in his eyes flashed. Blue eyes that were the color of nothing and everything. Not sky. Not sea. Not midnight. A pure blue that only existed in the unchartable depths of a rainbow.

She felt that flash snake up between her thighs, taking residence in her womb.

He wanted this conversation done so she would play with him. He wanted the preliminaries over so they'd get to the good stuff.

He wanted her.

She stared into those blue eyes and for a moment felt mesmerized.

For God's sake, Leigh, she berated herself in an effort to pull it together. *Rainbow?*

"Olivier," she prompted.

"I'm open to anything," he confirmed.

She threw her hand out, indicating the padded vault, the displayed tack . . . the stall.

"Anything?" she pushed.

He held her gaze like a dare. "Anything." Again his lips twitched. "Mistress."

She quieted and took him in.

Aryas would not let a voyeur past the front door. Amélie fancied he'd paid secret spy guys like the gentleman in the Bond film who created all the devices that got James out of a bind to set up a force field that would instantly eject anyone who wished to use the Bee's Honey as a curiosity or to get their rocks off observing and not participating (thus not embracing the lifestyle). Certainly not someone who found the whole thing amusing.

"Am I amusing you?" she whispered, the whisper holding a tremor that was not of fear but of anger.

His face set hard and his two words were so firm, the boulders again came tumbling.

"Absolutely not."

"Then can you explain your humor?" she asked.

He shrugged. "Sure. You are un-fucking-believably beautiful. You're also un-fucking-believably hot. But I wouldn't guess with the acres that make all of you, every inch of it so damned sweet, you're a walking wet dream, that when you get riled you're also un-fucking-believably cute. And there is no way in fuck five minutes ago, you told me a gorgeous redhead was gonna lead me to a room and make me her pony, I would be cool with that. But standin' here with you, I'm totally fuckin' cool with that."

It took a good deal, and she expended every bit of effort she needed to accomplish it, but at his final two points, Amélie didn't blink.

Instead, she decided to finish this part up.

Immediately.

"I must confirm you have no boundaries or rules."

"Got no rules or boundaries, babe."

Her voice held ice when she demanded, "You will refrain from calling me endearments I have not expressly allowed or you have not earned the right to use by pleasing me."

He was ready to roll, too, so he didn't miss a beat. "Yes, Mistress."

"And I'll remind you not five seconds ago you mentioned you wouldn't be . . ." she hesitated, as if using slang was beneath her (when it wasn't), "*cool* with pony play and I would mark words like that as a boundary."

"Mistress," he said softly, "there is a lot of shit that goes on in rooms like these that, if you told me somewhere out there in the real world I'd be deep in it, I would not be cool with it. That's the point of this gig. Am I right? You close yourself off to anything, you put your own damned self in a situation where you might be closing yourself off from *everything*."

He had a point.

An excellent one.

And that point proved he was no newbie.

She nodded.

"Right then, is there anything specific you don't particularly enjoy?"

"Humiliation," he stated instantly. "And, obviously, Mistress, if you agree, I don't wanna be on display."

There was a good deal there.

The instantaneousness of his first reply smacked the room like a boundary he refused, for some reason, to admit he had.

The second part of his reply—precisely the way he communicated it—was not in the normal language of an experienced sub. *If you agree* would be *if it pleases you*.

Again, it gave the uncomfortable impression of an untried toy.

However, watching him closely, the ease with which he held himself, the line of his frame that only tightened when he'd said the word *humiliation*, the obvious changes happening at the bulge of his groin as they moved through this conversation, bringing them closer to their purpose for being there, she suspected he did it deliberately.

That play was unusual. It was affecting, furthering his clear stamp as an alpha-sub, something she found magnetic. It was respectful and thus it didn't earn her censure.

But there was something wrong.

Before she could put her finger on it, he finished, "And I'm not real big on ass play."

It took more of an effort to control her reaction to that.

Not everyone enjoyed that.

In the outside world.

In the D/s world, full access, especially to places that had significantly heightened senses of vulnerability, was not only given, but toying with and manipulating them was entreated, yearned for, *craved*.

In fact, the foundation of their practice was losing control, or acquiring it, gaining access, exposing vulnerabilities, pushing boundaries, redefining comfort zones (repeatedly), leading, guiding, following, resisting your limits and then settling into understanding them.

For a sub, this boiled down to letting go.

For a submissive, letting go meant offering the gift of trust to their Dominant, a gift that was all the sweeter when you offered up your most guarded vulnerabilities and allowed another to exchange that gift with physical and emotional rewards that were beyond your comprehension.

For another moment, Amélie took him in. All of him. What she felt coming from him. The way he held himself. Harking back to his even tone, the matter-of-factness of confirming and sharing information. His easy acceptance of her mild remonstrations and quick corrections, adhering to her rules.

An untried or inexperienced sub would be a ball of nerves. Even with this powerhouse, he couldn't hide it. The anxiety would be palpable.

And again, there was not a chance Aryas would have allowed him to be open to selection without at the very least putting a note in his profile.

But he simply wouldn't do it. Aryas didn't believe in the art, he practiced the religion of the Dominant/submissive world from neophyte to high priest and priestess.

She made her decision.

"Very well, Olivier. Take your clothes off, please."

And it was a decision well made for there it was again. A flash in his blue eyes, there and gone, exposing his excitement, communicating his readiness, and if she had anything to do about it (and she was going to give it her all), an early indication of his need.

His need that would become her need.

His need that was not needy, it was just pure, flawless *need*.

His need that only *she*, in this moment, in this session, during this scene, could satisfy.

He shrugged off his suit jacket.

The revelation of his shoulders covered in nothing but his blue-black shirt made her mouth get dry.

She forced a swallow.

"Place your clothing on the hooks by the door," she ordered. "Shoes with socks tucked inside lined up beside the door."

She found herself curious when he turned immediately to the two hooks in the narrow area of wall by the frame of the door (most of the rest of the wall space that weren't beams where useful implements were hung were windows).

Her curiosity was that she would assume with a man of his beauty, he'd at the very least display himself to her.

And during play, he would know she wished him to do that.

But more basically, any sub knew they didn't turn their back on their Mistress, especially not in such close proximity and *most* especially not during a scene.

Instead, he'd done just that, moving to the hooks, putting his jacket there. His hands going to the buttons on his shirt, making light work of them.

Then, with a phenomenal shrug of his massive shoulders, the shirt was gone and Amélie didn't care if she had his front, back, side, or he was undressing behind a screen.

She struggled to keep her legs from trembling as her pussy started clenching like his cock was driving into her.

This struggle continued after shoes came off, he did as instructed with them and his socks, and down came the pants with his underwear.

She saw his thighs.

She saw his ass.

He *was* a beast.

A brute.

An incomparable *steed*.

The dents at the sides of his ass carved into full bulging globes that made her fingers actually *itch* to drag her nails over them.

And do much, *much* more.

On that thought, he turned.

And when he did, she gathered everything she had to keep her legs and hands steady, her eyes impassive, her face mildly interested, even as her heart beat a tattoo so deep in her chest, it seemed to thrum in the room.

She'd been very right.

He was a brute, an *incomparable* steed.

Hung long and thick, his hard cock stood out proud, but heavy. The mammoth length of it hard weighted his erection down, so much it nearly blocked her view of his sac.

However, his sac was as impressive as his cock, hanging high and tight between his legs, nestled with his impressive phallus in a nest of burnished brown curls. But his balls were so big, they, too, hung tight but heavy.

It was instinct and training that made her voice strong when she took two steps backward and commanded, "Come here, Olivier. The middle of the room where the ring is in the floor. Stop there, please."

The flash from his eyes again, the degree of heat emanating from it hotter, the length longer.

He moved as told and stopped where instructed.

"Lift your arms, hands clasped behind your head."

As she'd ordered, his gaze came to hers.

No flash then.

He was gone.

He was hers.

Amélie knew this because the pure blue of his eyes had darkened considerably and she saw no rainbow.

All she saw was night.

She dropped her gaze and noted the angle of his cock had dropped considerably as well. It was longer, harder, heavier.

She noticed his movement and watched with extreme pleasure as he lifted up his arms and clasped his hands behind his head.

She took him in, in this pose, all of him. The bulge of his biceps that she was certain she could wrap both hands around and the tips of her fingers would not meet. The chest scattered with the same burnished brown hair as between his legs, a good deal of it, but it was short, blunt, almost like it had been shaved and growing back, but she suspected, even so far as hoped, it was natural. This gathered and thickened in a line just above the navel in his flat, ridged belly, the line opening, widening, melding into the hair that based his cock. The hair was longer on his legs, but still relatively short and blunt, decorating the trunks that nature had appropriately seen fit to support his bulk, providing perfect appendages to complement a package that was an overall thing of beauty.

The hair on his head was not blond. It was not brown. It was lighter than it was darker, definitely lighter than the hair that adorned the rest of his body, and it had the same burnish of the hair between his legs.

She moved around him slowly, continuing to draw him in, memorize him, for if they only had this one session, she wanted to remember it forever. Savor the Adonis fate saw fit to drop into her sphere, even if he broke in fifteen minutes, which meant she'd never have such a moment again because she'd never select him again.

She slowly made her way around him, inspecting the dizzying array of muscles on his back, again appreciating the curves and hollows of his backside, allowing her eyes to caress the wealth of visible sinews carving along his forearms.

And his hands.

Strong. Capable. Long fingers that matched the rest of his body, ending in squared-off tips. They were oddly elegant and at the same time virile, and she fancied in studying them they were longer than most cocks.

Which meant just with the length, if he knew how to use them, he could bring her to orgasm thrusting them inside her.

He was no Adonis.

He was Zeus.

She drew her lips in, wetting them, feeling the saturated soak in her panties that was beginning to coat her upper thighs, gathering her wits as she finished her slow circle and came to stand several feet in front of him again.

His eyes were on hers.

Her eyes dropped to his dick.

Yes, he enjoyed this. His balls were even tighter in his scrotum, his cock hanging so heavy, it looked painful.

"Do I pass inspection, Mistress?"

Again with the cheek.

But there was now a thread to it, an edge. Not pure impudence. He could no longer pull that off.

He'd been affected by her perusal. He tried to hide it but he'd failed.

Amélie gave him her gaze.

"You do know . . ." she said softly and took a step toward him.

She allowed her eyes to roam his face.

God, she wanted to touch him.

Please, please, please do not let him break in fifteen minutes, she begged the fates and moved her attention back to his eyes. *Or ever,* she ended her plea surprisingly.

Before she could allow that thought rising unexpectedly to tear into her concentration, she took another step toward him.

He flicked his gaze down, it came back hungrier, and she watched him draw his lower lip between his teeth and slide it against that white ridge until it was free.

At the sight, her breasts grew heavy, her nipples strained the fabric of her bra, his exposure of his desire, to have her closer, for her to touch him, the baring of those teeth, oh yes.

She wanted very badly to touch him.

"That your opening line out there was unacceptable," she finished her earlier thought.

He looked boyishly confused for a second, it was intensely endearing for that second, as he muttered, "Uh . . . what?"

"The 'how you doin', sweetheart,'" she explained something they both knew didn't need to be explained. She drew infinitesimally closer, the barest of leans, but he was already so attuned to her, his eyes darkened further and he reciprocated her lean, drawn to her like the pull of a magnet. "Stand strong, Olivier," she ordered quietly.

She watched the beauty of him baring his teeth in a snarl of frustration he controlled before he swayed back and did as told.

"You know that's unacceptable," she repeated. "And obviously," she drew in breath, locking his attention on her, "I must do something about it."

He stood there, caught in her focus, hands behind his head, and said nothing.

"As I mentioned before, unless I forbid it, you're welcome to speak, just do it respectfully," she invited. She went on to prompt, "Don't you agree?"

"You gotta do what you feel you gotta do . . . Mistress."

The words were respectful, mostly.

That said, they weren't entirely acceptable.

What they were was voiced in a tight, thick rumble like each was a piece of gravel, and his mouth was full of the same he had to force them through.

At the same time she liked his acute reaction to her, she grew concerned at its quickness. She was taking her time, to be certain. But she hadn't been at him an hour and she'd done nothing to him but make him stand naked for her perusal.

He was going to break.

Fuck, she thought.

"Drop to your knees," she ordered.

Her extreme relief was only part of her reaction when he treated her to another of those bitten-back snarls, not a look of desperate neediness, eager to jump at her command.

In fact, he was so *not* eager to jump, it took several very long moments before he bent a knee, his big body teetering in a controlled fall that, when he hit that knee, it was a wonder everything in the room didn't jump at his landing.

His other leg came down.

And the new depth of emotion in his eyes as he looked up at her was astounding.

He did not like to look up.

She checked the expanse exposed below.

His cock had grown past impressive to legendary.

But he definitely liked to be *made* to look up.

Not easily broken, then.

Oh yes, her mind whispered.

"Behind you, Olivier," she said gently, "on the floor, there's a series of steel eyes set into the wood. They're in a number of lines. I want you to place your left calf against the outermost line, the same with your right on the other side."

He twisted to look behind him. She saw his chest heave mightily once as his predicament assailed him. He seemed to still and she watched avidly as he struggled with the mental constraints that separated him from his true nature.

She felt almost compelled to clap when he shifted his calves to where she'd told him she wanted them.

This left him still on his knees, a wide stance that would give him a nice stretch up his inner thighs but would cause no real pain.

What it was, was awkward and it made him vulnerable.

She went to the table where the bag she had packed for this room sat, put there by staff when she'd reserved the space. She riffled through it, finding what she needed. She riffled through it further, finding the things she'd need in a moment, setting them aside, at the ready.

Then she moved back to him.

He was twisted at the waist, hands still behind his head, watching her.

She nearly stuttered in her step, such was his beauty.

She finished her approach successfully, and in a closed-leg crouch, her knees shifted to the door so he couldn't even see them or any view her position could afford him, she started clamping down the straps.

A wide, fleece-lined one just above his ankle. Another fleece-lined one at the bulge of his calf. And, she had to shift and reach so she was still as distant from him as she could be, the same at the bend of his knee.

Repeat with the other calf.

And her steed was strapped to the floor.

She stood, looking him over, avoiding his face but feeling his eyes on hers, and nodded smartly.

"Lovely," she murmured crisply then moved back to the table.

She re-approached at his front, standing several feet away.

"You'll know how to put this on. Do that now," she commanded, tossing him the black leather with its mess of thin straps that had gold buckles, and in a variety of places, gold catches.

He caught it.

She stood back to watch.

He didn't move.

She finally looked at his face. "Olivier, now, please."

His head tipped back.

"Mistress—"

"Now."

"But Mistress—"

Please no, it couldn't be.

"Is there a word you wish to say?" she asked disbelievingly, her tone hiding disappointment that felt like acid burning through her veins.

"No," he replied immediately.

"Then put the cock harness on *now*, please."

"Mistress, I can see just looking at it, this won't fit me."

This could be true.

"Do your best, beast," she ordered.

His head jerked in silent response to her address for him. He recovered from that without comment but hesitated, his frustration clear, and also clear was that it was mingled with an edge of anger.

She hadn't had the latter in one of her playrooms in a good long while.

She liked both.

He strapped the harness on and Amélie thoroughly enjoyed watching him do it. It was a snug fit, the buckles on their last hole, and even so, he'd had to do some tightening which she could tell by the hardness in his jaw, the tensing of his frame, caused a twinge or two.

It wasn't just the harness along his shaft. There was a ball harness, too, a strap down the middle that separated each testicle, stretched them slightly, this connected to the strap of leather sitting snug at the base of his cock.

And trussed in this, his testicles were so large, they bulged out the sides beautifully.

He wore it well. So well, it took an almost torturous self-discipline not to rush through the rest.

But she didn't.

"The steel eyes in the floor, Olivier, to the front of you. Bend down please. Forearms lined up with the innermost eyes."

This hesitation lasted longer—not having the use of his hands, being strapped down completely, at her mercy (unless he could pull those eyes right out of the wood, which was a possibility).

She rode it through with him.

It was her wont to be patient, she was known for it.

Demanding respect from him, the proper address of Mistress was simply a play in response to his, one that communicated she would not be topped from below.

In future sessions, if they had them, as was also her wont and something else that was well known, Amélie would allow lapses in all the formalities. Her domination would be made clear through actions, trust garnered through affection, punishment thoroughly administered only when earned—not words, not strict adherence to the rules.

But their first session, she had to practice more than the usual amount of patience even if she could feel the need to see him strapped to the floor on his forearms and knees gliding down the inside of her leg.

Eventually, after another mighty battle it was a thing of beauty to behold, he bent forward.

Ass in the air.

Another thing of beauty.

Amélie shuffled her thighs together to wipe away the wet as she forced herself to move slowly to the table.

She came back with the straps, made light work of snuggly fitting them so his forearms were immobilized at wrist and the juncture of his elbow.

His head was back. He wasn't watching her restrain him. She could feel his focus on her face, the heat of it sensational.

She was an unknown. He'd placed himself in her hands. He had no idea what she would do. All he knew was that she had now wrested away his control. His bulk, his strength, there were likely very few situations, physically, that he would not best.

Now, that was stripped away.

There was fear tinting the air. Lovely, shimmering fear that was even more amazing drifting from this steed.

This mingled with the purple glint of arousal that a quick glance at his cock, which was straining, and not just the harness, proved fact.

Once done with both arms, she moved back to the table before returning to him.

This time at his other end.

The work she did there was practiced and swift.

The result everything she wanted it to be and more.

A leather strap around his hips, two thinner straps running down either side of the crevice of his ass, the other end attached to a catch on his harness at the base of his balls.

There was a distinct growl that throbbed through the air, a corresponding throb hitting Amélie in five places, as she tightened the buckles of the straps, this spreading open the cheeks of his ass, exposing perhaps (and she hoped she would eventually find out), his keenest vulnerability.

"Fuck me, *fuck*," he hissed.

She moved again. Settling into another crouch in front of him, she tore her gaze from the gloriousness of his readied ass and turned her attention to his face.

His was already on hers.

Oh my.

Oh yes.

There . . .

Good God, there . . .

The backs of his eyes. She saw it.

It flashed fiery, almost too deep to see, but she caught it before he blinked and blanked it, his face a hard mask, this an effort to hide what she was making him feel.

Regardless.

"How are you feeling, Olivier?" she asked quietly.

"You been strapped to a floor with your ass spread open?" he returned, voice still thick and now harsh.

"Another rule, I'm sorry that I didn't share before, but answering a question with a question is not acceptable," Amélie shot back. "Now, answer my question, please. How are you feeling?"

"Like my dick is being strangled," he replied.

"And?" she pressed.

"Pissed," he bit out.

There it was.

And she gave it to him. "You top from below."

A quick, blunt-edged, "No."

And in his face a strange hint of chagrin.

Oh my.

Unexpected.

He *wanted* to be topped. He just fought letting go.

Oh, she liked this. She liked this a great fucking deal.

In a shuffling step, still crouched in front of him, she came nearer. His attention intensified as he watched, anger melting, hunger honing his features.

He wanted touch. She'd barely brushed his skin strapping him down and he wanted her hands on him.

Even the barest touch might make him climax.

She wanted to test that.

But not yet.

She had other tests to administer. Tests he had to pass and lessons he needed to learn if he was to earn her time in the future.

"You need to let go, Olivier," she instructed.

Frustration then anger infused his expression.

"Think I did that, *Mistress*," he spat the last disrespectfully. "Seein' as I'm strapped to the floor with my ass, also strapped, I'll fuckin' add, in the air."

She let the disrespect slide.

"You know you bought punishment with your opening line. Indeed, you bought it watching me move toward you. And you know you bought more with your attitude when you hit this room."

He averted his gaze.

He knew.

"Look at me, Olivier," she ordered softly.

His eyes came back but the effort was apparent.

She tried not to smile or, actually, howl with glee.

No, not yet broken.

A miracle.

She lifted her hand, fingers curled in a loose fist, toward his chin.

He shifted, seeking the contact.

She stopped him.

"Don't move your chin," she commanded, her tone still soft but now also sharp.

He froze.

She held her hand just below his jaw and leaned forward so her face was an inch from his.

More hunger, this stark.

Eyes flickering down and up, knowing what he was giving away, unable not to do it.

He wanted her mouth.

This—the mutual test, the challenge relayed and accepted, the dare, the impudence, the taunts, the battle of wills—*this* was his favored game. She knew it to her fucking *soul*.

And it was hers as well, by far the sweetest trip you could take.

Ecstasy.

"And I will punish you, Olivier," she continued. "What you don't know, you can only assume, is that I'll take care of you. And that," she edged closer but not close enough, sensing his body trembling, feeling that tremble caress her clit, the walls of her pussy, wishing she could hitch her skirt, straddle his hips and ride it to climax, "I promise, *chevalier*, I . . . will . . . *do*."

She watched him force back a painful swallow.

"Yes?" she pressed.

"Yes, Mistress."

The two words were strangled, giving the impression he hated saying them, giving her that even as she suspected he got off on uttering each much, much more, he just wouldn't admit it.

Perfection.

She straightened away and turned from him, allowing the smile to curve her mouth when she heard his choked-back groan.

Amazing.

This soon in play with her, he simply fed off her nearness. Her attention.

One last piece. One minor adjustment.

Then she could begin.

She walked back to her toy with the length of gold chain in her hand.

She forced herself not to take in the glorious spectacle of his restrained body, which might cause things to get out of hand in a way that wouldn't test anything, except to see if he could ride her strapped like that, and kept her focus on his face.

He eyed the chain warily.

Handsome. Built. Hung.

And not stupid.

She moved behind him.

His ass tensed, the valleys on the sides coming out in even sharper relief, the muscular rounds fighting against the straps holding it open and exposed, and Amélie's mouth watered.

Then she crouched again and reached between his legs, expertly attaching the clasp on the chain to the catch at the back of the ring closest to the tip of his cock and running the length to the ring in the floor. Quickly and expertly, she did a mental measurement of how much slack she'd need in order to give him the movement *he* would need without causing undue pain or even harm. She wound the chain through the ring and caught the clasp at the other end to a link halfway up.

It hung loose, only its weight now pulling down his cock.

"Jesus, fuck," he clipped out, body unmoving, not about to test that slack.

"We're almost ready," she informed him.

He knew what was coming and he knew what it would mean.

She knew this when he dipped down, his forehead to the floor, ass becoming more prominent, back heaving with deep breaths, and she knew something else.

If he could take it, if she could give it to him, she'd have him again.

And again.

And again.

And again.

She moved to the panel by the door and flipped a switch. The multipaned windows surrounding each playroom had air trapped between the inner two panes for soundproofing. In the outer two, two sheets of electronically controlled blinds. One white and not quite sheer, but not opaque, to offer observers outside a view of what was happening inside as a silhouette. Another that was black, which would block onlookers entirely from enjoying the view.

The white sheet was down.

The whir hit the room as the sheet rolled up.

"Amélie—" he started, fear more than an edge in his graveled voice.

She liked her name in that tone.

Indeed, in that voice.

It was lovely.

"Sorry?" she interrupted him, using the word as a reminder, stopping as she made it back to the table.

"Mistress Amélie," he corrected swiftly.

She turned to him and his eyes riveted to the paddle she held.

"I think fifteen strikes will do. It's a lot for a first session, though you've earned it," she said conversationally, watching his big body begin to tremble, his eyes never leaving the paddle, her mind wondering if she could give that first crack without coming. "That said, it would be the switch if you were used to me, so I think the paddle is a good compromise."

She came to a stop at his side and his eyes shifted up to hers.

The plea was there, laid open bare.

He didn't want to be watched. He didn't want to be paddled. What he wanted, she was not yet sure.

But she would find out.

And in the meantime, she would make him love everything she gave.

"I said that I—" he began.

"I know what you said," she interrupted again. "However, this room is mine. When you're in this room, *you* are mine. I do as I wish. You submit to *any* wish. And frankly, Olivier, you are far too magnificent a specimen not to share."

A flicker of confusion passed across his face.

She had no time for that. He had to know his beauty. He wasn't blind.

"I would brace, *chevalier*," she instructed gently.

When her words penetrated, he had only a second to do so before, two hands on the handle of the long, wooden paddle with holes drilled through the wood, she bent her knees slightly, twisted her torso, and put her weight and a considerable amount of strength in the first strike.

Even braced, his body flew forward, the chain at his cock clinked as the slack disappeared, yanking it down violently.

"Fucking hell," he blew out, automatically swinging back through his recovery.

Thwack!

The second strike had more momentum and he again flew forward, the chain slammed taut, wrenching his cock at the last moment.

"Fucking *fuck me*," he ground through clenched teeth.

Marvelous.

Thwack!

After the third strike, she knew they had an audience, of how many, she didn't care so she didn't bother to look.

Her entire world was the tethered, muscled body and its cock harnessed and chained to the floor and the man who owned those (for now) named Olivier.

Thwack!

The fourth strike, as he swung back, his big frame shuddering violently, the visual so splendid, Amélie had genuine concerns she could finish his punishment without coming.

She persevered because she had no other choice.

Thwack!

The brutal forward sway, the vicious pull on his cock that was akin to a ferocious hand job, and he couldn't bite it back anymore.

His exquisite grunt filled the room.

It was music to her ears. It exposed, not with the lilt of pain, but with the edge of pleasure, along with his quick recovery and the almost imperceptible tilt of his ass, that he wanted more.

Thwack!

Another grunt, another pull, another recovery, his body now quaking in his effort to hold back his response.

Thwack!

And again, her nipples so hard she thought they'd pierce the material of her dress at watching him endure his punishment, especially since, with this recovery, the tilt of his ass was not nearly imperceptible.

He offered it proudly, no mistaking it.

It was a silent plea.

More.

The next one, his hips jerked at more than the pull and continued to do so as he shoved back.

Triumph filled her, and with a quick check, she knew what she suspected was true.

He was coming.

In rapid succession, but with equal intensity, Amélie finished his strikes. She did this watching with a fervor that she knew was complete adoration as he lost all control. Surging forward, grunting, flexing back, offering his ass, his legs shaking, his hips automatically thrusting his cock into the restraining harness like it was a pussy, his extraordinarily large offering of cum gliding down his chain.

When she was done, he was forehead to the floor, body quivering, hips still weakly thrusting through the aftermath of his orgasm.

She went to stand between his ankles and reached between his legs with the paddle, caressing his balls and cock with the flat of the wood.

And he gave his Mistress more.

Promptly angling back, he pressed down, accepting the caress and straining to deepen it.

He'd accepted his punishment so well, given her so much, it was time for a reward.

She shifted the paddle up, adding pressure against his sensitive organ, giving him what he needed.

He rode it, milking his dick in his harness, the final rivulets of cum gliding down his chain, and good God, good *God*, he was sheer perfection.

She continued to coddle his cock and balls with the paddle as she reminded him quietly, "It's customary to thank your Mistress for her ministrations."

His voice came deep and hoarse, spent, pleasured, but fucking *blissfully* unbroken as he hesitated a delicious moment before he murmured, "Thank you, Mistress Amélie."

She liked her name in that tone too.

"You were magnificent, Olivier," she told him.

She watched his shoulders slump and he settled back into his calves, not with shame. He'd come so hard, his body was forced to recuperate.

She carefully glided the paddle out from between his legs, twisted it, and ran the edge of its tip hard along the exposed crevice of his ass, stopping at his hole, pressing gently.

Another test. One it was essential he passed.

He passed.

Going inert at first, he then pressed back just as gently.

Another offering.

She gathered control and when she accomplished this, she whispered, "Well done, my beast."

His hips flexed, juddering either at her words or an aftershock of coming, but he said nothing.

She removed the paddle from his exposed crease and walked

swiftly to the table, her heels making dull sounds against the boards. She dropped the paddle there and then she moved to the control panel.

Stellan was outside at the window, just next to the door, the best view Amélie knew bar none in the house. A female sub was on her knees beside him, leaning against his leg, both were watching.

His eyes were not on Olivier, they were on Amélie.

She lifted her chin in acknowledgment, her friend looked down to it, and she flipped the switch that would bring both sheer and black screens down.

She moved back to Olivier, crouching in front of him.

"Chevalier," she called.

He didn't lift his shoulders, just tipped his head back.

Those eyes sated, warming her deep in her belly, the power of this statement when he could only tip back his head that she'd exhausted (perhaps temporarily, but she'd done it) this incomparable steed, was nearly her undoing.

It deserved another reward.

"I have not had a toy make me this wet in longer than I can remember."

His eyes rounded, his mouth softened.

"You are so beautiful, it's hard to believe," she said softly.

"Amélie," he replied but said no more.

The game was this. There was a reason he fought it. He had clearly not had a Master or Mistress who'd guided him in any permanent way around it (thankfully). He was intelligent enough to recognize he needed it as well as the importance of keeping it and he was courageous enough that he didn't allow the shame to keep him from seeking it.

He fought it, but when that flip was switched, he submitted to it spectacularly.

She didn't know if she wished to protect the beast that fought it so she could battle that beast (something she deduced the ones that had gone before her had done) or if she wanted to break him so she could take him straight to where he needed to be.

Or, to be precise, she didn't know which one *he* wanted.

It would be a puzzle she'd enjoy solving.

"I'm going to go home, doing this directly, and I'm going to touch myself, thinking of every moment with you. And I will come hard, my beast." She smiled at him and his eyes locked on her mouth. "Just visualizing that big brute of a cock you're hung with might take me over the edge."

"Let me eat you," he said quickly. "I'll stay strapped," he offered, like that was his choice.

Seeing as it obviously was not, it was an odd thing to say.

"Perhaps another time," she replied.

His reaction was gratifyingly quick, exposing he wanted another time to happen.

As it would at this juncture—his cock still snugly harnessed, his cum still dripping down his chain.

She just hoped he wouldn't go home and think differently.

It wasn't about convincing him not to do that. It was his choice. She only had to give him the honest her so he could make the right decision.

It came with a thread of tortured when he forced out, "I can smell you."

"I've no doubt," she agreed.

"I want that," he told her.

She was utterly delighted he did. She would relish the time when he'd earned her forcing his face between her legs, commanding him to make her come.

She leaned closer to him. It appeared he'd lift up to increase the chance of contact but he abruptly stopped.

Not stupid.

A quick learner.

"Is your cock getting hard again for me?"

There was the hesitation, the hint of anger at the indignity, before he hissed out, "Yes."

"A quick recovery."

"You're fuckin' gorgeous, somethin' I think I already shared . . . Mistress."

He was getting his fighting spirit back.

A quick recovery, indeed.

"You please me, Olivier."

"I'd please you more with my mouth."

"I hope that's true, *chevalier.*"

She lifted a hand as if she was going to stroke his hair, he tensed to allow her to do it, but she dropped it.

That got her the controlled snarl.

Yes, a quick recovery.

"I hope that's true," she repeated. "Saturday, please arrive at nine-thirty sharp. Ask the front desk staff to share with you my instructions. They will be fully briefed. I'll meet you when I'm ready."

His head jerked slightly. "We're done?"

Oh yes, he wanted more. Even coming that hard for her, he wanted it now.

Amélie beat back a smile.

"Yes, my beast, until Saturday. I'll send a member of staff in to untether you. It's unusual, and only a punishment, when I ask my toys to clean up. So no worries there. The staff will see to that too."

"You're leaving me here," he stated flatly.

"Yes."

"Like this?"

"The staff is responsive. I'll make sure they see to you immediately."

He very much didn't like that.

"Amélie—"

"They're discreet, Olivier, obviously. They've seen it all. If the room is black-blinded, they're not allowed to share what they see in

these rooms even with each other, much less members. They're exceptionally professional, and if not, they're in the middle of a lawsuit."

"Mistress Amé—"

She lifted a hand, finger extended, taking it a whisper away from
his lips, and he stopped speaking, focusing on the promise of a touch.

Incomparable.

Magnificent.

Then, in a fluid movement, she rose to her full height.

With unhurried strides and without a look back, a foolish move
that would be too tempting, she walked out the door.

three

Black Box

OLIVIER

The next day, Olly stood, leaning a shoulder against the open bay, his head bent, his eyes on what he'd looked up on his phone.

Chevalier: Knight. Soldier. Cavalry. Horseman.

Horseman.

He wanted not to smile but he couldn't fucking stop himself from doing it.

That room she'd led him to, to scare the shit out of him. The stall. The bridles hanging from its sides. The padded benches, vaults, saw horses with wide cushioned tops instead of two-by-fours.

Chevalier.

Fuck, he was in over his head.

He didn't understand what was the big deal. He thought he could handle it. With stupid-ass, cocky certainty, he'd convinced Barclay of it, Jenna, but not Whitney. That bitch had a mean streak and when he'd asked her to do what she'd done for him, he figured she did it to set him up to take a fall, either getting caught and bounced from the Honey or getting his ass right where it already was after one session with Amélie.

Over his head.

He blew out a breath, shoved his phone into his back pocket, and looked into the Phoenix sun streaming down to bake the pavement outside the firehouse.

He wasn't going back Saturday. He wasn't going back at all. He'd been approved by that huge fucking black guy for a scholarship but he'd still had to pay a membership fee based on his earnings and that shit stung. It cost a fucking fortune. If he didn't go back, which he wasn't going to, it would be a fucking fortune for one night strapped to the floor having his ass paddled and his dick jacked.

That fortune worth every penny.

"Shit," he muttered to himself, knowing that last thought should give rise to others, others that would change his mind, and he couldn't allow that.

He was not ready for this.

He didn't think he'd ever be ready for this.

Amélie had put him through the wringer and she knew the potency of everything she did, every look she gave him, every word she said, every fall of her sexy-as-fuck sandals on the wood floor.

And she'd guided him to the single most phenomenal orgasm he'd ever experienced in his life.

But she'd asked what he didn't particularly like for the sole purpose of using it against him. Opening the shades. Stretching the cheeks of his ass. Then leaving him on that floor to experience the humiliation of that girl coming in and letting him loose.

Amélie had been right. The girl had been professional about it. It was all the same to her, not about the scene, just about the job. She didn't take any jollies from it.

She just unstrapped him, not touching the harnesses, doing it quickly and efficiently and saying as she left, "Just leave the stuff on the floor, all of it. It'll be dealt with, honey."

Then she was gone.

But Olly had been seriously ticked. Getting dressed, freaking because he worried he wouldn't be able to figure out the way to get the fuck out in that maze of rooms. Seeing other people in the halls look at him and wondering if they'd seen Amélie work him.

He hadn't felt the full extent of his anger until he was home, in bed, and again hard as fucking rock.

What she'd done to him, how hard he'd come, how fucking beautiful she was, that clingy, dark-green wraparound dress she wore, tits that were high and full, hips curvy, a sweet round ass, all this on a slender, almost delicate frame, he couldn't get it out of his head.

He'd needed to jack off but wouldn't allow it to control him, trying to focus on what she'd done to cow him, telling himself that shit wasn't right.

And not allowing himself to remember that he knew the blinds were up, but once she started in on him, he didn't give a fuck about anything but what she was doing, what he was feeling, and how fucking hard she made him come.

He eventually fell asleep only to wake an hour later with a hard-on that was raging and wouldn't be ignored.

So he gave her more, jacking himself violently, thinking about what she'd done, and more he wanted her to do, and coming nearly as hard as he did for her.

Doing it knowing that he didn't even know where the woman lived, her last name, the kind of fucking car she drove, but he still stroked every tight stroke for her.

Fuck.

Barclay had warned him to go into the Honey the right way, the way they'd ease him in, even if it was Barclay who had told him in the first place, "Man, you do not belong in this scene. You need to get your ass into the Honey."

That scene Barclay was talking about was the Bolt. The club Olly had just started to go to. A club that was nowhere near the straight-up cool of the Honey.

From the moment Barclay shared what the Honey was, Olly had been obsessed with it.

He closed his eyes and opened them, no longer seeing the Phoenix sun.

It was that box. That fucking box. That box he found when he was fifteen and his mom sent him up to her and his dad's room to get something from the closet. Big and black and hidden, exposed only when he couldn't find what she wanted him to get for her so he went searching. At his age, he could have no clue what curiosity would expose when he'd opened it.

The ropes. The handcuffs. The blindfold. The vibrators. And a huge fucking dildo.

Not a box owned by parents any kid should see.

He'd buried that, but not deep enough. It was impossible.

He'd been jacking off by then for a long time and the shit that filled his mind so he could come even before he found that box was extreme.

But that box unhinged something he could not rein in.

And being a weak twat, he'd become *that guy*. That loser asshole that hit the strip clubs. The one who paid for lap dances. The one who found and paid for peep shows.

None of it doing anything for him.

It had been when he'd been out with buds and they'd met other buds and Barclay was among them when things got clearer.

Barclay was open about being a third of a partner in a BDSM club, that club being the Bolt. He also had skin of steel since the guys tried to take strips off him constantly, giving him shit about it, banter that could turn nasty and did, a helluva lot.

Barclay was not only immune, he was also observant. He noticed Olly never said shit, didn't participate in that, and often told the other guys to back off. This had the uncomfortable result of them turning that shit on him, accusing him of being in the closet, giving him crap about him liking to have his ass spanked.

Not knowing this was true.

Olly did not have skin of steel.

What he had, from a little kid, was a serious temper. A temper that fused fast, blew quick, and made words come out of his mouth that he might mean, but they could be communicated in a vastly different way. A temper his mother frequently told him, if he didn't learn to control it, would get his ass in hot water.

But bottom line, he still didn't like to be around assholes who acted like assholes and he was the kind of man who'd tell you you were being an asshole. They knew that, so it took a lot, but he didn't let their crap stop him. And he did it only partially because he didn't like to be around assholes, but also because, if he didn't continue to get up in their shit like he normally would do (his short fuse was both fortunately and unfortunately legendary), it might make them wonder if they were on to something.

Barclay found a time and had a word and did it smart, getting Olly half-shitfaced before he did it.

Feeling a massive sense of relief, half-shitfaced, Olly gave it to him. Something he'd never given anybody.

A window into those dark places in his head.

But Barclay had been cool. Extending an invitation, a guest membership to his club, and sharing that in that world, no one said dick. It wasn't an unwritten rule, it was an unbroken law. You feared your kink getting out, the person next to you at the club had that same fear, maybe even a bigger one with more to lose.

It took two months for Olly to accept the invitation.

Enter Whitney, who was seriously pretty with an amazing body, both of these meaning he'd let her work him once.

His first.

She'd sucked at it and was clearly into giving some serious pain without really bothering with the pleasure, so he never went back to her.

He almost gave up.

But then came Jenna, pretty, petite, sweet, and she'd orgasmed within ten minutes of having him in that room, doing it while she was shackling his foot to the floor.

He knew topping from below. In other words, attempting to control the scene even though you were the sub, using whatever way you could to do that, any way that was, in Olly's opinion, being underhanded in the part the sub was meant to play in that world. He hadn't jumped in like an idiot. He'd observed. Chatted with some of the other members. Got some of the lingo down.

Mistresses didn't do what Jenna did.

Regardless, he'd let her have him half a dozen times because she didn't suck, just got overly excited. She got better, but the experience wasn't what he'd hoped it would be.

When Olly didn't go back to Jenna, and couldn't find anyone in that club that interested him (not to mention, hanging around there he felt uncomfortable around all the leather and nurses outfits and spiked collars), Barclay had asked him out for a beer and told him about the Honey.

When the man gave him the intel, Olly told him he was interested, but not interested in the training period, which would mean he wouldn't be able to choose anyone he wanted to work him, but had a much smaller pool that Barclay admitted, if rumor was true, were mostly guys.

To be fair, at that juncture, Barclay had strongly advised against him trying to con Aryas Weathers, the Bee's Honey's owner, into believing he wasn't a rookie.

When they'd chatted about it in the club, Jenna, who knew the Honey (everyone in that scene did), advised strongly against it too.

Jenna liked him and wanted another go (or a hundred) so she wasn't hard to convince to write a reference that said he had what was required: a D/s relationship with her that lasted six months or longer (she'd said in her letter it was eight, which he thought was nice).

Whitney did it for her own reasons and her letter gave the bare minimum.

Before he jumped in on Olly's plan, Barclay, a switch-hitter (he could go both ways, Dom and sub), had demanded they meet so he could give Olly what he needed not to be found out and not to get his ass in a sling if he got in. This was because Barclay would have to substantiate Jenna's and Whitney's claims and give false information about the length of his membership at Barclay's club.

"You do not wanna get on the bad side of Aryas Weathers, man," he'd said. "And serious as shit, take that in. But more serious as shit, do not throw my ass under the bus with this because I don't wanna be on that man's bad side either."

They'd met. Barclay shared a shitload. He'd also told him what magazines to read, what sex shops to go to, what books to download, so he could learn more. Study up. Not only to be successful at the con but so he didn't do what he eventually did, get in over his head.

Olly went to the shops but didn't do the magazines or books.

This was the only reason he knew how to put on the harness Amélie gave him. He'd never worn one. It wasn't hard to figure out but if he'd had to fiddle with it, that could have led to uncomfortable questions.

And now that she'd done him with it, in his weaker moments, he was considering going to a shop so he could buy one of his own. One that fit.

In the end, he'd learned enough that he'd conned Weathers, but his approval as a member had been a surprise because, in the hour-long interview they'd had, he got the impression the guy saw right through him.

So he'd learned enough.

But he hadn't learned *enough*.

And it was clear practice made perfect.

He'd fucked up at the get-go, thinking all that "yes, Mistress," "no, Mistress," no eye contact, following-like-a-dog bullshit was a certain type of sub's kink.

But the way Amélie talked about it, it was expected.

This was something he did not know and something he figured Barclay, Jenna, and Whitney (the latter two had told him to call them Mistress, he'd done it enough not to trip their triggers, but he was his own man in the common sections of the club) thought anyone with any experience would know and this was why they didn't share it with him.

Time and again, he thought Amélie had made him and he had no idea what she would do if she did. She wouldn't work him, that was a given. Not that she wasn't into him, she *so* was. She made no bones about that. Just that it was clear she expected her subs to know how to serve, to take what she had to give, and she was impatient when he fucked up on the basics.

She got off on his struggle, though. Seriously got off on it. It tore him apart inside but she also made no bones about it being a turn-on for her.

Something that was totally fucked up.

And a big reason why he was not going back on Saturday, or ever.

He was in over his head. He was going to get found out. He'd be ousted, or something in that crazy-ass, *long* contract he'd signed meant Aryas Weathers would own his house.

"Bro, you gettin' a suntan or what?"

With a guilty start, like Chad could read his mind, Olly turned to his best bud and brother firefighter.

"Yo," he greeted.

Chad stopped close and gave him a look.

"Dude, you're in a mood," he stated.

"Standin' at the bay, lookin' outside," Olly pointed out. "This does not say mood. So what the fuck?"

"Plebes are fuckin' terrified, sure you're gonna make them wash the rigs with a toothbrush, *their* toothbrush, you been bein' such a dick all day."

This was why he'd moved to the bay. Not a lot of sleep but a lot of shit cluttering up his head, making him act like a dick. He didn't like assholes so it didn't need to be said he didn't like to be one.

He stilled.

Jesus.

Fuck.

He felt his lips slightly part as Chad went out of focus.

That was it.

By the time Amélie had made her round of inspection, his mind was clear.

Clear of everything.

Except her. Her beauty. Those tawny eyes that were never cold, always so fucking warm, when she looked at him it was like a touch on his skin. Her soft voice with that very soft accent, a pretty accent, like a lilt. An accent he couldn't place until she'd called him *chevalier*. What she'd done to him, barely touching him . . . no, the fact that she *did* barely touch him being part of what centered his focus. Nothing else got in but what was happening between them.

Nothing but what he was feeling.

Nothing but needing her to fucking touch him.

Nothing but unease that was mixed with a liberal dose of thrill at what she might do next.

Nothing but how hard his dick got, how heavy his balls became, how he got off on how tight the harness was, the bite of the straps running up the crack of his ass.

Nothing but how bad he needed to blow.

Nothing.

All his life, sexually, his mind had been cluttered. And because of those channels to the dark places in his brain that black box in his parents' closet opened up, this leaked into life. Women he'd banged, girlfriends—he got off. Like anything, he figured, if you were going to do it, you not only did it right but you gave the best you could give, so he was good at it.

But always in the back of his head, in those dark places, he knew those women would go because he'd send them away, never having the balls to tell them he wanted them to tie him up. To blindfold him. To play with his cock and not let him come until he thought it would explode.

Even with seeing as many people who'd been at both clubs he'd attended, everyone knew it wasn't right. It wasn't real. It couldn't be a part of him.

Especially not him.

He was a guy. A big guy. A big guy who liked women exclusively. He liked the taste of pussy, the feel of it. He fought fires for a living. He liked football and basketball and finding a stretch of road where he could ride his motorcycle fast.

That kind of guy did *not* like his ass strapped open. He did *not* ride the paddle that just spanked that ass like it was a woman's hand.

But he was the kind of guy who got off on that and there was no denying it.

Except the part he needed to find a way to fucking deny it.

"Uh . . . hello?" Chad called.

Olly shook his head and refocused.

"Sorry, bud," he muttered.

"You good?" Chad asked, studying him closely.

"Yeah," Olly answered. "Just didn't get a lot of sleep last night."

Chad grinned. "Hit the scene?"

More like the scene hit him.

"No, just had trouble sleeping," Olly replied.

"Dude, you need to find a woman," Chad advised, and he would advise that.

He'd been married to Annie for five years. They had two kids and one on the way. And Chad was one of those assholes who was an asshole because he got it all and got it early. Annie was a knockout. She was funny. She could be one of the guys and she still kicked ass in a dress and heels. She loved her husband like crazy. Was a good mom. And she got the life.

"Maybe, me bein' in a mood, we cannot go there," Olly returned.

"Annie's got a friend," Chad shared.

Olly felt his eyes narrow. "And, bud, been there, done that, *twice*, and your woman is the shit. But her friends are fucked way the hell up."

"Mandy just liked you," Chad declared.

"Mandy called me five times from the minute I dropped her at her house to the minute I got to mine and I live ten minutes away from her, which is about ten hours too close," Olly shot back.

Chad grinned again. "Okay, Mandy liked you *a lot.*"

"She was a stalker, Chad. I had to change phones."

"Sorry 'bout that," Chad muttered, not looking sorry. He'd always found the whole thing funny.

And luckily, Mandy had been so embarrassed by it (this being after a party at Chad and Annie's that they'd both attended, and she'd made her approach, which included a fucking *plea* for another shot), he now knew she always asked Annie if he was coming. If he was, she didn't show.

Which was a relief.

"Shannon was just psycho," Olly pointed out.

"Yeah, even Annie doesn't talk to her anymore. She's a little self-involved."

"She didn't tear her eyes off her reflection in the car window the whole time I drove her to dinner," Olly shared. "Bitch was gorgeous but no one is *that* gorgeous."

Except Amélie.

Fuck.

"Two strikes. This time, Annie says she's got a good one lined up for you," Chad wheedled.

"In this game, man, there is no strike three."

Chad kept grinning. "Just think about it. We'll have a big party. You two can circle each other. See if you wanna give it a go."

Circle each other.

Olly had far more interest in Amélie taking her sweet fucking time circling him again, looking hot and gorgeous and classy and in command, than he did whatever whackjob Annie had picked out for him.

"I think I've hit my quota of parties for this year," Olly announced.

Chad started laughing and through it said, "Bro, it's football season. That's sacrilege."

"Whatever," Olly muttered.

Chad lifted a hand and slapped him on the arm. "Shake off your mood. Pull your shit together. Come up to the kitchen and have lunch. Stare down the recruits and scare the shit of them. But don't stand out here any longer. Don't gotta remind you we live in the Valley of the Sun. Your eyes'll get burned out."

"That might be a better option then eating lunch with a smartass."

Chad never lost his grin. "Your call."

Olly said nothing and didn't watch Chad walk away.

He looked out into the sun.

Circle each other.

She was who she was. Amélie. Mistress Amélie. A woman who liked to tie men down and paddle their asses. A genius at that shit. And she was that, apparently, just like Barclay, with no hang-ups.

He was not that. He was not ready for the Bee's Honey. He wasn't thinking he'd ever be ready and he had some serious shit fucking with his head wondering if he even wanted to be.

So it sucked. She was gorgeous. He liked her voice. He totally got off on what she did to him. He wanted more and that included the fact he wouldn't mind actually getting to know her.

But it was done. He had to end this shit.

All of it.

It was tearing him apart.

So Olly was not going back on Saturday.

No way.

AMÉLIE

Word is, you gave quite a show last night, the text from Mirabelle read.

Amélie's lips curved as, late evening the day after her session with

Olivier, she moved through her house with her phone in one hand, a glass of chilled white wine in the other, doing this with practiced ease even as her cat, Cleopatra, wove through her feet.

She arrived at the couch that faced her wall of windows. Windows that showed a stunning view of Phoenix at night off Camelback Mountain, where her home was located in an exclusive neighborhood in Paradise Valley.

This view, of course, being beyond the negative-edge pool, clean-lined decking, contemporary but comfortable outdoor furniture and, before that, the open gas fireplace that sat inside her expansive living room between her and the vista beyond.

The evening proved enjoyable, she texted back, a smile curving her mouth.

Enjoyable.

A vast understatement.

Cleopatra jumped up to the couch after Amélie sat, took a sip of wine, and leaned forward to rest the elegantly curved glass on her equally elegantly curved coffee table. After she relaxed back into the couch, the Siamese put her two front paws to Amélie's thigh, knowing what she was demanding and knowing she would get it.

Amélie was a Dominatrix but she felt no shame admitting she was the dominated when it came to her pets.

Her eyes scanned for Stasia, her other furry darling. She was unsurprised when Stasia was nowhere to be seen.

Stasia loved her *Maman*. She was just exceptionally choosy about the times she wished to display that.

Cleo, on the other hand, was purring loudly as Amélie scratched her neck and occasionally gently rubbed both ears, able to do this now without Cleo racing away when she touched the mutilated one as had happened when Cleo first came home. The notch out of Cleopatra's ear had been one of several sad and infuriating reasons Dr. Hill had not allowed her to go back to her owners after they'd brought her in to his veterinary clinic.

These sad and infuriating reasons meant Amélie had no idea if it was the natural curiosity and intelligence of a Siamese that meant Cleopatra's spirit had not been broken in the first home she'd shared with humans (like, alas, her sweet but very shy Stasia's had).

She'd just painstakingly, with great love, an abundance of patience, and pure joy, made certain she reinforced that spirit so the second (and last) home Cleo would share with a human would be an entirely different experience.

Amélie heard a noise come from her laptop that was sitting on the coffee table in front of her. She looked to it to see the notification in the bottom right corner and felt her mouth get tight when she saw who the email was from at the same time another noise came from her phone.

She reached for the laptop before she looked to her phone.

The email was from her financial adviser, sharing yet again that, although they'd just returned from a series of travel to see to business, he was advising two more meetings, one in Seattle, one in San Francisco.

It wasn't her financial adviser that set her mouth. He was a good man, she'd known him a long time and he was absolutely trustworthy.

No, it was something else.

Amélie stared at the email, having hesitated after his earlier email on the same subject to pull the trigger on scheduling the meetings due to the fact that they'd just returned. She had a home. She volunteered at Dr. Hill's practice, and although she was a volunteer, she took the time she gave him as serious as if it were paid employment. Not to mention, she had pets who liked her around (even Stasia, although she rarely showed it).

She enjoyed travel but she'd been gone weeks, she didn't want to leave again so soon.

And last, the reason she wasn't pleased to see that email pop up reminding her she needed to make a decision, she found these business trips mind-numbingly dull.

Like waking anesthesia.

She detested them.

She just needed to attend them because . . .

Because . . .

She blinked at the computer screen.

She had no idea what that "because" was.

What she did know was that, now, she definitely wasn't going to schedule those meetings.

Not for a good while.

This was because she had a home. She had pets. She did office work at Dr. Hill's clinic. What she did was not essential in the aid of the animals he cared for, but it did assist his endeavors. And, regardless of the repetitive quality of the work, it was the only thing at the end of any day that Amélie felt good about in her life, something with more than a small amount of alarm she was allowing herself to realize.

And last, there was the very *not* insignificant fact that she had Olivier in a playroom on Saturday.

She felt her face get soft at that thought, a coil of anticipation in her belly, both highly welcome reactions.

It had only been a day and her mind had wandered to him repeatedly, and with each time she had that same exact response.

Highly welcome.

She dismissed the email with a clap of screen to keyboard and looked to her phone, still scratching Cleo, who'd hunkered down, eyes closed, purr loud, claws coming out to knead Amélie's thigh.

More play in the near future? Mira had asked.

That garnered another soft look because, yes, there would be.

And early indications screamed it would be *scrumptious*.

Saturday evening, she texted back.

Marvelous, my lovely, Mirabelle returned.

Absolutely, Amélie agreed.

She waited for more, even watched her screen, her heart feeling oddly suspended as she did.

It took time, time enough for Amélie to lean forward and take hold of her wine, have a sip, locate the remote that fired up the fireplace and wonder where she'd left the book she'd been reading, thinking about a contented night in for a change with wine, fire, book, and Cleo (and Stasia, if she'd deign to make an appearance).

In her life, she had a number of nights in . . . alone.

The change would be the "contented" part.

With Olivier to look forward to, that adjective could now be added.

This was also, obviously, highly welcome.

The text finally came and Amélie looked right to it.

Book club at yours?

That made her mouth turn down in a frown for this was not the text she expected, or more aptly, wished to receive.

She'd been waiting for word about what had (or had not) happened with Trey.

And yet there was no word.

Amélie wanted to ask her friend if the subject had been broached after their session last night. If Trey had asked Mirabelle out. Or if, perhaps, Mira brought it up.

What she did not want to do was ask her friend if the subject had been broached if it indeed *had* and this back-and-forth over texts was a brave face Mira was putting on to hide it had not gone well. For if it had, she would lead with that, not questions about Olivier.

Therefore she did not ask.

She replied, *Yes, darling.*

Good. And hey, have you heard from Evangeline?

This also set Amélie's mouth turning down, for she had not.

Evangeline, a fellow Mistress, but more, a close friend, had had the unspeakable happen to her. And unbelievably, the event had occurred at the Honey—the first of its kind, to Amélie's knowledge.

Aryas had lost his mind when it had happened and still carried guilt it was arguable, in Amélie's opinion, he should carry.

However it was so much guilt, he refused to speak of it. But there were times, with her relationship with Ary, her skills as a Domme, Amélie saw it show.

She said nothing, also knowing Aryas was doing what he could with Evangeline to see to her healing and not doing this simply to assuage his guilt.

Not surprisingly, Evangeline had taken a break from the scene.

Disturbingly, this was lasting a good long while.

Too long.

Worse, she'd nearly disappeared and not just from the club. Cursory returns of texts. No-show at parties and bad excuses not to make lunch or dinner plans.

Something needed to be done.

It was just that Amélie, unusually, didn't know what that something was. She'd tried gentle, at first. She'd tried firm. She'd even tried (carefully) insistent.

Evangeline was immune.

Or, knowing her friend, stubborn.

And if someone refused to heal, even a friend who cared deeply had to understand when the time came to leave them to that.

The only thing Amélie knew was that now was not yet that time.

No, Mira. I'll ask her to the next club meeting and urge her strongly to come, she texted in return.

Excellent. I will too. Right, heading for the bath. Talk soon.

Good night, Mira, Amélie finished it.

She took a deep breath before another long sip of wine, listening to Cleopatra's purring, giving her scratches down the length of her spine to her kitty-booty.

She did this sending her message to the fates that they'd take care of Mirabelle.

And Evangeline.

Careful to keep Cleo comfortable, instead of going to find her book, she shoved the laptop out of her way and curled her legs under her, now looking about space that was her space and had been for some years.

She was into minimalism, clean lines, modernism, with occasional statement pieces or flashes of color.

Throughout her large home, there were a lot of silvers, blacks, and grays.

There was also the phenomenal fireplace in front of her.

And the masterpiece of colorful glass art that was the chandelier that took over the full ceiling of her foyer.

Further, the five-foot-tall, four-foot-wide curvaceous, faceless goddess structure at the northwestern corner of the back deck—the goddess sitting on unseen calves, the sculpture starting at knees, leading to the juncture of the pubis and wide, rounded hips, back up, globular breasts, eyeless face looking straight on, arms raised up in curlicues.

A magnificent piece of beauty and power and femininity.

As she examined environs that were so familiar to her, she barely saw them anymore, suddenly, she saw them with new eyes.

New eyes wondering what Olivier would make of all of this. If she were to have him there, if he would like it, feel at home, share in her tastes.

And more, Amélie wondered what his home was like, and if he were to ask her there, if she would like it, feel at home there, share his tastes.

Practically the moment this thought entered her head, Amélie pushed it out.

One session and she was wondering if he'd like her goddess sculpture.

Not even one session and she was comparing the blue of his eyes to the hue in a rainbow.

You must be cautious, Leigh, she warned herself on another sip of her wine, eyes now fixed to the fire, hand now fully stroking her purring cat.

It was good advice. She knew it.

And she knew she had no choice but to take it.

But that did not diminish the coil of anticipation that twined deliciously in her belly.

One session. They'd had one session.

And they would have another one.

Her lips curved as she forced her mind to that. Just that. And with her considerable control, she was able to block out the rest and the hope that came with it, wondering about his space, wondering what he'd think of hers, how they'd fit into each other's lives if they were to do so outside the club.

Hope.

She knew she couldn't go there.

Not now. Not yet. Maybe not ever.

Amélie had to focus only on what there was and what she knew there would be.

They'd had one exceptionally fulfilling session.

And soon, she with her magnificent beast would have another one.

four

Lost and Never Found

AMÉLIE

Amélie entered the Honey and she did it with a carefully modulated gait, concealing her anticipation and impatience.

She greeted the front desk staff, giving them her purse to stow, forcing her words not to be perfunctory, but also not lingering.

She then moved to the left, from the close, warm confines of the foyer with its muted classical music playing, into the hunting ground.

This was where she should linger. Get a drink. See who was there. Chat with friends.

But it was just after ten. Olivier would have been waiting for her now for over half an hour. She knew how he'd be waiting. And she couldn't wait to see.

It said a good deal to all who were watching when she moved casually, but unerringly, toward the door to the playrooms.

She did glance around, though, offering nods, a curve of her lips, to Felicia, Romy, and Stellan, who, when she caught his eye, she found his attention on her in a focused way she'd only ever noticed he gave his subs.

She did not contemplate this. She simply lifted a hand to her lips, touching the side of her index finger there, and sending it slightly his way, like she was not quite blowing him a modified kiss.

He didn't grin at her like he normally would have done. Just kept his gaze steady on her as she moved through the room.

She had no idea what that meant and she had less interest.

She wished to get to her steed.

Moving through the playrooms, the only thing that caught her attention was Mirabelle working Trey.

He was naked, sitting on a plug screwed into the floor, his face stuffed by her hand clenched into his hair into the juncture of her thighs, where she'd completely zipped down the skintight, black catsuit she wore, clearly all the way to the back of her crotch. Her head was back and her beautiful face was flushed and close to coming.

Since texting with her Wednesday night, Amélie had called her friend, mentioning the situation casually, only to receive a quick, un-informative update. But Amélie now knew Trey had not asked Mira out to do something in the ordinary world.

She also knew Mirabelle still held hope.

Amélie would give this some time and attention, keeping her finger on the pulse and hoping her friend's heart didn't get broken.

It bit into her admittedly vast reserves of control not to hurry through the passageways to her special room.

But when she finally turned the corner that would lead her to the door, she couldn't stop a quiet coo of delight from floating up her throat.

There were a number of people, Doms and subs, standing (or kneeling) at the windows, looking in.

Of course, the sight would be one to see.

When her approach was noted, she got attention and gave nods, ignored subs, and walked right to the door.

She opened it, stepped through, and didn't bother flipping the switch to send the signal the room was in use as it had been now for some time and the employee who'd seen to Olivier would have done it for her.

The truth of it was, Amélie might not have even remembered to do it, for she'd been correct.

Olivier was a sight to see.

She closed the door, eyes to him, and walked on the spike heels of her red pumps to stand two feet in front of him, the wide legs of her cuffed-hem black slacks swaying along her legs, the snug fit of them at her hips suddenly seeming constricting, the choice of a light, loose, black silk blouse becoming a godsend.

His eyes were on her, too, dark as night, and they hit her the instant she entered, never leaving.

Her eyes roved over him, her *magnificent* beast.

"Hello, Olivier," she greeted quietly.

"Mistress," he bit out.

She felt one side of her mouth snag up.

But she took in his tone and studied him far more closely, honing in with keen eyes, seeing his distress.

She'd ordered him collared and bound, straps at ankles and wrists tied to each other at the back, a strap through the catch at the back of the wide band of black leather that circled his thick neck leading all the way down to his ankles. He was on his knees on the floor, thighs resting on calves splayed wide. As tied, he was forced back at a slight angle, but nothing too constricting.

This the staff would have done.

What was happening between his legs, he'd have been ordered to do before he was bound because no one touched her toy's privates but her.

His cock was ringed, the gold of it gleaming in the hairs at the root. His balls were harnessed, stretched apart by their strap, stretched from his body by another at the base. There was a long strap leading from the back of the ball harness that an employee would have had to deal with and would have been able to do so without touching what was only Amélie's.

This was tied tight, tethering him by his sac to the ring in the floor.

This meant he was strung back and tethered only at one point in his body, but still unable to move an inch.

He was being very good, his legs spread wide as she'd commanded.

The distress came from the cock ring. She'd worried it wouldn't fit without more than the pain she'd wish. She'd worried the same about the collar, which she didn't wish to add even a single twinge.

She wanted his attention between his legs.

It appeared the collar fit.

The ring, although the fit was not dangerous, visibly did not.

And his enormous cock was hard, weighted heavy. Regardless of the slight arch of his body forced with his bindings, it was so large, it was brushing the strap and the tip even hit the floor, the tight fit of the ring meaning in all likelihood he could think of nothing but his dick.

There was a sheen of sweat all over his body, including his thighs, as he struggled to control the pain and as he battled his reaction to his obvious pleasure.

He was beautiful.

She bent over him.

"How are you, my *chevalier*?" she asked.

Eyes flashed with ire and something else.

Both she liked.

"Peachy," he gritted.

Oh, how she liked his cheek. She shouldn't. She shouldn't allow it. Most Mistresses wouldn't.

But she liked it and she absolutely was not most Mistresses.

So she did.

And furthermore, she could play with it.

She tipped her head to the side. "I may be wrong, but you seem impatient with me."

"Impatient is a good word," he agreed.

"My poor steed," she whispered, letting her gaze trail down his sweat-slickened chest to the spectacular bound meat between his legs. She looked back at his face. "He needs to come."

"Yeah." It came as an exhalation. "That'd be good."

"First," she began.

Impatient frustration at the obvious delay her word conveyed saturating his hard features, she didn't fight the curve of her mouth.

When he spotted her smile, that brought more ire.

She smiled bigger and went on, "I think it important to share with you that I came three times after I left you Tuesday night."

His body suddenly surged up, yanked down by his rein, a suppressed rumble sounded like it came from trapped in his chest rather than forced between his tight lips.

She watched as he slid his knees farther out to give as much slack to the ball tether as he could while his chest expanded and contracted as he pulled in deep breaths through his teeth.

God, could he get any more beautiful?

She shifted closer.

His lips tightened so much, his body beginning to quiver with the effort to remain in place, those lips nearly bared his lovely, strong white teeth.

"Three times hard, *chevalier. Very* hard," she said softly, dipping even closer, coming toward his face, veering to his left at the last moment to say in his ear, "I haven't come that often that quickly in such a swift succession and so *hard* in *years,* my beast. Even during sessions, I have not received such pleasure. Just thinking of you, it seemed I couldn't stop."

"*Amélie.*"

That was also forced out, but the grit of it wasn't anger or frustration.

It was need.

She lifted her head and looked at him.

Oh yes. Stark. Amazing.

Need.

"Yes, Olivier?" she asked.

"Jack my dick, Mistress, fuckin' *please*."

She held his eyes. "Since you asked so sweetly, once I get you in position to perform for me, we'll begin. Now, if you would, rest into your bounds, *chevalier*. Your palms against the ties at your ankles."

He didn't delay. He leaned back, which arched his torso even farther. The flinch at the pull at his cock was such she reached out and quickly untied it from the ring.

He blew out an audible puff of breath, his thighs visibly trembling.

She watched and commanded, "Now arch more for me, please. Up on your knees. Round your back and push out your hips. Keep your hands to your ankles. Offer that big brute to your Mistress."

There came hesitation and she moved her avid contemplation of his body to his face.

As she did, Amélie was worried he'd indicate he was aware of, and was uncomfortable with, the onlookers.

He wasn't.

He was with her and his battle was within. He knew what she wanted. Hands to ankles, if he lifted to his knees, those knees wide, the position would be one of vulnerability, some discomfort, strain . . . and full-on display.

"Olivier," she said gently but warningly.

As he regarded her, she noted a wild to his eyes so early in their acquaintance that she had not yet seen.

It answered her earlier question.

He *could* get more beautiful.

Before she could open her mouth to reproach his lack of movement, he did as commanded.

It took a good deal to give him the comfort of her close proximity rather than step back and take in the fullness of the spectacle of Olivier lifting, arching, and offering his Mistress his big, hard cock.

"Thank you, my beast," she said, soft words that drifted around them, words only for *them* (not that anyone could hear anything unless she flipped on audio), words for *him*, words that settled the wild in his eyes.

When he gave her that gift, she reached out and took tight hold of his cock.

He grunted and the wild swept back.

"Do not thrust unless you're told to, Olivier," she warned. "This cock is my cock. As was my wont, you've sweetly offered it to me. Now I'll do with it as I will."

"Yes, Mistress," he hissed out, not anger, his breaths coming fast and uneven as he held back what she knew was an overwhelming desire to fuck her fist.

But it was more.

It was the first time she'd touched him in any real, direct way.

And she'd done it by claiming a man's most precious possession.

And he'd done very well. He was so very beautiful. And she'd looked forward to this all week.

She'd experienced more than a persistent anticipation all day, and the day before, and the day before that (and so on), knowing she was coming to the club.

As the time drew nearer, it was a want that kept her panties relentlessly wet.

So as her steed had performed very well so far, it was time for his reward.

She stroked him and did not go easy. She wanted to see the pull arch that powerhouse of a body to her will. She continued to fist him tight, tugging hard at the root and the tip, jerking his body into a deeper arc of offering to his Mistress.

His head dropped back and he fought it. Not the pull, the relinquishing of himself. She saw the tenseness that caused his muscles, all of them, already standing out in relief, to start straining.

With relentless and swiftly increasing tugs, she didn't give up.

It took time, long, glorious minutes before he cracked and she knew precisely when as he gave her some of what he was holding back, the grunts that grated up his chest and filled the room like explosions, pounding against her clit.

There was so much of him, so much she wanted to see, it was impossible to take it all in as she kept working him, harder, tighter, the pull more brutal.

She knew his ass was clenching, she was forcing it from her manipulation but more, he needed to do it to stop himself from taking over.

Her focus remained on his cock, his harnessed balls restrained but so fucking big, they still rocked with her pulls. But her mind was on his ass and how she intended to have him again, just like this, but fill him, perhaps with something special that would spread out on the floor around his calves and feet, swaying with her movements.

On this thought and the one that chased it, the one that made it difficult not to press her hand between her legs, it happened.

He broke.

The tenseness of his body vanished. He was hers to work at will.

He was *hers*.

He gave himself over to her, and if the sight of it etched in every line of his frame wasn't enough, he gave her more.

Lifting his head, she caught her breath and felt the gush of wet between her legs at the burn in his eyes, the look on his face so dark with need, she fancied it cast a shadow on them both.

"Yeah, Amélie . . . Mistress," he ground out. "Fuck yeah. *Fuck yeah.* Jack my dick. Jack my fuckin' dick." His words so affecting, her strokes came faster, rougher, testing his flexibility as he fully capitulated and gave it all to her. "Jack *your* dick. Jack your dick, Amélie."

Her voice was husky in a way she could not hide when she allowed, "You can meet my strokes with your thrusts, Olivier. Give my cock to me. Fuck my hand with that brute."

He didn't need to be asked twice, thrusting into her fist, forcing his own body into an impossibly beautiful arc. His head fell back again, the column of his throat convulsing with each grunt that came with each thrust, his jawline hard.

She felt the tension gather, shifted her grip from wrist up to wrist below, and ordered, "Offer your seed to me."

"Fuck yeah," he groaned and convulsed, his body staying arched, only his hips powered into her hand, the movements fluid yet spasmodic, coming in rapid succession, like an animal rutting.

And then on a muted roar, he spewed his seed, the milky jet of it soaring up his chest, wetting him from belly to nipple.

And it kept coming.

"Beautiful," she breathed.

She held him tightly throughout, even as his drives weakened, his back slightly relaxed, and his head began to loll on his shoulders.

"Stay in position," she ordered when he stopped thrusting altogether and she took over, gently milking out the last of his seed. "Stay offered to me, Olivier," she repeated.

Reaching her other hand out, she cupped his harnessed balls.

And carefully squeezed.

A final gush of milky cum splashed on his flat belly as his hips juddered violently.

"Jesus," he murmured, the tone one of stunned surprise, a shudder lightly shaking his body.

She stroked down and held him at the base, feeling the coolness of the ring.

"If you must, you may relax," she started and his head came up, that sated look on his handsome face one she could get dangerously addicted to, soft around his mouth and eyes, lips parted.

Hers.

In that moment, all hers.

"But I'd prefer, *mon chou*, if you'd keep yourself presented to your Mistress while I go about the task of cleaning you up and preparing you for more play."

He blinked.

He wasn't expecting more.

She fought a smile.

"You came very hard. It was stunning," she continued. "So I'd understand if you feel the need to relax. But as I said . . ." she trailed off, held his gaze, and then slowly released him before she straightened and moved to her bag on the table.

When she got what she needed and turned back, she could have wept with joy to see his head up, turned, and his body still arched for her.

She wanted to command him to sit back on his calves, straddle him on the floor, and kiss him so deeply, he'd wonder if their mouths had fused.

This before she rode that cock to another climax for him . . . and for her.

She didn't do either.

She moved to him, giving him a look that she hoped shared her gratitude as she took the wet wipes she'd gathered and swabbed the cum from his chest.

She felt him watching her as she walked to the unobtrusive bin and threw away the spent wipes.

Ignoring the shadows at the windows indicating they did indeed have an audience, a large one, coming back to him, she crouched between his knees.

He was still semi-hard but had reduced in size enough that she could slide off the ring without causing him pain or harm.

He was clearly sensitized for he allowed a long groan to roll up his throat, and in a lovely gesture of submissive gratitude, he followed his ring (and her fingers) with his hips like he didn't want to lose either.

"Seems I need to go shopping. My beast exceeds the size of my equipment," she noted.

She looked to his face and saw a small smile playing at his mouth—cocky, a bit—amused, mostly.

"That might be a good idea," he agreed.

"You'll stay harnessed, *chevalier*," she shared. "And you've greatly pleased me. *Greatly*. You can relax now."

Instantly, he settled ass to his ankles and came up as far as the slack would let him at his collar.

She straightened and went down again at his back, effortlessly releasing the knots that bound him, relieving him of ties and collar, dropping them to the floor.

"Sit forward, Olivier," she ordered from behind him. "You're at ease. You may need to do some stretches to get the blood running to your arms and legs. But when you feel you can take your feet, please do so and go display yourself for me on the vault. On your back, ass back enough your legs fall open at the sides, but close to the edge so I have access to your cock and balls."

He twisted his neck to look at her.

There was minor apprehension creeping in. He'd come. The experience was enough to sweep his mind free so he could give himself to her.

Rational thought, or irrational, however you looked at it (and Amélie considered it irrational), was intruding.

"As I said, my beast, you've pleased me greatly," she continued soothingly. "When a toy pleases me, I give rewards. I'm not done with you yet."

The last peaked enough interest he battled the beast and looked away from her, stretching his arms in front of him.

She left it at that, and moved to the table, lifting her hands to her hair at the nape of her neck.

She deftly pulled the pins out that fastened the soft twists of the chignon she'd curled there. She set them in a neat pile on the table, her back to the room and Olivier, her hands up, fingers moving through her hair.

When she turned, she was pleased to see she'd given him enough time. And he'd followed instructions. He was reclined on the vault, the old fashioned kind that was used in gymnastics competitions.

He was back far enough his powerful legs were spread off the sides, not quite dangling for they were too long. His feet rested on the ground but his legs were relaxed and falling wider open.

Next time, she'd have to remember to have the beam raised.

And, as well as the rest of him stretched across the vault, his cock and balls were exposed for touch and on display.

Yes, very much yes, he could get more beautiful.

She walked to his side, doing so seeing his head was up, chin in his neck, eyes on her in a way that was so deliberate, she knew he was focusing on her instead of the fact his beauty was exhibited to all in the club who wished to see.

It was crucial to focus him again.

She stopped close and looked down at him. His hands were up, resting on his chest.

She took one wrist and pulled it to her, flattening the palm against her breastbone above the opened neck of her button-up blouse.

Skin against skin.

His nostrils flared and his focus shifted.

Oh my.

She liked that.

There were no onlookers now. Just a touch from her and they'd melted away. It was Amélie and Olivier and his first touch of her, which he appeared to take as the gift it was.

"I'd like this, and the other one, *chevalier*, lifted over your head and holding on to the end of the vault, please," she ordered.

He lifted his other hand to comply but she held the one to her chest for a longer moment, giving him that nuance more.

When she let him go, his hand lingered only a beat before he did as he'd been told.

"Now, Olivier, I've inspected you but I'd like to take that multi-sensory tonight. You've been so sweet for me I'd like you to feel free to stroke your cock as leisurely or rough as you wish when it starts hardening again."

She swung back in surprise as the right arm whose hand she'd just laid against her chest came down and went right to his cock.

She looked that way and stared, fighting back an astonished blink.

He was not fully hard but he was getting there.

She turned back to him. "You seem to have a good deal of stamina."

"Amélie . . . Mistress, I don't think you're gettin' that I *seriously* find you not hard on the eyes."

She bent closer, as intended for this part of their session, some of her hair falling on his chest in another caress. She did this letting her amusement show, if not all of the emotion she felt at his compliment.

"I wonder, *mon chou*, if you think you can butter me up with compliments."

"I don't know. Maybe. Though not sure why I'd bother since I didn't give you one and you just made me shoot a huge-ass load the likes that have never come from my cock."

"And he gives another compliment," she said through a smile.

"You earn it, I'll say it," he replied, his lips twitching. "That is, if I'm physically capable of speech."

She was still smiling when she reached out a hand and delicately traced circles around his nipple.

His eyes darkened.

Her good humor increased.

"You're of course aware I should do something about you being so audaciously cheeky."

Another darkness crossed his face. "What?"

"I shouldn't allow you to be cheeky with me."

"Cheeky?"

"Impudent," she explained.

The look fled. "You mean, in uppity, hot-chick speak, a wise-ass."

Amélie couldn't help it, she laughed softly.

"She's got a pretty laugh, too, to go with that pretty accent," he murmured and she saw his eyes on her lips.

I could get lost in this one, she thought. *Lost and never found.*

She had the thought with no fear.

The fear she felt was at the hope that struggled to break through. The hope that their future held something outside of a playroom.

"Just sayin', Mistress," he stated her title like it was a nickname, something forbidden at the same time immensely alluring, "you don't want me to be a wise-ass, might be best not to invite me back to your barn. Think it's a part of me you can't get rid of by paddling my ass."

"Hmm," she murmured, smiling at him with her eyes.

"Amélie, I'm totally hard and shit is getting serious down there," he whispered.

She looked that way.

He did not lie.

She turned her attention back to his face and swept the hair off his forehead, running the tips of her nails down his hairline.

Obviously in a certain mood, a giving one, an acquiescent one, one she liked a great deal, he turned his head and kissed her palm.

This tender gesture came as a pleasant surprise and it made her bend farther to him. He held still as she ran the tip of her nose down the length of his.

That bump at the bridge, God, it was insane but she could fall in love with it.

Controlling the movement so it wasn't jerky at her growing-more-intense-by-the-second reaction to him, she pulled back.

"I ask you not to come, please," she ordered. "If you need to take a break, do. I'll let you know when you can give me your seed."

"Yes, Mistress."

She gave him another smile and then set about the serious business, for her, of this session.

That was touch.

And taste.

In an epic journey of discovery, she lavished his body with

attention. Touches as light as a feather. Scrapes of her nails. The whisper of lips. The sweep of her hair. Nibbles.

She mixed this randomly with rougher handling, the dig of her thumbs in his biceps, the scratch of her nails, the light twist of a nipple, sinking her teeth in his flesh enough he could feel the bite, but it wouldn't leave a mark.

It was with delight that she discovered him exceptionally responsive.

She found he had the usual sensitivity behind his ears and along the vulnerable strain of muscles down the sides of his neck, but farther, in the dip of his collarbone.

He also liked to have the lobes of his ears nipped.

His nipples responded to touch, but she discovered she'd need further exploration during sessions for they didn't elicit the response she'd expected. They'd need rougher play, pulled, twisted, clamped.

He had quite a lovely reaction to her digging her nail in the thick line of hair that led to his shaft just above and below his navel.

He was unsurprisingly, but deliciously more than normal, sensitive at the juncture of his thighs, her attention there with fingers, nails, and tongue taking his fisting of his cock to extremes before he'd stop, puffing out rapid exhalations of breath.

Inner and back thighs charmingly responsive, as were the backs of his knees. The fronts, not as much.

Tugs on his pubic hair brought a hiss that drowned a groan.

He liked that.

As did she.

She'd take that monster of a cock in her mouth on another, special occasion.

But when she'd noticed his body was taut with his increasing need for release, she finished her discovery, saving the best for last.

Laving his harnessed balls, sucking one, then the other, gently into her mouth, caused his hips to buck.

She watched, building her own need, the pull of his fist stretching the root of his cock as she relentlessly focused her attention on his sac.

As she did this, she found she liked his musk.

He wore aftershave and she liked that too.

But here, down here, the seat of his meat, he smelled *divine*.

"*Amélie.*"

There it was. The need.

She took one firm, final suckle of his ball sac, hearing his hushed explosion of, "*Fuck me*," before she lifted away from him but came to his left side.

"Do you need to come, *mon chou?*" she asked, staring (she knew because she didn't hide it) affectionately into his sweltering eyes and his dark, hard face.

"Yeah," he grunted.

"Keep stroking, Olivier," she ordered, reaching for his hand that was still over his head, now clutching the edge of the vault.

She took it and watched with great fascination the myriad of lovely expressions shift across his face as she moved it so he could comfortably accept what she was offering. Then she pressed his hand into the damp crotch at her center.

Unable to stop himself, he took what she gave him and beyond. Long fingers strong, he curled them in, shoving her panties into her pussy, palming her clit.

Right, he knew what he was doing down there.

That was good to know.

She drew in a sharp, delicate breath and whispered, "Very nice, Olivier."

"Let me fuck you," he begged.

She shook her head slightly, bracing her legs against the sensations and modulating her voice as his strong fingers forced themselves up and out, again and again. "Not this time, my *chevalier.*"

His hand curled into her roughly.

Possessively.

Her alpha.

She clenched her teeth to bite back a cry of pleasure.

"I need this," he growled, tugging on her, swaying her hips toward him, like she wouldn't know to what he was referring.

"You have it," she pointed out, slightly breathlessly.

"*Need* it, Mistress."

That was a plea.

"You have what I'm giving you tonight, Olivier," she informed him.

His hand shifted, middle finger finding her clit through her pants, up and circling, pressing hard.

Her lips parted.

"Fuck, Amélie," he whispered. "*Please.*"

"You'll take what I give you, Olivier."

"Put me on the floor. Sit on my face," he demanded, his fist jacking his cock brutally. "I want my cock in you, but right now, the minute you took me, I'd shoot."

"When I ride your face, you'll be restrained and at my mercy." His face darkened with more need. He wanted her to give him that too. "Olivier, you have what you're going to get. Now, take care of it, please."

The order registered and his focus intensified on what he was doing with his finger.

And he proved further he knew what he was doing.

All he'd given her that night, with delicate breaths whispering through her lips, she held his eyes and allowed his magic to work.

It took very little time.

Slowly closing her eyes, her hand coming to land on his chest, her fingers curling in, nails scraping through his hair, she trembled against his hand as she gave into the sweet release. Letting it wash over her, Olivier behind her eyes, his strength between her legs and evident under her hand on his chest, exquisitely elusive shivers slithered over her skin as she pressed her hips into his hand.

"Jesus, baby," Olivier whispered through her orgasm. "Fuckin' beautiful."

At his words, still climaxing, she felt her mouth curve up.

"Jesus." He was still whispering, now almost reverently.

She opened heavy lids and cast her gaze on him.

"Give me your seed," she demanded.

His face registered the order and then registered surprise, like he'd never been ordered to come on demand before and was shocked it could happen, before his head dug into the vault as his cum streamed up his belly.

He was milking his dick, his legs still prone to the sides, that outstanding display likely to be just as the first he'd provided that night, used mentally by whoever was watching to get them off later . . . and spectacularly.

She bent over him, reaching out a hand to his cheek.

He was still in the aftermath of his climax but that made it perfect when she bent deeper and took his mouth in their first kiss.

She added tongue, stroking his, and there was an enticing musk to his taste as well.

She lifted away and asked, "Is my beast appeased?"

Humor lit his gaze as he muttered, "Your beast got his rocks off twice in a big fuckin' way, Amélie. So yeah. Definitely."

"Cheeky."

His gaze stayed lit even as it grew slightly sober.

"Nice kiss," he whispered.

God, on his back on a vault with his cum on his belly, his orgasm witnessed probably by more than a dozen people, and he was flirting.

"Now you're a flirt."

The grin hit his mouth.

"Sit up, Olivier. On the edge of the vault, *mon chou*. I'll clean you."

She bent forward and brushed her mouth to his. Contrary to what he'd been taught, he pressed up to deepen the contact, but relaxed back before she could take him to task for it.

She moved away and found him sitting up when she came back to him.

She positioned between his legs, cleaned his cum from his belly, and then walked back to the bin.

She returned to her steed, again between his legs.

"You may hold me loosely," she allowed.

His lips quirked but he didn't hesitate to wrap his arms around her loosely. Arms that were so long, they crossed at the back and his hands rested at her front hipbones.

"Something funny?" she asked.

"You're cute when you're bossy."

She opened her mouth but he lifted his chin in a "shut up" gesture and kept going before she could get a word in.

"Cute but hot. When you're workin' me, it's just hot, Amélie. So don't get pissy."

"I decide when to get pissy."

Fucking hell.

That came out petulantly.

She never broke role. She never slipped. She never did because she wasn't *in* role.

This was her.

So she certainly *never* came across *petulantly*.

Wisely, Olivier caught it, she knew it by the flicker of hilarity she saw hit his gaze, but he kept his mouth shut.

Damn, but if he didn't let up, that hope this could become something more wouldn't break through.

It'd explode.

"I want you here Wednesday night," she demanded. "Nine sharp. I'll call you to my table or to a playroom when I arrive."

As she spoke, she saw his expression shift strangely.

"Olivier?" she called his name as a command for an explanation.

"Wednesday? Amélie . . . Mistress, that's four days away."

He wanted to see her sooner.

Oh God.

"Four very long days for you," she stated tartly. "Since you're not allowed to touch yourself until I have you again."

His brows went up before they relaxed but the instant they did, he blinked.

"Come again?"

"You may not touch yourself, jack off, shoot a load, *masturbate*, while you're away from me."

"Okay," he stated immediately. "Due respect and all, Mistress, but are you crazy?"

She couldn't fathom why he asked that and she had to tamp down her need to burst out laughing at the way he did.

"Explain why you think I'm crazy," she commanded.

"Right, well, I jacked off Tuesday night, and that was *after* the colossal orgasm you gave me and, Amélie, not sure you saw it but the slick you forced out of me onto the floor was so big, you could freeze it and make an ice rink."

She felt her body begin to tremble as she continued to fight back laughing.

"And, just sayin', that shit worked on me, as you know. So I jacked off in the shower Wednesday morning, when I got home from work Wednesday night, when I hit the sack, when I got up the next day . . . I need to go on?"

Powerless to fight it, and luckily being a Domme she could do what she fucking pleased, she melted into him.

And since she could also allow what she damn well pleased, after she did and his arms tightened around her, she let him do that too.

That said, there was a great deal he was saying, it was funny as well as gratifying, but it was also a little disconcerting.

"You've never had a Master or Mistress order you not to touch yourself between sessions before?" she asked.

"I've never had a Master, one. Mistresses only. And straight up, never had one jack my shit as good as you. So that question is moot since it's about the good you give which I can't get out of my head that makes that command, Mistress Amélie, damn near impossible."

Very nice.

Very.

"Then, my steed, you will please me greatly, which will mean I'll please you greatly, when you best that impossibility."

He stared into her eyes.

Then he gusted out the word, *"Fuck,"* to the ceiling.

"Olivier," she called, again grinning.

He looked back to her.

"Wednesday, *mon chou*. Be here at nine. Yes?"

"Yes, Mistress."

So good. So beautiful. Her magnificent beast.

He deserved one last reward.

She gave it to him, a long, carnal, wet kiss that included her allowing him to grope her ass while she ran her hands along his back and then fisted them as best she could in his hair.

She gave a light tug and he lifted away.

"Get dressed, my *chevalier.*"

He bent and touched the tip of that extraordinary nose to hers before he drew away.

She shifted from between his legs and assumed a position of side of her hip to the vault to watch as he put on his clothes.

A thought occurred to her as he moved away, his fingers going directly to the straps still harnessing his balls.

And she made a decision.

"Oh no, Olivier," she called. He stopped moving, twisted his torso, fingers still to his sac, and looked to her. "I want you to wear the harness home. You may take it off to sleep. You may leave it off except when you're alone at home. There, I want you to strap yourself so you can be reminded who owns those fabulous balls, who owns that big, gorgeous cock. Leave it on at least an hour. And wear it again when you come back to see me."

She watched, enjoying the show, but did so with bated breath, hope and fear fighting their own battle in her belly, as he waged internal war.

With jaw tight, the look in his eyes a mix of hunger and uncertainty, he nodded.

"Thank you, *mon chou*," she said, her words weighty with feeling, those words holding meaning he knew.

By allowing her to play with him out of the club, this meant their play had expanded significantly.

This utterly thrilled her.

And with terrifying honesty, she had to admit, it scared the hell out of her.

He went to his clothes on the hooks.

Her eyes moved to the windows only to assess that their audience had disappeared after the show was obviously over.

Only one onlooker remained.

Stellan.

He again was not watching Olivier. His attention was on Amélie.

And when he got hers, his handsome, dark head tipped slightly to the side and his gaze slid to Olivier briefly.

Then he pushed away from where he was resting his shoulders against the windows of the darkened playroom across from hers, turned, and with the loose-limbed grace of that long, lean body that for years she'd desired to have under her command, he sauntered away.

five

Courtesy

AMÉLIE

Wednesday evening at nine-thirty, when Amélie walked into the hunting ground, as it was not a difficult task, she spotted Olivier immediately.

He was standing, wearing another very nice suit, facing the door at a bar table in the middle of the room with his big hand wrapped around a pilsner glass of beer, three female subs sitting on stools around the table.

Amélie felt a pang of something she'd never felt before, it was unpleasant and extreme, before he noticed her arrival, smiled, and said not a word to his companions as he moved away from the table, taking his glass with him, and started walking toward her.

Denying her discomfiture even at the possibility she'd just experienced the wrench of jealousy, she watched his big body move.

He walked with an athletic bearing, but there was a slight lumber to his movements that she suspected any man of his size couldn't quite get past, his frame not that of a linebacker, but a defensive end.

She stopped to await his arrival, and when she got it, he looked into her eyes, then at her mouth as he said, "Mistress Amélie."

"Good evening, Olivier."

He seemed to find that amusing, something she found enthralling, and to control that reaction, which was far more intense than it should be simply being in his presence for three seconds, she looked from him to cast her gaze around the room.

She felt her focus shift when she saw Mirabelle, alone, in a booth. Where was Trey?

She looked back to Olivier and her focus shot right back.

She took half a step closer, and as he should when he didn't have her permission to do anything else, he held his place.

He was in the mood to be good tonight.

That was titillating.

Though, she hoped he again felt in the mood to misbehave, and soon.

"Did you come to me as I asked?" she queried.

He gave her the gift of his teeth appearing, scraping his lower lip for only a beat before he answered, "Yeah."

An altogether different pang hit her at knowing he'd harnessed himself for her.

She rewarded him by edging a little closer. "And, my *chevalier*, did you follow my instructions?"

This time, his answer was a disgruntled, "Yeah."

She studied him, pleased to see it wasn't that he disliked what she'd asked him to do, just that, in a good way, he disliked what she asked him to do and now was *very* ready to play.

"Excellent, *mon chou*. Go back to your friends."

His heavy brow drew in at the bridge of his nose but she kept talking.

"Finish your drink. I need to have a word with Mistress Mirabelle."

He shifted as if to scan the room but obviously decided against it, likely not being around long enough to know who Mirabelle was so taking his attention from her wasn't worth it as he wouldn't know where to look.

She lifted her hand and rested it lightly on his broad chest.

He looked down at her and she again had his complete attention.

"When I move toward the playrooms, you'll follow me. Yes?" she ordered.

"Yes, Mistress."

She struggled against her need to caress his cheek, sift her hands through the hair on his forehead, run her fingers along his jaw.

This struggle further concerned her as to her reaction to Olivier, for Amélie was known to be affectionate with her toys but not so publicly, unless it was a rare occasion where she led one to the social room.

He's getting under your skin, Leigh, and fast, her mind warned.

"Go, my beast," her lips said.

He nodded, stepped back a step that for other men would be two, shifting to the side.

Yes, he was being good. Not turning his back on her, as a good toy would do, he simply got out of her way.

She gave him an upward curve of her lips before she made her way to Mirabelle.

"Not going to immediately pounce on that?" Mirabelle asked as Amélie slid in the opposite side of her booth.

"I was," Amélie replied, eyeing her closely, "until I saw you here without Trey."

Mirabelle looked to the hunting ground. "He's got a business meeting tonight."

"He's got a meeting and you're here because . . . ?" Amélie prompted.

Mirabelle looked back to Amélie, and clearly done with holding it in, she let fly.

"He's not giving me any signs. He's not giving me any openings. He's certainly not asking *me* out. He's not giving me anything. Except it's clear he wants me to play with him, make him come hard, then he's good to go away."

Amélie harked back to Trey's silent response to Mirabelle's words about Bryan, obviously misinterpreting them as his Mistress having interest in the other sub, and not liking it.

It was unusual for Mirabelle not to be exceptionally attuned to her subs. She might miss something if she wasn't looking, but if the reaction Amélie saw indicated how Trey felt, he would be giving other things away.

Perhaps with her heart getting involved, she was missing things.

Or perhaps Amélie had misread his reaction.

"So I'm just checking things out," Mira went on. "There are some fresh, sweet babies out there that Aryas has approved. Trey has been all I've done for weeks. Maybe I need a new experience to clear my head."

"So now it's not once bitten, twice shy. It's once bitten, two thousand times shy."

Mirabelle, a friend but also a Mistress, narrowed her gaze sharply.

"You were the one who advised I be cautious," she said in a tone as sharp as her gaze, a tone Mira was usually incapable of when speaking with a friend.

In fact, a tone she was usually incapable of using outside the occasions she'd need to use it in a scene.

A tone she took that shared with Amélie just how deeply rooted her feelings were, feelings that Mirabelle was assuming were unreciprocated.

"And now I'm the one who's wondering if you're doing this for the sole purpose of it getting back to Trey so you can see if he's jealous," Amélie remarked with care.

"You're the reigning Domme at the Honey, Amélie, and respect for that. You know you have that from me and everybody. But this isn't my first time doing this. I've been around the block."

"I know that," Amélie said calmingly. "But just to ask, this block you've been around, particularly with Trey, is he serving you outside the club?"

"You know I'd tell you if we did my house, his, or had a play weekend away."

"What I mean is, are you giving him instructions to carry out when you're not here?"

She looked to her glass. "Yes." She looked back to Amélie. "But you know that doesn't mean dick. Just that he likes serving me."

"It's eking into life, *chérie*," Amélie pointed out, trying not to think about how she felt about Olivier allowing the same thing and so soon in their play. But she finished pointing out what was in most cases quite true. "So it often can mean a great deal."

"It's still part of the game," Mirabelle made her own very good point.

Amélie nodded, conceding it.

Then she made a very difficult decision but it was one that had to be made.

As Mira could often come under the spell of her subs, the lovely Mira could also often do things that were rash.

They weren't always destructive.

But they were sometimes thoughtless.

And unhealthy.

An odd trait in a Mistress and one that she strictly controlled in a playroom, which made Amélie wonder if it was one of the reasons that drove her to a playroom.

"Can I make a request?"

"Sure," Mirabelle replied.

"Please don't make a choice of someone to take back to the rooms until I've taken care of Olivier and returned to you so we can talk some more."

The stubborn set of Mirabelle's face softened. "My lovely, it's sweet you want to look out for me but I'm not going to wait for hours while you—"

"What I have planned for tonight"—or what she'd just changed her plans to for that night—"for right now won't take long."

Mistaking her, Mirabelle grinned.

"Go take care of that stallion. I'll be here." She lifted her hand when Amélie opened her mouth to speak. "And I won't choose a playmate until you get back."

"Thank you, Mira."

"No worries, Amélie." As Amélie slid out of the booth, Mirabelle finished, "Enjoy."

"Oh, I will, darling," she murmured, casting a look that made her friend laugh softly then turning her attention to the room.

She caught Olivier's eye momentarily but she didn't need to check to see if he was watching. He'd returned to the table as commanded but now his body was at an angle so he could see her and she barely took her first step before he lifted his beer to down it.

God, she could climax just watching him drink.

She'd reserved a different room that night, and feeling Olivier fall behind her close to her heels, after the annoying delay of needing to step aside so he'd open the door to the playrooms for her, she led him right to it.

The light in the playroom could only be seen at the edges of the dark blinds that had been let down.

She went to the door and put her hand on the handle, only to hear Olivier's quiet rumble of, "New digs."

She looked over her shoulder at him, not controlling the small smile that played at her lips, openly showing him her amusement at his terminology.

But she did hide the disappointment that the reasons behind her choice of this room would not be availed that night.

"Indeed," she replied.

She pushed in, flipping the switch to declare occupancy, and he came with her.

He closed the door and stood at it because he had nowhere to go. She had only taken two steps in.

His eyes quickly took in the room and the variety of complicated apparatus. She saw disquiet enter them along with a tightening of his jaw as well as his entire frame.

Fear and excitement.

Oh, how she wished she could have carried out what she'd planned this evening.

However, friends making bad decisions you might be able to do something about before they brought those decisions to fruition always took precedence.

"Do not move from there, Olivier," she ordered.

His focus cut back to her as she negated the space between them then lifted her hands to pull the suit jacket off his shoulders.

He drew his arms back for it to fall down and she felt the quickening between her legs just at that.

Yes, he was affecting her. Yes, he was affecting her intensely.

But she had no idea at this early point in their play whether to guard against it or let it fly.

Now was not the time to make that decision. Now she needed to take care of her steed and then look after her friend.

Therefore, once she'd divested him of his jacket, she leaned around him and hooked it by the door herself.

She then moved back, eyes to his face, lifting her hand to rest it lightly on his chest.

His total focus was on her. Neck bent, eyes darkening, she could feel his heart beating an accelerated, heavy beat.

"It sometimes startles me how handsome you are," she said quietly.

"Amélie."

Her name came gruff and, just as any way he'd said it, she liked it like that.

Slowly, she slid her gaze down his chest to see the bulge of his cock straining the front of his pants.

The gruff was still in his tone, but he'd controlled some of it, when he asked, "Can I touch you?"

She slid her hand down and her gaze up as she answered, "No."

A flash of defiance and annoyance in his eyes that set the lips of her pussy quivering.

She engaged her other hand to tug his light-blue dress shirt out of his slacks.

Just that had him setting his teeth into his lip.

She took that in gladly, almost gleefully, knowing she affected him too.

She knew this already but now she knew just how intensely.

She lifted the front of his shirt and found what she was looking for. Trailing her fingernail through, digging in at the waistband of his pants, she followed the thick trail of hair nearly to the base of his cock.

"Do you know how wet it makes me, knowing you're harnessed for me?" she asked.

"I'd like to check," he said by way of answer.

She dug her nail in and his hips reflexively swayed back as a hiss of breath passed through his teeth.

Then he pressed back into the touch.

Being so good.

"My beast," she breathed.

Turning her finger, she unlatched the hook of his pants and slowly slid the zipper down.

His chest started visibly moving with his breaths.

"I'd like to touch you, Mistress," he requested, the unguarded gruff back.

"And I've answered that request, *chevalier*. If I change my mind, you'll be the first to know."

His jaw got hard, forcing a muscle to leap up his cheek.

He just kept getting more and more beautiful.

She again engaged both hands as she ran them along the waistband of his trousers, hooking her thumbs into his boxer briefs. Holding his gaze as his hips swayed at the unexpectedly quick, powerful move, she yanked both down to his middle thighs.

She looked down. "Hold your shirt up so I can see you."

Quickly, his hand went to his shirt, yanking it up.

She quelled a smile at his readiness, both in pulling up his shirt

and in the huge erection he had for her. She saw the harness beautifully banding his balls and licked her lips.

"Keep that shirt held up," she ordered, reaching out and wrapping her fingers around his cock. She gave a gentle tug, looking up
at him. "You've not touched this?"

"No."

That was a near-to grunt.

She tilted her head to the side. "No?"

"No, Mistress. The shower, to get it out of the way to put the
harness on, other than that, as you askèd, no."

"Very good, Olivier," she whispered. "Now, keeping your pants
where they are, turn and put your hands to the door. And I want
your ass tipped up, please."

She let him go and allowed herself to fully enjoy the emotions
that flashed unshielded through his expressions—loss at her touch,
indecision, excitement—and finally he turned.

She moved to her bag, the tug of disappointment palpable that
some of the things in it that she'd intended to use that night would
go unused.

But they'd have another night (and another, and more) and she'd
make it up to him.

Oh yes, she absolutely would.

Repeatedly.

She found what she needed, slipped it from its wrapper, and
came back to him.

Settling in to standing behind him, she reached around and expertly rolled the condom on.

She'd prepared. She had a variety of things now to fit his size,
including magnum condoms.

"Amélie, what—?" he started.

She knew his question. In the variety of requirements of membership at the club, staying clean so nothing could limit play was
one of them. The contract required that every member submit samples monthly to the club for testing (and, as undignified as it was

for the Dominants, it was nevertheless mandatory that both Doms and subs gave these samples *at* the club so there was no cheating). Further, if you went elsewhere to have your fun, you were contractually bound to use protection.

"Your suit is lovely, Olivier. It wouldn't do to get anything on it," she explained.

She was now holding him tightly at the base of his cock, very tightly, so the gruff had turned to throaty when he said, "Right."

She moved in closer, so he could feel her breasts brush his back, running her hand down the side of his hip, stroking her other hand down his cock.

His head fell back as she whispered, "God, I love the weight of you."

"Good," he grunted.

She slid her hand around the lower swell of his ass then engaged her fingernail as she glided it along the crease of his hip and thigh toward his balls.

She cupped them and gave a gentle squeeze.

He automatically stroked her fist as his hips jerked.

"I like the weight of these too," she informed him.

"Good."

That was close to a groan.

She tightened her hold, getting nearer, now pressing her breasts to his back, feeling him trembling.

"Would you like to fuck my fist, Olivier?"

"Fuck yeah," he replied immediately.

"Is that how you answer your Mistress?" she inquired.

"Fuck yeah, Mistress."

She felt her lips quirk and pressed closer. His body stilled then continued quivering.

"Ask, Olivier, and ask nice. You want my answer to be yes," she ordered.

The response came immediately.

"Please, Mistress Amélie, let me fuck your fist."

She moved her hands from his balls, retraced her path along the crease of his thigh and smoothed it over his buttock, one thumb running along the side of the crevice in his ass.

His hips jerked again.

"Please, Amélie, I need to fuck your fuckin' fist," he gritted.

"Then perform for me, my steed," she allowed.

He nearly bucked her off with the power of his hips swinging back and he stroked her fist urgently. She held tight and incrementally held tighter, glad of the lubrication on the condom, making the glide easy for him, using her other hand to smooth, alternating with a light rasp of her fingernails on the skin of his hip, buttock, and upper thigh.

The strength and swiftness of his thrusts increased in speed, as did her grip, now not simply to give him pleasure but in order to hold on.

She heard his harsh breaths but the stubborn toy was holding back.

"Let me hear your need, Olivier." She phrased it sounding like a request but he read it and he gave her what she hungered for. The powerful grunts detonated in the room, intensifying, becoming more and more feral.

She knew he was nearly there when he groaned, *"Baby."*

That was when Amélie honed in with purpose, driving two fingers up his ass.

His spine and neck bowed, his head falling back, his legs spreading, caught by his pants gathered at his thighs, and he stayed in that position as he drove into her fist once, twice, three times, doing this meeting her thrusts up his ass.

"Yeah, *fuck*, Amélie, baby, *fuck*, give that to me," and then he convulsed. Still assaulting her fist, taking his finger fucking, his sharp, savage grunts, climaxing without her permission (but in this instance, she didn't mind), gushing heavy eruptions of cum into the condom with each drive.

After some time, he fell forward, his body spasming, now weakly thrusting, resting his forehead to the door between his hands.

When he settled, still shuddering, she milked him gently, now keeping her fingers still but firmly lodged up his ass.

She continued milking him, for her own pleasure and his, taking a great deal of gratification out of her powerhouse trembling in her grip, against her body, and asked, "How's my steed?"

"Good." The one word was deep and short because he was still fighting to even his breathing.

She went on stroking him until his breath became steadier, and then she moved her hand from his cock to cup his balls in their harness in a warm, gentle grip.

"You seemed to like me fucking your ass," she noted.

She felt the sudden tenseness he struggled to control and failed, only slightly making himself relax, perhaps in that moment not realizing as his hole tightened around her fingers that this reaction was far more easier than usual to read.

What he didn't do was respond.

"Olivier," she prompted, allowing impatience to thread that word.

"Yeah," he bit out.

"Yeah, what?"

The words still held a sharp bite when he said, "Yes, Mistress."

She pressed closer, he tightened against her in a lot of ways, and she lifted up to her toes in a vain attempt to get to his ear.

"Thank you for that but what I want you to share with me in words is what, precisely, you liked."

She sensed the struggle, pressed up against him she felt it, and she gloried in it and the length it took him to admit angrily, "I liked your fingers up my ass."

She pushed. "So you enjoyed your fucking."

"Yes," he clipped.

"I'm pleased you've said it, Olivier, even though I already knew since you showed it."

That got her a truncated rumble of annoyance that perhaps hid some discomfiture.

With his reaction to all she'd done to him so far, but particularly what she did tonight, something she'd wished to take much more time in breaking him into, she knew she could get him past the discomfort.

She'd done it before with him, delightfully and now repeatedly. She'd do it again.

And she was very, *very* much looking forward to it.

She gently massaged his balls and he truncated the rumble that caused, too, this time only to be recalcitrant because he knew she liked to hear his excitement.

She smiled against his lat.

"I'm pleased, my *chevalier*, because these balls are mine." She shifted her hand to his cock. "This beautiful brute is mine." She slightly wriggled her fingers up his ass and he pleasingly came up to his toes. "This ass is mine." She settled all movement and finished, "All of you is mine. *All*. And I'll play with it. I'll make you *beg* for me to play with it. *All* of it. And I'll give you my promise that I'll make it worth it for you to give that to me."

Before she could get lost in that thought and move on to doing just that, she tenderly slid her fingers out of him, releasing his cock.

She began to move away, but her eyes caught the control panel, the lever lifted up and glowing green to indicate that the room was in use, and a thought flashed, others tumbling in around it, taking her attention.

That and the fact she needed to get back to Mirabelle before her friend did anything stupid.

With these things on her mind, she left Olivier standing there as she moved to the table, ordering distractedly, "Pull up your pants. Clean up. I'll leave some wipes. The bin is under the table." She pulled out the wipes, her back to him, and cleaned her own fingers swiftly, continuing, "Then you may leave. We'll resume Friday night."

"You want me to leave?"

His incredulous tone made her turn to him.

When she did she saw not only that he'd pulled his pants up, and even gloved with a spent condom, tucked himself away, though he had not done up the fly.

But what was on his face took all her attention.

"Yes, Olivier, I—"

"That's bullshit," he grated, and even though she did not know him well at all, it was abundantly clear his fury had been unleashed.

Amélie blinked in shock.

"I put this fuckin' harness on for you every night, like you said. Made me hard as a fuckin' rock, doin' that for you, thinkin' of you the whole time I'm strapped for you, which is the fuckin' point and you fuckin' know it, a whole lot more than me. Got me so hard, sheer agony, wantin' to do somethin' about it, but I didn't jack my dick, like you said. I came here trussed up for you, like you said. You jack me off at the door, shoving your fingers up my ass, then dismiss me?"

She felt her shoulders straighten as her face got hard.

He might not be handling what she'd done very well but if he had issues, they discussed it. He didn't lose his mind.

"*Chevalier*, you need—"

"Fuck that," he bit out, interrupting her and pushing a hand in his pants. He prowled her way, doing it seething physically and verbally. "You get off on the struggle, baby, I see that. You know it tears me up and you help me push through. You fuckin' know that and don't pretend you fuckin' *don't*. So this shit is bullshit and you know that too."

He tossed the spent condom in the trash then dove back into his pants. Even as he spoke again, she heard the snaps on his harness release.

"I get how this goes. I know I'm your *toy*." He spat out the last word. "I know you got a fuckuva lot more experience than me and I ride that because you're fuckin' good at it, hell and gone, fuckin' *great*. I put myself in your hands because I know you know what to do with me."

He tossed the harness on the table, and the soft noise of the leather hitting the wood felt like a lash scoring her heart because both of them knew what his rejection of her symbol of ownership meant.

"You got a lot more experience, Amélie, but we both fuckin' know that this shit, all of it," he threw a long arm wide, indicating the room, "is about courtesy. And it isn't 'yes, Mistress,' 'no, Mistress,' 'please fuck my ass, Mistress.'" He lifted a finger and jabbed it toward her face. "*You* are obligated to extend courtesy too. And, babe, you know *exactly* what I'm tellin' you. I can see it on your face. And I do not have to stand with my hands to the door and my pants around my thighs like a naughty boy with your fingers shoved up my ass and take your shit."

With that, he stalked to the door and Amélie struggled to pull herself together because he was right. She'd made a grave mistake.

It was her duty to read her subs. It was her duty to give them what they needed.

And it was her duty to take care of them.

As surely as it would be unthinkable that a Dom would continue with play after a sub uttered a safe word, it was unthinkable when a sub gave of themselves, communicating *their* requirements, that a Dom ignored them.

The bottom line was, a sub gifted their Dom with extreme trust, making themselves vulnerable in ways that would be unimaginable in the vanilla world, depending *completely* on their Mistress or Master to hold that trust precious.

It was the control a Dom found pleasure in, but that was only part of it. The beauty of play was *earning* the treasure of that trust and the honor of holding it precious.

He had not hidden the way he was and what he required of her and everything that happened in that room, no matter she was ordering it, it was her job, her fucking *calling*, to give it to him.

He controlled that room, they both knew it, and with the battle he constantly waged and didn't hide, she knew that foremost in all her play with Olivier, much more than usual with her toys, she needed to handle him with care.

Not dismiss him with a used condom on his cock and his pants around his legs while she hurried to get to her friend.

"Olivier, stop," she called.

"Fuck that," he clipped, turning the handle on the door.

She just managed to keep the urgency out of her voice when she stated, "I have something to do. It's important."

He looked to her. "Then you tell me that, Amélie. You don't have to go into detail if you don't wanna give that to me but you can still give what you gotta give so I know you're lookin' after me. I know I'm your *toy* but still, I'm not that. I'm a man who consents to be your fuckin' toy. And in this room, I gotta trust you'll never forget that."

With that, he pulled open the door with such strength, it was a miracle it didn't fly off its hinges, and prowled out.

Amélie stood frozen, her mind scrambling, easily falling upon where she'd made her mistakes.

In order not to get lost in him, having him here, the only place she had him, needing to turn her mind to other things, she'd overcompensated.

She *had* dismissed him.

Her beast who'd groaned during their first session simply because she took her presence away.

He craved attention. No, he craved *her* attention. He followed her with his eyes not simply because he'd been ordered to do so or he liked the look of her, but because she was his anchor in their world, a world he grappled with his place in, and he *needed* to look at her. He needed *her*. He could sit bound for her for thirty minutes, but he did it knowing she'd be there eventually to take care of him.

She was entirely focused on him when she'd played with him that night, and please, to the fates, she hoped he'd felt that.

But then she lost focus and that was not acceptable in this room.

She only had to hope that he would return so she could find some way to talk this through with him.

She had a valid excuse, concern for her friend. If he consented to listening, she felt certain he'd understand that.

And allow them to move on.

If he did not understand, then that said a good deal about him and it would then be Amélie who would have what she needed to know if they *should* move on. Especially in the way she was wanting more and more with each interaction with her beast.

She swallowed, throwing the wet wipe she still held but had completely forgotten into the bin. She then exited the room with quick, irate strides, furious with herself, furious with Olivier for not taking a breath and allowing a conversation to be had, and unfairly furious at Mirabelle for taking her attention.

She'd managed to calm down slightly by the time she hit the hunting ground. She saw eyes on her and had no doubt that Olivier stalked out looking as pissed as he just was.

A sub doing that would cause a sensation.

Her sub doing this would cause a stir.

She didn't care about this.

She was more concerned about the fact she had to expend large amounts of energy not to lose her fucking mind at what she saw.

A sub whose name Amélie did not know as she was a female and Amélie didn't pay much attention to the females was standing close to Mirabelle. She'd been selected, it was clear to see. They were just waiting for Amélie to return so Mirabelle could take her back to play.

It was a fact that Mirabelle didn't often select females, though if she was in a certain mood, she could swing that way.

Thus Amélie saw Mira's play immediately.

Picking another sub, Mirabelle was hoping, would raise jealousy in Trey.

However, if he held feelings for her, expected things of their relationship as it had already progressed, selecting another male could cause the connection they were building irreparable harm.

Choosing a female might not have that same consequence.

Amélie knew this to be true, and seeing what she was now seeing, she knew Mira did as well, although it made little sense to her.

Intimacy was intimacy and it was all cherished, regardless of the sex of your partner.

Many men's minds, Amélie knew, especially when it came to same-sex play with women, did not work the same way.

"My God, Leigh, your stallion thundered out of—" Mira started when Amélie made it to the table.

"If you would, please," she snapped. "Ask your toy to remove herself for a moment."

Clearly thinking Amélie wished to discuss what happened with Olivier, Mirabelle did this immediately.

After the woman left, instead of sliding into the opposite side of the booth, she shoved in right next to Mirabelle.

"Fuck, Leigh, what happened?" Mirabelle asked, the sides of their legs and hips pressed together, they were so close.

"Do not, Mira, my beautiful friend, sabotage your own happiness."

Mirabelle blinked before her face went soft and warm but then almost instantly turned cold.

"Don't you—" she began.

"Yes, I have more experience than you, but not in that. Not in hoping for something, going for it, and losing it because you are what you are. Something you can't change. Something that's not only integral to you, but something you love about yourself. I have had two close calls with men I grew to care about, as you know, but neither broke my heart. Because I didn't have the strength of will to go for it. I want what you want, and you know that too. The beauty of you is that your strength is so powerful, you still allow yourself to hope. To even consider going for it."

"Leigh—"

Amélie put her hand on Mirabelle's on the table.

"Please let me finish, darling."

Mirabelle closed her mouth.

"If Trey could be something more to you, he's an alpha-sub, you know it, and you declaring ownership of him and then enjoying play with another, his pride will take a hit that he might not be able to recover from. This would be *you* causing that damage."

"This is our world, Leigh."

"We're not talking about our world, Mira. We're talking about your life."

She again shut her mouth.

"He did not like it when you said Bryan was a waste," she shared and Mirabelle's eyes widened. "His reaction was more than irritation. It smacked of jealousy. He didn't know you have no interest in Bryan. Trust me, female, but definitely male sub, no matter, you take one that's not him at this juncture, you could possibly sabotage your own happiness. And I hope like hell I can stop you from doing that."

"You saw him react to that about Bryan?" Mirabelle asked.

"Yes," Amélie answered.

Her friend began to look angry. "Why didn't you tell me?"

"Because I was being cautious, too cautious, perhaps, but you have to let me have that because I'm your friend and it's my job. And because I was hoping if he showed that so easily, he'd show more and you would find your time to *go for it.*"

Mira cast her eyes to the table and muttered, "Perhaps Trey and I should have a talk."

"I think that's wise, and if you'll allow one last piece of advice, make it one without a plug up his ass," Amélie tried to joke.

Mirabelle looked to her, the hope back, and also concern.

"What happened with your stud, Amélie? I get you're intense for me but it's obviously something else."

"It's no matter," she lied.

Mirabelle paused before she burst out laughing, controlling it enough to say through it, "You just shoved the big sister act right in my face and a sub, a chosen toy of the Grande Domme Mistress Amélie, storms through the hunting ground looking like he wants to murder somebody and you say 'It's no matter.'"

"If you don't mind, *chérie*, it just occurred and I'd actually like time to give it some thought to assess what actually *did* just occur.

And then," she smiled softly, "as you're so good at doing, we'll get together and I'll share it with you and then you can do the big sister act."

Mirabelle leaned closer. "Oh, lovely, did you fuck up? Push him too hard?"

"He's so attuned to me, so connected to me, I'm honestly not certain I *could* push him too hard." She shook her head against the beauty of that thought, and the alarm she felt at what she'd done that night that might have broken them. "It's humbling, Mira. And it's fragile. And I do believe that perhaps the fact that I wasn't as attuned to him tonight genuinely hurt his feelings. I'm quite sure it's made the rounds he's significantly endowed, so it isn't a surprise, hung like he is with that equipment, that his reaction would take reacting like a man to reacting like a *man*."

Mira looked instantly repentant. "You were worried about me."

"You know that it isn't your fault. It's my slip and I'll fix it."

"I hope so, Amélie, because you're right. It's made the rounds and everyone is saying that your play with him is like a work of art."

They were not wrong.

"I hope you can fix it, Leigh," Mira's eyes lightened, "because I haven't been able to watch."

Amélie gave her a smile. "And I hope you gather your courage, because I'd like to see you happy."

Their hands on the table shifted so they were clasped. Amélie gave her a squeeze, felt its return, and they let go.

"I think I might go home now, unless you want to sit with me for a drink? Or we can go somewhere and have twelve of them, Uber it home," Mirabelle suggested.

"That last sounds like a plan," Amélie agreed but leaned in a bit. "You need to release your toy. I'll meet you in the foyer and we can decide where to go."

"Right. It'll be about five minutes and I'll see you in the foyer."

Amélie nodded and slid out. She moved to the foyer. She waited for Mirabelle. And they went out to do the best thing a woman could do when she'd had a tough night.

Spend time with her girl.

Two evenings later, Friday, Amélie was at the club.

To her despair, the strength of which she tried to quell, Olivier did not show.

six

Miracle of Miracles

OLIVIER

On Saturday night, Olly walked into the Bolt, Barclay's club, and was assaulted by the loud music and flash of disco lights coming from the main club that were hitting the dim space of the front area.

He saw the girl at the glass counter that served as the membership check-in desk. Through the glass, the desk offered an array of condoms and tubes of lube, bottles of oil, and other sexual staples, most of these edible.

That was just what was available at the counter. There was a shop with a much larger selection inside the club.

The girl had on an outfit he could see all of, as she was perched on a high stool that cleared the top of the counter. It was made of that plastic-looking material, a black strapless dress with a short but wide skirt lifted up by a load of black netting, fishnets held up by garters. She had cat's whiskers drawn around her nostrils, her nose had a black dot at the tip, her eyes were lined with a thick, black sweeping slash, and she wore a thin black collar with rhinestones around her neck and a band with cat's ears on her head.

She was cute.

But not something you'd see at the Honey.

"Hey, gorgeous," she greeted then said, "Clay's waiting for you up in the office."

He stopped at the counter and asked, "Do I know you?"

He'd been there a number of times and she was cute enough, he'd remember her.

"Nope," she replied, grinning. "He just said if a big guy comes in who looks like he can rip my head off with his bare hands, send him up."

Barclay. He was a wise-ass too.

Olly shook his head before he jerked his chin up and moved to the narrow doorway that led to narrow stairs that would take him to the club's office.

Before he hit the doorway, she called, "Like my head where it is, but, sugar, you wanna rip something else off me, you just shout."

"Raincheck," he muttered and moved in the doorway, taking the first step.

"*C'est la vie,*" he heard her mumbled reply.

He knew it was a saying but he wished she hadn't picked French.

His shoulders actually brushed the walls as he made his way up to an equally narrow landing at the top. A landing that had one door.

He knocked.

"Yo!" he heard Barclay shout from inside.

Olly moved in.

He shut the door behind him and the music from outside could still be heard but not nearly as loud.

Olly turned to his bud in the dimly lit room filled with a large cluttered desk and a lot of furniture in plush fabrics that you could easily lounge on, and fuck on, which he suspected was done. That meant any time he was in there, shooting the shit and sharing a beer with Barclay, he'd never actually sat down.

Barclay, a decent-looking guy, as far as Olly could tell, dark hair, kinda slight build (but it was evident he took care of himself), average height, was behind the desk, brown eyes on Olly.

"Oh fuck," he muttered.

"I fucked up," Olly announced.

"Okay, first, that look on your face, not to make this about me but gotta fuckin' make it about me. Man, please tell me you did not get made at the Honey and right now I gotta gather all the cash I got on hand and get the fuck outta Phoenix 'cause Aryas Weathers is gonna hunt down my ass."

Olly moved into the room, telling him, "I didn't get made."

"No offense, Olly, but I'm as surprised as I am impressed and that's sayin' a lot, brother."

Feeling some guilt about the worry he'd caused his friend, not to mention feeling a lot of other things, nevertheless, since he had a dick, Olly turned to the smoky window that looked down at the club's dance floor and muttered, "Fuck you."

He heard a fridge open and looked Barclay's way just in time to see he'd twisted back from a short, square refrigerator behind the desk and a bottle of beer was sailing through the air his way.

He caught it as Barclay invited, "Just use the edge of the desk to wedge the top off. We lost our bottle opener and none of us lazy fucks have bothered to get a new one. Desk cost us a fuckin' shit-load but my asshole partners have no class so now it's ruined with that shit. Since I got absolutely no desire to fuck 'em, might as well join 'em."

He then stood and used the heel of his palm against the cap set against the edge of the desk to open his own beer.

Olly followed suit and Barclay moved around the desk.

"Park your ass, man, and give whatever shit you're carrying to me."

"No offense back at you," Olly started, eyeing furniture that looked like massive sculpted pillows, no legs, flush to the floor, slouchy and misshapen. "But maybe I should see a cleaning bill before I park my ass on any a' that."

He heard Barclay chuckle as he collapsed into a chair that could fit two (or three), falling into it, which was the only way to get into it. Another concern of Olly's since he had farther to fall . . . and more bulk to pull up.

"I know it looks like the lounge area of a low-rent porno company but we all agreed to no fucking up here. None of us wanna sit in someone else's dried cum so I can promise, even with my partners, there's been no fucking up here," he assured.

Olly could believe that so he moved to a couch and found his way into it. It was comfortable, but his feet to the floor, his knees were nearly in line with his shoulders.

"Christ, Clay, serious should think of maybe getting a real couch."

"I'll take it under advisement." There was humor on his face when he said that but suddenly, Olly saw him wipe it clean away before he invited, "Lay it on me, Olly."

Olly took a pull of his beer. Then another.

After that and a deep breath, he laid it on Barclay. No detail, the basics, some of it uncomfortable, making him feel vulnerable, a feeling he did not like (unless Amélie was there), laying it out just because Barclay needed to know it so he could help him out.

Except his totally losing his cool with Amélie and stomping out. That last, he gave detail.

When he was done, he said, "And that's it," and took another pull of beer.

"Right, that isn't it 'cause, see, you gave me all that and I don't know what it is, I can only assume. And I'll just go on here and say what I assume is that you came here to share all of that so I could give you a clue as to how to get back in there with your girl."

His girl.

Shit.

Yes.

That was why he was there.

Because he'd spent days trying to convince himself that it was good that was done. It was an excuse it *all* could be done. He got what he got from her and she proved the way she handled him last that it was fucked up, so now he could put that part of his life behind him. Now Olly could finally close the channels to that shit that fucked with his head and finally move on with his life.

And this all came on the heels of him spending more days kicking his own ass for being weak. For making the decision he was not going back for a second time and then going. His mind screaming at him to back down, not get in his truck, not put his foot on the gas, not drive to the Honey, his body not listening to a fucking word it said.

And she took him there again, better than before, both times she'd made him come.

But she also gave him more that second time and then it became *all* about how she was, the second session, with him.

It was the play, fuck yeah, absolutely. Mind-blowing. The world expanding like he wasn't on the same planet but in a different universe, even as it physically contracted, being only that room they were in. Even less, just the space the two of them occupied.

And it was more.

She was that miracle of miracles, sexy-as-fuck, gorgeous-as-hell, and still cute. She had a sense of humor. She had a beautiful laugh. She could be affectionate and sweet. Fuck, spread out on top of a vault with his dick and balls on show for the people at the windows, when they bantered, it was like they were on a date.

He wanted more. Of all of it. He couldn't fight it and was beginning to wonder why he did.

Then he began to wonder if he had to. If he could just be who he was, fight that fight, but allow himself to go to her so she could take care of him. Take him where he needed to be. Make it all clear for him. Make it all right. Make it so he was safe to be in that room, which meant safe in his head for unbe-fucking-leivably amazing moments of respite, but only when he was with her.

Then she'd acted like he actually was her fucktoy, a cock, balls, and ass she could play with and put out of her mind.

And that shit stung.

He was not wrong in what he said. What she'd done wasn't right. Both Barclay and Jenna taught him that and Jenna was like that when she'd worked him. Olly knew it and Amélie knew it. He saw it in her face.

It wasn't about her taking his ass. Whitney had tried to shove a huge dildo up it and he'd bit out his safe word so fast, she'd blinked and asked him to repeat it. She'd also gotten pissed about it.

But she did not have near the finesse as Amélie.

He had to admit, he was not totally down with the fact he liked her fingers up his ass.

That did not negate the fact he fucking *liked* her fingers up his ass and the fact he blew almost instantly was evidence of that he couldn't deny.

But as he could do ever since he could speak intelligible English, and do it big, he'd lost his mind and let loose. And after he cooled down and thought it through, struggled past the shit, he knew he might have been right to be pissed, but that didn't mean he didn't fuck up with the way he'd shared that.

And he'd fucked up huge.

Olly leveled his eyes on Barclay and confirmed his assumption, "That's it. You got it. I fucked up and now I have no clue how to get back in there with her, I just know, somehow, I gotta find my way back in there."

With a visible struggle which would be funny if Olly wasn't there for the reasons he was, Barclay pushed up from his lounge to rest his forearms on his knees, the beer hanging from one hand.

"First, man, straight up, do not *ever* talk to a Domme that way. Not during a scene."

It was voiced quietly, somberly, *seriously*.

"It was after the scene," Olly corrected him.

Clay nodded. "I see you might think that and you might be right. She might see it another way and it's up to her to end the scene."

"Not entirely, Clay," Olly said quietly. "And not with where we were at. It was definitely the end of the scene."

Barclay gave him that one with another nod.

"And anyway, it wasn't about the play," Olly reminded him.

"No. You're right. It wasn't. You had a beef, man, totally. But in that scene, that club, definitely the playrooms, in the majority of cases, that kind of reaction is out. There's ways to tell her where you're at. That was not the way and, bro, bein' cool here so you don't think I'm an asshole, what I'm sayin' is, blowin' your stack like that and not lettin' her get a word in is not the way to deal with *any* woman at *any* time."

Olly felt his mouth get tight, his turn to give the point because Barclay was right.

The reason Olly was fucked.

"You entered the game, Olly, you play it the way it's played," Barclay went on. "It cannot surprise you that, especially in the way that's your nature, you can't bend it to your will. And you find a Domme who's good with you not constantly offering verbal subservience or formality of address, ride that, man," he advised. "It isn't rare but that's somethin' I think will suit you so you go with that, but you don't push it. And as I told you, in social places, you gotta dig in and give it. Downcast eyes. Mistress. Master. Speak when spoken to. Come when called. Ask if you even need to take a piss. You with me?"

Olly struggled to take the tight out of his voice when he confirmed, "I'm with you."

Barclay lounged back, legs wide, one straight, the other thrown over the side of the chair, his casual position a trick to catch Olly unprepared for his next.

"You ever had a Domme take your ass?"

Olly drew in breath through his nose, took another pull of his beer, and shared, "Whitney tried unsuccessfully."

"Yeah, not buildin' you up to that, I'm sure. Bitch is nasty." He tipped his head to the window. "If a number of souls down there didn't like the way she played so damned much, I'd find a reason to bounce her."

Olly couldn't imagine anyone liking her nasty but Olly had seen, and now done, a shit-ton of things he couldn't imagine liking so he said nothing.

"Right, bro, clinically speaking, the ass is an erogenous zone," Barclay told him.

Olly shifted in his seat. "Clay—"

"No joke. Straight up. And not just for gays. Seriously, Olly," he said. "Studies, and not one, but a bunch, where they interviewed people, guys state they like it. It's part of their play, even in the vanilla world. A lot more than you think, *a lot,* and I'm talkin' hetero. I get some don't like it but some don't like eating a woman's pussy and you'd think that was whacked, but they don't. It's just a thing like anything. You like it, you go for it because you're alive and you're breathing and you should suck all the good outta life that you can while you got it."

"Not sure why we're talking about this," Olly said it straight.

"Okay, then, first, we'll get back to the earlier shit and I'll say, your Domme is a woman. You made your point to her in a way she couldn't miss, not that she could miss it, that you're a man. But you gotta get she's a woman. And you fuck up with a woman, any woman, you got a couple of choices. You stand your ground like a moron and maybe lose her, or you find a way to communicate with her and get back in there."

"It's not that easy in this situation, Clay," Olly pointed out.

"It's just that easy," Barclay shot back. "You might have to wait until she calls you to her, but if she's into you, she will. You obviously have been communicating with her during your scenes. Find a way to work it out."

That was the rub.

If he went to the club and she blanked him, that sting would become a nettle he couldn't get out.

But the bottom line was, he couldn't make magic. Wipe it all away. Go to the club and make them be just as they were before.

He had to do what he had to do, make the point he knew she'd read that he wanted them to find a way back, and just hope like fuck she wanted that too.

"Right," he murmured.

"And, you know, bro," Barclay started, a big smile on his face, "you instigate that, you might wanna do it on a night you got the next day off. She'll let you back in but she'll whip your ass and you might not be able to sit easy for a while."

He felt his balls draw up in an automatic reaction to Barclay's words, but he ignored that and grinned at his friend, muttering, "Whatever."

Barclay got serious again. "She's gonna take your ass, Olly."

Olly straightened. "Bud, why don't we—"

"You're my bro in a way a lot of men aren't so let me do this for you, Olly, please, fuck, trust me. You want me to do this for you." Relentlessly, he went on without Olly even getting the chance to open his mouth. "She's gonna take your ass and I'm tellin' you, you're gonna love it. You just gotta be there mentally and let her take care of you. You gotta be prepared in more ways than one. And if you're smart and you let me, I'll give you what you need to be ready for her before and after."

"What?" Olly asked, confused.

"I'll just get the shit for you from downstairs and it'll be self-explanatory," he mumbled.

Fuck.

"It's good, man," Barclay said in a voice that made Olly focus more closely on him. "You got someone who gives it good, it's gonna rock your fuckin' world."

Fuck.

Barclay wasn't done.

"I'll say this to you and no one but me and the people I let play with me know it, Olly, so this is me trusting you, but I've even taken cock. A real one. Once, from a Dom whose talents are extreme. It was a miracle he picked me to play, everyone feels that way. He usually does chicks. I normally take Dommes. I always play with female subs. He picked me. Due to his reputation and watching him work, I went with it and he fucked me up the ass and it far from sucked. Had Dommes give me that, drew a line with taking a man, just a boundary I got. But he blew my mind. Wouldn't go for it again, not with anyone but him just 'cause I gave that trust to him and he seriously took me there. So listen to the voice of experience. Yeah?"

"Yeah," Olly grunted, surprised at getting this knowledge but not about to judge and not just because he was not in the position to do so. He was also honored in getting it. It said a lot when someone shared shit that deep.

Suddenly lightening the mood, Barclay again smiled big and said, "Mistress Amélie."

Shit.

"Figure she's also got a reputation," Olly noted.

"Never seen her, but yeah. What I heard, she's the motherlode, brother."

He was right but Olly wasn't super-hip on the idea that she'd been in the game for so long that she had that rep.

"Expel that shit," Barclay stated, obviously reading Olly's thoughts on his face. "You cannot hold her to the same standards as you would your prom date."

"I want her to be mine," Olly admitted through tight lips, something he hadn't even admitted to himself.

"And she is yours when she has you. Roll with that."

He had to because it was his only choice.

"It sucks you had this blip but I'm pleased as fuck for you that you pulled it off and got yourself someone who can give good." Barclay lifted his beer in a salute. "Pleased as fuck for you, bro."

Olly dipped his chin, lifted the butt of his bottle Barclay's way, and took a sip with his friend.

Barclay spoke again.

"She's got a brain in her head, and I don't know anything about the woman except she's good at what she does, but I still reckon she's got her shit seriously together, she's gonna smooth things out with you. So just get her to the place she can do it. She'll take it from there," Barclay encouraged.

"I hope so, bud," Olly replied.

"Me too," Barclay agreed, nodding. "Me too."

AMÉLIE

That same Saturday night, with her book club in her living room deeply discussing the many finer points of a novel they'd revisited (now thrice, for obvious reasons), Joey W. Hill's marvelous *Natural Law*, Amélie was in her kitchen, renewing the water crackers, chopped red onion, and cornichons around the pâté.

She was dallying.

This, she knew, was why Felicia walked into her kitchen, which was fully open to the living room, but due to the large extent of space was also removed from their friends who were lounging before a lovely fire on Amélie's modern, but comfortable, furniture.

Felicia was Mistress Felicia at the Bee's Honey.

Outside the club, she was not just a member of Amélie's book club but a trusted friend.

Amélie did not have as close of a relationship with Felicia as she did with Mira, who she talked to and saw frequently, in and out of the club. Felicia owned her own mortgage brokerage firm, a successful one, so she worked long hours. She also played often at the club to alleviate the stress of those hours.

But the kind of friends they were, the expansiveness of the relationship that took them out of each other's spheres due to life circumstances contracted in times like these.

Times of togetherness.

And, from the look Amélie saw on Felicia's face, times Felicia saw as times of need.

Though, it being Felicia moving into her kitchen, it was more.

During her turns hosting book club, Felicia put on a spread

that rivaled any Amélie had ever had the pleasure of encountering, and it was safe to say with her expansive range of friends and her equally expansive travels, she'd encountered a great many, some of them sublime.

None, however, as sublime as Felicia's.

Further, she wouldn't allow any of them to touch anything, except a plate, a napkin, a utensil, or a bottle of wine for a refill.

No cleanup. No help. It was Felicia's thing and she gave with gusto.

Alternately, having earned it, she barely moved from her seat when the club was hosted at another's home. She might get up to visit the loo, or, if pressed, reach an arm long to grab a bottle of wine.

But Felicia was the host with the most.

She was also that treasured guest who allowed you the space to be the same.

So her appearing in Amélie's kitchen meant she came to talk even if her extraordinary green eyes were aimed at the plate of pâté.

"Do you need some help?" she asked, swinging her half-full wineglass to the side in a deceptively casual stance as she leaned her hip against the counter just down from Amélie.

"I'm putting out crackers, *chérie*, this hardly requires assistance," Amélie answered.

Felicia turned those green eyes that were set in a pixie face with flawless rose and cream skin to Amélie. Felicia's face was one that could get quite stern in a playroom, but in most other times it was kindly, often playful, and always exceptionally pretty.

"Right, then, do you need someone to talk to about why, in sessions that should be filmed to demonstrate the elegance of perfection that can be found in the connection between a Dominatrix and her submissive, the entire club on high alert, hoping you'll reserve a playroom, then word flies the stallion you're breaking stalks through the hunting ground like he'd rip the heart out of anyone who got in his way, possibly doing this with his teeth?"

Amélie felt her muscles tighten.

"Felicia—" Amélie started softly in an effort to shut this down.

This effort she was expending because she had to.

She'd made a grave mistake.

And then, not surprisingly, but wretchedly, Olivier had stood her up.

It was the first time that had ever happened to her.

And it was an incident that was painful, Amélie suspected, not because it happened.

But because Olivier had done it.

Even as early as it was in what they had, even with the strict boundaries of what they had, Amélie could not stop the nagging hurt that plagued her heart that her mistake had ended something not only promising, but in the few times they'd had it, so very beautiful.

"Every one of us out there is worried," Felicia stated, interrupting Amélie and doing it swinging her wineglass beside her to indicate the living room beyond the long island. A room Amélie's gaze studiously avoided, even knowing they were all too well mannered to listen in (or, more to the point, be obvious about it). "You left us and took an hour to arrange crackers, so they nominated me to come talk to you about it."

"I haven't been arranging crackers for an hour," Amélie retorted.

Felicia shifted, sliding along the counter toward Amélie.

"Babe, you haven't even given it all to Mira, and you two are tight," she returned. "She's totally upset. Thinks her shit got yours in a bind."

It was time to talk to Mira (again) and allay her fears.

But at that moment, Amélie held Felicia's eyes.

Then she whispered, "I like him."

Her friend's eyes sparkled. "I like him too. Don't even know him, just gotta look at him to like him, and I'm not into big boys."

"No, Felicia, I like him *very much*."

Felicia's gaze grew intense as she murmured, "And thus the elegance of perfection of your connection when you work him."

That made the pain in her heart stop nagging and start thumping.

"I really don't wish to talk about this," Amélie declared.

"Did you two exchange numbers?" Felicia asked.

Amélie shook her head.

Felicia got closer. "Aryas will give you his number. Call him. Talk to him. Whatever happened . . ." She suddenly shook her head. "I watched. Both sessions you had with him. I had to take care of my slave so we missed the end of the work you did with him on the vault, but Leigh, I watched. I did it closely and I did that for more than one reason. And honey, seriously, he's into you."

Of course he was.

The operative word being *was*.

"I would have liked to think that but I lost focus during our last session, which was a private one, fortunately. I believe I hurt his feelings and—"

Felicia reached out and took her hand. "No, Leigh, I don't think you get me." She gave Amélie's hand a squeeze and stated, "I finished Domme training, what, three, four years ago?"

Amélie nodded even though she replied, "You would know better than I, but yes. It seems it's been that long, though," she gave Felicia a soft smile on a light tease, "it still seems like just yesterday you were a green newbie with a penchant for biting off more than you can chew, even not being into the big boys."

And this was true. Felicia almost exclusively took male subs. But she liked multiple-partner play, and in the beginning, they thought she was trying to build a harem.

Felicia ignored the tease and the subtle effort to change the subject.

"Well, now I'm not a newbie, and honest to God, never seen a sub so focused on his Domme as that man is with you."

Amélie felt her breath catch in her throat.

Felicia wasn't done, and spoke again on a gentle tug of Amélie's hand.

"We don't find this often. We don't find that connection. Many of us aren't searching for it. We're looking for a different kind of connection that's important, but it's not that. *All* that. All I saw you have with him. We get what we need through the play. But some of us . . ."

She let that trail off, also knowing what Amélie was searching for, not needing to tell her something she already knew.

But she didn't stop speaking.

"Talk to Aryas. He'd do anything for you. Even break that rule, giving you your stallion's number," she urged.

"It's not only inappropriate, but a breach of trust not only with Aryas to ask him for that, but with Olivier to get it," Amélie said quietly, hoping her words held no rebuke.

"This is a special circumstance," Felicia returned.

"In our world, that special circumstance doesn't exist. Not with the intimacy we share. Not with the trust we need to establish. If you were angry or hurt, putting distance between yourself and a sub, you wouldn't feel it was a special circumstance. You'd be angry your privacy was invaded. Because, if that were to happen, it would be."

"Leigh—"

Amélie lifted her free hand, palm out, but tightened her hold on Felicia with her other before letting her go, doing all of this talking.

"Felicia, I'm grateful, your concern is very sweet." She dropped her raised hand. "But Olivier and I had three times together. They were lovely. They were . . ." She tried to find the words but failed as there were none. Therefore she had to go on lamely, "*More* than lovely. But he's a man, very much a man, no matter how he likes his play, and if he's to forgive me for my lapse, he's the one who has to take that first step so I know he's forgiven me. Then I can take the rest."

"I hope he does," Felicia replied.

So did Amélie.

But after his extremely heated yet justified outburst, and as time passed and she neither saw him nor heard word he was at the club, she knew she'd be foolish to hold her breath.

"While we were waiting for those crackers," Felicia went on, her full pouty lips in that pixie face quirking (she could honestly be described as a living doll, but if a sub did such, they'd feel her switch), "we all made a pact. Because we all know, after you having him, he's not gonna come back if he's not coming back for you. So if we see him at the Honey, we'll text you so fast, our fingers might catch fire. And if you're down with it, we'll spread that word."

Amélie hoped she was right, that should Olivier return to the Honey, he would be doing so to mend things between them, rather than to attempt to find another Mistress to see to his needs.

She even so far as prayed to the fates she was.

So she was definitely down with their plan.

It was not normal operating procedure for Mistress Amélie, entirely because she'd never been in this situation.

But if Olivier returned to the Honey there was hope he did so to find her.

It was good she cared very little about what people thought of her, she was what she was, did what she did, wanted what she wanted.

And she wanted Olivier.

Therefore, she didn't care if that word was spread.

So yes, she was down with it.

Amélie smiled. "That would be most appreciated."

Felicia reached out and touched the back of Amélie's hand before she removed her own and asked quietly, "No word from Evangeline?"

Amélie shook her head.

Felicia sighed before murmuring, "What are we going to do with that girl?"

Amélie had no idea and this was troubling her more and more.

Felicia said nothing further on that subject, took hold of the finished platter of pâté, and declared, "Now it's time to feed that starving horde, not like we haven't hoovered through all the goodies you've got out there. Seriously, I don't know where you get this pâté, Leigh, but my mouth starts salivating for it days before we hit your house for book club. If you ever hosted our meeting and didn't serve this stuff, I might go on a hunger strike until you produced it."

Amélie had it flown in from a bistro with a particularly talented chef in New York City.

She didn't tell Felicia that.

She said, "It's a secret I'll take to my grave."

As Felicia made her way toward the door, she opened the drawer that hid the trash and recycle bins and pointed inside.

"It's on the box, babe. If I was into digging through trash, I'd find it. Since I'm *way* not into digging through trash, I won't. Just don't think we don't appreciate your relationship with Federal Express."

She shoved the drawer to, tossed a wink over her shoulder, this wink stating plainly she knew exactly where that pâté was from, and sauntered around the island in her best Mistress stroll.

Which meant Amélie walked to the living room to see relieved faces.

This was because she walked there laughing.

Her friends cared about her deeply.

They were worried.

Now, they felt some ease.

Amélie just wished she could, too, deep down.

But she couldn't.

Not until Olivier came back to the Honey.

If he did.

Oh, but she hoped he did.

But that nag of pain was still there because she knew with the depth of his anger, the session he had missed, the time that had passed . . .

She shouldn't hold her breath.

seven

Too Delicious to Be Real

AMÉLIE

With a studiously unhurried gait, on Monday evening, Amélie walked up to the Honey, her head bent, hand up, just a woman checking her phone.

But she wasn't just a woman checking her phone.

She was an idiot woman who was excited beyond reason and terrified beyond words who was checking her phone.

The text string included:

> **Romy:** *There's a big, brooding boy holding up the wall, waiting for his Mistress.*
>
> **Amélie:** *Thank you, darling.*
>
> **Romy:** *Would you like me to reserve a room for you?*
>
> **Amélie:** *Yes, please. Number 17. You're a love.*
>
> **Romy:** *17? My, my. I hope you keep the blinds up, sweetie.*

Oh, she was going to keep the blinds up.

If he was there to deal with what happened between them, they'd do just that.

And then for all the stress he put her through waiting for him to forgive her, she was going to crop his ass.

She opened the door of the club and it felt like the atmosphere hit charged just by her presence the second she walked in.

She knew he was still there. Even though she'd taken time to prepare herself (and give herself time to attempt to calm down, this not working), Romy would have shared he was leaving or had left.

So he was there. She just hoped he wasn't there to further make a point already well made by finding someone else.

She walked into the club with many eyes already on her.

She found Romy first to send her a nod of thanks. Her gaze caught Stellan next, and noted his attention was on her and he looked strangely unhappy. She further saw Felicia, holding court with two male toys, and she was smirking a knowing (but happy) smirk.

She also noticed Delia was looking at her, and her look was a look that, for some bizarre reason (possibly because Delia never seemed in a good mood and it further seemed she didn't like any-body), could kill.

Halfway through the hunting ground on her way to an empty booth, she turned her head to the wall and saw him there. Standing right where she first saw him, looking just like he not only was hold-ing up the long wall, but that he could.

God, she wanted him not to be as amazing as she remembered, so if he rejected her entirely and moved on, she could do the same.

But he was just that amazing.

And he became more amazing immediately.

This was because his attention was on her as well. And when her gaze caught his, he straightened from the wall and turned in her direction.

But he didn't move in her direction. He just stood there, show-ing her he'd come if called.

In order not to do the real thing, she visualized melting to her knees, such was her relief.

She dipped her chin and twisted it slightly to the side.

It was not a demand he attend her. It was an acknowledgment of his message.

It was also an indication she was going to make him wait.

This could anger him and throw her right back to where she was five seconds before, if not make it worse.

But she saw his lips hitch up at the side before he slouched back with his shoulder to the wall and watched her walk the rest of her way to her table.

She barely got her bottom on the bench when a waitress was there.

"You gonna sit long enough for a drink or you gonna go hit that right away?" the waitress asked.

Yes, they all were talking.

And they were all watching.

Not a surprise.

And Amélie could care less.

For Olivier was here to forgive her.

So all was well in her world.

She looked at the waitress, a new-ish hire she'd seen more than once, but since the woman had never waited on Amélie, she didn't yet know her name.

In that moment, she also didn't take the time to ask.

Allowing her lips to curl up, she requested, "A drink, darling, and bring whatever Olivier likes to drink too."

"Gotcha," she muttered and moved away.

Moving in the instant she did was Talia, who slid in opposite Amélie without invitation.

"Sooooo . . ." She grinned. "Do you think it'll be a stampede to room seventeen?"

That was likely.

"Romy has a big mouth," Amélie replied.

"Romy saw you jack him on his knees. An already legendary spectacle I unfortunately missed. She wants a repeat performance. We *all* do. And thus Romy's putting together your application to be admitted to the Dominatrix Hall of Fame," Talia returned.

Amélie laughed quietly. "Would that there was such a thing."

"Girl, you're giving Sixx a run for her money."

Sixx used to live in Phoenix. Amélie had trained under her for a time years ago.

She wasn't a talented Mistress. She was the stick by which everyone was measured.

It was a nice thing to say but it wasn't true.

"That's sweet," she said. "Though, I'll be taking some time to sit and enjoy my beast and a drink so seventeen will be vacant for that time."

"Want me to get a slave to call him over?" Talia offered.

"That'd be lovely. Thank you," Amélie accepted.

Talia didn't vacate the booth immediately.

She gave Amélie a sweet look and whispered, "So glad he came back, baby."

Amélie felt her mouth get soft.

Talia took that in then slid out and the drinks were at the table by the time Olivier arrived.

He stood next to her, eyes to hers before they went to her neck. "Mistress Amélie."

"Olivier, please slide in. All the way to the back," she invited.

Clearly thinking that was a lot easier than expected, he assumed a startled expression before he moved to the side opposite her and did as asked.

She slid in farther, closer to him. When she was where she wanted to be, she reached for the drinks, moving his in front of him and taking a sip before she put hers to the table.

"Thought I was supposed to do that kind of shit," he muttered.

She looked his way, saw him studying the beer, and informed him, "I'm in a benevolent mood."

"And I bet I should thank Christ for that," he stated.

He thought she could be cute.

He could be cute too.

She was not going to tell him that, but even if she was, he lifted his hand, curled it around the pilsner glass, and moved his gaze to the room, doing this speaking quickly.

"What I did was fucked, Amélie. I know it. I had a point to make but there was a better way to make it. I lost my temper and that was not cool. I got a bad habit of doin' that, a habit I gotta learn to lock down. It took some time to get my head together about it and I didn't come to the Honey like you wanted on Friday and that wasn't cool either. I fucked up, I wish I didn't but I did. And," he drew in a huge breath, "I'm sorry."

That took a lot and she knew it. He was not that man in life and he was not that toy in the playroom.

So every word meant as much to her as it took him to say them.

That said, she was surprised, with her transgression, it was he who apologized.

It was his place in this world, but again, he was not that man and had made that clear in a variety of ways, most specifically during their last, painful encounter.

This made his words all the more prized.

To show him that, she moved closer to him, close enough to brush his arm with her breasts, as she curled a hand high on his thick thigh.

He turned to her in surprise.

"Mistress Mirabelle, my friend I was talking to that night before I saw to you, had a minor, but important, decision to make. She was leaning the wrong way, a way that, if she took that path, might have caused her some pain. I care about her a great deal and I didn't want her to do anything she'd regret."

She squeezed his thigh, getting closer.

"My mind was on *you*, Olivier, when I was working you. Only you. And I had other plans for you that I felt taking care of a friend took priority over. Not that you aren't a priority, just that I, too, had a decision to make that night and I felt the right one was to look after my friend. That said, I was disappointed not being able to carry my plans for you through. Very disappointed, my *chevalier*. Because of that, I'm afraid my mind wandered."

She said no more. She did not explicitly apologize.

And she wouldn't.

If some miracle occurred and the them they were became another type of them, and she was more than Mistress to him, there were times when she would (maybe).

Now, she would not.

She felt her breath catch at the warm look he was giving her.

"Not my place to say," he started. "But with your girl, you made the right decision."

She felt relief sweep through her and her face got soft.

"I should have listened to you when you wanted to share that," he said.

She should have shared it before he had to lay it out.

She gazed deep into his eyes, squeezing his thigh, and replied, "There were several *shoulds* that simply *weren't* in that situation, Olivier. You're sitting here, let's move on."

"Works for me," he muttered.

She gave him another squeeze, saw his hand still on his drink, and realized she'd been remiss. "Partake of your beer freely, *mon chou*."

"My cabbage," he muttered, lifting his beer.

She raised her brows, surprised he knew what *mon chou* meant. "You speak French?"

"I looked it up."

Her belly melted.

"Means pastry too," he stated, putting down his beer and looking at her. "Which one am I to you?"

Oh, he was definitely a delectable pastry.

There was a teasing light in his eye and she leaned closer.

"It's just an endearment," she told him.

"I know. That's where I found it. On a list of French endearments. Wasn't sure about it but at least you don't call my *mon cochon*."

My pig.

She laughed softly.

He grinned and lifted the beer to his lips.

She slipped her hand lower, cupping his cock and balls.

He jolted and coughed, putting the beer down without sipping it.

But she was feeling something.

Gently, fingering around his hardening cock, she probed deeper.

"Olivier," she whispered at what she felt.

"Bought it for you," he told the room. "Wore it for you." He shifted as she traced the strap. "And it fits better."

He was harnessed.

She rubbed her lips together so they wouldn't tremble.

Her other lips between her legs she wasn't able to do that with so they carried on.

"This pleases me," she told him.

"Hoped it would." He looked to her and dipped his voice. "Glad it does."

She held him, stroking his lengthening cock with her thumb.

He adjusted again.

She smiled.

"How old are you, my *chevalier?*" she asked.

He lifted his beer and answered, "Thirty-two," before he took a sip.

"Hmm . . ." she murmured, still stroking.

"Can I ask, uh . . . Mistress, how old are you?"

"Thirty-three," she shared.

"You seem older," he muttered. "When you aren't bein' cute. Then you seem younger."

She gripped him semi-tightly and his lower body tensed. "You should never tell a woman she seems older."

He turned to look at her, "Experience, Amélie, not age."

"Ah," she breathed out.

She ungripped him only to unzip him.

His lower half went still again and she heard a noise he strangled back when she pulled him out.

"Fuck," he whispered.

She slid her hand in the opening and inspected the harness more closely.

"Jesus," he blew out.

"I approve, *mon chou*," she told him, lightly cupping his balls.

His, "Good," came thick.

She gave him a slight squeeze and he shifted in his seat again. "How did you come to the life?"

"What?"

His mind was on other things.

"The life, our life, Olivier," she explained.

"Used to go to the Bolt," he told her.

"I've never been there," she noted.

"You're not missing much," he replied.

"I'd heard that."

"Owner's a good guy, one of them, anyway. He's a friend of mine," he offered.

She looked up at him as she massaged his balls. "Yes?"

"Yeah," he pushed out.

"Please put your arms on the back of the booth on either side of you, Olivier. And don't take them off. Yes?"

"Fuck," he bit out. Not in anger, he was again shifting under her his attentions to his balls. "Yeah," he went on. "Yes, Mistress," he finished.

He did as told.

"And coming to understand your nature?" she asked. He didn't answer immediately so she stopped massaging and just cupped him as she pressed closer. "You don't have to tell. It's your story and yours to give. That's nobody's to command. But I'd be delighted if you decided to share it with me."

He turned his head and dipped his chin down so their faces were close. She didn't move and she didn't ask him to move. This made the setting intimate, just the two of them, when he spoke.

"Black box."

She was confused. "I'm sorry?"

"Boys jack off. I did a lot of that when I was a kid, all guys do. Shit in my head, though, wasn't women in magazines showin' their tits. I guess I had a good imagination. Didn't know where some of it came from until, well . . . I did."

She smiled up at him. "And black box?" she prompted.

"Accidently found my parents' toy box. It was black," he told her.

"Ah." She moved her hand out of his pants to start stroking the long, thick length of him as she said, "And from there you realized there were other worlds out there, that some people hide and are ashamed of, but even your parents participated in, if perhaps to a lesser degree, depending what was in that box. So that opened your mind to who you are and brought you to a place where you could explore it."

He looked disconcerted.

"Olivier?"

"I just thought they were fucked up," he told her.

She smiled, stroking him deeply. So deeply, automatically, he dropped his forehead to hers and she felt his breath escalate.

"And now what do you think?" she asked.

"Amélie, you're jackin' me, talkin' about my parents," he warned her that wasn't in his comfort zone.

And it was a comfort zone she couldn't push, but she did want to push to know more about him so she shifted around it.

"Yes. Parents who I hope you know now are not fucked up and neither are you."

"Mistress—"

She kept stroking him, doing it harder. "You do know there's very little vanilla in the world. Men who like to wear panties under their suits. Couples who enjoy erotic movies. Having sex in public places where the threat is real they'll get caught. Having multiple partners during play. Being deprived of their sight with a blindfold or their ability to communicate with a gag."

"I know all this, Amélie."

It was nearly a groan.

She stroked the length of him, swirling the tip with her thumb and went on like he hadn't spoken.

"And I'm going to enjoy you tucking that brute in your pants and walking with me through this room with a massive erection to get to the place I will give you the punishment you earned then take care of you the way you know I will."

"Jesus, baby," he whispered, the untamed beast stark in his eyes, fear and hunger at war.

She wanted that but closer, where she could give him the tools he needed to win that war.

So she let him go.

"Tuck yourself away, Olivier. We have things to do," she ordered.

"Christ," he muttered, not moving.

"Do not delay. You'll only make it worse," she cautioned.

That got him moving. And when he'd pushed his cock back into his pants and zipped up, she slid out of the booth.

He was at her heels when she walked through the room, all eyes on them, and it took a lot not to toss her hair in triumph and smile like a teenager.

She didn't dally in the halls mostly because she couldn't wait. It had been too long.

She missed him.

They hit room seventeen, the blackout blinds down, the lights on, and when they entered, she flipped the switch that declared the room occupied and moved into it.

He stopped at the door he'd closed.

"Remove your clothing, Olivier. Deal with it as usual," she commanded. "Then stand by the center table."

She was moving to the side table, the only thing outside a sink and its vanity in the room.

Except, of course, for the centerpiece in the middle that even a novice would know its use.

Olivier knew and Amélie sensed him not moving, staring at the table, knowing, partially, what he would get that night.

"Again, my *chevalier*," she said quietly, sifting through her bag. "I would not delay."

She found the things she wanted, brought them to the top, but didn't pull them out. It would not do for him to see some of them too soon.

She grabbed what she needed right then and turned to find him where she'd told him to be.

He was naked, hard, balls harnessed in a very nice set of straps, and watching her warily.

"Turn around and put your hands to the table, please," she ordered.

He hesitated only briefly before complying but she noticed his breathing go unsteady.

"Legs apart," she said when she was close behind him.

"Jesus, fuck," he muttered but did as told.

She made her way to him and once there moved economically, ring to his cock, straps leading from it up to his upper hips, one around his hips, she buckled it securely. Then she bent and reached between his legs to grab the other two straps.

"Right, Olivier, hands to your buttocks, open them for me."

Another hesitation, this one longer, as he puffed out a breath, two, then his hands went from the table to his ass.

He opened for her.

She clenched her teeth to control her reaction as she lifted the straps and fastened them to the hip strap, tightening them, spreading him further, strapping him open.

He'd had them before, but even so, the puffs of breath came out faster once she'd finished.

"Lovely, *mon chou*," she whispered, gliding a hand up his inner thigh. "You may let go then please position on the table on your back."

She stood back and watched as he did it. He did it slowly, but he did it.

She went to the control panel that, in this room, had a number of other controls.

She hit some switches and watched his chest heave as his gaze followed the apparatus trundling mechanically through the air, dangling from the ceiling.

She moved back to him. Coming close to his head, she laid a hand on his chest and stroked him there.

"You're pleasing me greatly, my beast," she said gently.

And he was. It was early in their play and she was already soaked.

"Fuckin' thrilled, Mistress," he replied, going for the cheek but the wild was in his eyes and she had to assuage it.

"Breathe, Olivier, deep, and look at me. I'm here. Right here. All for you."

"Yeah." A gust of breath. "Yeah, Amélie. Yeah."

"I'm not going anywhere. You'll see me or you'll feel me close. Tonight, like every night, every time we have together, is all about you."

He bit his lip, let it go, and said, "Yeah."

She nodded. "Good?"

He nodded back.

"Good," she replied softly and bent to touch her lips to his. She lifted away and asked, "Now, would you please lay your arms along the lengths?"

He swallowed, his throat convulsing, and did as asked.

She made light, but tender, work of it. Strapping him wrist, forearm, elbow, biceps, and shoulder to the long arms that led out from either side of the table. As she did, she touched him, stroked him, kissed him, ran her lips along straps, then moved on.

The same to the thicker, heavier straps that she pulled from under the table. One at his chest. His rib cage. His waist.

She moved back to his head.

"Now, Olivier, I need to ask you to give me more," she shared quietly.

He nodded, the wild still there, knowing what was coming, but she sensed he was beating it back, there to prove to her he'd put their last session behind him, just as she was there to prove to him he could trust her to make that worth it.

And with all that, she thought he was never more beautiful than in that moment.

"I'll guide you," she said gently. "Go where I'm guiding you. I'll be patient but don't take advantage of it."

"You got it," he rumbled, perhaps bravado, perhaps psyching himself up.

She bent over him again. "After this, you'll request this room from me. I promise you, my beast."

It took a moment for him to get there but he made it.

"Okay, baby," he whispered, staring in her eyes.

She gave him another smile, another brush of the lips, and soothed his hair off his forehead.

Then she moved to his legs. Lifting one at the heel, she set it in the padded stirrup cuff, tightening it around his ankle.

She did the same to the other so he was resting, his knees bent, ankles in stirrups.

She folded the table down in order that his buttocks were at the very edge, slightly hanging over.

She also saw his erection was hard and heavy, lying on his stomach, his balls bulging at the sides of his harness. She took needed time to pay attention to him there, too, with licks and strokes, giving it enough his cock was distended, looking like it was aching, his legs trembling in their stirrups.

She moved back to his head but reached out a hand to stroke his cock.

"First your punishment, *mon chou*," she informed him.

He nodded jerkily.

"Then your reward," she promised.

"Great," he gritted out.

She smiled and stood back, his eyes following her.

It was then she put her hands into the material on either side of her hips, pulling the clinging jersey of her cobalt blue dress up and yanking it off.

"Fucking hell," he breathed.

She was wearing a black lace bustier, sheer black panties that shadowed her but also exposed her, ties on the sides, black thigh highs with lace tops and stiletto-heeled black platform pumps.

"*Amélie.*"

The need.

He liked what he saw.

She smiled inside, not allowing herself mentally to admit that she was relieved he did, and went to the control panel.

"Fucking *hell*," he grunted as the electric pulleys lifted his ankles, up and up, until his legs were straight. She hit another button and they moved out, spreading them apart. When she noticed him straining, his jaw clenching, she gave it another inch and then hit another control, lifting him even farther so his bottom half was slightly raised, his legs stretched wide and taut.

She studied him, his chest now heaving, his hands in fists, his cock, Amélie fancied, was visibly throbbing, and decided she could watch him in this pose, at her control, *giving* her *all* control, making him vulnerable to her for anything, everything. Giving her access to hand him the world.

But she couldn't stand there forever.

It was time to hand her steed the world.

She went to the table, coming back with her crop.

He eyed it, the beast at the surface.

"Do not come, Olivier," she ordered firmly.

"Fuck," he whispered.

"Did you hear me?" she pressed.

"Yes, Mistress," he pushed out.

She nodded smartly and turned to his backside.

And there she cropped him, fighting back her own orgasm, one she knew would be extreme, as he took it magnificently. Legs and hips, indeed his entire body jerking and lurching against the restraints as she cropped his ass, his back thighs, his inner thighs, and again to his ass. She avoided his balls with her blows but stood at the end of the table, and with the folded-over leather tip of the crop, lightly slapped them side to side.

That was when she got him. He let loose his pleasure for her to hear, groans this time, not grunts, long ones, shearing through the room while his legs strained, his fists clenched and unclenched. His hips bucked in ways that she didn't know if he was free, if he'd push forward for more or rear away.

"*Baby*," he growled, sharing he was at his end.

There it was.

She smiled.

He'd push forward for more.

And he was going to have to take more. She'd say when it would end.

She gave his balls more.

Then she cropped him more.

His head was digging into the table, hard jaw totally exposed, body nearly inert with the effort to hold still when she went to the other table again, prepared her next and walked back to him.

His eyes shot wide.

"Amélie—"

"Do I own all of you?" she asked.

"Yes," he clipped.

"Then, as it's mine, I'll enjoy what's mine," she declared, moving to the control panel.

She hit the control and the blinds started sliding up, both white . . . and black.

She heard his rumble but ignored it as she moved to the table.

And she held his eyes when she put her foot still in its platform pump on the little step, lifted up to a knee at the table by his ribs, and hauled herself up.

She positioned, settling with her pussy over his face, her face to his privates.

His body kept straining.

"You do not even lift your head to get to me until I give myself to you, yes?"

"Yeah," he gritted.

She reached down to pull the ties and then tugged her panties away.

"Torture, Amélie," he whispered. "Fuck, so pretty."

And so wet. He wouldn't have to eat. She'd drip on him.

Time to get to that; he needed it and so did she.

She grasped his cock, lightly stroking as she set the tip of the liberally oiled plug to his hole.

"Tell me when you're ready for more," she ordered.

"Fuck," he bit off.

"I'll need you to tell me, my beast. My mouth will be busy and I won't be able to ask."

"*Fuck,*" he groaned.

"Will you tell me?" she prompted.

"Yeah," he confirmed immediately.

She took the head of his cock in her mouth as she slid the tip of the plug in an inch.

It said a good deal that even stretched taut, the stirrups and their chains rattled violently.

She gave him another inch.

"Fuck, shit, Christ," he chanted.

She stroked him with her mouth, not taking him deep, and stayed still.

She gave him time.

Then she twisted the plug.

"More," he blew out.

She gave him more of her mouth and he learned quickly the more he took the more he got.

She watched as he widened for her, accepted her, in the end lifted for her as she bobbed on his dick, taking as much as she could get, and then she took his plug home.

"Blow me, baby, fuckin' hell, I need this pussy, God, fuck, *please*," he begged. "Give me your pretty pussy."

She blew him, moving faster, stroking the parts of his cock she couldn't get to with her mouth in a tight fist (because she had a good control on her gag reflex, but as sad as the fact was, he was an impossibility), she went back to the plug and started gently fucking him with it.

He was bucking, trying to fuck her mouth and get his plug.

"Fuck yeah, Mistress, *fuck . . . yeah, Christ*."

She fucked him harder.

"*Fuck, baby,* fuck that. That's it. Fuck it for me, *fuck*," he grunted.

She gave him more every way she could give.

"Fuck me, Amélie, fuck my hole. Harder, baby. Suck my dick. Jack my ass. Please. *Fuck me*," he begged.

He was ready.

She rammed her pussy on his face.

He started eating immediately, laving his tongue from back to front, dipping it deep to pull out her juices, pressing it flat and hard against her clit, then rolling, then flicking.

He was good at that, too, a sub who was a master.

Ecstasy.

She rode his face, sucked his dick, fucked his ass, and the table shuddered as she shoved herself deeper into his face and he accepted, gratefully, eating her savagely.

She had to pump his dick with her fist, shoving the plug home to feel his grunt of acceptance reverberate up her cunt as her torso came up, her spine arched, her head flew back and she came.

She'd been right and wrong.

Her orgasm was not extreme . . . but instead *extreme*.

Rocking on his face, jacking his dick, crying out quiet, short, but constant mewls of pleasure as it rolled over her, everything her beast had offered, everything he'd built, everything they were.

Magnificent beauty.

He ate her through it, not stopping, not gentling, consuming her.

Still in her glow, she sat farther up, tugging on his dick. "Come for me, Olivier."

He blew at her command, his cum splicing up his chest, some splashing on her thigh.

And then he continued to blow, his body convulsing in its restraints, hips curling up as much as they could to fuck her fist, cum gushing and gushing and gushing.

She stroked him through it, gentling when his eruptions started easing, milking him to the end as he lapped at her, eating her clean.

She bent over him, kissing the underside of his cock, his balls, the insides of his thighs, before she said quietly, "I'm climbing off, *mon chou*. But I'll be back."

She lifted off his mouth so he could say, "Okay, Mistress."

She climbed off. Moving to her panties, she positioned them and tied them.

Then she moved to the control panel.

Down went the blinds to Talia putting her hands in prayer position, silently begging she not stop the show.

Amélie shook her head but did it with a slight smile on her face.

Stellan was there again, still watching her, still looking peeved.

Whatever was up his ass, he could communicate it. Frowning at her through a playroom window was ridiculous.

The blinds whirring down, she quickly went about the business of lowering Olivier's legs, elongating the table, cleaning his cum from his chest and her wet from his face and unstrapping him completely.

He didn't push up or ask to, especially when, right away, she mounted him again, lowering herself, straddling his hips, chest to his chest, eyes to his face.

"And how did you like your reward, Olivier?" she asked.

To her (delighted, it must be said,) surprise, his arms flew around her, holding her tight, squeezing the air out of her as he burst out laughing.

That filled the room, too, the deep resonance of it echoing through the air, gliding across her skin, a sound almost too delicious to be real.

She grinned at him and was still grinning when he got enough control to ask, "I don't know. Do you mean finally getting to eat your very sweet, seriously pretty pussy? And baby, your pussy is *very* pretty and *very* sweet. Or you blowing me while you fucked my ass?"

"All of that," she answered, still grinning.

"Then I liked it, Amélie, it fuckin' *rocked*."

She was *still* grinning so couldn't quite pull off an authoritative tone when she replied, "I'm pleased."

"I got the sense you came hard for me, Mistress, don't know. Too busy tryin' to keep my dick from exploding. But my guess would be I'm more pleased."

She started laughing, feeling her face flush because she was so scrumptiously excited he'd liked what she'd done, something that had been a given for so long for her, she'd lost the thrill of it, and hoping he thought that pink in her cheeks came with her humor.

He held her tighter.

When she sobered, she stilled at the look on his face.

"I fucked up. I was a dick. I blew my stack 'cause I got a temper. Been kickin' my ass for days, worried as fuck you'd blank me. I'm glad you didn't, Amélie, because I missed you."

God, that openness. His honesty.

He was sucking her in, in a way she didn't want to crawl out.

She kissed him, couldn't stop herself from kissing him, she let him kiss her back, and she let them both do this for a long time before she lifted up and admitted, "I made my own mistakes to loosen the hold you have on that impressive temper, my *chevalier*. You were not wrong in what you said, as we both know. How you communicated it, I don't have to mention because you've apologized." She touched her lips to his briefly before she finished, "But I hope you know, I missed you, too, Olivier."

At that, he lifted his head and kissed her.

And she let him, his hands in her hair holding her to him and everything.

It took a couple of tugs back to break the kiss before he got the message and they were both breathing a little uneasily when she lifted her head.

"I want you back on Wednesday, Olivier."

"I'll be here, Amélie," he said instantly.

"And I want you to consider a weekend with me up in the mountains at my ranch," she blurted.

He blinked.

Damn!

Mirabelle had been with Trey for weeks; all her vacillation, not jumping in. Amélie had four sessions with her beast and she was inviting him for a weekend away.

And she meant a weekend away. Not strictly a play weekend. They'd definitely play, but she wanted to know the man who laid under her.

Damn.

When he stared up at her with intensity, like he was trying to see through the windows to her soul, she quickly explained, "I have a setup. It's nice. I . . . it's play. A weekend of play. You'll like it. Trust me."

He grinned. "Bet I will."

She relaxed on him. "You will."

"You got a ranch?"

"House here, ranch where I can escape the heat in the summer. And where I keep my horses."

"Now how did I know my Mistress had horses?" he asked her like he wasn't asking her.

She lifted a hand and stroked his cheek, slid her fingers through his hair at the side, and watched, captivated, as he turned his head and kissed her wrist.

"They're beautiful beasts," she whispered.

He looked back at her.

"Yeah," he replied, but he wasn't talking about horses.

Good God, if she didn't stop this, she'd melt all over him.

"I'll figure out a weekend. Tell you, yeah?" he asked.

She nodded.

"Now, Mistress, am I gonna wear that thing home or are you gonna pull it outta my ass?" he prompted.

"That's much too big to wear home, *chevalier*. The ones I'll send you home in are smaller."

He looked to the ceiling and muttered, "Great."

"But tonight, and when you come back to me, wear the harness, please."

He looked back to her, giving her a squeeze. "Gotcha."

"And please don't touch what's mine, Olivier," she went on.

His eyes darkened and the tone was deeper when he repeated, "Gotcha."

"Thank you for my harness, it's lovely," she told him.

"I'd say you're welcome but not sure that's the way to go," he replied.

"It bought you less of a cropping," she shared.

His brows shot up. "Less?"

She nodded.

"Well thank fuck I'm generous with sex shit I buy that I gotta wear but it's for you."

She laughed quietly and stroked his jaw with her thumb. "Don't pretend you don't like your punishments."

His hand still in her hair cupped the back of her head and brought her face closer to him.

"That ball paddling shit you did? A light touch with a bite? Fuck, baby. That was inspired."

Another compliment on something she knew all too well was "inspired" and she fought giggling like a schoolgirl.

"Anything else you'd like to use to flatter me for reasons unknown?" she asked.

"You give phenomenal head."

She couldn't stop her laughter at that. "You're incorrigible."

He lifted his head up so their faces were a breath away.

"Yeah, Mistress, and don't pretend you don't like it."

She felt herself melting, she just couldn't stop.

And she did it gliding her hand to cup his jaw and slide her thumb lovingly across his lips.

"I allow you way too many liberties," she murmured.

"Thinkin', havin' some more time to check out the talent out there, it's time you had a challenge."

He was not wrong.

"Perhaps before you earn my switch, we should get that plug out of you."

He nodded but lifted his head farther doing it, brushing his lips against hers.

"Cheeky," she whispered, following him down and kissing him hard.

They made out like normal people on a torture bed in a public dungeon room until she stopped it, crawled off him, took care of his ass and its straps, and gave him leave to get dressed.

She pulled her dress on as he did and flipped the switch to say the room was vacant as he tucked in his shirt.

He came to her.

"Wednesday," he said.

"Yes," she replied.

Then she grabbed his hand and linked her fingers in his. That way, she walked them through the playrooms, through the hunting ground and to the foyer.

She stopped there and curled into him.

He squeezed her hand and dipped his chin deep.

She pressed up to touch her lips to his.

"Wednesday," she whispered there.

"Yeah," he replied.

She let his hand go, he let his eyes linger on hers, then he turned and she watched him walk out the front door.

eight

Soixante Quinze

AMÉLIE

On Wednesday night, Amélie walked into the Honey early, going to the front desk to give them her purse to secure.

She hadn't told Olivier when to meet her and she half hoped he'd be there, waiting for her, anxious to see her. But it was so early she suspected he would not be and that was good (in a way) as she had another reason for arriving early.

She'd heard word Aryas was back in town and she needed to speak with him about something she'd been rolling around in her head since the thought occurred to her.

When there was any space in her head that wasn't taken by Olivier, of course.

He was consuming her.

This caused alarm.

She'd twice had toys she'd played with exclusively for long periods of time, as they'd pleased her greatly, but also, they had other attributes—looks, body, but mostly personalities—that called to something deeper.

Fortunately, before she'd dug into that something deeper to explore it, the first had shared he'd started seeing a woman in the mundane world who he'd found was "kinda into this shit" (his words). He did not wish to stop his sessions with her, but it was appropriate for him to tell her he had another partner.

A partner it was not difficult to see he felt could fit in his life in that world, whereas he didn't feel the same about Amélie.

She hadn't ended things on the spot, but their next session was a farewell one.

The second nearly hit more dangerous ground. Amélie was getting in deep, and their finale was much more awkward.

She'd begun to have feelings for him and was gearing up to share she'd like to explore a more expansive relationship when she saw him out to dinner.

With his wife.

He had not told her he was married.

As mentioned, it was appropriate, but also expected, that as their play deepened and the time they spent together lengthened, that he tell her he had another partner.

Therefore when she saw him with his spouse, he'd looked utterly terrified when he caught her eyes, as he should have been.

She'd been hurt, and in order to deal with that feeling, she'd twisted it to rage.

Rage that nearly made her do something highly inappropriate, not to mention tactless and unseemly. This being walking up to their table and exposing him for the cheat he was. For, clearly, he had not told his wife either (as he should) that he had needs that had to be assuaged, and if she could not do that, they had the discussion and his wife had allowed him his extracurricular activities.

Amélie had not exposed him to his wife.

She'd also never spoken another word to him, even when the bastard showed at the Honey looking whipped and obviously desiring an audience.

This kind of information was not shared on their profiles or in their notes. Why they were not there was obvious. What was in their lives outside the club's walls wasn't anyone's business unless a member chose to make it someone's business.

But it was an unspoken agreement between Master or Mistress and submissive, if their play went beyond casual sessions, to offer transparency.

In the ordinary world, his taking a lover without his wife's permission was unforgivable.

In their world, it was his life, but in deceiving his Domme, not offering that transparency she would require for a variety of reasons, including the opportunity to keep emotions in check—she had no idea how it was in other clubs, but it was severely frowned on at the Honey.

As was her responsibility (in her mind, not contractually or expected in the scene), she had a quiet word in order to warn the other Dommes.

He had gone uncalled long enough that the last she'd heard, he was prowling places like the Bolt.

This, she knew, the other Dommes had done mostly out of respect (and in some cases affection) for Amélie, and as a show of support. Not all Dominants found transparency to be a requirement (though, if anyone had taken him again, as per the note Amélie placed in his file, it would only be with protection).

He was a high-powered attorney who came from money. The Bolt, he would feel, was beneath him.

A fitting punishment.

Far faster than the two that went before, Olivier had gotten under her skin.

If they were other people, their quick connection would give rise to Amélie staring at wedding magazines in their racks, finding her mind wandering to thoughts of if their children would have his lovely blue eyes and wondering how to find a contractor to build a large wall safe where they could keep their toys.

But they were the people they were, where thoughts like these had to be banished, for protection, until the golden time when connecting and sharing, openness and communication, brought them to the place where Mirabelle was now.

She and Trey had a planned session the next evening.

And if he didn't take the reins, she was asking him out either before or after she was finished with him.

Amélie was nervous for her friend but more nervous for what was happening with herself, falling deeper and deeper under Olivier's spell. His humor. His honesty. His warmth. Wanting more and more from him. Thinking of him constantly. Wondering where he worked. Where he lived. If he had any siblings. What he did for fun.

Everything.

She drew in a light breath to calm her thoughts as she walked into the Honey.

She spied Aryas instantly, in the center booth at the wall to her left, a booth that was exclusively his if he was in the hunting ground.

He was sitting on the outside of the booth facing the entryway. A petite, African American toy with wide eyes and bouncing black curls sat close to him, her eyelids fluttering.

He was playing with her.

Aryas noticed Amélie, too, and although seeing him with a sub would normally change her plans for that part of the evening, avoiding him and allowing him his time with his toy, he surprisingly jerked up his chin at her.

That meant he wanted her to approach.

She did as he turned his bald head (the only place he was bald; he had a full beard and an unscaped physique) and said something to his toy. Her dreamy expression became petulant. He said something else, her mouth set into a pout, but as Aryas slid out of the booth, she slid with him.

"Mistress Amélie," she greeted in a soft voice that stated clearly, in song, she'd be a gorgeous soprano.

"Pretty baby," she replied.

The girl scurried away.

When she did, Aryas caught Amélie's hand and lifted it to his mouth, brushing his lips against the knuckles, his short eyelashes that curled so perfectly it was impossible not to believe he didn't use a lash curler covering unusual gray-blue eyes, as he murmured, "Amélie," against her skin.

He could pull that off, Aryas. The only other man who she'd met in Phoenix who could do something like that without looking like they were trying too hard was Stellan.

"Aryas," she replied.

Aryas squeezed her fingers, let them go, and reentered the booth, going in deep, but stopped at the side of the curve. He then patted the seat beside him.

Amélie slid in and twisted, touching him cheek to cheek and moving to do the same with the other side as he slid a hand curved at her hip and gave her a squeeze.

She pulled away. "Welcome back."

"Good to be back, my sweet," he replied through a grin.

"You didn't have to stop playing with your toy for me," she noted.

"My exquisite Amélie showing at my place at eight-thirty looking like she had something on her mind, I disagree."

That was Aryas Weathers.

He was an utter gentleman. Even with his toys (to an extent).

Amélie had met his mother and knew why this was. The woman had entrenched respect, for men and women, the latter being of the gallant variety, in both her sons. She'd done this with an iron will, the only thing she could have when her husband left her, never to be heard from again, to raise two very big growing boys on the salary of a hotel maid.

She knew this was why Aryas was driven to use where his nature had taken him to build an empire. Starting in Phoenix, he'd expanded and now had clubs in San Diego, Los Angeles, San Francisco, Seattle, Denver, and Vegas. They made him very wealthy. And they allowed him to take care of his momma in the way she always should have been by a man in her life that she loved.

"Your sacrifice is appreciated," Amélie told him. "And as a return kindness, I won't take up much of your time."

He was still grinning. "I don't have a baby here, Amélie, you can drop the Mistress shit."

"Of course," she murmured.

"You'll still be formal. It's your way. It's sweet," he replied. "Now, give it to me. What's on your mind?"

"I wanted to talk to you about something that occurred to me in regards to Delia."

His full lips thinned and his gaze went beyond her and into the club.

Amélie looked, too, an encompassing sweep, and she saw no Delia.

It was early and there weren't many people there, though at that moment, Penn and Shane were arriving.

Honing in on their arrival, Amélie's attention wandered.

A beacon of hope, Master Penn and his slave Shane were a couple outside the club, had met there, had been together now for nearly two years, and it was a widespread expectation they'd soon be declaring they were engaged.

Thinking on this, how well it worked, how they were living together and had been for over a year, how they still came to the club regularly, it took Aryas calling, "Amélie," for her focus to move from the two men. "Delia," he prompted when he again got her attention.

"She's clearly claimed Tiffany," Amélie informed him of something he probably knew.

He nodded.

"I've known Tiffany outside the club since she was young, Aryas. And I've kept an eye on her here. I even monitored Pasquel as she was training her. She seemed to settle in and be enjoying herself. Now, she seems pale and afraid. Tentative. It makes me uncomfortable."

Aryas nodded, he'd noted that too.

Even so, he suggested, "It could be part of her game, a darker side she needs to explore that she didn't give Pasquel."

Amélie didn't move her gaze from her friend.

He knew better. "I'm monitoring Delia, Amélie," he reminded her.

"Does she trip her occupancy switch when she enters a play-room?" she asked.

An ominous crease of his brows before, "She has to. To get a room, you have to reserve a room."

"And if the blackout blinds are down, but the lights are on, you can see the lights around the blinds, so another Dom will know that room is reserved and avoid it. But you told me that the hallways have cameras that move on the monitors in the control room, too much hallway with all that needs to be observed to watch constantly. She could be missed slipping into a room. She could easily use it without being observed, her equals avoiding it because they see the lights."

She got closer to him and continued.

"With all your staff has to monitor, Aryas, it would not be difficult to miss that a room was being used but the occupancy switch not flipped. She could disappear from the hunting ground and they'd lose track of her. Although you track arrivals, you don't specifically require anyone to check in and check out."

"Since she's being monitored, Amélie, my staff in the control room would make a note if she reserved a room and watch closely what happens in it."

"Her play can seem finished and she can turn off the occupancy and continue the scene, Aryas. A toy knows about the occupancy switch but it isn't their responsibility. They might not notice it's been switched off. The lights are still on, Doms avoid the room, your staff thinks the scene is done, and they're missing something. Does your staff turn off cameras immediately?"

He looked to the club over her shoulder. "No. They turn them off when the players leave."

Amélie sat back, murmuring, "Then I was wrong."

"She could go back in."

Amélie looked to Aryas when he said this.

"I'll get my eye on that, sweetheart," he promised.

"I'd like your permission to approach Tiffany," she requested.

"Strictly speaking, and you know this and would lose your mind if I gave what you're asking to another Dom, if she's claimed by Delia, you need to ask Delia to approach Tiffany. And it'd be tough to make anyone believe you're going in there out of interest. You've never played with a female."

"Then perhaps I can talk to Mirabelle or Pasquel. They have. Ask them to make an approach. Or you can," she suggested.

"I will," he grunted, sounding perturbed.

"Thanks, Aryas."

He nodded and focused on her, his lips lifting up and spreading in a wolfish way from his strong, white teeth.

"So, I hear you're enjoying the stallion I approved for you."

It actually felt like Amélie's heart started to swell.

Aryas, a good friend, a kind heart.

"Would you not have approved him if not for me?" she asked.

His big smile got bigger. "Fuck yeah. I saw that big mountain of meat, I probably would have paid to have him in my club." He bent closer to her. "But the second I saw him, darlin', I knew we had to have him for you."

"Well, thank you," she said, putting her swelling heart into her words.

"Hear you've been having all kinds of fun."

"I've been enjoying him."

His body shook with his chuckle. "Mistress Amélie, a skilled Mistress at much, including the understatement. Heather asked for a raise after she had to clean up that load you made him blow on the floor. You may have been enjoying him but he probably would use different words."

She hoped so.

Oh yes.

She very much hoped so.

She gave him an impudent grin. "I think so far he's found me satisfactory."

"Yeah. Bet he'll be here in about two minutes to find you satis-factory again."

She hoped that too.

"Speaking of which, we're meeting and you have a sub to tend to so I'll leave you." She went in to touch her cheek to his and said in his ear, "So lovely to have you back."

When she straightened away, he replied, "If it's so lovely, you'd invite me to that book club of yours."

She started laughing. "Aryas, it's an all-female group."

"Discrimination," he muttered, eyes dancing. "Hear you mostly read erotica."

"It is a genre that's often chosen, yes," she confirmed.

"Then I definitely want in."

She leaned into him again, this time eye to eye, hers, she hoped, holding kindness. "You've never mentioned it before but now, I imag-ine, you want in because we invited Talia."

The dance went out of his eyes and another reason Aryas was so good at all he did, especially in business (and play), entered them.

His *don't fuck with me* look.

"Don't go there, Amélie."

"Mirabelle is asking Trey out tomorrow night."

His gaze flashed with pleased approval as his mouth said, "Excellent."

"Talk to her," she urged.

"She's not my flavor, Amélie."

"She subbed under your training, you require it," Amélie pointed out.

"She did. Stellan did that part. He approved her performance. That's all I require, I didn't ask for details. It's done. She's topping exclusively."

Stellan did that part when Aryas usually did that part because the temptation, and the frustration if Talia didn't enjoy it, would have been too much.

"Perhaps you can work an arrangement where you share while working a sub together," she suggested.

"Beautiful, I love you, you got a place in my heart, I dig where you're going with this but only because of the why you're going there. But this is the last time I'm gonna say we are not talkin' about it."

She sat back in the booth and fought crossing her arms on her chest and huffing out a sulky breath, deciding, since she'd irritated him already, to go for the gusto.

"Evangeline missed another book club," she announced.

Even for Amélie, his eyes got scary.

Regardless, she persevered, but did it quietly, "I'm growing more and more worried, Ary."

"As am I," he bit off.

She snapped her mouth audibly shut.

That was all he needed to say. He was Aryas.

Amélie was uncertain with how to proceed to bring her friend back into their protective circle.

But if Aryas was worried, he would not be uncertain how to proceed.

When the silence after his statement stretched, and he didn't fill it as she felt he should do as a gentleman, she narrowed her eyes at him.

"Stop being cute when you've annoyed me," he ordered.

"Stop being annoyingly stubborn and *male*," she shot back. "You can be such a little boy sometimes."

He gave her a different smile in his arsenal, the charming one. "You've watched me play, darlin'. The meat I'm packin', that's an impossibility."

He wasn't wrong. He was as impressive as Olivier.

She decided to slide out.

"Amélie," he called.

She looked to him.

"Good thought about Delia. Gratitude, sweetheart, for looking out for me and my babies."

"Do not be sweet when I'm annoyed at you."

"Take that shit out on your stallion, babe. I don't take orders."

She rolled her eyes but gave him a small smile to let him know her pique was just play and began to move to another booth, but Aryas's words stopped her.

"And fuckin' enjoy the shit out of," his eyes traveled the length of her, "riding that stallion of yours, sweetheart."

At that, she turned her head away haughtily and heard his laughter as she made her way to another booth.

She had dressed the part that night, of course. High-waisted, black, skintight, cigarette pants. A black silk blouse shimmering with gold thread, buttoned low to provide an expansive display of the cropped, black leather bustier she was wearing. Knee-high, stiletto-heeled, pointed-toed black boots she was wearing over her pants.

Not jodhpurs and a whip, but it sent a message.

She settled in and it pleased her greatly when Olivier arrived not ten minutes later.

He looked for her, found her and she gave him indication to approach when he did.

He stood at her side and looked down in her eyes before he looked down at her cleavage and his lips twitched.

"Mistress Amélie."

"Olivier, bend to me," she ordered.

His gaze came to hers before he bent and she lifted a hand to smooth it into the hair on the side of his head, running a thumb along his cheekbone.

"My handsome steed," she whispered.

His face warmed but his eyes sparkled as he replied, "Looked forward to seeing you too."

"Cheek," she muttered.

He grinned, and when her hand dropped away, he straightened.

Glancing to her half-drunk cocktail, he asked, "Can I get my Mistress a drink?"

"No, please, slide in," she offered, scooching over so he could slide in beside her.

As he did that, she gained the attention of a server, tipped her head to Olivier; the server nodded and turned to the bar.

Amélie twisted fully to Olivier and put her hand on his thigh, giving it a squeeze.

"Have you found a weekend we can play, Olivier?" she asked, and cursed herself the minute it came out.

It sounded too eager.

He turned his head to look at her and stated, "My friends, people I care about . . . Amélie,"—a hesitation—"they call me Olly."

She felt her belly clench and release, her hand gliding down to his inner thigh doing the same, as warmth spread from her middle, moving up and to the left, rather than down.

"Is that an invitation?" she asked, not quite able to control the breathiness of her question.

"Do I get to invite you to do something?" he teased.

"Certainly," she replied.

"Then yeah. It is."

She leaned to him, her breast to his arm. "I accept."

He gave her a grin and she tipped her head to the side.

"Olivier is not a common name in the States. It's French," she noted.

"Yep," he agreed. "Mom . . . strike that, Mom's grandparents were French. As in French from France. Makes her still French in a way but not like they were. She doesn't speak the language, all that kind of shit was lost. But they have that tradition. All my aunts and uncles, cousins. My little brother is named Jean-Luc, but we call him Luc. My baby sister is Collette, but we call her Letty."

"You're the oldest," she remarked.

His eyes twinkled. "Right again."

"Are your father and brother as big as you?"

"Brother, mostly, a couple of inches shorter, but about twenty pounds heavier."

"Oh my, that's a big boy."

He was still grinning as he replied, "Though, not strictly the good kind. Since college, he let himself go. Then again, no reason to maintain an offensive lineman's body when he's no longer an offensive lineman. Got himself a woman who likes a teddy bear so it's all good. Dad's big as a house. My height, beer gut. Mom liked a teddy bear too."

Amélie liked a beast.

"Did you play football?"

Tipping his eyes up to look at the server when he placed Olivier's beer in front of him, he turned his attention back to Amélie.

"High school, college, Luc followed in my footsteps. But I was defensive end."

She'd made that call accurately.

"Not feeling like being a teddy bear?"

He dipped closer. "Baby, I'd teddy-bear you in a heartbeat. But not with a gut."

Suddenly, for the first time in her life, Amélie wanted to be teddy-beared.

Even though, with all her experience, she didn't know what that was.

"You like to stay fit," she commented.

He pulled back and something crossed his face she couldn't catch when he replied, "Working out clears the mind. Gives focus." He gave her a smile that appeared forced. "And I gotta lug all this meat around. It's taxing. Dad and Luc are good sittin' in their loungers, watching football, drinkin' beer and eatin' nachos. I'm good with that too. But not all the time."

She wanted to know what else he did the times he wasn't working out or being worked by her.

She was trying to figure out a way to ask that when he got there first.

"The accent, Amélie. You French?"

She shook her head. "Half. The other half American. But I've lived in the States all my life."

He turned more fully to her. "But you got an accent."

"My mother was French." She smiled, giving his thigh a light squeeze. "As in French from France. Up until I was five, she took me to France often and we stayed extended periods of time. She claimed I was fluent then, but now, I can often get by when someone is speaking French to me, I understand what they say. It's irritatingly awkward attempting to reply in the same language. Though, I've kept some words, mostly endearments my mother called me, or my grand-parents or aunts and uncles called me, each other, or my cousins."

In all that, Olivier honed in on one thing.

"Up until you were five?"

She gave a slight shrug of one shoulder. "My mother and father divorced then. She had little here and part of their issue was she was terribly homesick and never got over it. So she went back to France. The divorce and custody battle were quite ugly, from family lore, but Dad won. I stayed in the States and as I grew older, it became harder to go visit her, with school, outside activities, friends, and the like."

"Tough, Amélie," he murmured, more warmth in his face.

"Not really, my *chevalier*, my mother was not an affectionate person. My father was. Even when I was young, I was closer to him. But she loved me and part of that loving me was not making me leave my friends and things I liked to do here and force me to go to France. She came often to visit me, often enough I knew she missed me and I mattered to her."

She pressed closer to him, fighting her desire to share more but thinking it was too early, so she didn't.

And anyway, it was definitely too difficult a subject to get into when she'd prefer this getting-to-know-you session to be lighter, so they could segue into their *getting-to-know-you* session without any-thing heavy weighing on their minds.

"The accent," she continued, "was mostly from being around her and her family at a young, impressionable age, not to mention going back with some frequency. It was something that just hap-pened. I noticed it when I was old enough to notice it and, I will admit to you, *mon grande,* I purposefully hung on to it. It made me different. It set me apart. And I *like* to be different."

He was watching her closely, another expression on his face she couldn't read, when she realized she'd again been remiss.

"You can drink your beer at your leisure . . ." she paused, feeling bizarrely shy, before she finished, "Olly."

That got her the warmth back and he turned to his beer.

Taking a long pull, she decided not to share just how enchanted she was with him to the whole room by allowing herself to be entranced by the muscles working in his throat.

She took a sip of her own cocktail, seeing him put his beer back to the table.

"And explain that poison," she heard him demand.

She looked up at him. "I'm sorry?"

"What you're drinkin', Amélie."

"Soixante Quinze," she answered.

"Uh . . . come again?" he asked, smiling.

"Soixante Quinze. French 75. It's gin, champagne, lemon juice, and sugar, with a twist."

He made a face that made her smile and press closer.

"You're a beer guy," she noted.

"Beer, rum, or bourbon. A good scotch whisky's to be had, I won't say no."

Whisky.

She started stroking his thigh.

He cleared his throat and reached for his beer.

"I doubt I need to ask, but did you come prepared for me tonight, my *chevalier?*"

He put his beer down after his sip and again gave her his gaze. "Yeah, Mistress."

"Good," she murmured.

"And we got off track. To answer your question, I can't do this weekend, or the next, but if you got the next one after that free, I'm in."

Not only planning their weekend, having already checked his schedule and being able to do it two and a half weeks from right then, indicating they'd have two and a half more weeks of fun, not to mention their weekend together.

She had to fight not to start purring.

"If I'm not free, I'll arrange it so I am," she promised.

Though he didn't know it, it was more of a vow.

He nodded, shifting his beer this way and that with his fingers around the bottom of the glass, before he said, "And it fucks me to say this, baby, but I can't do next week. I gotta work. Back to regular schedule the week after, though."

So much for two and a half weeks. All next week she wouldn't have him.

She fought pouting or even frowning and lifted her own drink for another sip.

"Sorry, Amélie," he said quietly, like he wasn't sorry but *deeply* sorry.

She put her glass down and again gave him her attention.

"Work is work, *mon chou*. It is what it is. There's no need to be sorry."

That said, Amélie wondered what he did that took him away a whole week.

Perhaps he traveled for business like she sometimes did.

Not that she really had a business, as such.

As such, she really didn't do much of anything. At least anything important.

Before thoughts that had been nagging her for some time about that part of her life could come to the fore, Olivier bent his neck to get closer to her face. "Doesn't mean I'm not still sorry."

She lifted a hand to cup his jaw. "My sweet beast."

"You can, I'm free tomorrow and Friday. Saturday until the next Sunday, Amélie," he shook his head, "no go."

"Then let's meet again Friday," she decided.

She watched his eyes crinkle. "You're on."

"You are very correct, Olivier, as I do believe it's time we begin to make our way to our room."

His eyes didn't crinkle at that. They started burning.

"Would you like to finish your beer?" she offered.

"Fuck no," he answered.

She tipped her head to the side.

"Unless my Mistress wants to finish her crazy-ass, pretentious drink," he went on.

She forced her look to be severe. "It isn't pretentious. It's delicious."

"Whatever," he muttered. "You wanna finish it?"

"Yes, *chevalier.*"

He sat back and lifted his beer. "As you wish."

She was beginning to have a lot of wishes.

Worse, she was beginning to long for the possibility they would come true.

nine

Alpha

AMÉLIE

After they went through the doors to the playroom, for the first time, Amélie took Olivier's hand and moved him slowly, dallying in the passageways.

There was not a great deal to see that early in the evening, however, what there was, she wanted to see his response not only to others at play, but also to being on the other side of the glass.

So she stopped at a window displaying Mistress Shoshana with a female sub.

Her sub was bound with rope horizontally all along her torso, hips, and thighs, trapping her arms to her sides, her forearms to her upper thighs. Her breasts were tied tight in a way that looked painful, nipple clamps affixed. She was on her knees on the floor, bending over with difficulty, kissing Shoshana's boots.

A glance at Olivier said this did nothing for him. He didn't look bored or uncomfortable, he didn't look much of anything.

Not a surprise. He was assuredly not a boot-kissing sub.

She didn't pause at a silhouetted room that looked like two Doms were working a sub tied down on his back.

She did pause to watch Master Penn with his Shane.

Shane was lashed tightly to a spanking bench with an abundance of straps, one nearly every inch apart on his skin. This being on his belly, his arms and legs bound to the legs of the bench.

His cock was wound round and round with silk rope, this binding him at the base of his balls as well.

He had a rather large phallus in his mouth that he looked to be blissfully sucking as Penn (plugged himself with a toy that was quite impressive) drove into his sub's ass with not a small amount of fervor.

Amélie kept Olivier there, holding his fingers laced in hers, but her thumb stroked his wrist in a soothing way that also helped her to feel his steady, not accelerated, heartbeat.

This did nothing for him either and it appeared, unusually, that Olivier didn't get much from watching.

She was about to move when Shane's head suddenly shot back and he spurted from his rope, his body bucking in his bindings. Following him closely, Penn buried himself to the root, arching back delightfully, his face a mask of ecstasy, as he poured his seed into his submissive. Even in the throes of an apparently intense orgasm, he had the presence of mind to slap Shane's right flank repeatedly, forcing more of an offering from his toy.

After giving herself the pleasure of watching Penn build a near-simultaneous orgasm with his partner, she tugged at Olivier's hand to start them moving again. They didn't run into anything more to watch as they made it to the room Olivier referred to as her "barn."

They went in, she flipped the occupancy switch, and Olivier closed the door after he followed her inside.

"Mistress Amélie, a second . . ." He trailed off and she turned to him to see his eyes serious and on her.

She moved closer, raising a hand to put on his chest. "Yes, Olivier?"

"Need this . . ." He shook his head. "We're in here but I need to talk freely. You and me. Just Amélie and Olly. Do you get me?"

She got him and sent that message by coming closer, resting her hands on his hips and saying, "I get you, Olly."

Relief hit his face and he dipped it closer as he moved his arms around her to hold her in a loose embrace.

"Do a lot for you. Take a lot from you. I want you free to do your thing with me. But I'm not thinkin' I want a plastic dildo, or anything like it, in my mouth, and I do not want you to share me with a guy, lettin' him fuck my ass."

So their leisurely stroll observing the playrooms got her something. Territory he did not wish to inhabit, play he found unacceptable.

But she found this mildly disturbing. Not his boundaries, in truth, the way she'd found he was, she'd expect Olivier to have both. But the fact it gave the impression that this was the first time he'd seen such play or considered the possibility it might be used on him. The play they'd witnessed was actually mild and often done, no matter the sexes involved.

If it wasn't his thing, he should have already expressed those were lines he would not cross.

Although she'd noticed it was very clear he'd had less experienced or talented Mistresses working him, it was the first time since their first session he gave that odd impression he was green.

"My ass is yours," he went on, pulling her closer, taking the loose out of his hold. "I gave it to you. I don't have to say that. You know it. You can do what you want, you'll guide me with you. But I don't . . . I . . . *fuck*," he hissed, looking over her head. His gaze again dropped down to her. "I guess I don't want you to share me."

That.

Now *that*.

That was another story.

"First, *mon grande*, those are boundaries and I can see in your eyes they're firm ones. You'll need to change your profile for hetero play only and find a way to share you don't want to suck cock in its variety of forms."

She expected amusement and/or relief but instead he seemed more agitated. "Share on my profile."

"It's a requirement, Olly."

"Yeah, and I'll do that, not a big deal, but this is me and you. Why would I need to tell everyone in the club if I'm with you?"

"Because it's a requirement," she repeated.

"No, baby, I get that. I'll do it. But you say it like I gotta do it in the next second when it isn't a big deal because it doesn't matter because," he gave her a squeeze, "*I'm with you.*"

She felt her lips part when she understood him.

He'd change his profile when he got to it because it actually *wasn't* important to do it as soon as he could because the only person who really needed to know was her and she already knew.

He was hers.

She wanted . . .

No, *needed* that confirmed.

"Are you saying, Olly, that it's also me who needs to make a note on your profile?"

"Come again?"

"I don't like sharing."

His arms tightened further and his face dipped closer, eyes darkening.

"It's your prerogative, *mon chou*, to be claimed as exclusive, not mine," she told him. "Are you saying I can claim you as mine, not in here, when I have you in a playroom, not when you allow me to do it by giving you commands to carry out when you leave me, but to the club?"

"You can not only do that, Amélie, I hope to fuck you do." He grinned. "Though maybe not in the next second."

She slid her arms around him, happiness filling her heart even if she felt the extent of it was too much to share with him at this juncture. So she hid it even as she gave him a firm squeeze to share at least some it.

"All right, not in the next second. Now, my *chevalier*, please take your clothes off and—"

"Leigh-Leigh, baby," he whispered.

She blinked, automatically melting into him at his giving her a nickname.

She swallowed so it wouldn't come out as a squeak when she asked, "Yes?"

"Before we slide into what we have, while we have now, thanks for givin' me now, sweetheart. Means a lot you'd step outta the scene and listen to me."

She didn't know whether to cry tears of joy or be insulted.

"I'll always listen to you, Olly, out of the scene or in it."

"I got that from you but you gotta get *knowing it* means a fuckuva lot."

Fuck, she could fall in love with this man.

"You do know that right now I've made it my absolute mission, when it was just my definite intent, to make you come harder than I've ever made you, right?"

He started chuckling, her body moving with his as he did, and honest to God, it felt better than any orgasm she'd experienced.

"Have a feeling your definite intent was enough, Amélie, but I approve of your self-appointed mission." He let her go, finishing, "So I best get naked so my Mistress can work over her beast."

"Do that," she said haughtily.

He gave her a cheeky grin and moved his hands to his suit jacket.

She moved hers to the buttons of her blouse, walking to the table unbuttoning them.

"Once you're done with that, Olivier, go to your stable. Stand in the middle, facing out, your gaze to the room, not me, please," she ordered.

She went through her bag, pulling out the things she'd need, arranging them, and took off her blouse to expose the cropped bustier, which bared an inch section of skin between the waistband of her pants and bra, as well as her arms.

The rest was covered but all skintight, leaving very little to the imagination.

She went to the opening of the stall, which had three walls that would completely hide most people, but Olivier was a head above them.

He was standing naked, semi-hard, but his pecs jumped, his abdominal muscles tightened, and his cock seemed to grow before her eyes when he saw her without her blouse.

"My *chevalier*," she called his attention from her chest to her face. "With your life in the outside world, I need to know how to cuff you. Do you need no visible marks?"

He nodded, swallowing.

She nodded back and moved again to her table.

She grabbed the fleece-lined shackles, rather than the metal ones, and came back. She started with his arms. Asking him to lift them above his head she cuffed him to the chains so his arms were up high with little bend, but he was not stretched and instead had a good deal of motion.

When he had his hands around the chains that would support him in order to accomplish what she asked next, she commanded, "Spread your legs to the outer rings in the floor."

He did that, too, though with a slight hesitation, when he'd not hesitated with the arms.

When she had him shackled to the floor, link on cuff directly to the ring on the floor, no movement for his feet, only slack provided for him to sway his body, she stepped back and looked him over.

Swollen cock, swollen balls in their harness, he was so splendid, she could throw her plans out the window, drop to her knees, and suck him off happily.

He would come hard but not as hard as she was going to make him do.

More than once.

So she set about doing that and took her time. Strapping his ass open first, she then went to her handle-less equine grooming brushes.

Returning to him, she curried him everywhere, taking her time doing it, enjoying every stroke but doing it with the goal of having every inch of him sensitized. She started with a soft bristled brush that he enjoyed and she knew it by his extended, heavy cock, his frame swaying to reach her strokes, his offering of flesh, his playful nips at her ear and neck when he could steal them.

She got serious with her next brush, a tougher bristled one that caused him to suck in breath on the first few strokes, but he eventually swayed into them as well, her mighty, sweet beast.

She spent extra time on his back and inner thighs, brushing from up high, close to his scrotum, forcing noises that she fancied sounded like a lion purring.

When he was roughened up everywhere, his skin pinkish with the grooming, she went to her oils.

This was what she took extreme care and even more time with. A warming oil that she slickened him with liberally. It smelled of eucalyptus, a soothing scent that opened the nasal passages, adding another heightened sense to their play.

She oiled and massaged every inch of him, from neck to feet, cooing to him, brushing him with her breasts, touching her lips to his glossy flesh, using her thumbs to dig in, enjoying the muscles she encountered loosening under her touch.

She finished behind him. Reaching between his legs, she massaged the oil into his balls as she concentrated between his ass straps, gliding slippery fingers in and out of his hole gently, not going too far, feeling him tighten around her as the purring turned to a heady, pleasured growl.

Yes, Olivier liked this. He accepted her at his deepest vulnerability with no hesitation this time, allowing her to see, hear, and feel his enjoyment.

Finding herself needing to control the trembling of her hands (and legs, and other places) at the intoxicating experience of grooming her beast, feeling his excitement increase, the easy way he now put himself in her hands, she left him and moved first to the control panel to pull up both sets of blinds.

Then she went back to the table to collect the final piece to prepare him to perform.

She came around the stall and his lazy, aroused eyes sharpened as the wild held at bay under her ministrations came creeping.

"Shh, Olivier," she shushed, moving to him. Sliding the bottle of oil she still held in her hand between her breasts with the control she'd already put there, she reached out to stroke his cock calmingly. "Shh, beast." She pressed close, still stroking, head tipped way back to catch his gaze. "I've got you."

The words came clogged when he noted, "That's big."

"Yes, though I will assure you that my aim is not to stretch you, cause you pain. I don't want you to become accustomed to that." She gave him a tender smile. "I wish you to remain tight. This is the biggest you'll ever take."

It was like he didn't hear her. "It's bigger than the other night."

"Yes, *mon chou,* but trust me. You'll like it."

The wild seeped into his eyes and he gave a slight yank on his bindings, chains clinking. "Mistress."

"Shh, my steed. Look at me. Take a deep breath. Look at me. I'm right here. Breathe deep. Then let me give you something."

He looked at her. He took a deep breath.

Then he jerked up his chin like a stubborn stallion, neck tight, eyes still untamed.

"You please me," she shared her massive understatement.

He said nothing.

She stroked him several more times to assure him of her care, her presence, before she moved behind him.

It was a juggling act, the plug under her arm, the oil, and the need to keep reassuring him as she dribbled the oil from his waist in a maddeningly slow line along the opened crack of his ass, the slick of it sliding under, dripping to his balls she was holding and gently massaging.

It took some time but he relaxed under her attentions, pushing back, tilting, offering.

God, but she wanted to take a bite out of that superior ass.

But it was time to give, not take.

She continued to assure at his balls while she held the toy to his coated hole.

She slid it in, out, not much, stretching, a little teasing.

She bent at the knees and reached deep to grab his cock and she started stroking, tight, commanding quietly, "Take it, press into it, accept what I'm offering, my steed."

She stroked faster and he got her message, gently fucking her oil-slickened fist, for fucking her fist meant fucking his own ass. He took it, shoving back more, more, widening, accepting, taking it into himself in his own time, until the widest part of the plug opened him beautifully through a ragged groan tearing out of his chest, and his rim closed around the root.

"Magnificent," she breathed, set the oil aside, and dragged the fingernails of both hands up his buttocks, watching with fascination, her pussy clutching, as they tautened against his straps.

Oh fuck yes.

Magnificent.

She pulled the remote out of her bra.

She moved around him, held his cock again in a fist, and looked into his burning eyes, dark as night, radiating need.

Her clit pulsed.

Yes.

Magnificent.

"Are you ready to perform for me?"

His voice was hoarse when he replied, "Yes, Mistress, whatever you want, baby."

She leaned up. Pressing her body into him, he strained his neck down and they kissed, tongues tangling, wet and deep.

She hit the switch on the remote and he ripped his mouth from hers.

She felt a mini-convulsion, like a small orgasm, and nearly had to grab on to him to stay standing as his face saturated with pleasure.

But when his closed eyes opened, she saw only fear.

"Calm, beast."

"What's that?"

What it was was his plug vibrating up his ass, the end inexorably thumping against one of the most sensitive places in his body.

"A vibrating plug, *mon chou*. Calm. Give into it. Feel it. Let it take over. Don't fight it. Let it guide you," she advised, releasing his cock and stepping back a step so she could watch.

"Mistress—" he started to protest.

"I'm right here."

She increased the vibrations (and thumping), taking it up two settings.

His head flew back, his back bowed, his hands wrapped around the chains he was dangling from rattled them.

"Don't fight it, Olivier."

He dropped his head down, his eyes scoring into hers, that dark shadow suffusing his face, shrouding them both in his need.

"Baby."

She increased the vibrations.

Unable to stop, he started thrusting, his powerful body swaying against his bonds, fucking the air so mercilessly, it was like she felt him in her pussy.

"You're so beautiful," she told him, fighting her need to go to him, touch him, sink to her knees in front of him and accept his rutting in her mouth.

She increased the vibrations and he gave her what she loved, his deep, decadent, animalistic, guttural grunts of pleasure filling the room.

And she knew he was gone.

But he also told her.

"More, Mistress, jack my hole. Please, baby. *More*," he begged, still thrusting.

She turned it all the way to high.

Immediately, his body formed a perfect arc, head back, cock

thrust proudly forward, shooting his seed gloriously across the floor.

She allowed the vibrations to continue as he convulsed through the last spasms, the final emissions trickling, and she turned the remote all the way to low.

Olivier went slack and hung from his shackles.

She took a moment to take small, deep breaths to calm her reaction to his glorious display before she went to him, telling him of her pleasure, running her hands over him.

Then she began to truly break him into their night's mission.

She increased the vibration. He expressed surprise, then fear, but quickly became hard again for her.

She took him there, with patience, with pleasure, to the point her stallion was performing beautifully, driving his hips through the air.

And before he could come, she took him down only to give him the shortest of breathers and begin to build him back up.

Once there, she'd take him down.

And up.

Hanging from his shackles, at an ebb, his ravenous eyes, the pupils appearing nearly black, semi-focused on her.

"Please, fuck, baby, let me come. Christ, you're killin' me. I need to blow," he begged.

She wanted to give him anything he needed.

He just didn't know it wasn't what he needed.

Not yet.

Amélie had to show him.

She moved to him, touched his chest, and the simple touch forced up a guttural growl she felt deep in her womb, he was so sensitized. She lifted up to his mouth to brush her lips against his, and he tried to deepen the kiss.

She pulled half an inch away and his lips curled back in a snarl.

"Not quite yet, my steed," she whispered.

The snarl went feral.

She increased the vibrations.

His jaw turned to stone and his head rolled back.

Amélie again fought against climaxing, just watching him.

Again and again she brought him close to orgasm and when she was on the way to building him up yet again, she commanded, "I'm going to unshackle you. When I do, you may drop your arms and I want you on your knees. Once there, don't move another muscle, Olivier. Is that understood?"

"Yes, Mistress," he gritted between his teeth.

She unshackled him, legs then arms.

He dropped his arms and went to his knees.

Beautiful.

She moved in front of him, taking the vibrations up a note, watching him battle the pleasure pulsing up his ass, his muscles straining, his hands fists, perhaps so he wouldn't tackle her, rip her clothes from her, throw her on her belly and mount her.

Oh, how she'd glory in that. Breaking his control. Experiencing firsthand that wild.

And she continued her torture, slowly taking off one boot, the other, then rolling down her pants, taking her panties with them.

He watched avidly, and when she revealed it, his eyes locked on her glistening pussy, his lips again pulled back in a snarl, growl rolling up his throat.

She moved in front of him.

And made her second mistake with him, her second mistake with anyone in *years*.

She'd pushed her beast far and her mistake was feeling she could push him further.

Lifting her leg to throw it over his shoulder, allowing him to smell her, see her, she did this saying, "You may now eat—"

She got not another word out.

One of his arms closed around the hip of her upraised leg. The other hand went to the inside of her other thigh and she cried out as he lifted her and swung that leg over his other shoulder. Shoving his face in her pussy, his hands going from her ass up her back, his long arms on either side of her spine as he fell forward, controlling her, holding him to her.

She had the presence of mind to keep her head lifted so when she hit floor, she didn't bang it against the wood.

But she had no time to recover or get control.

He clamped down on her hips by curving his long forearms around them, crossed at her lower belly, and in random, effective, mind-boggling jerks, he forced her to ride his face while on her back as he ate her, no finesse. Sucking her clit, fucking her with his tongue, dragging his teeth down the sensitive sides.

He kept rocking her against him as he took one arm from around her and put his hand between her legs. He drove two long fingers inside her, fucking her mercilessly.

Oh yes, he reached places others could not go with those long fingers.

Fuck.

Luscious.

"Olivier—" she whimpered, arching into him, rocking into his pulls. Not a demand to stop, a demand *never* to stop.

"You want a finger up your ass?" he growled into her flesh.

"Yes," she gasped.

He adjusted, his fingers gathering her wet and fucking her pussy and ass as he continued eating.

In no time at all, he drove her there and as she went, she had it together only enough to turn the vibrations up her steed's ass all the way to high.

The explosive growl he forced up her pussy sent her flying. She dropped the remote and grasped his head, holding him to her, shoving him deeper even if there was nowhere to go, calling out his name in soft mews, fighting for breath.

This was it. She'd never been there before.

Nirvana. A miracle. Arriving in heaven on an explosion with Olivier's mouth to her cunt, she never wanted to leave.

"*Baby,*" he groaned between her legs.

"Come on me," she pushed out, still climaxing.

She lost his mouth but her waning orgasm waxed when she was dragged across the floor between his legs. He put his weight in one hand at her side, gripped his big dick in the other, and arched back, shooting his cum over her belly and chest.

Still experiencing a colossal aftermath, she almost didn't notice his body stayed arched, his head back at a straining angle, his jaw so hard it looked like it would shatter, and his hips were giving desperate thrusts as faint spurts shot from his cock.

She felt frantically around for the remote, took it up, and turned off his plug.

He collapsed on her in a bone-crushing heap, giving her all of his weight.

Obviously recognizing he was cutting off her oxygen, about to suffocate her after giving her the best orgasm of her life (and she was unable to decide if she didn't mind that end), he lifted some of his weight up to a forearm at her side but kept covering her with his body.

She wrapped her arms around his waist.

He was panting into her neck.

Amélie was also panting, doing it holding him loosely and staring at the ceiling.

Then she said, "You lifted me up."

His body tensed.

"You lifted me up," she repeated.

Slowly, his face came out of her neck.

She saw his guarded eyes.

"You lifted me up and wrapped my pussy around your face," she told him something he was there to experience since he did it.

"Mistress, I—"

She burst out laughing.

Too caught in her hilarity, she didn't fully register his relief as she asked, "How many people in the history of the world could do that? You and an East German female shot putter, circa the 1970s?"

He grinned. "I thought you'd be pissed."

She moved a hand to cup the side of his face. "Darling, I'll paddle you some other time, when I haven't just been eaten out fucking *amazingly* by my beast."

He kept grinning.

"I'm not certain I can move," she shared. "We might need to curl up on our clothes and sleep here."

"Works for me."

She lost her humor and reflexively dug her fingers in his skin.

So easy, his ability to share he wanted more time with her.

Which for her meant time with Olly.

Sleeping with Olly.

Waking up with Olly.

God.

A magnificent dream to share all that with her magnificent beast.

He caught her mood change and dropped his head so his mouth was at her ear and he shoved an arm under her to hold her close even if the only way they could get closer was if they were connected.

And there he whispered fiercely, "I wanna fuck you, Leigh-Leigh. I wanna bury my cock inside you, fill you full, force you to release, give you what you just gave me."

Feeling everything at once, all the good things of life crushing down on her in that warm, exquisite, unrestrained way Olivier had just given her his weight, she slid her hand up his back, turning her head slightly, and whispered back, "Olly."

He paused before he kissed her neck and finished, "Think about it."

She didn't need to think about it.

She was taking his cock inside her on Friday.

He lifted his head and his somber mood was not gone. "I hurt you?"

"Um . . . no," she said firmly on a gentle smile.

"Baby, I'm a big guy and you took all my weight."

"For only a few moments."

"And I slammed you to the floor."

"It was a controlled fall."

"Amélie—"

She moved both hands so they were holding his face. "I'm fine, *mon chou*."

The somber stayed but it shifted, intensified, before he growled in a tone that vibrated in her soul, "Marked you."

She drifted her hands down to his neck and stroked his jaw. "Yes, you did, Olivier."

"You wanted that."

It was not a question.

It was a declaration.

"Yes, Olly," she whispered.

His stare stayed locked on hers as he announced, "I'm yours, you can claim me, but get me now, Amélie, or we gotta have another conversation. You claim me, I claim you. I get my place. I get you make this decision. But I'm fuckin' sayin' it anyway. You're mine."

She was his.

No Domme allowed her sub to claim her. Not like that.

But she already knew it.

She actually knew it the first time she'd had him.

He would be hers, and now he was.

And she would be his.

And now she was.

"I'm yours," she whispered.

He bent his head and took her mouth.

They kissed for a long time before he slid his lips to her ear and said, "You were right. I got off huge, but I gotta ask my Mistress to slide this thing outta my ass."

"Get up, darling, let me take care of you."

He got up, pulling her up with him, both of them holding on to stay steady, doing this several beats before he said, "You get this thing outta me, I'll get the wipes. You cool with that?"

She nodded.

They cleaned up. Dressed. As they did, vaguely, she caught the people outside floating away; the only one she focused on was Aryas smiling at her arrogantly.

She didn't roll her eyes. She didn't do anything. She had to concentrate on what she was doing as she could barely move.

She needed a bath and bed.

She just wished both would happen with Olly.

It was at the door when he curved an arm around her waist, pulled her close, bent his face to hers, and made that hope she was struggling with controlling burst forth in a blaze of glory.

"Babe, didn't know when you wanted me here tonight, didn't know how to get hold of you. We need to share numbers, yeah?"

"Yes, Olly," she agreed, shocked to her soul she didn't sound breathless to panting, such was her glee.

"Right, do that now?"

"My purse is at the front desk. We'll do it before we leave."

"Gotcha," he said, opened the door, and guided her through.

Their audience was gone.

Except one.

Stellan was standing there, looking beyond peeved straight to angry.

"Get rid of your stud," he ordered angrily.

Irritation flashed through her and she opened her mouth to speak.

Before she could, Olivier used his arm still around her waist to pull her behind him and he stepped in front of her, his aggression clear.

So was his possession.

And his protection.

She lost all thought, only had feelings, and two words drifted into her mind.

Oh my.

She came back to the situation when, pushing his shoulders off the glass of the room across the hall, dropping his crossed arms, Stellan ordered, "Stand down, slave, and run along."

An intolerable order for a Dom to give.

Olivier was *hers*.

"I said, *run along*, rutting steed," Stellan clipped when Olivier didn't move.

"And I say fuck you, asshole," Olivier returned.

Oh no.

Stellan's face turned to granite.

She put her hand on Olivier's arm.

"Get rid of him, Leigh," Stellan ordered her.

"She gives me my orders, not you, and I like what she gives me. But you know that, don't you, *Master*?" Olivier asked maliciously. "You're always on hand to watch."

So he wasn't totally oblivious to his audience.

"Olivier, *mon chou*, meet me in the foyer, please."

He jerked his head to look down at her.

"Please, the foyer," she reiterated. "I'll speak with Master Stellan and meet you there."

His eyes were communicating. He didn't like leaving her and she had reason to believe that it wasn't just protective possessiveness but that he felt he had reason to feel protectively possessive with what all three of them knew.

Olivier was right.

Stellan was always on hand to watch.

It wasn't like she hadn't noticed he held an interest, but not this much.

In fact, he'd never been so interested in her work with her toys.

"Mistress—" Olivier started.

"Olivier," she interrupted firmly, also speaking with her eyes and the hand she was using to squeeze his arm reassuringly.

It was a command he needed to obey, but still communicating she understood him and she'd be fine.

He hesitated magnificently then dipped his head respectfully to her in a way that was a thing of beauty before he sliced a scowl through Stellan and sauntered away, delivering his final cut to Stellan by doing it turning his back to the Dom without hesitation.

Amélie knew she shouldn't feel this way, what her beast had done in these hallways was not right.

But still, she couldn't help but feel Olivier's show of rebellion and disgust for Stellan's behavior was *glorious*.

"You allow a slave to talk to a Master that way?" Stellan asked.

"What I don't allow is a Master to talk to my sub that way," Amélie shot back.

Her point was more valid than his but he didn't give it to her.

He decreed, "You're in too deep with that one, Leigh."

"I think I can decide where I am and if I want to be there, Stellan," she retorted.

"He's wrapping *you* around his little finger. Fuck, you both *made out* after you worked him your second go." He lifted a hand high and stabbed his index finger over her head to indicate the room behind her. "And *tonight*."

"I'm sorry, I hadn't noticed you didn't kiss your toys," she returned.

His jaw got hard.

That was a point conceded.

That didn't mean he was finished.

"He's dragging you under, topping from below, and I'd never thought I'd see this from you but it's right in front of me every time you work him."

"Then you haven't been watching closely," she replied.

"Leigh—"

"No," she hissed, taking a quick step so she was in his space. "Your commentary on what happens in the playrooms is not welcome. It's highly unsuitable. And it's infuriating. Your commentary on where I am with the toys I play with is even more of the three.

How you can feel you have a say in either is beyond me but let's get that point clear, shall we? You don't."

"You can be affectionate with your slaves—"

"Not *can be*, Stellan, I *always* am and you know that."

He speared her with his gaze. "Yes. In there." He jabbed his finger to the room behind her again. "But you're practically fucking *cuddling* him in the hunting ground. This is more and *you* know *that*."

She drew in a steadying breath and agreed, "Indeed I do."

His anger grew; his eyes flashing to the room she and Olivier had just shared and back to her, he stated, "Guy like that will chew you up and spit you out."

Her heart clenched.

"Really, your commentary on your assessment of his intentions isn't welcome either," she fired back.

"Not the slave," he stated, getting closer to her, too, looking down into her eyes from the superior height she'd always found so attractive. "The *guy*. The man he is. You're falling for him, Leigh, and you've had him, what? Five times?"

"You would know, you seem to be marking them closely."

He continued to appear furious before his face warmed.

"Leigh—"

"Oh no, Stellan. I'm not one of your toys. You don't get to be a stern tyrant, bending me to your will, seeing I'm not going to break, noting the challenge and going in with the sweet. Fuck that. And as Olly said, fuck you."

She turned on her boot to march away but turned back.

"And if you ever speak to Olly or *anyone's* sub like that without their owner's permission, swear to Christ, I'll note that in your fucking profile, Stellan. That was not on. And *you*," she jabbed *her* finger at *him*, "know that."

"A slave is a slave," he bit out. "And *you* know that."

"Indeed, but do not pretend with your avid observation of all that has happened between Olivier and me that you don't get what

I'm saying. Aryas would lose his *mind* if he heard you speak that way to Shane, in front of Penn or not. My beast is *owned* and you fucking *know it* so stand the fuck *back*."

He looked like he'd paled when he said quietly, "Penn and Shane?"

She'd given too much away for he did not miss her meaning in the slightest at her mention of Penn and Shane, indicating openly where she was wishing things would go with Olivier.

She also didn't reply. She marched away, trying to deep breathe, calm herself, not wanting to get back to an angry Olivier, who'd shown, and admitted, he had a bad temper, while she was still so very angry.

A desire thwarted for she turned a corner and rammed right into him.

His arms wrapped around her and her head jerked back.

Her eyes narrowed as she lifted her hands and curled them on his biceps.

"I ordered—" she began.

"Spank me, paddle me, whip me, I don't fuckin' care. Do it for hours, gorgeous. It'll be worth it, seeing that and *hearing* that."

She snapped her mouth shut, terrified now of what she'd exposed with her words.

He smiled down at her hugely.

"Stand the fuck back," he quoted though his big grin.

"Olly," she said.

"That was not on and you *know that,"* he kept quoting.

Relief swept through her at his teasing, she slapped his biceps, got up on her toes, and hissed, "Olivier!"

"He stalked off in the direction of the Dom lounge, baby. He can't hear."

She had to admit, that gave even more relief.

"Olly, I told you to go to the foyer."

He dipped close. "And Leigh-Leigh, I'm an alpha-sub and the operative part of that in every sense . . . and I'll say that's even when you're jacking my ass, as I proved tonight . . . is *alpha*. No way I'm gonna leave any woman, much less one who means something to me, alone with a visibly ticked-off dude." He shook his head when she opened her mouth. "It's just not gonna happen." He grinned again. "Now I get you can take care of yourself, at least verbally, though I know for certain you'd swing a mean bat. But I don't give a fuck. I understand where you were and where you needed me to be in these halls when dealing with that fucker. But that's the way it is."

He gathered her closer and summed it up succinctly.

"Paddle my balls on Friday, but that's the way it is."

She stared into his eyes, standing in his arms, holding on to bulging biceps, still tingling from the orgasm he'd given her, hell, tingling from *everything* he'd given her, hearing all the words he'd said after *he'd* heard all the words she'd said to Stellan.

And she knew this time it was *she* who was gone.

All evidence was suggesting Olivier was the one even if it turned out he didn't agree.

And the last part terrified the life out of her.

ten

Clawing Right Under His Skin

OLIVIER

"Olly should go, just so he can get his ass laid."

"*I'd* go if it meant getting laid and I don't give a shit she turns out to be a psycho. Phonin' my ass, pantin' for my dick. How you let that one go, Olly, don't know. Bitch pants for my dick, I give it to her. Even if I gotta close my eyes 'cause she's butt-ugly. Not that your stalker was ugly, dude. I've seen her at Chad and Annie's, which makes me wonder at you more. She's just a stalker and any man should get past the stalker part, seein' as she's doin' it 'cause she wants his dick."

"Nope. I'm with Gary. Leave the stalker in your rearview and take this new bitch out. Then feel her out. She may dig kink. Then you can take her for some fun at Clay's place. Or maybe Clay can set you up, Olly, find a girl who likes to be spanked."

"Shut your fuckin' mouth," Olly growled and the way he did made his friend Todd's head jerk.

"Olly," Barclay said pacifyingly.

"Fuck that," Olly bit out in response to Barclay but did it not looking away from the guys. "What's all you assholes' problem?" he asked Todd, Emilio, and Gary, the guys he was out with at a bar for beer and Thursday Night Football, along with Chad and Clay.

The conversation had started with Chad digging into him again about meeting Annie's friend.

It had not gone well from there.

"Jesus, bro, lighten up," Emilio muttered.

"You got three sisters, Lo, and they're all really fuckin' pretty. You good with knowin' a bunch of assholes like you assholes sit around over beer callin' them bitches and talkin' about spankin' their asses? Because I can guarantee you, *bro*, there's so many assholes like you assholes out there, that shit happens."

Emilio shifted aggressively on his stool but the man knew he could never take Olly so he answered Olly's question through his, "Fuck you."

"I'll take that as a no," Olly shot back accurately and looked through them all. "Fuck, heard this kinda shit in junior high, high school, we're all way outta that and you're still spewin' it. When you gonna grow the fuck up?"

"We're just fuckin' with you, Olly. Grow some balls," Gary bit back.

"Wait, not sure, don't check, you tellin' me bein' a fuckwad and takin' a fuckwad's bullshit means your balls grow bigger? Shit," he leaned back, "no wonder you practice it so often. But seein' as you do, can't see how you're sittin' that stool."

"Calm down, Olly," Chad murmured low, and Olly turned to him.

"Annie's tight with Mandy. How do you think your wife would feel, knowin' you sat here listenin' to Emilio spout that shit about her?"

"Annie gets how it is with the boys," Chad returned.

Olly nodded. "You know? You're right. Most times, she does. That's true. Though, gotta say, known your wife a long time and not sure I'm convinced she'd be cool with that at all but especially not when it's about her friend. But whatever. You got a daughter, Chad, your baby girl isn't gonna be a baby girl forever." He flicked an irate hand to indicate the table. "You down with this shit for her?"

Chad's mouth tightened but he said, "It's just what guys do. Fuckin' with each other. Talkin' smack."

"So you *are* down with it?" Olly asked disbelievingly.

"Of course not. Don't be an ass," Chad spat.

"Think you need to walk this off, man," Barclay advised.

He did. Olly needed to walk a lot of things off.

In order to do that, he slid off his stool, pulling out his wallet, but he did this keeping his eyes on Chad.

"Said it enough times, won't say it again. I do not want a fixup. I dig you and Annie give a shit about my future happiness, but how 'bout you leave that to me?"

"You want that, you got it, bro," Chad bit off.

Olly threw some bills on the table to cover his beer and wings and shoved his wallet in his jeans, nodding curtly to Chad.

"We gotta walk on eggshells at the house, this newfound sensitivity you got, Olly?" Todd asked sarcastically.

"You know, I'd rather talk about the game, or the rig, or the budget cuts we're facing, or when we're gonna get together again and go up to the lake. Take a little shit about a new haircut. Give a little ribbing 'cause someone's into the new woman they're seein'. But this bent you guys got to cut as deep as you can and talk crap about women . . ." He shook his head. "You wanna call it sensitivity because you're right now feelin' like a schmuck because I pointed it out you should and you don't got a big enough dick to handle that, that's cool with me. But the right word for it is maturity. Look it up. They usually define big words in little ones you can understand."

He didn't give any of them a chance to say shit. He moved out of the bar and right to his truck.

He was at the door, hand to the handle, when he heard Barclay call, "Olly!"

He stopped and looked to his friend, then beyond him to make sure none of the other assholes had followed, and when he saw they hadn't, he gave his attention back to Clay.

"Jesus, brother, those long-ass legs of yours. You walk in a way that to me is running," Barclay said wheezily.

"What do you want, Clay?" Olly clipped.

Barclay studied him closely. "Things good with you?"

"Yup," Olly answered.

"I mean with, you know, *things*," he clarified.

"I know what you mean and I called you the day after we worked shit out to tell you it was all good with Leigh."

Barclay's brows shot up. "Leigh?"

"Amélie."

"Think I could figure out the nickname," Barclay muttered, getting closer.

"Well, it's all still cool."

And it was.

Absolutely.

Better than cool.

Brilliant.

And it also absolutely wasn't.

"Got a shorter fuse than normal with those guys, and before you get wound up again, Olly," Barclay said the last quickly, lifting up his hand, "they were just being guys. They weren't worse than usual." He dropped his hand and did a one-shoulder shrug. "Not better, but not worse."

"You dig that kind of ragging?" Olly asked.

"No, but they're good guys once they quit trying to communicate who they think has the biggest dick. It's just the male-bonding ritual, man. You know that."

"I know it. I also don't like it. And since I stopped doing it in the locker room when I was twenty-one, never did."

"One reason why I like you," Barclay replied. "And think you made your point back there. If it'll change them, I don't know. It doesn't and it gets on your nerves that bad, get out of their sphere. Don't crawl down their throats when it's obvious something else is fucking with you."

It was hard to get out of their sphere, seeing as, except for Todd, he worked with them.

Olly looked to the bar then blew out a breath, turning and practically collapsing a shoulder into his truck.

He looked beyond Barclay to the bar and admitted, "I like her."

Barclay totally knew what he meant.

"I hope so."

The humor in Barclay's reply got him Olly's attention.

"You don't get me, brother." He shook his head, weirdly unsure what to do with his hands, his body. "It's like . . . she slips out of the scene and suddenly, we're connecting. Not of the flesh, in another way. During sometimes, but especially when it's over. It isn't at all like we're where we are, doin' what we're doin'. It's like after vanilla fucking, when you like a woman, she likes you, and you shared something fuckin' great that got you off, you've got that and build on it in other ways that are also great."

"You seem surprised by this," Barclay noted.

"We're in a playroom at a BDSM club, Clay," Olly returned.

"It's still a club, Olly," Barclay replied. "It's a sex club, yeah. That's the only nuance of difference. All the people there are there for their own reasons. Some just want to hook up and get off. But some are looking for other things."

This was one of the things that had occurred to him last night that Olly was worried about. That something that was absolutely brilliant and absolutely not.

Christ, he didn't need to have his head jacked up with something *else*.

"Explain what your issue is, Olly," Barclay demanded and his ticked tone made Olly focus more fully on him. "So, she's giving you signs she might want something deeper and you're good with her jacking your shit but not good with going there. Is that what you're saying?"

"What I'm—" Olly started, but that's all Barclay let him get out.

"You're in that space and your head is that far enough up your ass you don't think you're gonna be able to get out of it, when she slips you outta the scene, Olly, you share that shit with her. Because she might be your Mistress but I keep reminding you she's still a woman. She wants something you don't, you gotta give her a heads-up so you don't crush her."

Guy like that will chew you up and spit you out.

The jackhole at the club's words came to Olly and he felt his throat start to scratch.

"Think I made it clear, man, I'm here for you with this shit if you need me. When I entered the scene, I didn't have someone like me to take my back and I could've used it. But that's on you, got nothin' to do with me, and you jack her shit in a different way, I don't want anything to do with it," Barclay declared, turning like he was going to walk away.

"Brother, something happened last night," Olly said and Barclay turned back.

Quickly, because his friend was pissed, Olly needed to let it out and Barclay had done a fuckload for him, he owed him the honesty; he gave him a rundown of what had happened after he and Amélie left their room the night before.

You're falling for him, Leigh . . . This is more and you know that.

Indeed I do.

The words said between her and that Stellan guy ran through Olly's mind after he told the story, a story that sent a lot of expressions racing across Barclay's face.

"My take from that is she's into me more than being into me," Olly finished.

"My guess is, you'd be right," Barclay replied.

"And that's where I'm at, because I honest to fuck didn't think it'd go that way, brother." He reached out, curled a hand around Barclay's shoulder, and gave it a squeeze before dropping it. "No offense. Not saying I thought everyone in the scene was out for nothin' but a way to get their kink. Just sayin' that I had so much fuckin' with my head, I didn't get that far to think about where it would go if you actually *connected* with somebody."

"And where are you willing to go if you keep *connecting* with Amélie?" Barclay asked.

"There's the rub."

The anger again entered Barclay's voice. "Because she's a Dominatrix and somehow with your place in that mix, you're too good for her?"

"Because she's a Dominatrix and not sure how I'd be, introducing her to my dad. And because she's a rich-as-fuck Dominatrix who obviously has more money than me, makes more money than me, and for both, always will."

"You bring a vanilla girl to your dad and share how you fuck her?" Barclay asked.

"Fuck no," Olly grunted.

"So that doesn't factor. It's none of his or *anyone's* business no matter what you do with a woman you got in your life. He doesn't even *want* that to be his business. And the other, man," Barclay took in a deep breath, "that's not something I can help you with. You either got it in you to get past that or you don't. I hear you on that. A woman I chose made more money than me, it'd give me pause. A *load* more money, that pause would last longer."

"Fuck," Olly muttered.

Barclay got closer. "I know this, Olly. I found a switch woman who gave it to me in *all* the ways I liked it that I connected with *great* who was loaded, can't say for sure, haven't found that woman, but not thinking that pause would last long enough for her to slip through my fingers."

Olly pulled breath in through his nostrils.

Then he nodded.

Barclay kept talking.

"What I will say is you gotta decide and let her in on that. Don't know how this Domme plays. That could be how she plays. Though

I will say, bro, that usually when a Domme plays it that way, she's opening herself up to other things."

The words sounded tight when Olly shared, "That asshole who got up in her and my faces said she was affectionate with all her toys and she confirmed that."

"That asshole also has a thing for her, straight up, Olly, something I figure I don't gotta tell you if you're into this woman to keep your eye on. You've tripped his trigger. So she might be an affectionate Domme, but what she's got with you is different."

Olly liked that a fuckuva lot.

And it freaked him the same amount.

Not to mention, it did not escape him that that Stellan asshole was carrying a torch for Amélie and that pissed him right the fuck off.

Which tweaked him all the more.

"I belong to her," Olly shared.

"That happens in the scene, man," Barclay said quietly.

"And she belongs to me. Claimed her. Said that shit straight. Not sure in the scene those go hand in hand, her owning me, me demanding that back, but she jumped right on that, brother."

Barclay studied him for a few very uncomfortable beats before he replied, "You need to get your head straight about her, Olly."

Yeah, he fucking did.

"Thanks for listening, Clay. Owe you a beer or seven," Olly muttered.

The intensity slid out of his friend and Barclay grinned at him. "Hold you to that. Go home. Cool down. Get your head straight. And I'll see you later."

"Right, later."

Barclay loped off.

Olly got into his truck and drove home, thinking what Barclay had said about Amélie meeting his dad was true. What they had was what they had and it was nobody's business.

He still didn't know how he'd handle that, but that was more about him still not being in the right place in his head about the shit he liked. The only person who got him to that place was Amélie in a playroom. If that translated to the real world, he didn't know.

And what he was struggling with now was if he wanted to find out.

No, that wasn't it.

If he let his mind wander and didn't think on it, he knew he *did* want to find out. It was just when the other shit pushed in, things became less clear.

What he also knew he would see if he brought Amélie to meet his dad was his dad having the same concerns Olly did.

His father was a man's man and a man provides. Amélie clearly being stupid rich, pure class, and not belonging in their world, his father wouldn't miss it. He'd worry about his son. He'd share that verbally and/or nonverbally.

If Olly's mother was alive, she'd probably worry too. She knew her kids. She knew her husband. She'd worked as a seamstress for a tailor since Olly could remember (this being the only reason he had nice suits, suits no way he could afford if his mother didn't get a discount). She'd brought in some money to help lighten the load but his dad made the bulk of what they lived on working foreman at a quarry. They were comfortable in that and never fought about money or shit like that. They fought about stupid things that didn't mean anything so they could get it out, get it over with, and move on without any baggage.

Amélie had his balls in a harness a lot of the time because he let that shit happen.

If the brilliance they had got better and both their minds went there, he was not a man who wanted his balls, figuratively, in a harness.

He drove to his house, went in, turned on the game, and got himself a beer.

But he sat on his couch with his feet to the edge of the coffee table, phone in his hand, tilting it around, knowing her number was in it.

He could be just a toy she petted and kissed like any other, maybe more because there truly wasn't a whole lot of challenge in that club for the likes of her and she got off with him.

But that fucking guy, Stellan, had lost his mind about them making out like it was something she didn't do (and he hoped like fuck it wasn't because she was a fantastic kisser, her mouth tasted almost as good as her pussy, and he liked the idea of that being for them).

You're falling for him, Leigh . . . This is more and you know that.

Indeed I do.

She was falling in deep. She'd nearly straight out admitted it.

And in play, she looked out for him.

Out of it, no matter what they were to each other or what they became, it was absolutely his job to look out for her.

He should get that straight with her.

Or end it.

"Shit," he whispered, engaging his phone.

He put it to his ear, considered hanging up as it rang, and if she called back or asked about it, telling her he'd accidentally dialed when she picked up.

"*Chevalier,* is everything okay?"

That sweet voice sounding worried.

Worried.

About him.

Everything he'd been thinking flew from his head.

"Yeah, baby, everything's cool," he lied.

"I . . ." She hesitated more than a beat before she went on, "I'm surprised you called. It's football night. Aren't you riveted to your screen with your laptop open beside you, assessing your rankings in your fantasy league?"

He started chuckling. "A woman who drinks pretentious drinks knows about football?"

"Olly, big men tackling each other . . . please." She drew out the *please* in a cute way. "What do you think I'm doing tonight?"

That was unexpected.

"You watch football?"

"Do I need to repeat myself about the tackling?"

He chuckled again and suggested, "I think we need to stop this conversation before you ruin football for me."

"Perhaps that's a good call," she replied, also sounding like she was laughing.

And it sounded nice.

"So, if everything's all right, Olly, why are you calling?" she asked.

She was calling him Olly.

She called him Olivier when she jacked him. She did that exclusively. He'd noticed last night after sharing his nickname that she didn't use that name in play. She called him other things when she was working him, but if she used his name, she only used his full name. Never Olly unless she'd slipped them out of the scene.

Now she was calling him Olly.

And she was bantering with him. She wasn't ordering him to go find his harness and put it on. And that worry had crept in her tone again.

Maybe she was worried he'd called for the reason he'd actually called.

Because she knew he heard what she said and he needed to find out where both their heads were at and maybe, if his wasn't where hers was, move what they had in the direction it needed to go.

"Olly?" she called.

More worry, her voice beginning to sound stiff—not with authority, like she was closing down.

He didn't like that wrapped around his name.

Not one bit.

"You just . . ." Fuck, fuck, fuck. "You said something the other night and you looked . . . I don't know, gorgeous. When you were talking about your folks, you looked like you left something out."

And what he didn't mention, she'd talked about them in past tense.

He hadn't pushed at the time even though he'd really wanted to, especially when that expression crossed her face.

And this wasn't the first time he'd thought about it since last night, wondered about it.

He wondered about a lot of things when it came to Amélie. What she did when she wasn't at the club. What kind of house she lived in. How she made her money.

Everything.

Fuck him, he was again in over his head but now in *two* ways.

One, he was treading water until she pulled him up to surf a killer wave.

The other one could have him going under.

"They've both passed," she said softly.

His throat got tight, his stomach clutched, the reason he called flew out the window . . . and yeah.

He totally fucking could go under.

"I'm sorry, sweetheart, I shouldn't have asked."

"That's fine, Olly."

"It isn't."

"It is. It's sweet you noticed and called to ask. And it isn't like it happened yesterday. This year, it'll have been eleven years."

Eleven years.

Fuck, she'd been twenty-two.

But he was confused.

"Eleven? For both?" he asked.

That was shitty luck and meant they both had to die young and when Amélie was young, taking that double hit around the same time.

"I know, it's strange. They fought in the beginning but time wore on." A smile entered her voice. "Dad would have *lady friends,*" she said this like it was amusing and he'd get why when she explained it.

"I don't think he chose any of them due to the fact he doted on me. And you can read that to the point he spoiled me rotten, if you wish, because it's true."

Olly had no doubt. If he had a beautiful, auburn-haired little girl with pretty tawny eyes, he'd dote on her too.

Fuck.

"Mom got remarried," she continued. "They eventually got over it, also for me. And when she and my father were married and *Maman* was still with us, she did a lot of charity work. Her work with that meant a lot to her, so when she'd come back to see me, she remained involved in some of the organizations she'd worked with when she was in the States. They were both patrons of one and continued to be, eventually, when they mended fences, doing this together. There was an event and they went to it together. They were leaving, and I don't know..." She paused. "The investigation showed there was something wrong with the man's car..."

She paused again and with his gut tight at her words, Olly got concerned.

"Leigh-Leigh," he whispered.

He heard her clear her throat and she finished, "Dad was helping *Maman* get in the car. The out-of-control car hit Dad's car. Dad got crushed under his car and died within minutes. Mom was thrown mostly free but hit her head on a cement step." Her voice dipped. "She lasted longer, but after a couple of days, we decided to turn off the machines."

"Christ, shit, fuck, baby," he ground out, feeling like a twat. "I shouldn't have said anything. Made you relive that. I'm so sorry, Leigh."

"I live with it every day, Olly, so you didn't make me relive anything."

The pain was in her voice, not deep, but she didn't hide it, so she was right. But he could have done it when he was close so he could hold her.

On that thought he knew he was not going under.

She was.

Crawling under his skin.

"Nothing else to say, sweetheart. That sucks," he murmured soothingly.

"You're very right," she replied softly. "I was exceptionally close with my father. We always had been. My mother, she didn't know what to do with children." Another smile in her voice, this one weak. "It could be why you think I act older than I am, because she always treated me like an adult. Unfortunately, we never got along. This, I see belatedly, is because we're very similar. My mother's brother and sisters say I'm an Emmanuelle clone. They say it's uncanny. I even look like her, which I'm grateful for, she was lovely."

If Amélie looked like her, she'd definitely been lovely.

She drew in a breath that he heard.

He waited for it and she gave it to him.

"After feeling angry, I got to the point I realized I have no re-grets about Dad dying. As much as I would like it to be different, I came to hard terms with the fact that there's nothing I can do to change what happened and he left me with something precious. This being that he made sure we had everything we could have while we had the time to have it."

Another breath and Olly stayed braced even after she carried on.

"But I was only beginning to understand *Maman*. I was an adult and we were finally connecting in a place where she was comfort-able. But I was still young, and stupid because of it, so I was resist-ing that. That resistance was slipping, we were beginning to share something wonderful, and now I wish I'd just let it go. Realized ear-lier what a remarkable woman she was and all she'd given me so she could have gone knowing I appreciated it and adored her, like I did. So, like I said, I live with it every day, darling."

"I'm still sorry I brought it up, Leigh-Leigh," he replied.

"Yes, I can imagine, but strangely, it feels good talking about it. It always feels good talking about them, sharing with someone what a wonderful dad I had and what an extraordinary mother too. It's like introducing them to you, or anyone I talk to about them for the first time, which is usually the last time because losing them both that way was such a tragedy, people learn the story and then don't bring them up. I'd obviously rather introduce them personally, but at least I get this. So it wasn't easy, but in an odd way, it feels nice."

"Glad you can twist it that way."

The smile was clear in her voice when she returned, "I'm not twisting anything, Olly."

"Well, babe, all I can say is I don't get it but I do. My dad's alive and kicking, in a way. Mom died two years ago. It started when she was sitting next to him, watching TV. Pulmonary embolism. She died in Dad's arms while he was phoning emergency."

"Oh God, Olly," she whispered.

"Sharing war stories, Leigh," he said unemotionally, because he had to. After two years, he wasn't over losing his mom in a way that remained so fresh, he knew he never would be. "It fucked up my dad. He's with us and he can laugh his big laugh and give us shit but he lived for her. It's like he's there but he's a ghost, just existing until he can get back to her."

"That's as heartbreaking as it is lovely," she noted.

"I just see the heartbreaking, baby," he replied quietly.

"I'm so sorry. Of course you do."

"Not bein' a dick. Just miss my mom, get it about my dad because I saw how they were with each other my whole life, but even though I get it, I hate seein' Dad so unhappy."

"And that must be horrible, to want him to be happy and not at the same time."

"Yeah," he muttered.

"Oh Olly," she whispered in his ear.

She said nothing more but the way she gave him that, she didn't have to give him more.

"So, how about we quit talkin' about this shit," he suggested.

"I'm all for that," she agreed.

"Now, gotta admit, Leigh, I was born and raised in Phoenix.

Had no idea we spawned gorgeous but pretentious, uppity women like you, even with French moms," he teased.

"That would be because Phoenix didn't *spawn* me," she returned, her voice trembling with laughter, giving him relief because hearing it he knew he'd taken them both out of the heavy. "I was born in New York City."

"That makes more sense."

"Yes, and raised there, mostly."

"Outside of France. Yeah, you told me," he reminded her.

"Actually, what I mean is, when I was thirteen, before I started high school, Dad moved us here. He hated the weather in New York, hates humidity more so Florida and Texas were out..." There was a pause that Olly again braced through but he didn't need to when he heard her again speaking through laughing, "And he had a daughter he spoiled rotten who was obsessed with horses and you can't have horses in the City. So we were always in a car going to our house in Connecticut so I could be near my horses. He hated the traffic too. So good weather and I could be near my babies, we moved here."

Their house in Connecticut.

Her ranch in the mountains.

Horses.

"Olly?" she called when he got stuck in his head.

"Nothin' to say, Leigh." He injected humor into his tone when thoughts of all she had that, if they went there, he didn't give her and never could, weighed him down. "Not a big surprise you like horses."

"No," she agreed, still sounding like she was smiling. "I can imagine it also won't surprise you that when I was eighteen, Dad hired a man to manage the stables on our land. A big man who was, as you put it, not hard on the eyes. So when he did, I had very interesting visions of fettering him in a stall and taking my crop to him."

Surprising the shit out of himself, overriding the stitch of jealousy her words caused was him busting out laughing.

"Needless to say, when Dad was away on business, I managed to accomplish this feat when I was nineteen," she said through his laughter.

"I bet he was gagging for it, baby," Olly remarked.

"As we did it more than once, I believe that was true," she replied. "Though, he was my first and I think I was able to handle that because I'd taken a crop to so many flanks before his. But even though he was my first, I'd come to terms with my nature before that and having him made me realize I couldn't take that further until I knew what I was doing."

Olly said nothing to that, unable to ignore that stitch as it was now vicious at the thoughts those words brought, because he was in the position to know she'd had a lot of training.

And further jealousy she'd "come to terms" with her "nature" before she was nineteen.

He wondered what that felt like—to be free to just be.

"Olly?" she called.

"I'm here," he grunted.

"Darling, you're aware that training for a Domme is often observing. Participating only to assist the Masters or Mistresses you're training under. Sometimes, you don't even touch a—"

"You don't have to explain this, Amélie."

"I think I do, sweetheart," she whispered.

"There were others before me, I get that."

"And there were others before me as well, Olly."

He said nothing because that was true.

"I've never asked anyone to my ranch," she declared.

Olly blinked at his knees.

"Say that again?" he demanded.

"Although I had certain things installed, no one has used them, not even me."

"Baby, that means a lot,"—understatement, it meant a fuckuva lot, all of it great, and all that great tweaking him even more—"but like I said, you don't have to explain this. I didn't come to you a virgin."

"This is true," she replied.

"I mean, some things were virgin, but you took care of that."

That got him a soft laugh.

"There's enough judging in the world," he went on. "The things we give each other mean too much to bring that kind of shit into it."

He said the words and he had to live by them.

Since they were straight-up true, he had a feeling he could.

"He's handsome, sweet, *and* wise," she said quietly like she wasn't talking to him.

The compliment hit him warm and sweet all the same.

"As well as a wise-ass," he reminded her.

That got him more laughter.

Right, so having a normal conversation that didn't end in her rocking his world through his cock, balls, and ass, instead rocking his world other ways when that was the last thing he intended with this conversation, now he needed to end this before his head got any more fucked up.

"We shared war stories. I now have proof the rich girl fucks the stableboy." He continued through more of her laughter, "I can pretty much guarantee my Leigh-Leigh is gonna try me in a variety of ways tomorrow night, so I need to finish my beer and hit the sack. You cool with that, sweetheart?"

"I'm cool with that, Olly." Her voice dipped. "And I'm glad you called. Though I would have preferred not to depress you with the story of my parents, it's sweet you listened."

"Anytime, baby."

He said it. He meant it. He was fucked by it.

Clawing right under his skin.

"Thanks, Olly. See you tomorrow. Good night."

"'Night, Leigh-Leigh, sleep good."

"I will," she promised, something in her voice he felt in his balls.

And just like his Amélie, she hung up, leaving him wanting more.

AMÉLIE

After hanging up with Olly, Amélie sat in her TV room with Stasia in her lap, the television on a game but muted, her hand in Stasia's thick long, gray, black, and white fur.

Unlike with Cleo, Amélie avoided the mottled, bare patches missing from Stasia's haunches for reasons too hideous to call up.

So she did not.

She just enjoyed a rare moment of connection with her sweet kitty.

At the same time she enjoyed a moment of sweet relief that Olly had called.

Called and chatted.

Called and chatted, curious about her, concerned about how she'd been after her talk of her parents.

Called and chatted and bantered, just to call and chat and banter.

All this after all they'd shared together at the club.

All this after he'd heard what he'd heard when she'd spoken to Stellan.

All these gifts she gladly received, using them to help to sweep the fear away, incapable of stopping them from nurturing the hope that refused to slow its blossoming.

She'd been concerned all day about how Olly would react to her altercation with Stellan once his amusement had worn off. Once he'd had time to think about all she'd said and all it meant.

When he'd called, that concern escalated sharply.

The tone of his voice, so hesitant when he was always so open, turned that concern into a piercing pain that he'd called at the very least to be certain they established appropriate emotional boundaries.

But at worst, to gently end things as he was aware her emotional boundaries were already very blurred.

But now, her eyes on the television screen, her fingers tenderly stroking her furry baby, the feel of Stasia's quiet purrs vibrating, she had no concerns.

She'd enjoyed a double delight that night, Stasia coming out for some love and Olly phoning her just to connect and more, do this connecting outside the activities of the club.

No, Amélie had no concerns.

Just sweet relief.

And that sweeter spiral of anticipation starting up yet again.

For she'd see him tomorrow night.

She had it all planned.

And it was going to be *fabulous*.

eleven

Baby

AMÉLIE

On Friday night, after Amélie gave her clutch to the staff at the front desk, she walked into the hunting ground of the Honey and saw Olivier immediately, sitting with a male and female sub at a table just off the far side from the entrance.

But he was turned on his stool, facing the entryway, and she'd barely walked in before his eyes caught hers.

She allowed her lips to curl in a small smile and lifted her chin slightly, telling him she wanted him to come to her.

After their conversation last night, she didn't want him to come to her.

She wanted to take him right to the playroom she'd selected for the night and ravish him.

Literally.

But after tonight, she wouldn't see him in more than a week and she wanted to enjoy a drink before they played, this allowing her to get to know her sweet beast.

Her *very* sweet beast, if the way he reacted and handled her after she'd told him what happened to her parents was any indication.

And Amélie was guessing it wasn't any indication.

It was every one.

She wanted more of that time with Olivier over drinks, and as she moved through the room, watching him slide off his stool, grab his beer, and say something to his companions, she knew after he instigated last night's phone call, he wanted that too.

That call, not chatting but talking, sitting in her living room with Olivier's deep voice rapping a soothing tattoo into her ear, lulling her into sharing, lulling her into dreaming.

Amélie now understood, acutely, Mirabelle's pain at feeling a connection grow with a sub that might blossom into something more in her life and the paralyzing fear such a gorgeous feeling could cause. Not to mention the desperate need that grew with every encounter to read every sign as hopeful as your mind screamed to be cautious and keep yourself safe.

Therefore she'd resolved to have their time together that night, and then their time apart (which hopefully would come with Olivier phoning her sometime during it), and when he came back to her they'd continue to explore what they were building.

Until their weekend.

At her ranch, they would play.

And they would talk.

Olivier moved in just behind her several feet from the empty booth where she was heading. When she felt him there, she reached back, searching for his hand, unsure if she found it or if he found hers, his fingers curling sure and warm, making her heart light even as something she wasn't sure of felt heavy in her belly.

They arrived at the booth and she turned into him, tipping her head back to watch him move into her space and dip his chin down to catch her eyes.

"Olivier," she said softly.

His lips twitched, his eyes traveled more than her face, taking in the slinky, deep V-neck (that had a deeper V-back) of her jet-beaded dress.

"Mistress Amélie," he finally greeted, his gaze roving up to hers. "Want a drink?"

She tore her attention from him just enough to see the Friday evening crowd at the Honey was thriving. She wanted a drink and it might take longer to wait for a server than she wished to do.

"Please, Olivier." She glanced down at his mostly drunk beer. "And refresh your own, if you like."

"Gotcha," he muttered then started with, "Swahsoh—"

"Soixante Quinze, darling. But you can say French 75 or just that you're getting a drink for me. They'll know."

"Gotcha," he repeated, squeezing her hand, perhaps to give her a squeeze or perhaps to remind her she was holding him and needed to let him go.

She didn't wish to, could stand for an hour looking up into his eyes, but she forced herself to do so.

He moved off and she slid into the booth, the heavy beading of her dress slightly digging into the flesh on her buttocks and thighs, this reminding her of her plans for the evening, and she licked her lips in anticipation.

"I see your prized stallion can actually behave properly when it suits him."

The surprise of Stellan's voice coming from over her shoulder had her twisting her neck to look back at him.

He was standing there, leaning insolently against the side of the booth where she was sitting.

"I'm in no mood, Stellan," she warned.

He crossed his arms and looked down his nose at her. "Then it would seem you're in the wrong place, Leigh."

"You know what I mean," she rapped out impatiently.

"I know we need to talk," he returned.

They did. He might not be her closest friend but they were more than acquaintances. They'd often sat together in a booth, sharing about themselves and their lives while they idly surveyed the specimens on show, both on nights when there wasn't much that interested them as well as getting caught up in their conversation and not finding anything interesting because of it.

And he'd been to her house on more than one occasion for parties she hosted. She liked to entertain, to cook, to have people around her she cared about, and as her life wasn't filled with much that she enjoyed, except the Honey, her pets, her horses, and that, she did it often.

"Perhaps," she agreed. "But that won't be happening now."

"You're still angry," he said, but not accurately.

Since the incident, her thoughts had been on Olivier. How he'd reacted to what he heard. What he would do with that. The aching concern that assaulted her when he'd phoned, thinking at first he'd called to discuss it and put them on a different path than it appeared they were heading. Then, of course, her relief this didn't happen and her struggles with tamping down the joy she felt that it was something else altogether.

None of those thoughts had been on how she felt about Stellan doing what Stellan had done.

"Actually, you're wrong. After our altercation, I didn't think much of it," she told him and watched with deep surprise as he didn't hide that her words stung.

His tone had changed a good deal when he cajoled, "We still need to talk, Leigh."

She changed hers to quiet and cautious when she replied, "And we'll find that time, Stellan. It just won't be now."

It was then she watched with stunned surprise as he lost eye contact with her, dipping his chin and bowing his head in a gesture that was inherently submissive, something she'd never, not ever, seen of a dyed-in-the-wool, extreme alpha-Dom.

Something she would never guess anyone would receive from Stellan.

To be honest, it was something she wouldn't even think he could do. If his mind didn't stop it, his body would instinctively rebel.

And he was an extreme alpha. She knew what he did for business. She knew he was a shark. Cutthroat. Aggressive. Proudly open about being insatiably greedy for money or anything he could acquire.

In business.

And in play.

She had not been wrong during their quarrel. If his subs didn't bend to his will, and he, like she, picked those who were a challenge, he could be a tyrant.

He could also be unbearably sweet, even romantic, definitely chivalrous, anything he needed to be to get what he wanted, whatever that may be.

And at that moment by her booth, he said no more. Didn't even lift his eyes to hers. He just straightened with his gaze toward the bar, his jaw getting tight, and turned and walked away.

Amélie looked to the bar and wasn't surprised to see Olivier standing there, his attention on Stellan, his expression sharing openly that Stellan being close to his Mistress did not make him at all happy.

Suddenly, Olivier's focus shifted to her.

She shook her head and gave him a soft smile.

It took a moment before he nodded, only once, and she watched him turn back to the bar where the bartender had put her drink and was now turning to pull Olivier a fresh beer.

But as he moved, something caught his attention because he did a double take, and she could just make out in his profile that his eyes had narrowed.

She followed his gaze and saw the back of Delia, Tiffany pinned to the wall just visible beyond the Domme (who was, like Amélie, also tall, though Amélie would guess she had at least two inches on Delia).

That creeping sensation came back as, even with the little she could see of Tiffany, the girl looked scared out of her brain.

Seeing that, Amélie had to tell herself that Aryas was aware and would no sooner allow any danger to come to any of his members than he'd allow his own balls to be cut off. This was true before what happened to Evangeline, but especially after.

Whatever was happening there, Aryas would discover if Tiffany wanted it.

And if she didn't, he'd deal with it.

Olivier came back with their drinks and she slid over when he did. He slid in beside her, setting her champagne glass in front of her.

"Enjoy your beer, *mon chou*," she gave him leave to drink as she reached for her own. "And thank you."

"My pleasure, Amélie," he muttered distractedly.

She finished the sip she'd been taking as he spoke and looked to him to see his attention was still across the room where Delia and Tiffany had been.

"Olly?" she called.

"That shit ain't right," he stated.

She put her drink down and put her hand to his thigh, giving him a squeeze.

He turned his head her way.

"Sorry, Mistress," he murmured. "Something I saw—"

She nodded. "Mistress Delia and Tiffany. I've noticed too. So have many others. Aryas is monitoring the situation."

Amélie had to admit that Olivier's notice of this was a vague relief to an even vaguer nagging feeling that Olivier had not only experienced unskilled Mistresses in his past but he'd not had very much experience at all.

A rookie sub might not notice or translate what was happening with Delia and Tiffany.

He caught it immediately.

"Figure Weathers'll fuck her up, she's fuckin' up one of his subs," Olivier noted.

And again, that nagging feeling came back as there was the green.

Amélie got closer. "*Weathers* is usually Master Aryas in this room, Olivier."

Olivier got closer, too, and as he was mercifully always able to do, he quelled her nagging feeling by saying, "I know, baby. I'd be cool to his face if I was talkin' to him direct or anyone else could hear me. Respect. Who he is in this scene, just this scene being this scene, and what he's created for the players, which is the shit. But gotta ask, when it's you and me, just sayin', that shit doesn't sit well with me."

"A lot won't, as a sub, as you know," she replied, watching him closely.

"Leigh-Leigh, what I'm sayin' is," his big hand folded around hers at his thigh, "this is you and me."

"Ah," she breathed out, understanding him.

They were in a booth, sharing a drink and talking. This was Olly and Leigh. Not Mistress Amélie and her toy.

"You down with that?" he asked.

"You're asking a great deal, Olly," she answered.

His face softened at the name she used. "I know, sweetheart. I'm still asking, you down with that?"

She liked Leigh and Olly so she gave in.

"If you show respect to my equals, *mon grande*, then yes."

"That asshole gets in your space again, Amélie, you gotta know, the others, I'm in the game. Him. You gotta take care of that for me because I can't be sure I'm gonna be cool with him."

He was talking about Stellan.

She nodded. She already knew that.

"You're heard, Olly."

"Good," he muttered, turning back to his drink.

He took a sip and she watched his mouth quirk as he put the drink down and spoke again.

"Hear your girl's out on the town tonight."

She leaned into him and he turned to face her again.

"Yes," she said, trying to shove down her excitement, and her apprehension, neither she thought Olivier missed as his eyes crinkled when he looked into hers. "Mira and Trey are on a date tonight."

And they were. Another phone call Amélie got last night that made her happy. Mirabelle had barely left the club when she'd called, phoning Amélie in the car on her way home, ecstatically happy, telling her Trey not only wanted to go out with her but shared that he, too, had been looking for an in to ask Mirabelle out.

"How did you know?" Amélie asked Olivier.

"Everyone's yammering about it." He took another sip of beer and said, "Everyone seems to dig her. Him too." He grinned at Amélie. "They see good things."

"I hope so," Amélie replied before she took her own sip.

"You hope so, you like this dude for your girl, I hope so too."

She smiled up at him.

His grin turned boyishly playful and she immediately decided to rank his smiles.

This one, for the moment, was on top.

"My Mistress likes watching men tackle each other." He arched his brows. "You in a fantasy league?"

She laughed, leaning ever closer. "No, but I've been known to whip up some nachos for friends on a Sunday as we watched games."

He didn't hide his surprise. "You eat nachos?"

"There are many culinary delicacies a spoiled rich girl enjoys, Olly," she teased.

"Never heard nachos described as a delicacy."

"Then you haven't had any that have the exact perfect balance of sour cream and guacamole."

His smile turned amused and took the top spot.

"Maybe not, though not for lack of trying," he returned.

And now she wanted to make him nachos while they watched football.

Damn.

"You got friends?" He lifted his beer to indicate the room. "Outside this place, I mean."

Amélie didn't know how to take a question that seemed oddly offensive.

"Of course," she answered, moving back a smidge.

"Leigh," he called the instant she did, taking her attention from picking up her drink to look at him, and she knew he read her retreat even before he spoke again. "You own this room, gorgeous. Even if everyone didn't say it, you'd know it just watching you walking through it. The life, this life, it's a part of you." He erased the distance she put between them by dipping closer to her. "It's sexy as fuck, Amélie, not just how you reign supreme in this joint, but how you live the life honest, totally and openly cool with who you are and what you like."

"That's sweet, Olly, but still, my sexuality out there in the ordinary world does not define me, like it doesn't anybody. I have a life outside this space. Including friends who mean a lot to me who know nothing about this part of my life."

"Okay, but you could see how it would define you, though. How it's a part of you where anyone who'd know about it and think shit about it or say shit about it would just get a 'fuck you.' And you also know enough about this part of life and the people who live it that that's amazing, Leigh."

She squeezed his thigh and noted aloud what he'd been giving to her during play, "You struggle."

He looked to his beer, and before taking a sip, murmured, "You know I do."

"So it's more amazing that you have that struggle, but you don't let it stop you. Instead you've still got the courage to be who you are."

He didn't respond.

"It's amazing, Olly," she pushed.

"Yeah," he grunted.

She decided to let that go for now. Outside the battle waged during play—being with her in the hunting ground, phoning her—that didn't seem a battle for Olly.

That came easy.

For both of them.

"I do have friends outside the life," she shared to get them beyond what had become awkward. "My book club is all Dommes, however."

He turned back to her. "My hot-as-fuck Mistress makes nachos, watches football, and has a book club. Careful, baby, I'm gonna start thinking you're a real person and not an angel sent from heaven to jack my shit."

She started laughing, through it saying, "I'm sure you'll agree I'm no angel."

He moved his face close to her. "Don't know about that."

Amélie got closer to Olivier. "Stop flirting with me, Olly, or we won't finish our drinks."

"If you think I got a problem with that, just sayin', you're wrong."

That set her inner thighs to tingling.

She pressed closer, sliding her hand from the top of his thigh to the inside and up, very close to his meat.

"Does my Olivier want to play?" she whispered.

His eyes dropped to her mouth and he whispered back, "Yeah."

"Then take one last sip, my beast, and we'll go to our room."

He held her gaze then did as told. She did the same and let his thigh go as indication she wanted him to move out of the booth.

He read her sign, slid out, and offered a hand to help her out.

She took it and didn't let go. They again held hands as they walked through the hunting ground, through the door to the play-rooms and the halls she guided them through to get them all the way to the back room. A special room. Aryas's room. A room de-signed specifically for his appetites, where Aryas did the majority of his playing.

However, on the way, it was Olivier who stopped Amélie. Not with a tug on her hand. When he halted and their linked hands stretched out their arms when she kept moving.

Amélie looked back at him to see his attention had been taken by a scene. She moved closer and as she did, he curved their arms so their linked hands were held behind her back and he tucked her into his side.

A lovely, intimate gesture she liked greatly.

But he did this with his attention firmly directed to the scene.

Amélie gave it the same and saw Talia working Bryan again. He was strapped, legs up, fronts of his thighs to his torso, knees bent, calves to the backs of his thighs, all of this bound to his torso. He was thus curled into himself in restraints and also restrained to a high bench, arms also strapped, but straight over his head. His buttocks and outer thighs were red in a way that stated he'd taken a whip or cat.

And Talia was fucking him rhythmically and clearly enjoyably (for both of them) up the ass with a strap-on.

"You ladies like your ass," Olivier muttered.

Amélie turned fully into him and replied, "We do when you do."

Olivier looked down at her.

"Does that disturb you?" she asked.

"You gonna want that from me?" he asked in return.

Since she finished training, she'd eschewed the strap-on. There was something that just wasn't aesthetically pleasing about it. She'd considered having one specially made that might alleviate this aversion but found other toys offered her what she needed so she'd never bothered.

She didn't share this with her steed.

"There are many ways I'll be taking you, Olivier. And all those ways you'll give to me."

His expression darkened in a manner she couldn't quite read but since she wasn't going to fuck him (that way) tonight, they didn't need to continue this conversation (for now).

"Come, *mon chou*, you're delaying our play," she ordered, curling their arms from her back and tugging on his hand to follow her.

He moved and they strode to the room at the very back.

This one was twice as large as the general playrooms and the dim light shone through a mostly opaque screen that was down. It was not white or black, but red.

When Amélie led Olivier to the door, he murmured, "I see tonight is going to be interesting."

She hoped so.

She said nothing, just opened the door, flipped the switch for occupancy, and pulled him through.

She let him go and moved directly to where she wanted to be, knowing what he was seeing.

The opulence of the rich red watered taffeta papering three walls (only one wall in this room was windows).

No toys or equipment on display, as Aryas's gear remained here. It was all in ornately carved walnut chests and not available for use by other Dominants.

Amélie's things had been stowed for her in the empty chest Aryas provided for others who used his space.

There was a variety of furniture to be used for a variety of reasons—armchairs, stools, a chaise lounge, upholstered benches—and rugs on the floor (all this meaning this room was the only one that required controlled ejaculations for it was disallowed to make a toy come on any of these things).

And there was a canopied, king-size bed, dressed in red satin sheets, an abundance of pillows in the same, a beveled mirror on the ceiling above it, one behind the headboard, sturdy black ties with black velvet-lined shackles easily visible at the bottom, the same with black velvet-lined cuffs at the headboard.

And last, a plethora of candelabrums all throughout the room.

"Remove your suit jacket, shoes and socks," she ordered as she moved. "Put them by the door as normal. Otherwise, stay dressed and sit on the stool facing the bed, please."

She went to the long matches on one of the bureaus and was about to strike one when she heard a sweet, quiet, deep rumble of, "Baby."

She turned and saw Olivier's eyes on her, his face soft, his expression warm.

It not being difficult, he'd read the scene (or part of it).

"Please do as I ask without delay, my steed," she replied, turned away so he wouldn't see her face had also gone soft at the idea of giving him something he so obviously desired (this being her) and struck the match.

She moved through the room, lighting candles, and then more, and more.

She felt his eyes follow her as she did, there being so many candles, having to put out the match she was using to strike another and keep going.

Halfway done, she ordered, "Stay seated. Untuck your shirt and unbutton it. But just unbutton it, Olivier. Leave it on."

She didn't look at him and only knew he'd followed her direction when she finished with the candles and moved slowly to the bin to deposit the spent slivers of wood in her fingers.

As told, Olivier had one bare foot down, one foot on the first rung of the high stool where he was sitting. He was not lounged against the curved back but instead on the edge of his seat, his eyes hungry and on her, the crotch of his trousers lifted with his arousal.

She knew she'd enjoy this night.

She knew it better then with one look at him, the casual posture, the aggressive masculinity, the power of him at rest.

She deposited the spent matches in the bin and walked his way, demanding, "Don't move."

He didn't, watching her approach, his hands resting lightly on his upper thighs, his gaze devouring her, head to black, strappy-sandal-shod feet.

She stopped close and dropped her attention to his chest before she put her hands on it. Roaming it with her fingertips, feeling the silk of his skin and the steel of his flesh drift from fingers to nipples to pussy, wondering if it would take minutes or hours to memorize every swell and dip and hoping she'd one day be able to answer that question.

Sliding one hand in his shirt and around his ribs, she rubbed his nipple with her other thumb and looked in his eyes.

"Are you harnessed for me, my steed?" she asked quietly.

"Yeah, Mistress," he answered, thickness to his voice, laziness to his eyes, banked fire there ready to be stoked.

She slid her fingertips down his side, over his waistband, honing in to cup him through his pants.

"And you're hard for me," she noted, rubbing the heel of her palm down his length.

"Always, Amélie." That was uttered thicker, his arousal growing against her hand and in his tone.

She took both hands away. "Stand for me, Olivier."

He seemed disoriented at the abrupt change in circumstances, hesitated momentarily, then slowly unfolded out of the seat.

She moved close and put her hands back to him, roving the skin inside his shirt, around to his back and forward to his stomach, doing this with her head tipped back, watching the uncertainty leave him as the lazy came back.

Holding those lazy eyes, she moved her fingers to his fly, unhooked it, and slowly slid it down.

His white teeth emerged, skimming his lip, his lids lowering, hooding his gaze.

God yes, he was going to make it fun to watch.

She lifted her hands up, running them along the waistband, hooking his underwear in her thumbs, and she pulled them down slowly, swaying his hips, until she got them mid-thigh.

She took in his cock, which bounded clear of his shorts, his strapped balls declaring her ownership, and her mouth watered.

Amélie tipped her head back. "Sit again, Olivier, as you were sitting, one foot on a rung, but I want your pants to stay right where they are."

There was a flash in his eyes. Rebellion. Perhaps a memory of how she'd had him before in that way, but against a door. Perhaps uncertainty because he wasn't quite sure he liked where she was leading him.

She rode it through with him, unwilling to give him too much patience. He should know by now they were beyond what happened when she'd taken him at that door and definitely he should know he should follow where she led.

Before she could remind him, he sat and she felt her own eyes get lazy, lifting her hands and pulling his shirt over his shoulders just to the tops of his biceps, shoving the sides back so she could see all his chest and his belly, along with his cock and sac.

She leaned in and at his ear, whispered, "Cup your balls, *chevalier*, stroke your cock slowly. Let me see all your beauty."

She stepped back one step, two, and watched his hands move to do as commanded. She hit the end of the bed and lowered herself on it, *her* eyes now hooded, her pussy saturating, taking in Olivier exposed to her *en déshabillé*.

Watching his big hand stroke his long cock, his harnessed balls resting in his cupped hand, she said softly, "You must know how beautiful you are." She lifted her gaze to his. "But you can't possibly know just how *beautiful* you are."

"Amélie." This was a near growl, the thickness giving into rough.

"Squeeze your balls just slightly for me, *chevalier*," she ordered.

He did, and when he did, his head tilted marginally back, giving her more of his throat.

"Yes, Olivier, so beautiful."

She watched for some time until she saw his movements get faster, his stroking turn jerky.

"Slow, my beast," she whispered.

He didn't want to do as told, she could tell. His excitement was palpable. He liked touching himself, as he would. He liked more that she liked watching.

Even not wanting to do it, he did it.

So very good.

Rising from the bed, keeping her eyes on him, she moved to the chest where her things were placed for her use.

She came back with a bottle of oil, coming to a stop in front of him.

"Hold your cock tipped up for me."

"Mistress—"

She had no idea if he wished to say something or dissent.

It didn't matter.

"Do it, Olivier," she commanded.

He did as she asked.

"Now hold it gripped just under the tip," she ordered.

He stroked up, holding the head upward.

She opened the bottle of oil and in practiced, slow drops, she dropped it on the head of his cock.

"Fucking hell," he whispered.

"Don't stroke," she demanded.

One drop. Two. Four. Eight.

"Killin' me," he muttered.

She suppressed a smile.

She eventually stopped torturing her beast with the drops and looked in his eyes. "Now, stroke, Olivier," she ordered and he immediately complied. She bent close to him. "You'll be stroking for me a good deal tonight, *chevalier,* I'd like it to be in comfort."

There was dark in his eyes and his tone when he asked, "Please, Amélie, kiss me."

"Perhaps later," she replied.

"Fuck," he muttered.

"Stroke, my steed," she said as she leaned back. "But uncup your balls. Shift so your arm is hooked around the back of the chair. Both of them, actually, but careful not to lose hold of your cock. I need you arched for me."

That got her more dark and another hesitation, though less this time, as he moved to do as she wished.

The new pose left him pants at his thighs, cock rigid, balls harnessed, chest displayed beautifully with his back arched, the frame of it all with his blue shirt—extraordinary.

Before she let the sight of him overwhelm her so she lifted up her skirt and climbed that lap, she went to the candle.

His eyes followed and there was a bite to his, "Mistress Amélie."

She drew out the taper and came back to him.

His head was up, his body tense, his hand around his cock gripping it at the base not moving.

"Did I tell you you couldn't stroke?"

He was staring at the flickering candle.

"Relax into position, beast, and stroke your cock for your Mistress."

His gaze cut to hers. "Baby—"

She bent over him, getting close quickly, and the snarl curled his mouth.

"I love it when you call me baby, Olivier. I feel it right in my pussy. Sometimes it floats up inside me sweet, sometimes it thrusts in like it was your big brute of a cock. This is why I allow you to use that word when I play with you, but right now, you use it and do as you're told."

He stared into her eyes.

"Now, Olivier."

"When I drive inside you, Amélie, fill you up to your throat with my dick and pound my mark in you, you'll feel *that* every time I call you baby."

She felt a tremor go up and down the insides of her thighs at this shift in the game.

A shift back to the beginning.

The dare. The taunt. The defiance.

He was uncomfortable with what she was doing but that discomfort came from the fact he liked it and was fighting giving in.

And the night got better.

"Is that a promise, Olivier?"

"Yeah, it fuckin' is, *baby.*"

"Stroke yourself," she ordered. "And relax."

They battled, eye to eye, will against will.

"Do it," she whispered, "or you're over my knees, getting a spanking."

She knew by the flash of fury in his eyes that would never happen and marked it as somewhere to go only proceeding cautiously.

Not that she could take him there if he didn't allow her to, physically.

But it got him stroking and he semi-relaxed into position.

"Thank you, Olivier," she said softly.

He said nothing, lips tight.

She bent to him and touched those lips with hers.

He didn't open.

Yes, defiant.

She slid her lips to his ear and worked him there, at his neck, down to his collarbone, down to his nipple, where she nibbled, holding the dripping candle in her hand extended from their bodies, the wax sliding down, giving a slight burn to her fingers.

The same except direct from the flame she'd use on him.

She moved to his other nipple and when they were both tight nubs, she brought in the candle.

"Fuck," he grunted.

She tipped the flame and watched, wetting her lips, feeling the slick of her pussy coat her thighs, as Olivier took his wax, his chest tightening, his hips shifting, his hand stroking. The wax would drip, drip, drip, she'd shift it, mold it, squeeze his nipple under it, peel it off, and give him more.

"Amélie—" The gruff was there.

She moved to the other nipple. "Shh, stay still as you can and stroke."

"I need to stroke faster, baby."

She lifted her eyes from the flame to his.

Need.

She'd taken him there.

"Then stroke faster, darling."

He stroked faster.

She worked his other nipple until she saw his jaw tighten.

"Mistress . . . Amélie . . . gorgeous, need you," he grunted.

She lifted the candle away, peeled off the wax, and moved to the holder. Sliding the taper back in, she stood in front of him. His cock now distended, his balls high and tight, his eyes wild.

"What do you need, *chevalier?*"

"Climb on, Amélie, need your pussy."

"Not this?" she asked.

Putting her hands behind her to draw down the short zipper at the low vee in the back, she shrugged the heavy beaded dress off her shoulders and let it fall to her ankles, exposing her entirely naked underneath.

He tensed and lurched like he was going to burst from his seat as he bit off, "Christ," his eyes roaming everywhere.

The beast was nearly unleashed.

"Keep your seat and keep stroking yourself," she ordered as she moved slowly closer. "Do not touch me until I offer myself to you."

He lifted the dark need in his eyes to hers. "You're beautiful, Leigh-Leigh. Fucking amazing."

Fuck, she loved that.

Fuck, *fuck*, she loved that he gave that to her.

She lifted her right hand to her right breast, circling her nipple with her thumb.

"You want my pussy?" she asked.

"Take anything you wanna give me," he answered, his eyes watching her thumb.

She moved. Putting the sole of her sandal to the rung between his legs, she lifted up. Fingers curling around his exposed shoulder, she steadied herself and just barely moved forward toward his mouth with her nipple when he moved in and seized it.

"Yes," she breathed, her head going back as he sucked it deep, the tip of his tongue swirling. "More, Olivier."

He sucked harder, gave her more, but suddenly let her go and begged, "Baby, closer, sit on my cock. Arch your back. I'll take your tits and your pussy."

Carefully, beating back her body shaking, Amélie shifted position and hands. Lifting her left breast, she guided it to him.

His rebellious eyes were on her. "Mistress, want that, fuck, want it, but need your fuckin' cunt."

"What my beast needs is to learn to accept what he's offered or he might lose it."

He pierced her with a look of fury before he dropped his eyes, turned his head, and if he'd seized her right nipple, he marauded the left one. Sucking so deep and flicking it with his tongue, she had no choice but to arch her back, allow him to pull it deeper.

Unable to control her breath anymore, she panted softly, whispering, "God, yes, Olivier."

Proving precisely why he was so good with his mouth between her legs, when she thought he couldn't give her more, he did.

"*God*, darling," she breathed.

She was going to come, knew it, and pulled away, stepping on shaking legs away from him.

She stared into his face.

He was there.

"Pull off your shirt," she ordered.

Damn, her voice was shaking.

She backed up toward the bed.

Olivier ripped off his shirt, his eyes to her feet, watching.

"Stand and take off your pants."

If she were to blink in that moment, she wouldn't have been able to before his pants were gone.

Her calves hit the bed.

"Does my beast want me?" she asked.

He didn't answer and he did, his growl surging through the air, and she didn't know if his "baby" would do it after he fucked her, but that growl thrust deep inside her.

"Then take me," she whispered.

Before she knew it, she had his arm around her waist and she was up, being dragged into the bed. Then she was down, her legs spread, knees jerked up, her eyes just focused on his before he drilled her.

Her head shot back and his mighty thrust forced a soft "Hah" from her throat.

He didn't relent and she was glad he didn't. God, so big, after their play, she was so fucking ready to be filled full of him, she took his fucking, grasping him with her pussy, reaching blindly and taking every inch of skin she could touch, feeling his dick to her throat and wanting more.

She got more.

He pulled out abruptly, flipped her to her stomach, and yanked up her hips.

When Olivier was driving back in, Amélie moaned into red satin.

"Fuck me, Olly," she panted. "That's it, baby."

Her words set him loose, his thrusts unchecked, God, so damned deep, his grunts scoring the air in a way it drove into her skin, the noises made by the pounding of his flesh into hers making her body start to tremble all over.

He felt it and pulled out again, flipping her again to her back, giving her most of his weight, one arm around her waist, driving her down, one hand curled around the back of her neck, holding her steady for his pummeling.

His eyes locked to hers, dark as night.

"Eyes are sweet. Mouth is sweet. Pussy so fucking sweet. Tastes sweet," he rammed in and the bed shook, "feels *fuckin'* sweet."

"Olivier."

"You're takin' all of me."

"Olivier."

"Mark you deep, Leigh. Gonna mark you deep."

"*Olly,*" she gasped, her head driving back into the satin. Scraping her nails deep up his spine, she felt him arch into her at the pain, his grunt tear through her as she came. Her world exploding so forcefully, fear she'd never felt coursed through her veins and she grasped on to the only thing that could keep her safe.

Lifting her head and shoving it in Olivier's neck, she wrapped her arms and legs around him, held tight and whimpered into his ear as it ravaged her.

"That's it, Leigh, hold on, baby," he grunted, still taking her hard.

"Give it all to me, Olly," she gasped. "Now, darling."

"You got it, Leigh," he grunted again then groaned, driving her into the bed as he shoved the top of his head into it, his hand at her neck sliding up into her hair to hold her face in his neck. He pounded into her, shuddering as she felt his release.

They came down, both trembling, and she felt his hand relax at her head but hold her there as he turned his and nibbled her neck.

She sighed, melting beneath him.

He moved his lips to her ear.

"You good?" he asked.

"Yes," she answered.

"You took me—"

"I'm fine, darling."

He lifted his head and looked down at her, remorse heavy in his features.

"Normally, I start gentle. My size, I got to. But you took all of me, Leigh-Leigh, fast and hard, baby."

"I wanted all of you, Olly." She slid a hand down, around, and up to stroke his jaw. "I knew what I was doing." She gave him a grin that was weak because she didn't have the strength to give more. "With the pussy wrap the other night, slamming me to the floor to eat me, you made it pretty clear what happens when I push you too far."

"The pussy wrap," he muttered, lips quirking, relief sifting through his features before the amusement set in, eyes to her mouth.

She cupped his jaw and his gaze came to hers.

"Kiss me, Olly."

She was surprised and moved when the dark need filled his face, shrouding them in that warm shadow, before he slanted his head and took her mouth.

They kissed, deep and wet and hungry, like they both just hadn't come magnificently.

It was the best kiss of her life, lying under, holding close, and connected intimately with a man whose last name she didn't know.

He nipped her lip before he ended the kiss, lifting his head, but not very far.

"Blind down, you do that to keep us in or keep him out?"

The answer meant a lot to him, she could see.

But the way he phrased it was interesting.

Not keep *them* out, but keep *him* out.

Stellan.

"Actually, until he approached me tonight, I hadn't thought of him." She lifted her head and touched the tip of her nose to his. "And after he left my booth tonight, I didn't think of him." She dropped her head back down and managed to give him a bigger grin. "Though, now that you mention it, two birds . . ." She trailed off and watched, heard and felt his soft chuckle.

Yes, he was terrifying because she was beginning to understand that, in having him, *really* having him, she wouldn't be gaining something.

He'd be her everything.

"You go with your flow, Mistress," he said playfully but his eyes were serious when he finished, "But pleased as fuck what we had tonight was just for you and me."

She knew that. That was why she gave it to him.

But she loved it that he could express it.

She lifted up again but this time to take his mouth.

She didn't need to take it. He gave it to her.

When she ended it, he went back to nuzzling her neck, up to her ear where he noted, "My dick buried inside you, you called me *baby*."

She allowed her hands to drift over his back, belatedly seeing their beauty (well, mostly his beauty, as she could barely be seen), connected and framed in red in the mirror in the ceiling, unsure how to reply.

"Felt you come hard for me, Leigh-Leigh, buried deep, so any time you use the word *baby* on me, could be pissed as shit at you, on another continent, and just hear you giving it over the phone, I'll feel it in my dick."

She shouldn't give more. She knew she shouldn't. It said too much too soon.

She gave it anyway, like she, Mistress Amélie, had absolutely no control.

"I've never called anyone 'baby' in my life."

She felt him still completely over her, all around her, before he slid his lips again down to her neck, where he muttered, "So totally gonna feel that in my dick."

She smiled at her reflection in the mirror.

"After you . . . after our break . . ." she began and he lifted up to look down at her. "I'd like to see you Tuesday."

His head tilted to the side. "Got something on Monday night?"

"No."

"You're dissin' our reunion for football," he guessed inaccurately, and teasingly.

"I'll amend," she said, again fucking *grinning*. "After our break, I'd like to see you Monday."

He dipped close, lips to her lips. "Right then, Amélie. I'll be here Monday."

She saw his eyes were smiling.

He liked that.

He liked what she gave him.

He liked what they had.

He liked her.

And she liked him.

Fates, keep me safe, she whispered in her mind as she slid out her tongue and touched his lower lip.

Olivier sucked it into his mouth.

She let him kiss her and she kissed him back.

And Amélie could only hope the fates listened.

twelve

Lipsticked Lips

OLIVIER

Olivier could only hack it until Monday morning.

Since starting it with Amélie, he'd used most of his markers to change shifts with the guys so he didn't work nights or midnights.

In order to keep that going, rebuild his markers, he was giving them, taking a week of midnights.

Now, having her completely Friday night, all they'd shared before and after she took him to that red room, Amélie giving that room to him, just them, no one else, he felt her almost constantly digging deeper under his skin.

All day. All night.

Even in his dreams.

And clearly with no willpower and losing the fight to find it, he didn't stop it.

So that morning after shift, Olly lay naked in his bed, the blinds closed against the Phoenix sun, the curtains drawn, needing sleep.

But needing his Leigh-Leigh and his Mistress more.

So he called her.

"Olly," she answered. "Is everything all right?"

He gave her what he needed to give her to tell her what he needed to get.

"Mistress."

There was a hesitation before he knew she got him when she ordered, "Cup your balls, *chevalier.*"

His cock, already hard, got harder as he moved to do what she said.

"Have you done that?" she asked.

"Yes, Mistress," he answered.

"Good, Olivier. Now, put the phone on speaker and place it where I can hear you and you can hear me but it won't be distracting."

He had her voice coming at him, his cock hard, his hand cupping his balls because she told him to do that, he could balance that phone on his dick and it wouldn't be distracting.

But he did as told, increasing the volume and pushing the phone into the pillow by his head so it'd stay put.

"Do I have you, *mon chou?*" she called.

"You got me, Amélie."

And she did.

Christ, she *so* did.

"Good, now how much time do we have?"

He closed his eyes, a sweet agony.

Because there it was. Amélie looking out for him in all the ways she could.

She probably thought he had a day job, and that early in the morning, but still not *that* early, she'd think he had to get ready to get to some office.

He didn't. But he did have to get good sleep, get up, get fueled, work out, shower, do life shit, like laundry, and get back to the firehouse.

A lot of the guys on midnights slept in the bunkbeds at the house. Since Olly was acting lieutenant on the nightshift, he felt it necessary to stay alert so he didn't do that.

So they didn't have a lot of time.

"Not much," he told her.

"Okay, Olivier," she said softly. "Let's begin then. At the same time, slide your middle finger in your mouth and give your balls a squeeze."

He did what she asked, fighting the urge after he'd given them a squeeze to take his hand from his balls to jack his dick.

"Extract your finger from your mouth, please," she ordered.

He did. "It's out, Mistress."

"Lovely, Olivier," she purred. "Lift your knees, legs wide, feet in the bed. Tell me when that's done."

He did it and grunted, "Done."

"Excellent, now please grip your cock at the base but don't stroke."

"Done," he said, his voice rougher.

"Are you hard for me?" she asked.

"Very," he answered.

"Oh, Olivier, how much I wish I could see." She said it and she meant it, he could hear it and it made him even harder. "Are you prepared for me?"

"Yeah," he bit out, and he was. He needed to stroke.

"You're harnessed?"

Shit, he hadn't thought of that.

"No," he admitted.

"Mm," she said before she made a tsking noise and murmured, "There'll be punishment for that when I have you again."

Fuck.

Yes.

"Now, let's focus. Wet your middle finger again, Olivier."

He did.

She must have known it because, as he was sliding it out of his mouth, she ordered, "Please, seat that finger up your ass and then stroke your cock for me."

Fuck. He'd never done that to himself.

"Amélie."

"Do it or your punishment might not end in a reward."

He wondered what that meant and doubted she could pull it off. Anything she gave him was a reward.

"Fuck," he muttered it verbally this time.

Then he took his time, reaching between his legs, and he gave himself his finger as he started to jack his dick.

Nice.

"Fuck," he puffed out.

"Are you as I want you?" she asked something she knew the answer to.

"Yeah, Mistress."

"Stroke harder, Olivier."

He did.

"And fuck your ass with your finger."

"Christ," he ground out and he did that too.

Brilliant.

A growl surged up his throat.

"To be taking your ass myself, listening to your pleasure right there with you, I want that right now, *chevalier*," she whispered.

"Me too, baby," he grunted, jacking his dick harder as he fucked his own ass.

"When I have you again, after your punishment, I'm going to show you off."

His fist pumped faster and the noises he was making escaped as they did, and for once, Olly didn't try to stop them.

Without her there, he wanted her to hear.

"Take you to the social room," she shared. "Parade my beast. Bask in their envy that that magnificent body of yours is mine, that brute of a cock is mine, those beautiful balls are mine, that ass is mine."

God, he wanted that.

How could he want that?

He just did, and him starting to raise his hips, fuck his own fist, his finger up his ass, made that undeniable.

Which meant Olly could no longer deny that he liked that she liked to show him off. He liked she was proud of him. He'd been beginning to understand as he saw that Stellan asshole watching her work him why he'd feel the sneer of conceit spread on his lips, watched the corresponding sneer of pure jealousy spread on that asshole's mouth, knowing that guy might say he was a Master, but he wanted to be right where Amélie had Olivier, taking anything she wanted to give.

Fuck, Olly even got off on seeing what became only shadows beyond that glass when Amélie was opening his world, arrogant, even smug that she'd chosen him and he was hers as she was his.

Olly loved she'd claimed him and was so deep in that he got off on the fact she wanted to rub the others' noses in what she gave him.

And what he gave her.

"Amélie," he bit out.

"Oil you before we go. Prepare you. Bend you over a table, your legs spread, your ass on display. My ass. They can look, they can't touch."

"Plug me," he grunted.

"If you wish, my Olivier," she sounded pleased, hot and pleased.

"Only yours," he told her.

"Only mine as I'm only yours, darling."

"Fuck," he grunted.

"Bent over a table in social, would you ride the handle of my crop in your ass, performing for me?" she asked, her voice hotter, breathier, the purr hitting extremes so it was almost like he could feel it on his skin.

"Do anything you want, Amélie," he groaned.

"Then right now, my stallion, offer me your seed."

He came on demand, driving his finger up his ass and shooting up his stomach and ribs, grunting her name through it.

His orgasm not close to what she could give him, but it far from sucked, he was so deep in it he almost didn't hear her command of, "Milk yourself dry for your Mistress."

But he did hear her and did as told, muttering, "You got it."

"Slide your finger out, Olivier, and stroke your cock gently."

He did that too.

Like she was attuned to him completely from whatever distance they had, after a while she whispered, "You can stop stroking at your leisure, Olly."

And that was it. They were out of their scene and back to Olly and Leigh.

"Are you okay, darling?" she asked.

"Oh yeah, Leigh-Leigh."

"Good." It was still a whisper but he could hear she was pleased.

"You come, baby?" he asked, wishing he'd heard if she did, though wondering if he would since she looked great coming but she didn't make a lot of noise.

"Mm, next time." She was back to purring.

"Right," he said through a grin. "And when do you want this next time to be?"

"Tomorrow morning, at this time, Olly, if you're free."

He would be.

"I'm free," he confirmed.

"Prepare for me, Olly. Harness and a towel on the bed."

Fucking hell.

He had a feeling, with a heads-up, she was going to give him even better.

"And, your decision, but if you text me your address, I can have some things delivered that will make times such as these between us much more interesting."

When he didn't answer that immediately, she continued, her voice softer, reassuring.

"It will come direct from me, courier delivery. No way to know what's inside. And I'll do nothing but use your address for the delivery. Your space is yours and I'll only occupy it on your invitation, darling."

Yes, she took care of him.

"Then send what you want to me."

"It'll be there this evening."

The amusement he felt was in his voice when he replied, "Awesome, Leigh."

"I'll let you go, but before I do that, I just want you to know that I'm pleased you phoned."

"You not comin' means I'm more pleased."

The amusement was now in her voice, as well as something richer, warmer . . . happy, when she said, "Good."

Shit, him, her, the both of them were getting in deep.

He just couldn't stop it.

And what they had was so good, in a playroom, a booth with a drink or on the phone, Olly was also beginning to wonder why he was allowing it to fuck with his head to even try to stop it.

"Gotta go, sweetheart," he returned, knowing he should hide the regret in his voice and not stopping that either.

"Okay, Olly. Until tomorrow, *mon chou.*"

"Yeah, Leigh. Later."

"Good-bye, darling."

He hung up, laid in bed on his back with his cum on his stomach, the feel of his finger up his ass, his cock sensitive and still semi-hard, and he waited for it.

The uncertainty.

The shame.

But it didn't come, mostly because all Olly could do was wonder what she'd send, wanting to hear her come for him too. He'd been up all night, was right then seriously relaxed, so he needed to shut his eyes and sleep.

To that end, he swung his carcass out of the bed, went to the bathroom, cleaned off his cum, and climbed back into bed naked, throwing the covers over him.

Nothing, not that barest inkling fucked with his head as he fell right to sleep.

Olly got the delivery before he went to work.

He opened it like a fucking kid at Christmas and felt his dick jump at what he saw inside.

A small plug, some lube, a remote control, a cock harness with attached ring, and a Bluetooth earpiece to allow him to be hands-free and have her sweet voice right in his ear.

He opened the thick stock, classy-ass, light beige notecard that had an elegant but contemporary embossed AMÉLIE HÉLÈNE STRAND on the flap at the back.

And there it was.

She gave him more.

He had her full name.

Damn, that felt good.

The good he felt knowing her name got better when a chuckle burst from him to see she'd sealed the note with a kiss from lip-sticked lips.

Cute.

Leigh-Leigh.

He opened the note and read:

Olivier,
Our time tomorrow, on your knees in bed, Bluetooth in position, towel before you.
Entirely harnessed.
Full, please.
Yours as you are mine,
~Amélie

Shit.

Yeah.

In deep.

Yours as you are mine.

And suddenly, with a feeling he didn't know if he'd ever felt in his life, he couldn't wait for the morning.

Exactly as required, balls and cock harnessed, Bluetooth earpiece at his ear, plug up his ass, on his knees with the towel spread out before him, he made his call the next morning.

"Olly," she answered.

"Like my presents, baby," he whispered.

"Then please, my *chevalier*, turn on your plug then put your hands behind your head. First setting only, please."

He grabbed the remote, did as told, and she guided him through it. Doing it swiftly because she undoubtedly thought their time was limited.

And he listened to her get hotter and hotter in his ear as she told him shit she wanted to do to him, shit he wanted, and she jacked his ass as what she was giving him made him automatically and desperately fuck the air in his harness that was tightening as his cock swelled inside it almost like she had her fingers wrapped around it.

"My stallion needs a tail," she whispered when he was holding on by a thread, ready to blow. "Long, so when I have you in his position, your tail seated deep, and I'm pulling your seed from your cock personally, your tail will spread out behind your ass that's full for me like the beauty all of you is to me."

Without her command, at her words, his groan came deep and surprised as his body arched way back, shoving the plug deeper, and he shot his load across the towel on the bed.

He was still shooting when he heard the soft noises she made when she came.

At her noises, he kept shooting, jacking the remote to top speed before she told him he could, pumping his cock through the air, grunting through a prolonged orgasm (almost) the likes of what Amélie could give.

Though she was still giving it, she just wasn't there.

When he was coming down, he shifted the plug to low and whispered, "Sorry, Mistress."

"Can I take it from that you'd like a new toy?"

A tail up his ass? Fully her pony?

"Amélie."

He said no more because he didn't know what to say.

How that was her asking more from him than she already had, he had no idea.

But it was.

And the shit of it was, he'd come the minute she suggested it.

"Many things, Olly," she started softly, taking him to the place she could sense he needed to be, and he turned the vibrations of the plug completely off, "even with what we have, what we give to each other, can remain a fantasy. You can like it in your mind, as can I, we can use it in times like these, but you can share you don't want it in reality."

"Am I at ease?" he asked. She'd called him Olly, but he wanted to be sure.

"Of course," she answered gently.

Carefully, he dropped to a hip away from the towels, and then to his back, cocking his knees to accommodate the plug still seated inside.

And then he went where he wasn't sure he should go, over his head once more, not knowing if he should ask this of a Mistress and also not knowing if he should ask it at this juncture with Leigh.

But he asked it.

"You ever have a pony, baby?"

She didn't reply immediately and he felt his gut get tight.

"Not mine to have," he stated quickly, his voice as tight as his gut. "Forget I asked that, Leigh."

"I think we both can agree we're at a place where this is yours to have, Olly. And no. I've never had a pony. Not like what you mean. I've often looked at tails to enter that into play but . . ." She hesitated before she went on, "Oddly, I think you understood even before me why I didn't buy them."

"And why's that, Leigh-Leigh?" he prompted when she didn't share.

He knew the answer but he needed to hear it.

"When I found him, to earn that honor, he needed to be magnificent."

His gut relaxed and at the same time warmed.

"I'd like to give you a tail, Olly. Only if you think you'd like it."

"You give me what you want, baby."

"Do you think you'll like it?" she asked, and fuck him, he could hear uncertainty from his Amélie.

It was cute.

It was looking out for him.

Even when she had it all together, when it came to him, it was still so fucking *her*.

"I think you can make me like almost anything."

The uncertainty was still there when she murmured, "That wasn't a wholehearted affirmative."

"Leigh, you want to give the honor of tailing me, no doubt you'll make it rock my world. So I love it that you'd discuss this with me instead of springing it on me but you take care of me, if you're right there or you're over a phone. I trust you, sweetheart. So give that to me and doing it, let me give you something."

She sounded surprised, and unnerved, when she returned, "You give me something, many somethings, many somethings that mean the world to me, and you do it constantly, Olly."

"You get me," he said low and firm.

"Ol—"

Okay. Maybe she didn't.

"You know you give me more, Amélie. You know I'm only me with you."

Fuck, was he giving her all this?

Fuck.

He was.

And he kept doing it.

"Only time, even with the others before you, I was able to just be me."

"I'm . . . I honestly don't know what to say, *mon amour*. With this, it's me who's honored."

"Good, 'cause it's an honor." That was again low and firm. "One you earned and I'm glad you did."

She made a noise he'd never heard, like a feminine growl he felt in his balls, and when she spoke, he felt it somewhere else completely.

"I'm finding this immensely frustrating because I'd very much like to kiss you right now, darling."

He started chuckling, doing it to fight the sensation that seemed to be wrapping his chest, and through it said, "Good, 'cause I'd like that, too, very much."

There was a smile as well as a sweet hotness to her purr of, "Hmm."

He stopped chuckling and was grinning at the ceiling when she went on, no smile, her tone still sweet but serious.

"We'll enjoy ourselves together next week, Olly. But while we'll play at my ranch, I'd also like to ask you to think about us taking the time to have . . . a chat."

Oh, they needed to have a chat.

The thing was, Olly didn't know if he was looking forward to it or dreading it.

But he needed to give it to her. He needed for both of them to get out where they were so they could figure out where they were going.

And he needed that so he could sort it in his head and be sure to protect her in their future.

He didn't know if they had one. He knew that he didn't want this to end. Just thinking of it sent a stabbing pain in his side like someone sunk a blade in his ribs.

He also knew it'd be hard work, undoubtedly painful work, and perhaps too much to ask from both of them to get there because, when she found out who he was, what he did, there were ways he wouldn't fit in her world outside the club that she would feel.

Though, he figured he'd feel them more.

It was going to be Olly who'd need to make all the compromises, compromises that to a man like him would be sacrifices.

So they needed to go over that and make that decision.

But before that, before they went there, he needed to weigh what she gave him along with all the other. Not the orgasms but her cute and her sweet and her taking care of a friend or worried about another sub or asking him how much time he had so she could take care of him without making life difficult for him. And he had to weigh that against what their future could be and how he knew down to his bones he didn't fit in hers at the same time he wasn't sure how she'd fit in his.

Not Mistress Amélie and Olivier. That worked fucking great. He felt it. He knew it. She took him there and he was settling into it. And touching that kind of freedom, learning to let that go in his mind, finally, after having it fuck with his head for so long he barely remembered a time it wasn't doing that, he'd owe her huge.

No, it was everything else.

So during this chat, it might mean the end. And he fucking hated that.

But if that's what it led to, he needed to give that to Amélie because she was digging under his skin and doing it deep.

However, he had a feeling he was already under hers.

She was right, they needed more time together before their chat so they could come to terms with what that chat would bring.

Because it also might not mean the end. Olly just needed to lay it out for her so she'd know who he was and where he stood and they could both have the information they needed to find their way in whatever the future was going to bring.

"Yeah, we'll have a chat," he agreed, unable to keep the unease out of his voice. "Definitely."

"I must let you go, darling," she said quietly.

"Yeah," he lied.

He could talk for an hour, two, four, and he was feeling that lie. Feeling that she didn't know what he did, how he was at the Honey under scholarship or that he'd come to that club green.

She didn't even know his last name.

And in feeling all that, Olly was finding it was time to share all of it too.

Fuck.

"Would you like more tomorrow morning?" she asked.

That was it. That was his focus.

He had her.

For now.

And he'd take all she could dish out while he did and give her all he could in return.

"Yeah, gorgeous."

"Okay, Olly, but only tomorrow. No more after. Not anything, sweetheart. I want you prepared for when I have you next."

Yeah, he'd take all she could dish out while he had her.

"Fabulous," he muttered, both not looking forward to that at the same time knowing the payoff would be huge, leaving his cock be so she could take care of it when she had it again.

There was a smile in her voice when she said, "Tomorrow, my Olly."

"Tomorrow, Leigh-Leigh."

My Olly.

Fuck.

Yes. Goddamned yes.

He was under her skin.

And in thinking that, he remembered something Jenna had told him, giving the knowledge to him not hiding that she wanted to get what she was explaining *from* him.

This being that a good sub *subbed*. Gave up everything, gave over everything, trusted implicitly. And when they got what they got in return for that, they shared in every way they could that they liked what they were getting, how good it felt, but most, how much it meant. And doing all that, he or she controlled their Dom, owned their Dom, for that Dom would live to push those boundaries so they could give their sub everything.

Olly had a feeling he was there with Amélie.

And he liked knowing he was there, a lot, maybe too much.

He just needed to get the shit sorted in his head if that was actually too much.

Or if it wasn't.

If too much wasn't too much.

If instead it was everything he needed to be free.

Of a lot of things.

AMÉLIE

Thursday morning, at precisely the time Olly had been calling so she could play with him over the phone, Amélie paced the hotel room, her phone in her hand.

She had to catch a taxi in one hour to go to a business meeting. She'd decided, if Olly was unavailable, it was the perfect time to get these nuisance meetings out of the way.

Definitely a much better time than having to leave town when Olly wasn't unavailable due to work commitments, instead she was, meaning more times of separation.

That wouldn't do.

She was ignoring what that said about how deep she was with Olly and instead obsessing about calling Olly.

He'd phoned her once just to talk.

The other times he'd phoned and made it clear he wished to play.

He'd also sounded strange when she said she wanted them to have a chat at her ranch. It was a strange she didn't like. It seemed wary, hesitant, and Olly was neither of those, not while he was communicating.

That could mean anything.

But Amélie's overactive mind was centering on only the possible meanings that were dire.

They'd had their last phone date yesterday morning. It had been fulfilling for them both. She'd then ordered him to prepare for their reunion by abstaining.

She was not expecting him to call.

That didn't mean she didn't want him to call.

However, the minutes were ticking by, she'd soon have to leave, and she wanted to talk to him. Hear his voice. It had been twenty-four hours (and fourteen minutes).

That was fourteen minutes too long (it was actually about twenty-three hours and fourteen minutes too long but she wasn't admitting that).

"Blast," she whispered, stopping her pacing and dropping her head to look at her phone.

She touched the screen, found his listing in her contacts and felt an instant, irrationally intense desire to have a picture of him in the little circle by his name.

"Now I'm acting like a besotted teenager," she muttered to herself.

This did not make her stop her finger from touching the button to make the call.

She put the phone to her ear, listened to it ring, and again began pacing.

She halted abruptly when Olly's voice came through, sounding deeper and husky, oddly like he'd still been asleep when he should be up by then, preparing for his day.

And her belly clenched when he answered with, "My Mistress feels like bein' sweet."

She stood staring unseeing at the shiny toes of her nude Louboutin pumps, completely at a loss of what to say.

He thought she'd phoned to play.

He wanted her to be phoning to play.

Did that mean he didn't want her phoning just to connect, *not* through play?

"Leigh?" he called, sounding more alert, more himself.

Her head snapped up. "Olly . . . um, Olivier, yes . . ."

She wasn't prepared to offer him what he clearly wanted.

It was highly likely she could be in the mood for Olly at a moment's notice.

But there was something dragging at that mood as worries

assailed her that he didn't want to hear from her unless she intended to, as he put it, "jack his shit."

When he'd phoned just to talk, he was worried about how she'd been when discussing her parents.

Perhaps, as it could for any human being with a modicum of sensitivity (and Olly had more than a modicum), this worry overrode his boundaries. But just for that.

Only for that.

"Leigh-Leigh," he said softly. "You okay?"

"I . . . uh . . . I . . ."

God, she was stammering.

Spit something out, Leigh! her mind shouted.

"If you . . . if you're in the mood—" she began.

"Leigh, talk to me," he ordered. Now fully alert, his voice had taken a tone she'd never heard from him. Demanding. Authoritative. Inflexible. "Is everything okay?"

Entirely contradictory to her sexual nature, she felt a pleasant shiver skid over her skin at his tone.

Entirely consistent with the female she was, the man in her life exhibiting a fierce protectiveness at the hint something might be amiss with her, she felt that shiver gather, giving her a warm, sweet feeling in her throat.

Like she'd just swallowed a healthy dose of fine whisky.

"I'm out of town," Amélie blurted.

"Fuck," he bit out then spoke again swiftly, concern coating every word, "What is it, sweetheart? Something happen to a friend? Someone in your family?"

She closed her eyes.

There was her sweet beast.

She took in a deep breath, feeling the release of the tension that was beginning to make her feel sick to her stomach.

God, she should have been far more sensitive when Mirabelle was going through this as her relationship bloomed with Trey.

The breath she took was a breath she needed to take but she

knew she took too long to take it when Olly demanded, "Leigh, baby, tell me what the fuck is going on."

"I just wanted to let you know I was out of town. For business. There's nothing wrong. I was just calling to, well . . . let you know," she finished insipidly.

She closed her eyes tight.

His words sounded in her head.

Leigh, talk to me.

She shook her head sharply.

What is it, sweetheart? Something happen to a friend? Someone in your family?

Damn.

Everything from him meant everything.

Was she falling in love with a man whose last name she didn't even know?

That staggering thought barely came before she realized he hadn't said anything.

It was her turn to call his name.

"Olly?"

"Here, Leigh-Leigh," he said quietly.

"I just . . ." *Speak, Leigh!* "I'm in San Francisco. There were some meetings I was putting off. I thought with you tied up with work, now would be a good time to see to that. I'll be back for our date at the club on Monday."

"When'd you leave?" he asked.

"Yesterday afternoon," she answered.

"Was this sudden?"

She shook her head even if he couldn't see her. "I decided to go on Monday and started making the plans then."

"And you couldn't tell me when we talked on Monday?"

Her eyes slid out the windows, where she had a lovely view the Golden Gate Bridge, doing this while she reminded him, "We were doing other things when we spoke Monday."

"And then we got done doin' other things and we were just talkin'," he returned.

"Well, yes," she confirmed, confused because he sounded like he was becoming irate.

Irate was not a good thing with Olly.

"And now you're out of town," he remarked flatly.

"And another yes," she stated cautiously.

There was a long pause before he started, "Babe, you know—"

But he cut himself off and said no more.

"I know what?" she prompted.

"Right, not really my business but we went there last time we were together, as in *there*, me inside you, ungloved, so it also is. You got another man in your life?"

She felt the strange sensation, like her heart actually slid up into her throat, and again, with a question like that from Olly, she didn't know whether to be delighted or offended.

"Of course not."

"Okay, then—"

But this time, Amélie decided to be offended so she cut *him* off.

"And just to say, Olly, it actually *is* your business as we *are* lovers."

She could swear he sounded like he was choking back laughter when he replied, "Yeah, think I know that, gorgeous."

Amélie found nothing funny.

"Is there another woman in your life?" she snapped, fear gripping her belly yet again, but she hung on to the anger to hold the strength of that fear—strength she knew would be paralyzing if she gave into it—at bay.

"Not sure we totally understood each other, or at least not sure you totally understood *me*, babe," he began, no longer sounding amused at all, "when we had our little chat after the pussy wrap."

She understood what he was saying.

And again she felt the release in her midsection but this time she actually bent slightly with it, it was so extreme.

Olly apparently felt no release.

"I'm fuckin' you, you're fuckin' me, that's exclusive," he declared.

"I definitely agree, Olly," she said, now speaking soothingly because he was again sounding irate.

"Fuck, we should talk about this when we're together," he muttered.

"I agree to that too," Amélie replied. "Though we're talking about it now and for a variety of reasons it's important to know we're both on the same page with that."

"We're both on the same page with that," he declared immediately, but he wasn't quite done. "And I'll just say, what we got, where I'm at, Leigh, is that, you take off on a plane, or you go to your ranch, I wanna know. You don't gotta report in, tell me your every move, share what kind of soup you're buyin' at the grocery store, but you're outta town . . ." He paused then stated, "Anything can happen and I wouldn't know until I walked into the club and that's only if someone else knows and shares it with me. If I know where you are and I don't hear from you . . ."

He let that hang and she moved on her Louboutins to the window in order to lean her shoulder against it, the stunning view lost on her, his words all that were in her head.

Olly wanted to know where she was. He wanted to know this because he wanted to know wherever she was she was safe.

Outside her father, she'd never had that. Not with a single man in her life.

She felt that warm whisky sensation in her throat again.

"I should have told you I had plans to leave town," she admitted softly.

"Yeah, you shoulda told me," he affirmed, his words still slightly curt but she could hear he was letting it go.

A good thing, with Olly's temper.

"That won't actually be happening again once I'm back, not for some time," she informed him, and she hoped she spoke true. Her business, as it was—which was mostly her attending meetings that bored her out of her skull because she wasn't needed in any form except to nod her yes or shake her no—was beginning to feel like it was wearing on her very soul.

"Right," he grunted.

Amélie didn't know whether to smile, burst into tears, or collapse in a bundle of nerves.

So perhaps it was best to let him go so she could turn her mind to other things that might, for brief moments, not be obsessing on all things Olly.

"I have a meeting soon and you'll be needing to get on with what you're doing as well," she noted.

"Yeah," he said like he wasn't too enthusiastic about what he was going to be getting on doing, which again made her wish she knew what he did for a living.

She didn't ask. Her call had been embarrassing, encouraging, heartwarming, promising, and nerve-wracking, a mixture that was more than a little disconcerting.

In the time they had before they met at her ranch, they needed to enjoy themselves and keep it light.

This was *not* light.

"So I should let you go," she continued.

Olly didn't allow her to let him go.

"You called just to talk, didn't you, gorgeous?"

"Well . . . yes," she admitted warily.

"You want me, Leigh-Leigh, you call me. You wanna talk. Something's up. You wanna play. Don't hesitate, okay?"

She drew in another big breath, accepting that gift and trying not to allow herself to admit how precious it seemed, but she let it go a lot quicker than the other to reply, "Okay, Olly."

"When's your meeting?" he asked.

She looked at the thin, gold diamond watch on her wrist before answering, "Three-quarters of an hour I have to catch a taxi."

There was more amusement in his voice when he said, "That's not actually soon, sweetheart."

She smiled but replied, "You have pressing things as well, I'm sure."

"You called to talk, that went south, now I got a little time, not a lot, but I'll give it to you."

Yes.

Her sweet beast.

"That's very kind, darling, but—"

He interrupted her to ask, "You do vanilla?"

The interruption and abrupt change of subject took her off guard.

"I'm sorry?"

"Vanilla, Leigh. You ever fuck vanilla?"

"Well...I..." she started hesitantly, but didn't finish.

"Baby, been through this," he said gently. "Not gonna hunt down all your past boyfriends and erase them from the earth so I can fool myself into thinkin' I'm the only one."

That caused another smile.

"Then, yes, Olly. I do vanilla."

"You like it?"

"If done well, anything is enjoyable," she told him before asking her own question. "Are you saying that you'd like us to have that?"

"Just gettin' to know you, gorgeous."

That kept the smile on her face but he wasn't finished.

"And just you and me for our weekend, I'll say now, we're not doin' our other thing, want that option available to me if it's something you get off on."

She wanted that option too.

She'd had him between her legs in a variety of ways. With this he'd demonstrated beautifully that he had a variety of talents and he was very gifted in using them.

So yes, Amélie wanted that too.

She wanted it very badly.

"That option's available, Olly."

"Good," he murmured.

"So, I take it you also like it," she stated unnecessarily as he'd shared he wanted that option so that meant he did.

She heard the tease in his voice when he replied, "Done well, anything's enjoyable."

"Absolutely," she returned, hearing the humor she felt injected her tone.

"Not enough on its own," he said quietly.

"No," she agreed, feeling their connection snap taut even with the distance. Who he was. What he liked. Who she was. What she liked. How that worked so magnificently for them.

As did other things.

More and more of them.

She felt all that draw them closer, even with their distance.

And she liked it.

"Had women in my life and they never . . ." He stopped speaking but quickly started again. "I never shared."

Oh, her Olly.

But she understood.

She'd had the same.

"It's not easy to do that."

He didn't reply quickly to that and the silence stretched so long she almost called his name.

But eventually he filled it.

"Guys you had, was it the same?"

She wondered if the delay was jealousy, even after saying he wouldn't hunt them down and erase them from the earth, the alpha that was him not wanting to get too deeply into this subject.

But the alpha-sub that was him, not quite one with his nature, would find a reciprocating struggle reassuring.

"Yes, Olly," she told him the truth.

"You, my Leigh-Leigh, not able to be all you are," he said, not like it was a surprise, or a playful tease, but like he felt exactly how distressing those situations could be.

And he'd just told her he did.

"I'll just go on record, darling, officially, to state what you must know already. That even though you struggle, I'm glad you're strong enough to win that struggle. It's quite . . ." she searched madly for the right word that didn't say too much but also didn't say too little, "soothing not to have that in between."

"Well, gorgeous, glad you went on record officially with that, though I won't because I think you already know I agree."

That was a partial playful tease.

What he said next wasn't.

It was quiet but firm.

"But yeah, I totally get you."

"I know you do," she replied softly, then she finally allowed herself to ask something she'd been curious about for a good long while. "How long have you been in our world, Olly?"

"How about we get into that at your ranch, baby," he replied, and before concerns he was prevaricating could rise, he continued, "Face-to-face, no one around, just you and me and we can get into the deep stuff."

That was much better than talking about it over the phone when they were miles away from each other and only had a limited time to talk. Or in the club, even in a private playroom.

So she agreed, "That's a plan."

"Good," he murmured and then carried on, "Though, gonna wanna know how you got your place as the Queen of the Bee's Honey. Not that I don't know exactly how you earned it, just that, sub talk, you're not the leather-catsuit-wearing, whip-wielding, kiss-my-boots Mistress who uses bodies as footstools while she reads a book and still, all the dudes are gagging for it and most of the women too."

"Would you like me to use you as a footstool, Olly?" she asked in a tease, for she knew the answer.

"Fuck no," he replied, giving her the answer she knew and sounding like he was smiling. But there was a solidity to that statement took that option off their play table.

Not that it actually was ever on it.

He was right; she was not that type of Mistress.

"How about we get into that over beer and French 75s at the club?" she suggested.

"You're on."

She would look forward to that.

Then again, she looked forward to everything that involved Olly.

"Okay, Leigh-Leigh," he said quietly, causing more warmth to heat her throat because he sounded very much like he didn't want to say his next. "Now I actually do gotta go."

"All right, sweetheart."

"But just to repeat, glad you called and glad I know you're fuckin' states away, if after the fact, but you'll be back with me on Monday."

She was yet *again* smiling when she replied ridiculously, "I'm glad you're glad."

"Cute," he muttered.

She felt that in her clit.

"Gonna hear from you tomorrow?" he asked.

"Probably not, darling. I'm trying to pack a good deal in so it'll be done."

And when she did, she would no longer have to have her mind numbed by her unwanted activities. She wouldn't even have to think of them.

At least for a while.

"That's cool. So I'll see you Monday."

"Yes, Olly. See you Monday."

"You call, you want to, babe."

"I will. And same with you."

"Workin' this weekend, all weekend, Leigh. So, just so you know, you don't hear from me, that's why."

He didn't want her worried she wasn't on his mind.

Olly.

So very sweet.

"Okay, then Monday, Olly."

"Monday, baby. Lookin' forward to it."

"Yes, me too."

"Right, Leigh. Later, sweetheart."

" 'Bye, darling."

She rung off swiftly so she wouldn't be tempted to wait and listen to him disconnect.

God.

Absolutely a besotted teenager.

Amélie remained standing at the window, running down their conversation, and she couldn't stop herself from staring unseeing at the bay, her lips curved up and doing that deeply.

Okay, so she was acting like a besotted teenager.

But really, except for a little hesitancy, she could find nothing that would give her any reason not to glory in being just that for a change.

Hopeful without the fear.

And just happy in the moment, what she had, what *they* had.

Rolling with it.

Getting everything she could out of it at the same time giving and doing the latter even more, if she could manage it.

What was the harm in that?

Nothing.

Not a thing.

So Amélie was besotted with a beautiful, sweet man called Olly whose last name she didn't know and this thought didn't make her smile fade. No fear clutched her belly. Not that single nerve end frazzled.

Because she actually *was* a thirty-three-year-old woman who was besotted.

And for the first time in her life, she was perfectly fine with that.

thirteen

Took Us Deep

AMÉLIE

Monday evening, after handing over her purse to the front desk staff, Amélie walked into the Honey and looked immediately to her right.

Olivier was standing there, where she'd first seen him, holding up the wall.

She then did not go to a booth. She also did not scan the hunting ground.

She turned on her high-heeled sandal and walked in his direction.

She watched Olivier push from the wall and he moved her way but stopped, awaiting her.

She didn't take her time getting to him.

And when they met, they did not speak or embrace.

They found each other's hands and moved to the door to the playrooms.

Once Olivier opened it and guided them through, as they kept walking, his hand gave hers a squeeze and he muttered a rough, "Barn?"

Her "Yes," was breathless.

He led, practically dragging her, not looking left or right, his sole focus their destination.

Amélie looked left nor right either. She hurried her step, nearly trotting to keep up with his long strides.

They made it to her room and Olivier opened the door. And it was he who flipped the occupied switch as he tugged her through.

He also shut the door, slammed her back to it, and moved in.

He had his hand fisted in her hair, his other hand fisted in the material of her dress at her ass, his mouth brutally crashing down on hers before she could make a peep.

Amélie had no intention of making a peep.

She took his tongue, she took his kiss, and with her fingers, she yanked up her dress.

He let her go with his hands only and she felt him working at his fly.

She pushed down her panties and they barely fell to her ankles before she was up; he surged forward and her head flew back and hit the door when he impaled her on his big cock.

She tipped her head down and rounded his shoulders with her arms as she whispered, her eyes vague but still gazing into the heat of his, "Yes, baby, fuck me."

Olivier did, hard, banging Amélie against the door, audibly and literally, their lips attached but not kissing, his grunts scoring down her throat, her whispered breaths filling his mouth.

"Come," he grunted.

"Olly," she breathed.

"*Come,*" he barked.

He drove deep, pressing her into the door, one hand again fisting in her hair as he held her head stationary and she panted her orgasm into his mouth, her pussy squeezing his cock, whimpers finally releasing.

When Olly got the whimpers, he pulled out and drove in one last time and she felt, heard, and watched him climax deep.

He held her up and kept her full as he came down, using her hair to shove her face in the side of his neck.

Amélie held on and kept that hold tight in every way she could, the climax he'd given her and the one she'd given him very slowly receding.

As she'd shared with Olly, she'd had vanilla sex. It was rare and only with men she'd dated outside this world.

And as they'd discussed, it worked in its way. If done right, it could be enjoyable.

But it was never really fully satisfying.

However, she'd never had a man in any situation take that control, take what she had to give, and give so much in return.

It was another indication that there could be something more with Olly.

No, that there *was* something more with Olly.

One could play Mistress with a toy during every sexual encounter, she had no doubt.

But it was too good by half to know that if this was what it seemed to be building up to be, there would be variety.

And that variety would be delicious.

Slowly, gently, actually *tenderly*, Olly lifted her off his cock and set her on her feet, doing this pressing her into the door, allowing her to take her face out of his neck, and once she did, before she could even make eye contact, he kissed her just as tenderly as he'd disconnected from her.

Yes, to the fates, *please let it be yes* there was something more with Olly.

She melted into him and gave him his kiss, giving herself something even better.

Getting that kiss.

When he lifted his head, his eyes flashed and his lips tipped up in a grin.

"Now you can bring on the Mistress if you want, gorgeous."

Amélie felt her own lips tip up. "You're incorrigible."

"And you fuckin' love it."

God, she did.

She absolutely did.

She allowed herself to revel in that moment just a bit longer, keeping her arms around him, lifting up, brushing her mouth against his and smiling into his eyes.

Then she pulled back half an inch and ordered, "Naked, my Olivier. And bend over the vault facedown, feet to the floor spread wide. There's a matter of your punishment to see to before we can truly begin."

She got another eye flash as his arms convulsed around her.

Then his gaze dropped to her mouth and he murmured, "As you wish, Mistress Amélie."

She had a feeling her eyes flashed too but he let her go and she moved to the side so she could watch him pull his pants (that he'd dropped to his thighs to take her against the door) all the way down. He flipped off his shoes. Then went the rest.

He hung his clothes as she liked him to do.

Then he gave her a look of challenge before he sauntered, casual and beautiful in his nakedness, over to the vault and positioned as told.

She watched him do this, his cum sliding down the side of her thigh, her clit still tingling, her sex bruised from his battering, beside herself he was back. Beside herself *they* were back. Beside herself that she couldn't wait to get to this room, but more, he couldn't either, all but dragging her there and giving her nothing but a kiss before they both lost control and fucked at the door.

As with many things with Olly, she'd never had that. Not in her life.

Only Olly gave it to her.

That was them.

And she stood there, seeing his now only semi-erect cock hanging down between his legs, his balls harnessed for her, positioned, waiting, right there, not over the phone, ready to take so she could give, she realized this was them too.

Indeed, all indications were not saying but almost *screaming* they could have it.

All of it. Here. Out there. Their lives. Their worlds. Not colliding. Not separate.

Tangled exquisitely.

On that marvelous thought, Amélie went to her bag.

She used a towel to clean him from between her legs and then got what she needed.

She approached him from behind, seeing his neck twisted, his eyes to the short paddle in her hand.

"I'll not restrain you, my beast. You'll restrain yourself. Eyes to the vault unless what I give you naturally tears them away. But this time, you do not look at me."

Even after just climaxing, he was ready and she knew it when he gave her the need, his face saturating with it, before he murmured, "Yes, Mistress," and looked to the vault.

When he did, Amélie did not delay.

She paddled his fine, sculpted ass.

She didn't give him much, his transgression didn't deserve it. Though she reddened his ass significantly, and in so doing, felt another, lazier quickening between her legs.

This was reciprocated by a visible quickening between Olivier's legs.

Oh, her sweet beast did take pleasure in his punishments.

So Amélie moved their play to other things they both enjoyed.

Immensely.

They ended up on the floor, with Olivier on his back, Amélie having ridden him to splendid orgasms for them both, and she lay atop him, still filled with him, his arms around her, her face in his neck.

Amélie knew he wanted to see her face when she felt one of his arms move so he could use that hand to draw the hair away from her cheek.

She lifted her head and looked into sated blue eyes.

And she knew, staring deep, she'd move heaven and earth to give Olivier that look as often as she could for as long as she could.

When he had her gaze, he kept his fingers tangled in her hair, holding it back.

"Right, dig all you do to me, Leigh-Leigh, but leaking your wet on my back, feelin' how much you like makin' me dig it, that wasn't inspired. That was beyond inspired, whatever the fuck that is."

Thinking yet again that he'd had untalented Mistresses in his past, she right then thought they also sadly lacked imagination.

But she didn't and she gave him that, he enjoyed it, all this making her grin at him.

He pulled her face close and did not grin.

He was nothing but serious when he demanded, "I want tomorrow night."

He'd missed her.

She knew that with the way their evening began.

But she loved the reminder because she'd missed him too. They hadn't spoken since she called him Thursday morning.

Though, Friday morning when she was at a meeting, at the time they'd been phoning each other all week, he'd texted her with, *You're on my mind, sweetheart.*

She'd texted back, *And you are as well, darling.*

And Saturday, she'd texted, *I'm home safe, Olly. Try not to work too hard this weekend.*

His reply came hours later, likely because he was busy as he said he'd be, but he replied with, *Good to know, baby. See you Monday.*

Even with all that, the break had been too long.

And now it was thankfully over.

"I very much like to please my sweet beast so I'll give you tomorrow night," she granted his request, which was actually a demand.

That was when he grinned at her before the grin faded, something lovely taking its place, and he pulled her down and kissed her.

As was their wont, this moved to making out.

When they were done, he tucked her face back in his neck and they lay on the floor, still connected, but she could feel she was losing his cock.

They didn't move.

"Tomorrow, we'll be going to the social room, Olly."

With his communication before their first scene that he didn't like to be on show (albeit he seemed to have accepted that in a playroom), she expected him to tense. To make a noise. Give some indication this made him uneasy.

He just said, "Whatever you want, Leigh-Leigh."

And with that, and all that had gone before between them, Amélie had a feeling she'd gotten him there.

Tamed the beast.

This did not trouble her in the slightest.

"Would you like to get cleaned up, dressed, and go out to have a drink?" she asked and fought her own body tightening, worried about his response.

She didn't have to fight hard or long.

And she shouldn't have even worried.

His response was immediate.

"Fuck yeah."

She smiled against his skin.

It was not unheard of, but usually it was Doms and subs like Penn and Shane, and quite often Aryas and his babies, who played then returned to the hunting ground for a different kind of togetherness.

Amélie had never done it.

Not once.

But she found herself doing it, Olivier helping her off his dick and to her feet. Walking her to her bag with his hand in hers. Crouching in front of her to wipe him from between her legs. Then she pulled on her panties and stood close, touching Olivier, kissing him, with Olivier often returning those touches and kisses as he dressed and she did as well.

Together they walked back out to the common area, again hand in hand.

She guided him to a booth and she did it knowing everyone was watching.

As ever, she cared not in the slightest.

She slid in first, Olly followed her and a server came to them immediately, giving them both a look, a smile playing at his mouth, for he'd been around awhile and he knew what Amélie sitting in a booth with Olly after play meant.

They gave their orders and off he went.

After they'd been served, Amélie took a drink but noticed that Olly was just twisting his pilsner glass on the table this way and that with his long fingers at its base.

So she looked to his face.

He had his gaze to the door to the playroom.

"Olly?" she called.

He turned to her, looked into her eyes, and muttered, "Sorry, sweetheart. That woman just hit the playrooms with her girl. And the bitch gives me a bad feeling."

Amélie turned her attention across the space to the now closed door before glancing back to Olly.

"Mistress Delia?" she guessed.

He nodded.

Her interest piqued. "Did you see something untoward?"

His lips quirked and he murmured, "Untoward. Cute."

She set her champagne glass down, turned to him, and pressed into his side.

"Untoward. Troublesome. Inappropriate," she explained.

His eyes flickered with a playful light. "Know what it means, you're just the only woman I know who'd say it. And it's cute."

She loved he thought she was cute.

However.

"Olly . . . Delia," she prompted.

A look crossed his face she didn't quite understand but he didn't make her ask about it nor did he make her wait to explain it.

"Want my arm around you."

That made her catch her breath.

He wasn't quite done.

"Wanna be at ease right now, most I can be when we're in this room. That cool with you?"

Oh yes.

It was cool with her.

Amélie nodded.

He immediately pulled his arm from where she was pressed against it and rested the upper part on the booth behind her. His forearm, however, he curled possessively around her, doing this tightly, pulling her close so she was pressed against him again.

That felt much better.

She rested a hand on his thigh.

"Mistress Delia," he took them back to what they were discussing but dipped his face closer so their conversation would be more intimate . . . and not overheard. "Nothing untoward," he gave her a small grin when he used that word, "just, I'm a sub and when you and me go back there, I don't know what's gonna happen. I just know it's gonna be good. So whatever's gonna go down, I might be on edge about it, but that doesn't mean I'm not lookin' forward to it. That chick she's got, she looks like she's being led to an electric chair."

"I've noticed the same," Amélie remarked.

"Told you that shit ain't right. It's still going on and it *still* isn't right."

Amélie pressed even closer. "We must trust in Aryas."

He gave her a close look, one she found mildly strange. "Do you trust him?"

She was surprised at the question.

"Of course," she immediately answered.

"Heard about some shit that's gone down here, Leigh-Leigh," he told her.

He was talking about Evangeline.

"I think I know what you heard, Olly, and that happened to a friend of mine. It was the first such occurrence at the Honey. And the person who felt it most, outside my friend, was Aryas. Even after that transpired, he had his reasons for taking Delia on. He has his reasons for keeping watch over her. And he'll not allow anything else like that to occur. I'm utterly certain if he could erase what happened to my friend, he would. But he can't and to be honest, we were all fooled by the sub who harmed her. Everyone was surprised at what happened. Including my friend. No one blames Aryas, though he blames himself. Thus he's being very cautious with Delia. But that said, he would have been the same even before what happened to Evangeline."

Olly nodded and his gaze wandered to the door as he muttered, "Stil not feelin' good about not bein' more proactive."

She liked this about Olly.

Very much.

Then again, Amélie was beginning to think it was time to stop noting all the things she liked about Olly.

She just liked it all.

She gave his thigh a squeeze and when she again had his attention, she noted, "The strictures of this world, *our* world, make it very difficult for me to wade in."

She tipped her head to the side and lowered her voice even further before she confided in her Olly.

"I've known that sub, Tiffany, for years, darling. Even before I knew her inclinations and she came here. Her parents were friends of my father's. They're rather . . . tyrannical. At least her father is. Her mother is mostly . . . I'm not sure how to say it except the word negligent comes to mind. Her position in society, her preoccupation with herself, her clothes, shoes, hair, face, these took precedence over her children. One never knows what one is working out in their lives, not only sexually, and when that's sexually, it's not only in our world. Even in the mundane, people work issues out sexually. With parents such as hers, Tiffany still so young, she may be working out those issues with Delia and therefore, *mon grande*, into something darker."

"I can see that, gorgeous," he replied. "But she'd still get something out of it, a release, or she wouldn't keep going. She might not be skipping through the halls to the playrooms because whatever they're doing makes it harder for her to get in the zone. But once that woman starts working her, she's gotta find that zone or she wouldn't keep going back. Am I right?"

It was then Amélie's gaze wandered to the door as she murmured, "Yes, Olly, you're definitely right."

"Talk to your guy," he ordered and her gaze skittered up to his at again getting his authoritative, inflexible tone. "You been around longer. You know this place a fuckuva lot better. He'll be more receptive to it from you. I get you trust him. I also get what you're saying about what went down with your friend. One bad apple doesn't actually rot the whole barrel, it sure as fuck doesn't rot the farmer who owns the trees. He seems trustworthy and it's clear he takes the running of this place and the care of the people in it seriously. But just sayin', Leigh, that shit so isn't right, you don't talk to him, I will."

They were not in a place she should respond to his authoritative, inflexible tone in the way he clearly expected she would.

But in their cocoon of just Olly and Leigh, she also was.

And that was where she was, she realized, at the same time she realized with a warm feeling beginning to shroud her heart, it was part of who they were.

Or who they might end up being.

Olly was Olivier, her alpha-sub, she his Mistress.

But when not in the scene it was different.

It was Olly, the alpha, and Leigh, his woman.

Further, it wasn't like he wasn't giving her a choice. He was just stating the way it would be, what her part in that could be, what his part definitely was, depending on her choice.

Damn, even though the knowledge of it shocked her quite deeply, she had to admit she liked that too.

"I'll speak with Aryas, sweetheart."

"Good," he muttered, finally lifting his beer and taking a sip.

Amélie did the same with her drink.

When she placed it again on the table, Olly asked, his tone quite changed from serious, now it was downright roguish, "You ever have a footstool, Mistress?"

She turned her gaze back to him, her lips curled up. "Once, during a week of training with Mistress Sixx, who used to be the premier Mistress at the Honey before she moved from Phoenix."

"Once," he said.

Amélie nodded. "Yes, darling. Just once. I do understand the concept, the need of some subs to be relegated to that position, how their excitement heightens not only because of that but the anticipation of waiting for attention from their Dom, not knowing when it'll happen, just knowing that with each second that passes, the time that attention will come, comes closer." She shrugged one shoulder. "It's just not for me."

He lifted his brows, still teasing. "No catsuits?"

"The first BDSM catsuit Valentino creates, I'll buy it," she returned drolly and enjoyed every second of it—as did others who were either openly (like Stellan, she noted, across the way, though he appeared not to be enjoying Olly's humor) or furtively, like most of the rest, listening in—after Olly burst out laughing.

"My Leigh-Leigh, all class," Olly muttered when his laughter died down, taking another sip of beer.

She fought melting into him.

Or sliding into his lap.

Instead, she shared, "I must admit, I'm unusual, though all Doms, as all subs, have personalities in the scene. Things they enjoy more. Things they're quite talented in doing. Things that do nothing for them so they avoid them or don't do them at all." She smiled at him. "I do require service, submission, obedience, as you well know."

"Yeah, gorgeous, I well know that," he replied, also smiling, and Amélie couldn't help but note one other thing she liked.

This banter about who they were, how they were, how easy it was, a casual connection that was all theirs.

Penn and Shane likely had the same.

Trey and Mirabelle possibly had it or were growing toward it.

But Olly and Amélie now had it.

And Amélie had to admit, she didn't just like it.

She loved it.

"But I don't desire *subservience*," she carried on, then shook her head lightly. "I've dallied in it and found it's just not my thing."

He was still smiling when he noted, "The reason they're all gagging for you, even if they get off on the other shit. You prefer to be more hands-on with the buildup. But you definitely don't hold back on that buildup."

"You well know this too," she remarked, lightly stroking the inside of his thigh with her fingers, not a sexual touch, though an intimate one.

But also an affectionate one.

"Yeah I do," he agreed, the skin around his mouth softening. An intimate look.

And an affectionate one.

"Buildup is a good word, darling," Amélie stated. "I prefer the buildup, not the tearing down."

She noted something potent pass through his eyes but she didn't comment on it when he didn't share verbally what it was.

Though she did continue speaking.

"I probably don't need to note that I don't judge those who desire that, feel that need. I actually understand it. I just don't enjoy doing it." She pressed her breasts closer to his side, another intimate touch but this one hinted at sexual, a reminder of all they shared, and if the heat flashing through his gaze was to be read correctly, Olly didn't miss it. "As you know, my sweet beast, I like the challenge. I'm not looking to tear down someone's defenses to reach that sweet spot of trust any Dom savors. I'm searching for the break. The difference between the two is a nuance. But that difference remains."

"You were searching for me."

At these words, automatically, Amélie straightened against him.

With his long arm, he'd been able to slant it down her back, curling his fingers in just under her ribs.

But at her movement, those fingers came up and he stroked her upper arm as he voided the minimal space that was between them by leaning in and dipping his face close to hers.

"First Mistress I had, she tried to shove a big cock up my ass, didn't even prepare it with lube. Barely touched my dick and balls or anywhere before she went in for the serious shit." He hesitated before he shared his last in a way Amélie didn't know if he didn't wish to admit it or if there was more to it he wasn't giving her. "Only time before her or after I ever said my safe word."

At that, her body tightened further.

In fury.

"You must be joking," she bit out.

"Nope," he stated.

With this knowledge it was little wonder he'd declared in the beginning he wasn't "big on ass play."

"Olly, that's . . . that's . . ." she couldn't find the word so she put severe emphasis on, "*wrong.*"

He grinned in the face of her fury as he returned, "Know that, babe."

"Every Mistress I know would take deep umbrage with one of our own doing that to anybody," she announced.

"Know that, too, Leigh-Leigh. Not just from the look on your face but because the ones you know are here where that shit won't happen. Except maybe with that Delia woman. But that's not my point."

"What's your point?" she asked, still angry but now curious because Olly had never gotten this deeply into this particular topic and she'd been curious from the first.

"My point is, if you got something out of it, I'd be your footstool. Totally get off on that just knowin' you would too. But that isn't it. It's how I know you'd get me there. It's how you'd read me. It's how you'd know how to do it to make it something that'd work in a big way for me. And that isn't somethin' anyone in this room, no matter how good they are at what they do, could give to me. It's you. And it's me."

His fingers stopped stroking her arm and curled around it before he went on even as several expressions chased their paths across his face, none of which she could catch before he simply allowed it to be soft, his blue eyes warm.

"So you were searchin' for me, Leigh-Leigh. And I was lookin' for you."

These words meant so much, Amélie shifted her hand from his thigh to rest it on his flat stomach, only able to whisper his name.

"Olly."

He used his free hand to find hers at his stomach and he linked them, curling hers so the tips of her nails rested against the insides of his fingers, and likewise his with hers.

"That took us deep, baby," he said softly. "And I don't regret it but deep is for our weekend away. Got a lot to tell you about me. Lookin' forward to knowin' more about you. I'm fuckin' glad we had this now. But you . . ." He shook his head, appeared strangely uncertain for a moment before he started again. "But now let's get out of the deep and in the meantime, Leigh, let's have a fuckin' good week."

The promise that their weekend would hold the key to many doors behind which were facets of Olly, Amélie could wait.

So she held tight to his fingers and replied, "That's a deal, darling."

They stayed in their intimate bubble in a booth in the hunting ground of the Bee's Honey, holding each other's hands and staring into each other's eyes and they did that for a long, golden moment, solidifying the equally golden promise of what was yet to come, before Olly gave her fingers a squeeze and let go.

He reached for his glass.

Amélie followed suit.

They sipped but neither of them moved out of their snug position as they talked for two hours.

During this time, Olivier had two beers.

Amélie only one cocktail.

They finally walked to the front desk, Olly waited until she got her purse, then he walked her to her SUV.

They kissed at her car door.

Just like lovers do.

And he stood there, she knew he did because she watched in her car mirrors, not moving, but watching her drive away.

That night (amongst other things, nothing weighty after the beginning, all consequential because it was about him, or her, but they both felt the need to keep it light, the important discourse would come during their weekend), she'd learned his last name was Hawkes.

It was a strong name.

Perfect for him.

But his last name could be anything, and Olivier Hawkes was so perfect himself, he'd make it flawless.

fourteen

Senseless

AMÉLIE

The next afternoon, Amélie listened to Aryas responding to her concerns about Tiffany and Delia over the phone.

"I'm handling it, Leigh."

"But Aryas—"

"My sweet, *I'm handling it.*"

His tone made Amélie shut her mouth.

Aryas did not shut his.

"I get you're concerned. I get why. You know I am too. So trust me, I'm handling it. And if I need you, I'll call you. Yeah?"

"Yes, Aryas," she replied.

"It'll all be good, honey," he said reassuringly.

Aryas wouldn't lie.

"Right, Aryas. Thank you. And I'll be there for anything you need, if that need should arise."

"Knew you would, babe. Now, hear you got your room reserved for the night. Have fun with that big stallion of yours."

That made her smile. "I always do."

She heard his return smile in his next words, "Right, Leigh. Later."

"'Bye, Aryas."

She took the phone from her ear, disconnected the call and went right to her texts.

Spoke to A. He says he's handling things with D and it'll all be good. I trust he's doing as he says. So it will all be good. Does that work for you? she texted Olly.

She didn't have to wait long for the reply, *It'll have to.*

He sent that and then sent another right on its heels.

For now.

That made her smile bigger, Olly's concern for Tiffany, a girl he didn't even know.

See you tonight, darling, she returned.

Yeah you will, was his reply.

And unsurprisingly, that made her smile even bigger.

That evening, Olivier stood before her in her "barn," ready for his introduction to the social room.

That was, with him standing naked and with the command of motionless in front of her, she'd soft brushed him, oiled him all over, strapped his ass open, plugged it and harnessed his cock.

He'd arrived, as usual, with the same done to his balls.

She moved to stand in front of him and saw the wild was at the surface, unhidden.

All right, so maybe she hadn't tamed the beast.

This was a lot to give, she knew, for many subs. Mistress and toy in their place in their room, even with onlookers, was a controlled situation. A situation that Amélie sensed Olivier understood (correctly) that, in the end, it was he who held the control.

And also, even with an audience, there was an intimacy to it that could not be denied.

A social room was much different.

She moved close.

"No one can touch you without my leave, beast," she assured gently.

He gave her one of the many things she loved to get from him.

An upward jerk of his head, like a stallion fighting, showing his defiance, at the same time knowing he had no choice but to relent.

Amélie allowed her fingertips to touch his stomach lightly, getting closer.

The wild in his eyes darkened.

"You've never done this," she noted carefully.

"The Bolt doesn't have a social room," he shared. "Members want that kind of thing, they take it off premises for a private party."

Well, that explained that.

"And you haven't gone off premises for such a party?" Amélie queried.

He shook his head in a sharp no.

She nodded, hiding her surprise.

It was another indication either of inexperience, or what she realized with their time together was more likely—he'd never had a Mistress he trusted enough to give this gift or enjoyed himself enough with to go there with her.

From what little she now knew of one of his Mistresses, this really was actually no surprise.

She just hoped he'd enjoy himself once he'd gone there with Amélie.

"Right then, *chevalier*, I'll explain," she said softly. "I'll lead you by your magnificent cock. I'll take you to a table I select. I'll guide you to the front of it and when I release you, you'll lean over the table. You'll spread your legs wide. You'll cross your arms under your head on the table. You will not speak at all unless I give you leave, even if another Dom addresses you. And you'll turn your head my way."

Amélie got closer and finished with giving him what she knew he'd need.

"I'll be in your line of vision all the time. I'll be right there. And remember, my steed, you are mine, no one else's."

She got even closer. Flattening her hand on his stomach, slowly, she slid it down the length of dense hair to his cock, feeling those muscles ripple as she did it, at the same time she held his eyes.

"You are *mine*," she repeated. "Nothing will happen there I do not wish. And I've made my desires clear to you but I'll do it again. I do not share. What you give in there, you give to me. It is you and me, *chevalier*, like always."

By the time she stopped talking, she'd wrapped her hand loosely around his cock and was rolling the tip with her thumb.

His teeth came out and scored his bottom lip.

"Are you ready?" she asked.

"Ready, Amélie," he answered, the answer gruff, not firm, a hint of unease in his tone, but his eyes stayed locked to hers.

"So good, my beast," she whispered with approval, ran her thumb harder around his cock head and watched his lips curl back in that amazing half-snarl. "So good," she repeated before she released his gaze, turned, and pulling him gently by his cock, she walked to the door.

She also walked him out that door.

And she walked him down the hall.

She did this with her head held high, shoulders straight, gait slow, one foot in front of the other, like she normally walked.

But there was no mistaking the pride in her pose.

It was beyond the elegance ingrained in her by her mother. Beyond confidence.

Straight to haughty.

And she didn't care. Not that she would normally, but she owned the marvelous stallion following her because she'd earned that claim.

And it was making her wetter and wetter with each step, feeling him follow her, his trust in her, giving her even *more*, letting her lead him into the unknown, allowing her to show him off in all his glory.

So she deserved to be fucking haughty.

And she was so deep in that glorious moment, she barely acknowledged Master, Mistress, and definitely not toy as she opened the door to the social room and led him in.

This room looked much like the hunting ground, bar at the end, surrounded by curved booths.

However, it was smaller.

And there were raised, oblong stations down the middle, all of them like stages, only the center one having a pole in the middle.

The bright light beaming down on the stages was mostly what lit the room, although there was elegant blue lighting around the bar and that same blue at the edges where the walls met the ceilings, plus very low watt bulbs providing minimal illumination from sconces dripping with crystals over each booth.

This meant that most of the rest of the room was quite dim and there were even some corners that were downright dark.

This, Aryas's genius way of providing a chic atmosphere at the same time allowing, should a Mistress or Master have desire of it even in that social setting, privacy.

She noted distractedly that when they entered, there were a goodly number of people there, but only two of the five stations had a sub performing for (and with) their Dom.

Amélie barely glanced at any of them. This was because, if those performances were getting attention, they'd lost it the minute Amélie and Olivier entered the room.

She felt Olivier hesitate and rounded the head of his cock with her thumb reassuringly even as she didn't miss a step and kept pulling him inexorably to a booth on the opposite side of the room, its situation centered, her intent to parade her steed for all to see.

She did and she almost wanted to guide him right back out, return to their room, so she could unharness the splendid brute she held in her hand, climb his big, powerful body and bury him in her pussy.

She didn't do that.

She stopped him at the front of the table at the booth she selected, released him and looked to his face.

He was looking down at her, the wild even in the dimmed, blue-tinted lighting unleashed. So out of control, she feared he'd bolt.

She felt her clit swell, her nipples harden and her stomach warm when his jaw clenched but he did not bolt.

He bent over just as instructed, legs wide, arms crossed, head on them, torso to the table, strapped, plugged ass offered for display.

She slid her hand over the cheek of his ass, gliding her fingernail lightly down the outside of the strap as she murmured, "You please me."

As instructed, Olivier said nothing.

She then moved into the side of the booth, her gaze going direct to his to find his locked on her, and he didn't hide his desperate need for her to be right where she was.

Amélie again reached out, this time stroking the small of his back.

"Calm, Olivier, I'm right here."

He didn't settle so she stroked him and continued to do that.

"It's in your power to share with me if you need to leave. And I'll share with you that this will not displease me," she assured him. "Now, *mon grande*, do you need to leave?"

It took a moment but he held role and instead of answering audibly, he shook his head on his arms once.

She flattened her hand on him and showed him her pleasure through a soft smile.

"A drink, Mistress Amélie?"

She turned to the female server and nodded. "Yes, please."

Astutely, the server made no mention of Olivier at all, which would call to his attention that he was the center of attention, not only from the server's admiring eyes on his backside, but from most of the room.

It was, to Amélie's shock and considerable dismay, Delia, fortunately without Tiffany for once (the only fortunate thing about it), who approached first.

"Please tell me that hole is on offer and not just for show," she begged and regrettably continued, "I'll have my cock strapped on and fuck him raw before any of the boys can get their bids in."

Olivier tensed under her touch, an unfortunate response for it made Delia's eyes drop and her face fill with greed as she stared at the bunched muscles of his ass.

"Pay you to drive deep in that," she muttered reverently.

"If you do not take your eyes from my Olivier, you'll struggle to see through them after I put all my effort to scratching them out."

Her tone was no threat.

It was a warning and Delia's attention snapped to her.

"You brought him to social and displayed him," she rapped out.

"He's mine to do that and we both enjoy that fact. Alas, I didn't know you lurked in social or I would have selected another evening, one when you were not here."

"I can put my eyes where I wish, Amélie," she bit out.

"Not if that's my steed," she returned coolly.

"I'm no slave, honey," Delia shot back acidly. "You can hardly tell me where to look."

Amélie shifted only an inch and her voice was ice-cold when she retorted, "Try me."

"I think this Mistress has made her wishes clear as it comes to her stud, Delia."

Amélie's gaze moved to Aryas, who was standing close and positioning closer, shuffling Delia back and away at the same time hiding Olivier with his considerable bulk from the odious woman's eyes.

"I would assume you'd require her to respect your wishes if you asked the same for one of your slaves. Respect that's mandatory at the Bee's Honey, as you know. So I believe with no further exchange, we're done here," Aryas concluded.

"I'm uncertain how I feel about how you run your club, Master Aryas," Delia sniffed.

"I'm uncertain I give a shit, Mistress Delia," Aryas fired back.

She gave him a glare, another sniff, then stormed off.

Aryas turned his attention to Amélie.

"Thank you," she said shortly, still angry.

"Don't mention it," he murmured, glanced down at Olivier, gave her an audacious grin that was reminiscent, if not as effective, as one of Olivier's, and he strolled away.

Amélie looked down at her beast.

He was biting his lip and she didn't know if he was doing this to stop laughing, stop speaking, or stop himself from shouting.

She glided her hand from the small of his back up to his lat and bent close.

"You may say one word, *mon chou*, are you all right?"

"Yes." It was again gruff but this time gruff with amusement as well as something else that was pleasant.

Amélie felt her eyelids go hooded and she leaned back, gliding her hand to retrace its movements but not stopping at his back.

She stroked the cheek of his ass and partially down his back thigh.

She continued to do this as Mira slid in the booth opposite her.

Amélie blinked at this new surprise.

"I didn't know you were going to be here tonight," she noted.

"Well hello to you too," Mira replied on a happy smile and Amélie smiled back because she knew why Mirabelle's smile was happy.

Suffice it to say, the first date—as well as the three after it— had gone well for Mira and Trey.

Putting new meaning to that "well," Mira turned her head and ordered, "On your knees, please."

Trey, standing at Mirabelle's side, dropped to his knees beside her.

Without hesitation, Mira shifted so she was straddling the end of the booth, put her hand to the back of his head and shoved it between her thighs.

"Hold it there. I'll let you know if I wish your tongue," she commanded.

She looked up from her sub/new boyfriend to Amélie and Amélie couldn't help the fact her smile was huge.

Mirabelle smiled huge back.

Neither of them noted why they were smiling, as they wouldn't with the two male specimens (one of whom would be the topic of that discussion) right there to hear, regardless of their submissive postures.

"So, of course, word spread wide about two seconds after you led this beautiful brute into the halls that social was the way to go tonight," Mirabelle noted. "Beware the doors opening and we're treated to the Honey's version of the bull run at Pamplona in this room."

Amélie felt Olivier tense again but she ignored it, didn't look to his face, and kept stroking, widening her range as best she could without reaching, her touch as light as she could make it.

She did this grinning at Mira in response to her quip.

But she shared, "We won't be performing," doing this for Mirabelle's information as well as to assure Olivier.

"Too bad," Mirabelle replied, her lips twitching. She looked down and pulled Trey's head from between her legs using his hair. "Would you like to perform for me tonight, my handsome slave?"

"I'll enjoy doing whatever pleases you, Mistress Mirabelle," Trey answered.

She slid her fingers along his jaw. "You always do," she whispered affectionately. She then slid her fingers back up his jaw to his hair and tenderly pressed his face between her legs again. "As before, my slave," she ordered adoringly.

Ah, yes.

Things were going *very* well with Mira and her Trey.

The server brought Amélie's drink and asked Mirabelle if she wanted one. Mirabelle declined and by the time her friend looked back to Amélie, Amélie could not contain the glee she felt at witnessing Mira's tender handling and Trey's seemingly easy shift from Mistress and submissive to more, that more still including Mistress and sub.

"Stop grinning like a goof," Mirabelle ordered.

"Make me," Amélie retorted, taking hold of her drink and then taking a sip.

Mira rolled her eyes but focused on something beyond their table as she rolled them back.

"Mm, Talia's taken a shine to that big boy and he's performing beautifully for her," Mirabelle noted.

Amélie put her drink down and looked over her shoulder to see one of the stages was taken up with four players, but two more were standing at the edges.

In the middle was Bryan on his back, his legs up the chest and over the shoulders of another male slave, his ass being fucked by that slave as another male slave had his weight in his hands over Bryan's head, fucking his face.

As for Bryan, he was stroking his dick madly, clearly finding pleasure in what he was getting and putting on quite a show.

The two slaves' Mistresses were standing close to the stage, enjoying that show, while Talia stood on the stage, calling the shots.

"She's finding interesting ways to keep him from speaking," Amélie remarked, her eyes on the stage, her bottom sliding slightly down the booth so her hand had more access to Olivier.

With this access, she cupped his balls.

"Indeed he is," Mirabelle agreed.

Amélie barely heard her.

Moving her attention from Talia and her sub to Olivier, she ordered quietly, "Legs wider, *mon chou*."

He did not look amused and he did not look desperate when he immediately acquiesced.

He very much liked his Mistress paying attention to his balls.

He was hers, only hers, and she his, only his, right there in a room full of people.

She gave him a smile that told him precisely how much she liked that.

She also gave him more.

Moving from his balls, she went to his plug and gave it a slow twist.

His lids lowered and he came up on his toes.

"Beautiful," she cooed.

He bit his lip, not scoring it with his teeth, pulling it in and keeping it in.

Performing well, doing as told, keeping silent, her sweet beast.

She went back to his balls, taking her eyes from his and sensing something.

She looked to the room and noticed Stellan across it, standing, no slave in attendance this time, back to the side of a booth, arms crossed on his chest (again, what a bore), his attention on her.

She didn't give him hers for very long but she did give it to Olivier.

"Slide closer to me," she ordered on a light squeeze of his sac.

He slid from the center of the table her way.

When he did, she switched positions with her hand, reaching under the table to cup his balls in one hand and she manipulated them while stroking the skin of his ass and thighs with the other.

She looked from her fascinated perusal of Olivier's face turning languid with the slow build of lazy desire, delighted at the ease with which she'd been able to guide him to a *just them*, even in social, to Mira when she felt her friend's gaze.

"I suspect I'm grinning like a goof now," she declared.

"Please shut up," Amélie requested, any bite of her words not there due to the smile infusing them.

"I think I'll do that since I'm feeling some alone time coming on with my handsome boy," Mira returned, pulling Trey's face out from between her legs. "On your feet, handsome. Time to eat."

Amélie watched Trey's face grow hungry and she liked that so much for her friend, she squeezed Olivier's balls tighter than she meant to.

She heard his low noise and looked to his face.

He'd lost the wild. It was gone.

He was hers. In her hands in every way he could be.

That meant so much to her, Olivier settling in so beautifully, she tore her gaze from his, having just enough courtesy to look up to Mirabelle and bid, "Enjoy."

"You, too, my lovely," Mira replied, yanked on the leash she had attached to Trey's cock harness, and led him out of the room.

Amélie looked back to her steed.

She shifted her attention to the inside of his straps, light, so soft, and he again went up on his toes.

"God, you're amazing," she whispered in a tone she knew was just as adoring as Mira's had been, maybe more so, doing this leaning toward him.

Olivier licked his lips.

Amélie leaned closer.

Suddenly, looking through the dim at her tamed beast with his sultry eyes, she wanted to know everything on his mind.

And since she could, she set about learning that.

"You have this moment to speak freely, Olivier," she granted.

He didn't hesitate.

"Is he here?"

She felt her brows draw together.

"Who?" she asked.

"Baby, you know."

It came to her that she did.

"Master Stellan?" she queried to confirm.

He jerked up his chin and it was alluring, masculine, magnetic, even with his head down on his arms.

"He is," she shared. "Why?"

"Is he watching?" Olivier asked.

"I only glanced at him but yes, as usual, he was, *chevalier*."

"Then make me perform."

Amélie blinked.

"Sorry?" she asked.

"I'm yours. Make me perform."

"Onstage?" Her voice had risen for this surprised her.

She would not expect Olivier would want to do that.

And further, she herself never made her toys perform in social. This was because *she* was also performing and that was something she didn't fancy.

She actually didn't often go to social for she rarely had a toy who she wished to display. She happily lifted the blinds but she preferred the barriers and the intimacy the glass provided, and the undistracted closeness of what she could offer her toys behind it.

"No," he grunted. "Unless, do you—?"

"Absolutely not." She made her feelings clear on the subject.

"Then here."

She didn't understand.

"Olivier—"

"If you claim me here, Mistress, then I'm claiming you. Right?"

With that, she understood.

"Fuck me," he ground out. "You wanna make me come, make me. But I want him to know where we are, you and me, but also fuckin' *him*, and I can do that my way or you can make that crystal right now."

His way, she was sure, Stellan would dislike immensely and even Aryas might frown on.

Amélie, however, wouldn't mind witnessing it.

Though she was absolutely certain it would be worth the headache it might cause, it wouldn't be worth it if Aryas frowned on it significantly.

Even with these thoughts, his request (which was more like a demand), was beyond titillating and not because she wished to make him serve her right there at the table.

But *why* he was making his demand in the first place.

A declaration of possession, through her of him, to him of her.

All this to Stellan, and due to their locational circumstances, to everybody.

For Olivier might not know that she'd never, not once, done such with another toy (this was when she wasn't training with another Dom).

So everyone who was in the know through history, and it would spread by word of mouth, would get the message Olivier wished to send.

She got closer and she actually felt the sparkle in her eyes even as she felt something much more lovely between her legs as she cupped his balls and covered his plug with the palm of her hand.

"You do know, my steed, this isn't topping from below. This is actually telling your Mistress what to do."

"You don't wanna do it, up to you. I'm just telling my Mistress what I *want* her to do."

"I see the difference," she murmured sardonically.

"Your call," he stated the obvious.

"Stop speaking, Olivier, and no more, unless they're noises you can't control."

She saw his expression darkening.

He was getting what he wanted and he liked that.

And so did she.

"If you need to adjust to hold on to the edge of the table, please do so," she invited. "And please be aware that you'll need to retain some stamina for I intend to ride your face when we return to our room. And it would please me greatly for you to offer more of your seed while I stroke you when I do that."

"Baby," he growled.

With that, Amélie had him where *she* wanted, not because he had a statement to make to Stellan but because he wanted what she was going to give.

She moved to his cock and started unbuckling the harness, her eyes searching the space. Avoiding Stellan's, she found a server and inclined her head.

The server approached.

"Please bring me a receptacle," she requested.

"You got it," the girl replied, moved quickly away and Amélie removed the harness from her toy.

She again gave him her attention.

His face was dark, his eyes riveted to her, his jaw clenched, a muscle jumping up his cheek.

"Now, you serve me, my Olivier," she said softly.

As his show of submission, he again lifted up on his toes.

And at that show, Amélie felt a tremor between her legs, gripped his cock, took hold of his plug, and she made her toy serve her.

She fucked him with his plug, stroked his cock roughly, and didn't even notice the server setting the pail under to the table to catch Olivier's cum.

Amélie's eyes were glued to his and his to hers, giving her all the communication she needed.

Then his head came up, his arms slid out, and he gave her *everything*.

Arching his back, flat stomach pressing into the table, hips tipped up, he came up to his forearms, fingers curled around the edge of the table, but his head dropped down in a submissive gesture that had her clit buzzing.

"You may express your pleasure audibly but quietly, only to me."

His burning eyes cut to hers and he hissed, "Fuck me, baby. Take my ass. Jack my junk and goddamned *fuck me*." Before she could demand it, her training kicked in, and he finished in a way that was *so . . . deliciously . . . Olivier*, "Motherfucking *please*."

Her clit and womb spasming, she took him there and nearly came, sitting in the booth beside him, wondering if he'd rip the table right out of the floor as he bucked violently, lifting up to arms outstretched, head bent back, hips pistoning, and shot into the pail, thrusting through her fist to do it.

She slid the plug in gently, milked him as minimally as he needed before she slid out of the booth with more than a little urgency.

"Up, Olivier," she ordered huskily.

He lifted up, sated eyes, face soft, all that for her, all that she'd given him on show to the room.

She moved in, hand back to his cock, and he bent his head down. She kissed him.

Then he kissed her.

After she pulled away, she led him out by his semi-hard cock to their room, kept the blinds down, pushed him on his back on a bench, and climbed on his face.

He ate her wet pussy ravenously as she stroked him in order to get him hard yet again.

She was so primed, she came before she could take him to climax and collapsed on his chest and stomach, her face nuzzling his hardening cock (regrettably hardening because she was spent, Olivier had made her come exquisitely (as usual), and she didn't have it in her to do anything about it).

With a noise of surprise, she found herself moved, turned and rolled so they were face-to-face and he was on top.

She looked into his eyes.

"I think that made my point," he declared, his deep voice rolling through the room, coating it and her in complete and utter possession.

The feel of that was warm.

Amélie still shivered under him.

He was right. He had. She'd had no control, barely allowing him to recover from his orgasm before she dragged him from the room to get him to herself.

To give herself to him.

That was not her modus operandi. Amélie was in control at all times. She gave. She took. And always, she did so with attention and affection, but still with an air she could take it or leave it.

She did not smooth her toy's jaws as Mirabelle did, not in the hunting ground, definitely not in a prolonged scene in social.

She most certainly didn't make a mad dash from the social room so she could ride her toy's face.

But with Olivier, she'd shown much affection, as Stellan had accused, holding hands and cuddling with him openly wherever she felt like it. Indeed, doing that for hours with him just the night before.

And obviously, she'd made that mad dash from the social room so she could ride her Olivier's face.

But she didn't care.

He may well be her Shane. Her Trey.

Just hers.

Completely.

In fact, everything they shared made that seem more and more real.

God, she could not *wait* for their weekend.

To that end, she lifted a hand and smoothed it over Olivier's jaw and into his hair.

"You do know he's no competition," she noted soothingly, for there was a new beast to be tamed, she could see it in his eyes, and she enjoyed this one just as much.

But he wouldn't so she had to do something about it.

"I know he wants you and he wants that bad," he returned.

"He's a Dom, Olly," she told him something he knew.

"He wants you to bend him over a table and he wants to take his fucking from you, Leigh-Leigh. He wants to thrust his cock in your hand. He wants you riding his face. He wants you to string him up and jack his ass so deep, he spews across the room for you. He wants to fuck you senseless. He wants," he dipped his face close, "what's *mine*."

Oh yes.

There was a new beast to be tamed.

She melted under him even as she shook her head. "I've known Stellan a long time and I don't think—"

"He wants what's mine and it's mine," he bit off, interrupting her. "He can't fuckin' have it."

Amélie fell silent.

"Fuck," he ground out, nudging her legs open with his knee. "I need to fuck you, Leigh."

"So fuck me, Olly," she invited.

The heat of possession in his expression only intensified as he positioned, brushing his mouth against hers, before he drove inside her wetness, filling her full.

Then her Olly proceeded to fuck her.

Senseless.

Thursday evening in the bed in the red room, Amélie collapsed on top of Olivier after she rode him to a stunningly gorgeous simultaneous orgasm.

When she did, Olivier did not wrap his arms around her.

He couldn't. His wrists were cuffed to the bed over his head, as his ankles were cuffed, legs opened wide down below.

When her breath again came easy, as did his, she nuzzled his neck.

She'd had book club Wednesday night. He'd had plans with his friends that night.

He'd ditched (his words) his friends and came to her.

"You got the text with my address?" she asked.

"Babe, wanna hold you."

She lifted her head and looked down at her bound steed.

"I like you at my mercy."

His gaze flashed and she grinned. Leaning in to sweep her lips across his, when he lifted his head to get more, she pulled away slightly.

"Olivier, did you get my address?"

"Yeah, Leigh-Leigh, on the way here. Was more interested in getting inside than texting you back. Thought we'd have a drink and I could share the pressing news that the global communication system is still functioning, all systems go, and I got your text. But you hightailed our asses in here so I didn't get to confirm that yes, I got your address."

She laughed softly because he was funny.

Then, she asked, "You'll come after work tomorrow?"

Tomorrow began their weekend at her ranch.

"Yeah. Drive means I'll be there late, though, sweetheart. Eight, earliest. Probably more like eight-thirty."

Disappointing.

But she'd work with it.

"Fine," she replied.

"Baby, uncuff me. Wanna touch you." He gave her that then whispered, "Please."

Since that was sweet, she brushed his lips with hers, moved them down his jaw, his neck, his throat, and at the dent at the base, she murmured, "Come to me harnessed."

"Of course," he grunted, half insulted, half turned on.

"And plugged."

His body tensed under her.

She trailed her lips to his nipple and took a bite.

"Fuck," he growled.

She licked his nipple and ordered, "Plugged, Olivier."

"Okay, Amélie."

She lifted her head and saw him dip his chin in his throat to look down at her.

"If you aren't hard when you arrive, when you arrive, you stay in your car and make yourself hard for me. If you arrive late, I want you to arrive ready."

"I'll be ready," he rumbled, lifting his hips into hers still straddling his cock.

"We play, we spend time together." She slid up his chest so they were again eye to eye. "We enjoy. We talk on Sunday."

"Works for me."

Excellent.

"Now, I feel the urge to lick your lovely sac until you beg to come for me."

"Christ," he gritted, his head digging into the pillow but his eyes remaining on Amélie.

"Would you like that?" she asked playfully.

"Are you joking, asking that shit?" he asked back impatiently.

"Would you like my pussy while I do that?"

His eyes narrowed. "Babe. Again. Are you joking, asking stupid-ass shit?"

She got closer, her lips touching his, and lost the playful, watching him carefully as she reminded him, "Darling, I'm filled with you."

"Gorgeous, that pretty pussy of yours can be drippin' three loads of my cum and I'd still fucking eat it."

He was simply *perfection*.

Amélie grinned against his mouth.

"You gonna grin at me all night or you gonna lick my balls?" he queried irritably.

Her playful came back. "I wonder," she started musingly, "if my steed wants my tongue on him more, or if he wants his mouth on me."

"Pussy, absolutely," he answered. "Now, if you were wrapping that sweet mouth around my cock, that'd be a different story."

She grinned against his mouth.

"Baby," he growled warningly.

"You please me, Olivier."

"Thrilled, Leigh-Leigh. Now, how 'bout you shake a leg and let me keep doing that."

She allowed her eyes to smile.

Then she slid off his cock, repositioned, and let him "keep doing that."

He did not lie. He had no hesitation eating her and him out of her "pretty pussy."

So she rewarded him by spending a good deal of time on his balls but when his growls into her flesh turned pleading, she gave him that different story.

She tasted herself while she did, but in the end, it was just Olivier Amélie took down her throat.

fifteen

Flawed Perfection

OLIVIER

Friday night, Olly drove to Leigh's house, knowing he was getting close from the GPS.

And knowing that, he was hard as a rock, straining his jeans to the point of mild pain.

Even having had her the night before, he still couldn't wait to see what she had in store for him that weekend.

But he knew what he had in store for her.

It happened when he was bent over that table and Amélie took on that bitch. He watched her and listened to her and he knew if that woman didn't take her eyes off Olly, Leigh would have launched herself at the cunt and given her all to do bodily harm.

As he watched that, Olly felt something release deep in his brain.

Something that had been strung tight for so long, threatening to snap, it snapping meant *he* would snap. He'd lose hold. He'd lose himself. He'd lose something integral he needed to be Olly.

Amélie was right. He was not defined by his sexuality, no one was.

But it was a part of who he was. An important part. One he couldn't bury without losing a crucial element of himself.

And what got him off . . .

No, finding Leigh and being free to be just how he needed to be, it all sunk in.

All of it.

He'd watched Amélie take on that woman finally getting with all Leigh had given him—not just to get him off, but in everything—that she'd take care of him. And that was not just with what he liked to get worked, but in every way.

Not simply as his Mistress, but that *and* as the woman in his life.

And as that hit him, that thing fucking with his head loosened. Melted clean away.

And her giving him that. Her yanking down her panties, as desperate as he was to connect after they'd been apart—no preliminaries and they were fucking against the door. Her opening her legs so he could take her pussy after he delivered his message through her in the social room. Her obvious happiness that things were working out for her girl and her new man. Her calling him to let him know she was out of town, doing that on a pretense just so they could talk, connect. Her sweet. Her candor. Her teasing. Her upfront excitement they were spending the weekend together. Her being there for him any time he called. The real they had, the ease of it, the honesty, while playing or sitting in a booth having a drink, the magnitude of what they shared and how deep it went.

Leigh giving him all that, Olly wanted this to go somewhere.

He had no idea how to make that happen. There was honesty he had to give to her about how he came to the Honey. And his greatest concern, there were serious differences between them—the money she had, his lack of it, and the lives they led because of that—that had to be hashed out.

But she was Leigh-Leigh. She found a way to release that torture that had been screwing with his mind since forever, so he sensed that together, they'd find a way to build something more with all they already had.

Olly knew that because, in understanding all this, he'd come to understand they'd already begun to build it. There was the scene then she sensed innately when it was time to guide him out of it and give him the rest of what he needed.

Not a feeling of normal. He no longer cared about being what others would think was normal (and she'd taught him that too with the ease and dignity with which she lived in that world).

What he needed was to have the sense that he was always Olly, even when he was Olivier, and he always had his Leigh, even when she was his Mistress Amélie.

The GPS in his truck told him he'd be turning left in a third of a mile.

He searched a dark that no city could have, vast stretches of land, a plateau in the northern mountains of Arizona, and he saw it.

Two lights illuminating two sweeping adobe fences that marked either side of a drive. One had the house number of her ranch on it in purposefully rusted iron numbers. The other side had another rusted iron piece, this a horse trotting, neck proud but head bowed.

Something about that made Olly's mouth quirk.

Even if he'd come to his decision about their future, he was still relieved to see there was no grand entryway over the lane to her ranch with some pretentious name sweeping across it.

It was clear since he'd passed the last house half a mile ago that she had land but as he turned in, he saw the house he was driving to and it wasn't pretentious either.

It wasn't small but it wasn't large.

Compact.

Classic adobe, including the beams. He saw some blooms around the front courtyard as his headlights hit the house. The front light was on, showing the courtyard was welcoming, but not elaborate. There was a fountain trickling at the side of the front door that was not ostentatious, just pretty, undoubtedly the sound it made calming and making the entry even more inviting.

He stopped his truck in the neat gravel of the big circular drive, doing this next to her Mercedes SUV coupe, and watched her open the door.

His ass tightened around the small plug he wore that she'd given him during their week apart, his balls drawing up in their harness as he saw her for the first time in jeans.

They were low-slung, tight, faded in a way that came from wear, not made that way in some factory. She wore them with a thick belt, utilitarian, no ornamentation, but it was still cool. She had on a turquoise, flowy blouse that fell off her shoulder, a mess of southwestern necklaces dangling from her neck, and he could also see big hoops at her ears.

Her feet were bare.

Leigh at her ranch.

Not a beautiful woman with a French mother, a load of money, and a way of calling her man "darling" that didn't sound moronic, but instead amazing.

No. A northern mountains of Arizona rancher who had money but nothing about her shoved that down your throat.

Oh yeah.

They could find a way to work.

He was no longer hoping for that, but instead, with everything she gave him, he was beginning to count on it.

She stood in the door, leaning against the jamb, as he grabbed his duffel off the passenger seat and angled out of the cab.

He walked to her and saw the courtyard had some comfortable-looking furniture, a table, two chairs, intimate in that small space. A place for two people to hang in the morning with a cup of joe, not a place to have a party.

And that courtyard was teeming with lush bougainvillea growing up the walls that delineated the courtyard space as well as the front of the house.

Prettier up close than from afar.

The same could be said for the woman standing in the door.

Olly stopped in front of her.

"Hey," he greeted.

"Olivier."

He felt the name she chose throb in his cock.

She wanted him too. Just as badly.

It was play time.

All right.

He fought back a triumphant smile.

"Come closer, *mon chou.*"

Olly came closer and stopped. She tilted her head back to keep hold on his eyes as he moved.

This meant he missed her hand moving but he didn't miss it when she cupped him over his jeans and at the same time asked, "How was the drive?"

"Over," he grunted.

He watched her lips tip up.

"Drop the duffel, *chevalier,* we'll come for it later."

He tossed the bag close to the side of the door but other than that didn't move.

This was good since she did. Slightly.

Her hand twisting, she slid his zipper down and didn't hesitate even a second to dive in then pull him out.

Olly clenched his teeth against the goodness he felt when his heavy cock finally sprung free of his confining jeans.

She kept locked on his gaze even as she shoved in roughly, tugging him, his lower half swaying as she inspected his balls, then she slid under, jerking him to her as she slid her hand back and found his plug.

His hole tightened.

Oh yeah.

"Mistress," he whispered.

"Are you ready for our weekend?" she asked.

"Fuck yes," he answered gruffly.

"Good," she replied softly. Her gaze still direct on his, she found the tip of the plug and twisted it.

That drove straight up his ass, through his balls to his cock, and unable to stop himself, Olly lifted a hand and grabbed the jamb over her head.

"I have much planned for you, my stallion," she said softly.

It was his turn to say, "Good," but his came out harsh.

"I have a gift for you too," she told him. "Would you like it now or later?"

"Which way do you want it?"

"The way I want it is to know if you'd like it now or later."

He stared in her eyes, his focus shifting from his ass to the look he saw shining there, and he knew the answer.

"Now."

Her lips tipped up at the sides again, this time slowly, and as they did, she slid her hand out of his jeans but latched onto his cock and gave it a gentle tug.

"Come," she ordered.

If she wasn't careful, he'd do that in way she didn't mean.

By his dick, she led him into her house and he had the presence of mind to close the door behind him.

Other than that, he didn't have the presence of mind for anything else so he didn't take much in. He felt his boots hitting rug under his feet, distractedly saw the tile at the sides of the runner, the adobe walls, paintings, furniture, other decorative shit, felt the coolness of the air, the smell of piñon vague but pleasant.

But his attention was riveted to the back of her rich, shining, unfettered auburn hair hanging down to past where her bra strap would be and all he thought was that he didn't mind at all his Mistress could lead him around by his cock.

She turned into a room that had soft lighting, candles glowing, and a big four-poster bed in the middle with white sheets, lots of fluffy pillows, and towels laid over the comforter.

It also had restraints dangling from the back posts, more coming up the sides and end of the bed.

Fuck yeah.

She released him, turned to him, and immediately went for the buttons of his shirt.

"I'll be undressing you this time, Olivier," she shared as she started doing just that.

He nodded before he dipped his chin down and Olly watched as she exposed his chest. And he kept watching as she pulled the shirt over his shoulders and a look settled over her face he was getting used to.

A look he fucking loved.

Her face got soft at the same time hungry.

In a room at the club, she'd get that look but she withheld from him until she found it time to give in to what she needed.

This was always after she gave him what he needed.

Here, she did something about it.

Even as she moved her hands to his jeans to undo the top button, she bent in, nuzzling her face to his chest, and it took a lot not to lift his hand, cup the back of her hair, and plant her face there.

Olly managed not to do that just when she tipped her head back.

"Please take off your boots and socks," she ordered.

She then stepped back to allow him to do that.

He did it, straightened, and she came right back to him. Fingers in his waistband, she yanked his jeans and shorts down.

"Step out," she commanded, crouched in front of him, holding his clothing steady so he could step free.

When he was, she straightened, latched onto his cock again and gave a tug.

She led him to the foot of the bed, let him go, and curled into him, front to front. Sliding her hands from his waist back and down, she cupped his ass, again with her head tipped back.

"When I release you, climb on the bed, on your knees. Settle them near the restraints."

"You got it, Amélie."

She grinned, rolled up on her toes, and touched her mouth to the base of his throat.

Olly again fought the need to hold her head there, among other things.

She slid away.

He climbed into bed, settling as he was told.

When he was there, she didn't fuck around. She touched him sweet but she didn't take her usual time when she restrained him at the bend of his knees, his ankles, this with his thighs spread wide.

"Now lift your arms, beast," she ordered.

His eyes to her, he did and she shackled him with what felt like fur-lined cuffs, his arms up and outstretched. There was slack, not much. There was less movement in his legs.

Once she had this done, she glided a hand around his hip as she walked on her knees on the bed to get to his front.

As for Olly, restrained, hers to do with as she would, his dick was hanging low and heavy, his balls ached, and his jaw was again clenched, now against begging her to touch him. Take his cock in her fist. Squeeze his balls. Do fucking *anything*.

He kept his silence because he knew she knew better.

And she did.

To his disbelief, and pure fucking elation, while he watched, she pulled off her necklaces, her hair swaying as she did.

She dropped them to floor at the side of the bed.

Then off went her blouse.

She wasn't wearing a bra.

After that, she undid her belt and jeans and drew them down, with her panties, to her thighs, falling on a hip to allow her access to clear them from her legs.

She tossed them aside then she was again on her knees, unusually naked before him.

His dick started throbbing as his eyes took her in, her full tits, the swell of her hips, that sweet pussy with the strip of trimmed hair leading to her gorgeous nub he wanted in his mouth so bad he could taste it already.

"I've told you often but I'm uncertain you know how beautiful you are, Olivier."

His eyes went from her clit to her face.

"Perhaps you'll understand after I'm done with you," she went on.

"Do you know how beautiful you are?" he returned and got that look on her face, her eyelids lowering, features softening.

"My sweet beast," she whispered, but she didn't touch him, come in for a kiss.

She shifted back on her knees, and fuck him, *fuck him*, she bent, and with no preliminaries what-so-fucking-ever, she sucked his cock deep in her mouth.

His head dropped back automatically but Olly forced it forward and his eyes locked to her heart-shaped ass up in the air. Seeing that, the pressure of her hot, wet pull, he couldn't stop himself from thrusting.

She drew him out and gripped his balls in a hold that had pain shooting through his ass and cock. His head dropping back again, he felt a muscle jump in his cheek with his effort to hold back the grunt.

"Be good, Oliver."

"Yes, Mistress," he gritted.

She released him and then his Mistress went down on him and Christ, *Christ*, watching her gorgeous ass rock, her hair glide across the smooth, pale skin of her back, her mouth working his dick, Olly was clenching his plug up his ass and every other muscle he had, twisting his hands to grasp the bindings in order not to take over.

And then he'd had enough.

"Baby," he groaned.

As was her way (fucking brilliantly), she kept at him.

God. Fuck. Fuck.

"Baby," he growled.

She released him and worked her way with her mouth up his stomach to his nipples and Olly panted, trying to pull his shit together as she did. His cock was pulsing, ready to blow, so if she wasn't ready for him to come (and she wasn't), he was grateful for the relief.

She lifted a hand to his neck and extended her thumb to stroke his jaw before she moved away, sending a lazy glance over him as she did, giving him a view of her ass again as she crawled to the night-stand.

She came back with a chain.

And he felt his grip tighten on his bindings when he saw at its ends were nipple clamps.

He knew what they were. He'd seen them in the stores. On subs at the Bolt and the Honey.

He'd just never had them used on him.

He didn't share this.

His eyes went to her and she took in his look, he knew she liked it, the struggle he was waging against the fear of the unknown, how those would feel, if they'd hurt too much, or if they'd give him more.

But it didn't stop her from going in, pinching his nipples, twisting them, pulling them, as Olly let go at the sensations this was causing, free in this space that was all hers, alone with his Amélie, allowing the noises to roll up his throat. Noises that felt like they started in his nipples, his cock, his plugged ass, tearing through his body and rumbling from his lips.

When she had them as she wanted them, blowing on them, just that against their sensitivity set his hips thrusting, she put the clamps to and twisted them closed so he felt them.

Fuck yeah.

He felt them.

There was weight with a definite tightness and hint of pain and it felt fucking *great*.

Then she yanked the long chain that hung between them and he *felt them* as it dragged his nipples down and she added a pull to the tightness that increased the brilliant pain, and the spectacular sensitivity, when she hooked the chain tight around his ball sac.

"Fuck, baby," he grunted, his attention scattered, the focus broken, nipples, balls, ass, cock, all of it not good, all if it fucking *great*. "Fuck," he grunted again.

"Now it's time for your gift, my steed," she whispered, moving behind him.

Twisting gently, he felt the tug and the release of losing his plug, a feeling that was sweet.

But he'd learned being full felt a fuckuva lot better.

He turned his head to look at her, that movement yanking on the chain, drawing it up his balls and pulling at his nipples.

Christ, fucking *brilliant*.

Fuck, but she knew how to work him.

"Amélie."

He said no more but how he said it gave her what she needed. He knew it when her face warmed with satisfaction at the same time it filled with more craving.

She moved off the bed and he twisted again, gritting his teeth against the pull of his chain, as he watched her move across the room behind him.

She did something at a dresser that he couldn't see before she turned.

He felt his body lock solid as she came back to him, and in her hands she held a plug of substantial size and from it trailed a tail that looked like it matched the hair on his chest, legs and around his cock fucking perfectly. The tail was long, at least three feet, and if he was in another state, he might find it handsome.

Or alarming.

He was not in that state.

And he was not in the state to deny her tailing him.

He was in the state that he wanted to perform for his Mistress, do it with intent and do it fucking *now*.

"I had it specially made, my steed," she told him, approaching the bed. "It has many functions and I'm hoping all of them are pleasing."

"Baby," he growled.

She looked into his eyes and what she saw made her lick her bottom lip.

He jerked at his arm bindings.

"Baby."

She got to the side of the bed. "Are you ready to be tailed, beast?"

"Yeah," he grunted.

"Are you ready to perform for me?"

He was ready driving up to her house.

"Fuck yeah, Amélie."

"Oh, you please me," she whispered, entered the bed on a knee and gave him what he needed.

She needed.

She settled at his side, slightly behind him, and slid the lubed end of the plug through his crack until she found his hole and he watched her face, his neck twisted, his chain pulling.

She turned her gaze to his.

"Tail me," he growled.

She drove that plug home.

At the swift, unbelievably outstanding feeling of fullness, a grunt tore from his chest, exploding in the room, and he heard her soft noise of pleasure but he got no more from her. Or he did, he just was so gone, he couldn't focus on it.

This was because Amélie turned it on and she didn't take him there easy. That thing vibrated up his ass, thumping right where he needed it, doing it violently.

And Olly performed.

He had no choice but to perform but that didn't matter.

He'd do it for hours. Days. Years.

It was just that . . . fucking . . . *phenomenal*.

He drove his hips through the air, his body arcing, giving all his weight to the bindings at his wrists so he could thrust up, fucking nothing, feeling everything, including Amélie sliding a hand soft and sweet down the back of his thigh, up the inside, over his clenching ass, through his long tail.

He could take no more.

He turned his head, his chain pulling, his hips still pumping, and thought he caught her eyes but he couldn't tell.

He was gone, hers, all hers, everything she gave him was everything he was free to be, everything he *could* be.

Everything he just fucking was.

For her.

Focused on nothing but the sensations she'd created coursing hot through his body, his cock an aching pulse, his balls drawn up feeling so full they'd burst their restraints, his nipples shooting equal measures of pain and pleasure up to radiate over his scalp and down to grip his cock, balls, and hole, his ass clenched around his tail.

Not to mention he was too busy begging, *"Mistress, please."*

"Come, Olivier."

He instantly arched and did it insanely.

And goddamned fucking *proudly*.

Driving his cock into the air, he shot, his plug thumping up his ass, his dick exploding, the position of his body yanking violently at the clamps at his nipples at the same time it pulled up his balls at the scrotum.

It wasn't phenomenal.

It was goddamned motherfucking *sensational*.

And he couldn't stop his groans of, "Yeah, fuck yeah, *fuck yeah*," as his cum arced through the air and hit a towel.

He thought his orgasm wouldn't stop, didn't want it to stop, wanted to have that as long as he could have it, wanted to give it to Amélie, and as ever, she knew what he wanted.

So she didn't allow it to stop when she cupped his balls and gave them a firm squeeze.

Her touch rocketed every-fucking-where and his back arched even deeper.

"Fuckin' fuck," he grunted, cum still streaming. "Yes, baby," he pushed out.

When finally he was spent, she released him, took the vibrations of his plug down low, and Olly sagged immediately, hanging from his bindings.

He heard rather than saw the towels being swept away and felt his arms being released. One then swiftly after, the other.

Unable to stop himself, he dropped forward, face in the bed, ass in the air.

He felt Amélie settle at his side, her hand light and soothing on the skin of his hip, curving over his ass, her voice gentle even as she said, "Get used to this particular positon, Olivier. You'll be in it a lot."

"Great," he muttered.

He heard her soft, contented laugh and his hips bucked when she threaded her fingers through his tail.

Fucking hell, she did it for him.

Christ.

She was perfect.

And Olly knew in that moment that he'd do anything for her.

For as long as he had her.

Which he hoped like fuck was a very long time.

"It suits you wonderfully, *mon amour*," she purred admiringly.

"Glad you like it," he told the bed.

Her hand left his tail and came to his hair where she gripped it and he lifted his head because he had no choice.

Olly was looking at her.

She was looking at her hand in his hair.

"You haven't cut it since we met," she said reflectively.

He had other things to do, like work, sort through the stuff fucking with his head, and getting his shit jacked by a beautiful red-head who he was falling in love with.

"No," he agreed.

Her gaze came to him as her grip tightened. "I like it like this."

Then she'd have it like that. He was not a man-bun, lumbersexual type of guy but if she wanted to take a grip on his hair, he'd give it to her.

Fuck, tailed ass in the air, it was pretty much a given he'd give her anything.

Suddenly, she let him go but just as sudden, she gripped him by the hair again. This after she shifted up from his side toward the pillows, throwing a leg over his body, and then she slid down.

With her hand forcing it there, Olly had his face buried in her pretty pussy before his mind caught up to what she was doing.

Then he had his tail up his ass vibrating deeper.

"Baby," he whispered against her cunt, not even going soft, his dick started getting hard again, but needing her permission, wanting nothing more than to bury his tongue deep.

"Eat," she ordered.

He ate. Fuck, he took everything from her sweet pussy, drenched with her response from watching what she'd given him, he'd given her, cupping her ass and pulling her into him so he could devour her.

She gave him more with his tail as she did it. She gave him more with her noises as he did it.

And when both of them were desperate and his hips were thrusting, rocking the bed, she grasped his hair again, yanked his face out of her sex, and slithered down.

She turned the plug up all the way and rasped, "Fuck me, beast."

He didn't even feel himself positioning. He just drove into her hot wet and drilled her. Out of control. Wild. Savage.

Just like his Amélie liked it.

He felt her come and distractedly heard it, his focus again scattered, ass, cock, balls, his chain pulling, the taste of her in his mouth, the smell of her, their noises, he knew he wasn't going to be able to wait for her order to blow.

Luckily, she gave it.

And he blew, driving her by her pussy up the bed while doing it, only stopping and clamping down on her to hold her to take his fucking when his restrained legs wouldn't allow him to move with her.

He was spent, bucking weakly into her, his face in her neck, his breaths coarse against her skin when she turned the plug all the way off.

Olly again sagged, resting some weight into a forearm but giving her the rest of it.

Amélie didn't seem to mind, her hand drifting on the skin of his back, his ass, his hip.

Not phenomenal. Not sensational.

Motherfucking *colossal.*

Everything, from releasing his dick from his jeans at her front door to right then, her hand moving on him gently, petting him, soothing her beast.

He caught his breath and gathered his wits.

Just as he did this, she asked, "Are you hungry, Olly?"

His head came up and he looked down at her.

Then he burst out laughing, his head jerking back with that, his laughter having a grunt as his chain pulled, so he dropped his face and shoved it in her neck again.

When his laughter died, she asked, "Well, are you?"

Something struck him and that wasn't funny.

He looked at her.

"You tailed me."

There was something there, if he accepted it, which he'd done, and they both knew it.

Jenna and Barclay both told him that Doms gave subs things to lay claim. Mostly jewelry. Bracelets, cuffs, necklaces, chokers, nipple chains, cock rings.

Usually, these things could be worn visible so that out at a club or at a party, another Dom would know a sub was claimed. Or even out in the ordinary world, a Dom would know their sub was walking around, wearing their mark. Sometimes, these things were from past relationships and a sub would wear them simply to indicate which way they swung so a Dom eying him or her would know.

But Olly knew what was up his ass was that kind of gift.

She hadn't given that to anyone else.

And he wouldn't take it from anyone else.

Yeah, he'd made his decision about how their chat would go on Sunday.

And Leigh had made hers too.

As these thoughts cycled through his head, feeling great, Olly watched uncertainty wash across her face before she hid it but she couldn't quite control it seeping into her words when she stammered, "Are you . . . you seemed keen—"

He cut her off so he could take her out of that place in her head.

"It's beautiful, Leigh-Leigh."

She relaxed under him.

"And packs a punch," he went on, giving her grin.

"I had asked for added power."

"Well, you got it," he confirmed.

"Good," she whispered, lifted up, brushed her mouth to his, and then dropped back down. "Now I asked my Olly if he's hungry."

"Plug up my ass, hard most of the drive, you think I'd stop for food rather than get here fast so you could jack my shit then make me a sandwich?"

He felt her body tremble with her laugher under him.

It felt fucking awesome.

"Then let's get you some food," she said and it seemed she was making a move to slide out from under him but he lifted both hands to cup the sides of her head and Olly again got her complete attention.

"Thank you for my tail, baby," he whispered and saw her face soften but her eyes started shining, almost like they were getting moist.

With that he knew it meant just what he thought it meant.

He also knew just how much that was.

"And my chain," he continued and dipped low, touched his nose to hers and slid it down the side, down her cheek so he had his lips at her ear. "Rocked my world again, Leigh-Leigh. Fuckin' beautiful."

"I'm glad you enjoyed it, sweetheart."

He kissed her neck and didn't confirm he enjoyed it. When she wasn't part of the show, she'd watched.

She knew.

He lifted up. "Now feed me."

She smiled then ordered gently, "Back to your knees, Olly. I'll take care of you."

He pushed back to his knees and she took care of him.

In his jeans, his shirt on but unbuttoned, with her pulling on a soft green kimono-type silk robe and tying it tight, they walked hand in hand to the kitchen.

And he finally took in her place.

The Amélie he met who harnessed his cock to the floor and paddled his ass before she made him ride that paddle with his dick was a woman who, if he was told she owned this house, he'd call the teller a liar.

Leigh, on the other hand, belonged there.

All around, white adobe walls, dark beams exposed in the ceiling, but splashes of color everywhere. Native American inspired rugs over the tiled floors. Slouchy, comfortable-looking furniture you wouldn't feel like a twat if you spilled your beer on it. Big, colorful toss pillows. Prints on the walls.

It was all rugged, rustic, southwestern or Indian or Mexican, nothing contemporary or elegant, nothing to break the feel this was not a place to see, it wasn't a place to be, it was a place to kick back and *hang*.

Though, in the great room (which wasn't strictly great, it was snug and smallish, and downright cozy, another indication this wasn't a place she entertained, this was intimate to her, private) he reckoned the print over the adobe fireplace was an original DeGrazia.

She took him to a kitchen that had a high bar lined with stools that marked it from the living room and let him go to keep moving.

Only there did he see the money. Restaurant-quality fridge and stove. Imported Mexican tile, and not the kind you could buy in bulk at some tourist place. Battered copper backsplash behind the range with the only hint to her heritage, slanted fleur-de-lis stamped in the corners.

"My assumption was, that body of yours needs a good deal of fuel," she stated as she rounded into what looked like a short hall at the side of the kitchen. "Though I didn't know your preferred fuel. So I got a lot of everything."

Olly really fucking liked the idea of Leigh going grocery shopping, getting food in, trying to find things he wanted.

He'd have to share what he liked.

And he was looking forward to discovering the same from her.

On these thoughts, he heard a door open and stood in the kitchen, staring down at the tile when a gorgeous, sapphire-eyed Siamese cat with chocolate boots, face, tail, and ears slunk into view.

The thing was weaving around the legs of his jeans before he noticed a hefty notch had somehow been taken out of one ear, there was a slight hitch when it moved its right hip, and that it had lost some of its tail.

But Olly stood frozen, staring down at it, doing this because he was unable to process Amélie having anything less than perfect, most definitely her ownership of another being. Even this house, as laid-back as it was, was still perfect, every inch.

"That's Cleopatra."

He tore his eyes from the cat to look at Leigh standing six feet from him, watching her pet with a look of pure affection on her face.

Fuck him.

Fuck.

Him.

Jesus, she was beautiful.

"She needs to be contained in the laundry room." Her attention came to his face. "She's far too curious to be able to roam free while we play."

"Looks like she's got a limp," he observed before asking, "And what happened to her ear and tail?"

The affection slid from her face as some strong feeling slightly twisted it and she turned away, giving him her back to open the fridge.

"She's a rescue," Leigh shared. "They thought she was about eight when I got her a year ago. Malnourished. Dehydrated. The vet who cared for her liberated her from her old owners, who apparently had a child who liked to inflict pain." She leaned back to look beyond the fridge door to him.

Leigh had adopted an older, abused cat.

Fuck, it was rare anyone adopted older pets and taking one on that had been abused and might have issues . . .

He looked down at the cat sitting in front of him now, staring up at him with curious, intelligent eyes.

"She like to be picked up?" he asked.

"She likes all forms of attention," Leigh answered.

He bent and lifted the cat.

She started purring and trying to climb his shoulders, snuggle his neck, and she did both immediately.

"Stasia is probably hiding," Amélie continued. "She's older. I rescued her when she was twelve. She's fifteen now and very friendly once she gets to know you. This will be around the time you have duffel in hand, ready to leave. And this she'll watch you do with some satisfaction from a window far away."

"So I take it you're an animal lover," Olly noted.

She came out with arms full of deli bags topped with three bags of bread.

She dumped it inelegantly, and he thought adorably hilariously, all on the bar counter.

"Yes," she declared. "And for your information, your fabulous new toy as well as your cuffs are not real hair or fur. They're synthetic. The best of synthetics but they absolutely are not real."

He grinned at her, massaging her cat's neck. "So you're an *animal lover*," he repeated.

"I work at a vet."

Olly blinked.

Leigh stared down at the shit on the counter. "All right. I have roast beef, turkey, honey ham, provolone, Swiss, Cheddar, every condiment under the sun, and white, sourdough, and rye bread."

"You work at a vet?" he asked.

She looked to him.

"Well, volunteer. The vet I took my last cat to, and sadly, the cat passed, has a heart that veritably bleeds. He does so much pro bono work, it's a wonder he doesn't sleep on the couch in his office, which he does, but not because he doesn't have a home, because he works too much. He also is known not to take pets abandoned by their owners at his practice, something that happens shockingly frequently, to a kill shelter. He shelters them and re-homes them. Because he's known for this, people drop other animals at his business. Dr. Hill shelters those and re-homes them too. Recently, he had to increase his space because of this. I donated to help with that, and to assist in keeping his overhead down, two and a half days a week, I work for free in his back office doing billing, answering phones, and scheduling appointments."

"You work for free for a bleeding-heart vet," Olly intoned.

"Yes," she easily confirmed. "It's not tremendously enjoyable work but a bonus is I get to play with the animals when I'm there. Now what kind of sandwich do you want, darling? Because it might take me a year to list all the kinds of chips I bought and we should get to that."

Olly's dad had three dogs, two cats, and four parakeets. Olly's dad and his mom had always had pets while Olly was growing up and they'd taught him, his brother, and his sister not only how to respect but give a happy life to animals.

Olly's father would be cautious and unsure of an Amélie in her expensive heels and clingy dresses.

He'd have absolutely no problem with a woman in faded jeans and southwestern necklaces who volunteered for a vet and adopted flawed animals no one else would want, no matter how gorgeous they were.

"Roast beef," he whispered and at his tone, her head twitched and her focus on his face intensified. "Provolone. Mayo. Rye. And I'll pick the chips after I go get my bag."

"Olly—"

"I love animals, Leigh-Leigh."

Her gaze dropped to her cat still in his arms before it came back up to his.

And she gave him the soft.

She said nothing to what he said nor did she bring attention to the moment they'd just shared.

At the same time she did.

"Don't let either of my babies outside," she said quietly. "And watch for Stasia. She's the master of the great escape."

"Wouldn't dream of letting her out," he returned but took Cleopatra with him and kept hold of her as he got his duffel, shifted it from its position outside to that same place inside.

He went back, asked where the chips were kept, found she did not lie when she said it'd take a year to list them, and went for the old standard. Taco-flavored Doritos.

He set Cleopatra free when he sat on a stool opposite Leigh at the bar and she put a full plate of food in front of him, going back to the fridge to get him a beer.

She placed the opened bottle next to his plate while he took a bite of the massive sandwich she'd piled high with beef and cheese as she asked, "Do you have pets?"

He shook his head, chewed, and swallowed.

"Lost my dog 'bout four months ago. Giving it time. I'll know when it's right and then I'll get another pup."

"I'm sorry, Olly."

"Me, too, babe. He was a great dog."

She nodded. "They all are."

"So you volunteer at a vet, what else do you do?" he asked.

She shrugged but her expression shifted in a way he didn't get.

"Not much, actually. I have an adviser who assists with the investments and board functions I inherited from Dad, but I do have to have a hand in all that and it takes time, if not much."

"Lady of leisure," he remarked, hoping it came out teasing.

She looked to the countertop and muttered, "Unfortunately."

But Olly didn't like that from her, not the look on her face, not the tone of her voice.

Not at all.

"Leigh," he called and got her attention again. "What gives?"

"I don't like charity work," she told him immediately, and confusingly. "For my ilk, that means fund-raising. Mother was gifted with that. I abhor it. I also don't like sitting on boards as it's tedious in the extreme, and I have a seat on eight. My great-great-grandfather made our money. Assembly lines. He built them. He made a fortune from them. My grandfather saw the merits of selling that business and investing in technology. He was ahead of his time and had an uncanny knack for seeing in the future. He invested and taught my father to invest in things that no one would ever imagine would soar. Xerox. Google. Those kinds of things. My father loved it, buying, selling, taking risks, monitoring the rewards. Me, I don't have that love."

"So, young age, you inherited all this from your dad and took over but don't like it much."

"That's the gist of it," she said.

Olly swallowed a chewed chip and asked, "You trust this adviser?"

"Yes," she answered. "Implicitly. He also worked with Dad."

"So hand the shit you don't like over to him and find something you do like."

"It isn't that easy, darling."

"How isn't it that easy?" he pushed, throwing another chip in his mouth.

"There's only one thing I'm good at," she smiled, "and I give that away for free."

He didn't find her amusing and his tone was low when he stated, "You aren't your sexuality, Leigh-Leigh."

She hesitated a moment before she replied softly, "Touché, Olly."

"Okay, babe, Xerox? Google?"

"Yes," she repeated. "Though we've long since sold our shares in those."

"So you got money."

"I do," she confirmed.

"Then stop investing it in shit you don't care about and invest it in you. You like animals, go to school and become a vet tech. Fuck, be a vet. You find it's not that that trips your trigger, it's something else, find what it is and do it."

She looked startled for a second, genuinely, *deeply*, not hiding from him how much what they were discussing troubled her, something he hated but also fucking loved that she gave it to him so he could give back to her, before she gave him the soft again and whispered, "My sweet beast is also wise."

Sensing the importance of what they were discussing, honored by it, even so far as moved by it since it was coming from his Leigh-Leigh, Olly gave her the soft, too, feeling it in his face and hearing it in his voice when he replied, "Easy to look in from the outside and have the answers, sweetheart. It's always that way. Harder to be up to your neck in it and find your way out."

"Yes, wise," she reiterated.

Man, but that felt good, the first and the second time she said it, not only that she felt that way, said it and meant it, but that "it" was indication he *did* have something to give to her.

Something important.

Something meaningful.

Something that wasn't about wealth or class.

Something that meant a fuckuva lot more.

Olly wasn't moved by that.

He was thrown by it.

In a seriously good way he really fucking liked.

"You're giving compliments, do it closer," he ordered, making an effort to keep the rough of emotion out of his voice, and luckily succeeding.

The time to lay that on her was their talk on Sunday.

Now, her laying this on him, it had to all be about his Leigh.

He saw her shoulders straighten. "You're being very bossy, Olivier."

"Good, that means you might paddle my balls later. Now, get your ass over here so I can kiss you and finish eating."

She looked adorably irked, and it was totally fake, before she stomped over to him.

He took a tug from his beer as she made her way, turned only so he could curl his arm around her waist, pull her to him, and he dropped a short, wet kiss on her mouth.

"Great sandwich, gorgeous," he said when he lifted away an inch.

"I'm glad you like it." She snuggled closer. "I'm hoping you enjoy dinner tomorrow much, much more."

His eyes dropped to her mouth. "Thinking my Leigh-Leigh has something special planned."

"Oh yes."

"Lookin' forward to that, babe."

She grinned.

He touched her mouth with his and kept his arm around her waist as he turned back to his plate.

"Hurry, Olly. Before we go to bed, I want to take you to the stables and show you my horses."

He turned again to her and looked down at her robe. "In that?"

"I'll go get dressed."

"Good call."

She leaned in and kissed his jaw then pulled from his arm and he twisted on his stool to watch her ass in her silk robe as she moved down the hall.

When she disappeared, Olly caught sight of a fluffy beast lurking at the side of the couch. It had a mess of gray, white, and black fur, some of it missing in patches around its haunches, yellow eyes inspecting before she saw she had Olly's attention and she slithered out of sight.

Leigh and her beasts, in search of flawed perfection she could give everything.

Olly finished his late dinner and did it grinning.

After their tour of the stables (she had two horses, both palominos, but a stable with four stalls), the bedroom she led him to was not the bedroom she'd worked him in.

It was a master, roomier but still cozier because it was more lived-in, master bath open to the room at the back through a double-wide arch.

The king-size bed also had four posts, distressed wood that looked untreated, spirals at the posts, carvings at head-and footboard. Creamy sheets and comforter set off with lime, orange, bright purple, and red toss pillows, some of them having embroidered Mexican crosses on them.

He had no idea what she'd planned. His guess, Amélie leading him to her personal space, it was going to be Olly and Leigh.

Regardless if she intended to play with him, right then it was just Olly and Leigh.

And he had to give her the honesty, so until he was done doing that, it needed to stay that way.

Therefore before she could say or do anything, he tugged on her hand and took her to the bed.

"Olly—" she started.

"Shh, Leigh," he shushed and said no more.

He guided her to the bed, sat on it, and tugged her again until she had no choice but to come up on the bed, one knee at his hip, the other knee swinging up on his other side, straddling him.

"Sweetheart—"

"I need ten minutes to talk to you, Leigh."

She studied his face then her body tensed in his hold.

"We're talking Sunday," she declared.

"Not about this. This has to be out there. And, baby," he pulled her closer, "I've trusted you a lot and you've never let me down."

A small flinch hit her face and he quickly amended.

"You let me down once for a good reason. But now, I need to ask more of that trust. I need you to listen to me. Hear me out. And try to get where I was coming from when I perpetrated a fuckup that, because of you, ended up not fucking me up. This isn't about our chat on Sunday. Been living with this for a while and I gotta come clean."

She was staring at him, lips parted, eyes uneasy, frame still tense in his arms when he was done speaking.

"You perpetrated a fuckup?" she asked when he didn't go on.

"I lied on my application for the club. I'd been in the life a couple of months, had two Mistresses. One who I'd had only one session with, that one I mentioned to you the other night. And with the other one, not many more."

Her hands were at his shoulders, but as he spoke, they slid down to press against his chest.

He gave her that distance but locked his hold to share when he was done with that.

He waited.

She made him wait.

Finally, she gave it to him.

"Olly, that wasn't smart."

"I knew I was in over—"

"I could have hurt you."

"You didn't, Leigh. You—"

"You could have ended up with someone like Delia and who knows how she plays."

He felt the sneer twist his mouth as he declared firmly, "That wouldn't have happened."

"A Domme could have bound and gagged you and done things—"

"A Domme didn't do that. My Domme is *you* and you took care of me. All's well that ends well." He tried to pull her closer. She resisted but he didn't give up and she relented, all while he finished, "and it all ended well. You saw to that."

"This life is not a game," she snapped. "A risk. A dare. An adventure."

"Bullshit, babe. It's all that and it's more."

She saw his point but kept right at him.

"Then it's a game you take seriously and you don't enter it unprepared."

"I knew that my first session with you. I told you I got a friend, he part-owns the Bolt. He's been unbelievably fuckin' cool with me. So if I had something I needed to work through, he helped me out."

"Well, thank God for that because the person who *should* have been available to you to work things through was *me*. And although I had concerns your previous Mistresses were severely lacking in talent, I did not have the information I needed to guide you through. And to make my point so you won't mistake me, I absolutely would not have worked you the way I worked you our first session, our second, our third, our fourth, you'd see the social room perhaps in *months*, are you following me?"

She was pissed.

Seriously.

But he had a point to make too.

So he was going to make it.

"I needed that."

"I know how it goes, Olly. I understand that need. It lives in me as well, but also I've been in the *game* longer than you."

"That's not the need I'm talking about," he shot back. "It is and it isn't. What I'm trying to say is, I didn't need anyone I didn't connect with dicking around with me and I needed a Mistress who would not *dick around with me*. I needed precisely what you gave me even though I didn't know it at the time. I don't know what powers are at work, Leigh, that led you to me, but I'd had shit jacking with my head for so long, swear to Christ, I thought it'd break me."

Her body loosened with despair at his words, her face suffusing with it, and Olly took advantage. He yanked her closer and didn't stop talking.

"I needed you to try me. I needed you to push me. I needed from you what you said you needed from a sub. I needed you to *break me*. I needed someone to throw me in the deep end and force me to learn how to swim. But I needed to do that knowing she was right there to pull me to the surface. And you were right there, Leigh, not pulling me to the surface. Leading me up and forcing me to surf a fucking killer goddamned wave."

Not surprisingly, she was stuck on what he'd said before.

"You thought that shit jacking with your head would break you?"

"A man like me does not let a woman lead him around by his dick . . . literally," he bit out.

Her hands slid from his chest to curl tight around his neck.

"Darling—"

"But *I* do. I get off on it. Fuckin' love it, if *your* hand is on that dick. I'm a man like me and that's how I like it. It took time to come to terms with that and it was half you working me, half watching your don't-give-a-shit attitude, deep in that life and reigning supreme in your place in it, doing that with pride and dignity. If I got some Mistress pussyfooting around with shit, not narrowing my focus, it'd keep half my mind open to the possibility I'm jacked up and I can't have that. I can't live with it. I can't live with who I am, what I need. And if I was left open to that overwhelming me, I'd turn it off, bury that part of me, let it infect me even as I forced myself to lose it forever."

"Then maybe you being *incredibly* foolish by lying to Aryas about your experience was a stroke of good luck."

He hadn't realized his own body had gotten tight, as well as his grip on her, until he relaxed both at her words.

"But only because it was me who claimed you that night and that's only because I'm exceptional at what I do," she finished snobbishly.

Olly fought a grin. "That's part right, part bullshit, baby. Always, in anything, it takes two to tango and you tailed me tonight so I'm gettin' that you're exceptional, fuck yeah," he said the last two words lower, rougher, pulling her closer. "I get that totally because I'm the one who gets that good. But you get it good, too, and you let me know that which was part of what I needed."

Even though she was melting, she still held on to her pissy, declaring, "For a rookie, you've got excellent instincts."

Olly shoved his face in her neck, murmuring, "Latent talents an exceptional Mistress had the chops to pull out of me."

"Indeed," she muttered.

"You done bein' pissed?" he asked.

"There's no going back. You're correct, all's well that ends well. It gives me the shivers to think of what you'd encounter if you'd found someone other than me, but you didn't."

She drew in breath but she wasn't done.

"And it's important to note that even if we'd discussed all of this in the beginning, any good Mistress, this goes without saying including *me*, would have sensed what you needed through that discussion, as well as while working you, and given it to you while they played with you."

He pulled his face out of her neck and looked to her.

"It had to be you," he whispered.

Her tawny eyes warmed so much Olly felt their heat on his face as she moved closer, smoothed a hand over his cheek and cupped his jaw.

"I love that you think that," she replied softly. "And I think you know what you did was reckless. I actually think you knew it at the time. But it's done. I just need to know two things. The first, trust goes both ways and I have to trust you're always honest with me."

He had more to give her but he hadn't lied about it. It was just that it wasn't until Sunday that she'd get it.

"Other than that, I've always been honest with you, baby."

She nodded, thankfully letting that go without busting his balls or digging into it for the next seven hours so he regretted giving it to her in the first place.

Said a lot about her. A lot he liked.

Then she asked, "Is that shit still jacking your head, Olly?"

"Fucked, but truth of it is, bent over a table, ass strapped open, on display, my Mistress throws down for me after a woman I don't know but know I detest says she's gonna fuck me raw, that shit didn't break in me. After enduring it forever, watching you do that, it just..." he paused, unable to fully explain it so he used the only word that came close, "disappeared."

Relief infused her features, she totally melted into him as she stroked his cheek with her thumb.

"This makes me happy, darling."

"Not as happy as me, Leigh-Leigh."

"I'll bet," she whispered.

"Now, we done?"

She kept stroking his cheek as she nodded.

Fuck, that was a helluva lot easier than he thought it would be.

Then again, this was Leigh.

"Good," he muttered.

And it sucked but he had one more thing to get into before they got past this and he wanted this in their rearview so he didn't delay.

"Fooled Weathers during my interview, Leigh," he noted.

She studied him a beat before she gave him the knowledge that she caught his meaning.

"You're worried Delia did the same."

"Yep," he replied.

She gave him a small grin and shifted a hint closer. "Although I do believe you might have partially got one past Aryas, I'll also note that you did the same with me. However, Aryas had his reservations in accepting Delia's membership and this is why she's watched. As for you, he had no reservations and he told me quite plainly he was keen to have you at the Honey, having you there for me."

She said this to assuage his concerns but Olly did not like it one fucking bit, seeing as Weathers doing that, especially with Olly's size, and strength, if he was another kind of guy, it might have put his Leigh in jeopardy.

On this thought, his brows drawing together, he said low, "I got the impression I wasn't pulling one over on him but he approved me anyway, and you're sayin' he did this just to give me to you?"

"There aren't many who could pull one over on Ary," she replied airily. "Or any of us, really. This why what happened to Evangeline so rocked all of us."

"That put you out there, Leigh," Olly pointed out.

"I do believe we both can agree it didn't," she said softly, still stroking his cheek with her thumb.

And fuck him, she was right.

But that didn't mean they were done with this topic of conversation.

"That might be true, but this doesn't make me feel better about the current situation at the club, Leigh-Leigh," he told her.

"You had references," she stated.

"Yeah, and they all lied," he reminded her.

She nodded smartly, not appearing like this bothered her at all. "What I mean to say is, at least one of your references must have convinced him, perhaps not of your experience, but of your character."

Barclay.

"My bud who owns the Bolt is a decent guy," he murmured.

"And Aryas knows the scene and most of the players. He'd definitely know the owners of the Bolt. If this *bud* of yours," she said that last with her lips twitching, "spoke for you, and Ary respects him, that was all he needed."

At least that made sense.

And it made him feel better.

Which meant this conversation could be over.

Thankfully.

Snaking a hand up her back into her hair, he pulled her mouth down to his and he kissed her.

Then he rolled her in the bed.

And after that, Olly took his time, and so did she, memorizing every curve and swell of her beautiful body while he made love to his Leigh.

Including fucking her against the door, vanilla sex was never as good for Olivier.

Then again, maybe it was just that, in their present moment, whatever that moment was, it was always the best when it was with Leigh.

And after she came back to him once she'd cleaned up, both of them naked, he fell asleep for the first time with Leigh tucked into his front, a cat curled at the small of his back, another one he could feel curled on the pillow behind his head.

Stasia melted early.

Olly wasn't surprised.

She was Leigh's.

sixteen

Dream Come True

AMÉLIE

Amélie's eyes opened when the arm curled around her belly tightened and a deep, drowsy voice sounded at the back of her hair.

"There's a cat that needs feeding and there's a beast that needs to be worked, baby."

After that, Olly pressed his hard cock to her ass.

She felt her eyelids drift down, enjoying the hardness at the curve of her ass, but more, the contentedness she felt finally waking up with Olly (after she'd finally slept with Olly), not to mention all that had happened last night and anticipating what would happen that day.

Then she turned in his arm.

She took another moment to revel in Olly, snuggling in to his big, warm body, nuzzling then kissing his throat as she snaked her arm around his waist.

"I'll go feed the cats," she said there.

"Good call, but if you tell me where their stuff is, I'll—"

She tipped her head back and when she did, Olivier interrupted himself to dip his chin down to catch her eyes.

"No, Olivier. You'll have ten minutes to prepare for me. Today, all day, you serve me."

She saw the banked fire stoke in his eyes, felt his arm tense around her and she pressed closer.

"All day, Olivier. Do you think you can handle that?"

"Try me," he challenged.

Oh, she was going to.

She grinned slightly.

Then she ordered, "When I get back, I want you in this bed on your back, head to the pillows. And I want three towels down on the bed under your hips."

"You got it, Mistress."

She liked he was ready for play.

But she was not done.

"And I want your knees up, legs spread, hands at your inner thighs, keeping them open for me. No harness."

The fire in his eyes blazed and the drowsy was gone from his voice, but not the gruff, when he replied, "Yes, Mistress."

"Right." She touched her lips to his. "Prepare for me, *chevalier.*"

Without hesitation, Olivier rolled one way.

Amélie rolled the other.

She pulled on her robe, went to the guest bath, brushed her teeth, opening one of the new toothbrushes she kept there for use of guests who might have forgotten to bring one to do it. She then splashed water on her face. After that, Amélie went to the kitchen, fed her cats, and made coffee.

She was hips to the counter, sipping said coffee, thinking it'd probably been over fifteen minutes since she'd left him so she contained a now-grouchy in the laundry room Cleopatra before she grabbed the bowl she needed and went back.

But she also retrieved his tail before she entered her room.

He was in position and more than ready for her, his big cock hard and lying on his stomach, his blue eyes going immediately to his tail.

Not saying a word, Amélie approached the bed, swung the tail out and set it at the side, doing this before she skirted the bed and went to the bathroom to prepare.

She came back with the big fluted glass bowl filled with warm water, as well as shaving cream, a razor, and several hand towels, one of which she'd wet with hot water and wrung out.

"Mistress," he grunted.

He knew what was coming.

Her rookie with the good instincts.

He wanted to be thrown in the deep end?

She'd help him surf that killer wave.

"Stay in position, *mon chou*, you'll want to remain steady," she ordered as she sat on the side of the bed, not hesitating a second to place the hot towel where she needed it. She then looked to his eyes and got a hint of that wild she was growing to love, with it coming the delicious understanding she'd never quite tame her sweet beast. "We won't want any accidents while I shave you."

"Amélie."

She said nothing, just held his gaze steady.

"Fuck," he whispered his surrender.

"You're beautiful, beast. As you are. We'll see how I prefer it when that pretty cock is entirely exposed to me."

He dug his head in the pillow and muttered again, "Fuck."

Fighting a contented grin, she set the bowl on the bed, the towels and razor down, and she filled her palm with shave cream.

She gave the towel a few more moments to do its work before she pulled it away.

She lathered him.

At this touch, his hands automatically clenched at his thighs, drawing his ass up, pressing his legs wider.

Her clit pulsed.

Lovely.

"Yes, Olivier, I like that position better. Retain it," she commanded.

"Christ," he groaned.

She picked up the razor, swished it in the warm water, and went to work.

She was wet before the first stroke.

On her last, she felt herself dripping as his body shuddered, his balls heavy, his cock red and distended, his noises choked back.

Amélie threw the razor in the bowl and took a towel, wiping away any residue.

"Pretty," she whispered.

And he was.

She liked him like this and she'd have him this way often.

But so she could groom him, he'd also need to grow it back.

She looked from his pretty dick to his clenched jaw, which was all she could see, his head pushed back, his throat moving with a swallow.

And she felt more wet gather between her legs.

She could have no idea if he liked how he now looked, but it was clear he'd enjoyed being shaved.

She ran a lazy finger on the smooth skin, then around his balls and down to his hole, where she touched it to his rim.

His legs trembled and he pressed in, forcing the tip of her finger inside.

She liked that so she bent over him and ran her tongue along his sac between his testicles and up the underside of his cock.

"Baby."

She straightened away, pulling her finger from his ass. "You're taking your tail now, Olivier."

He lifted his head to look at her.

Wild gone.

Nothing but need.

My.

There was simply no way to express how delighted she was Olivier so liked his tail.

"Yes, Mistress," he pushed out.

"Stay in position."

"Yes, Mistress," he gritted, impatient to be filled.

She gave him a smile, reached to the tail, shifted the other way to reach to her nightstand, and she grabbed what she needed.

She prepared the plug, tossed the tube aside, and looked to Olivier.

"You'll take it all at once?"

"Yes," he bit out.

She tilted her head. "Rough?"

"Whatever way you want to give it to me, Mistress."

She straightened her head.

"Please," he forced out.

Amélie knew precisely how she wanted to give it to him.

So she positioned it and in one smooth stroke, drove it home.

Her inner thighs quivered watching his hands at his thighs jerk his entire bottom half up as he dug his head in the pillows.

Even better than expected.

She gave herself a long, lovely moment to enjoy the scrumptious view before her in her bed before Amélie retrieved the remote control and set the toy to vibrate, medium low.

"Turn, Olivier, offer your tail to me. On your knees. Cheek in the pillows. Arms out."

He didn't hesitate.

Amélie didn't either.

She moved from the bed and pulled the hidden sashes out from under the headboard, lifting them up. She bound one lash of silk around his wrist, holding his arm firm and wide, then she moved around the bed and lashed the other.

After that, she took the bowl, the towels, and the razor to the bathroom and she tidied.

Done, she went back to the bed, stroked his ass, and leaned in close.

"You'll remain this way for me for some time, Olivier. I'll be back to play."

His cheek in the pillow, she saw his eyes widen and cut to her. "Baby—"

"If I come back and see you've moved, this will annoy me."

"Mistress."

She twitched his tail. "Be good."

And then she walked out, setting the vibrations from medium low to medium.

So she smiled when she exited the room as she heard his groan.

Twenty minutes later, she hit the remote to a setting she had not yet used two steps before she entered her bedroom.

She heard his, "What the fuck?"

But what she saw was her custom-ordered tail that she'd had made on a rush (and at great expense) was a thing of beauty.

On its own, Olivier's tail was twitching.

"Amélie," he grunted.

"Yes, Olivier?" she asked, entering the bed from behind.

"Baby, give me something."

"All right," she answered agreeably, and she reached between his legs, grasped his cock in a tight fist, and ordered, "Perform for me."

"Thank fuck," he grunted as he jacked her fist, his ass moving through the air, and she bit her lip. Enjoying the show tremendously, she reached with her other hand to part her robe. Honing in on her target, she lazily circled her clit.

Oh yes.

Much better.

"Stop," she commanded, her voice husky.

"No, baby."

She gave him a hard tug.

"Stop," she snapped.

He stopped.

He was breathing heavily.

She turned his vibrations up.

"Mistress, fuckin' *fuck*," he growled.

"Perform," she ordered.

He thrust into her fist.

She gave him that until she felt his excitement ramp.

"Stop."

He came to a juddering stop, now puffing out air.

"Whatever you want, whatever you want, Amélie. Just let me come," he pleaded.

"Perform."

"Fuck yeah," he gritted and pumped her hand.

She gave him time, took him higher.

Then she ordered, "Stop."

"Fuckin' *fuck me*," he groaned as he stopped.

She pulled her finger from her clit, her hand from his cock, and heard his, "No, baby, please."

She stopped his tail twitching and lowered the vibrations.

"Mistress—"

"On your belly."

"Christ, Amélie."

She cracked a hand against his right flank. "Now."

He slid off his knees on an incensed growl.

She liked that sound but she didn't revel in it.

She pulled one of her beast's long, heavy legs wide and lashed it that way with another silk sash that was attached to the bed but hidden under it, tugging it tight at his ankle.

The same with the other.

She moved to the end of the bed, took in his magnificent beauty, and cooed, "So beautiful."

It was an understatement.

He was simply glorious.

"Mistress, fuckin'—"

She set the vibrations to high and watched with great delight as Olivier humped the bed, all that power leashed except at his hips, his fingers fisted around his bonds, the bed creaking, his tail swaying, his hips thrusting violently.

His grunts came fast and deep, his movements jerky and desperate, and she turned the vibrations all the way to low.

"Please, God, fuck, baby . . . Mistress, jack my ass. Let me come. Fuck."

"I'll be back, Olivier."

She watched the bed jerk with his nonverbal denial.

Glorious.

So again, Amélie was smiling when she left the room.

Fifteen minutes later, she walked back to the room, stood outside the door and turned up the vibrations.

She heard his groan of pleasure and fury.

So she was once again walking away smiling.

Twenty minutes later, she did the same, heard no groan but a warning rumble and again wandered away with a grin.

Half an hour after that, she walked into the room and felt the shudder roll up her pussy at the sight of her beast, his entire body slicked with sweat, lashed spread-eagle on her bed.

She turned the vibrations down low and even though he was prone, she saw his large, powerful frame slump into the bed.

He saw her, too, and begged, "Baby, please, fuckin' let me come."

"You'll come, my steed," she assured.

"Now, Amélie, in you, loosen the ties and slide under me."

She sat on the side of the bed and held his eyes.

"Mm," she purred. "Perhaps another time."

His eyes tilted to the side and locked on her, the heat there, the fury she'd heard, the deep, dark, delicious need shadowing him, her, even dimming the sun in the bright room, he growled, "Let me have your pussy. I won't eat it. Just hold my face to it."

"Another excellent suggestion, *mon chou*, but today I've decided on something different."

"Mistress, I'm beggin' you—"

Suddenly, she darted a hand between his legs, gripped his balls, and rolled the remote all the way to high.

His head jerked back.

Top to toe a thing of beauty.

"Perform, beast," she ordered.

She didn't have to order it. Holding tight in order to keep hold, Amélie watched as he fucked the bed.

"Come at will, Olivier."

"Yeah, fuck yeah, fuck, *fuck,* squeeze my balls, baby."

She squeezed.

And he blew, his grunts thundering through the room, the entire bed shaking as Olivier ejaculated his seed into the soft towels under him.

When his noises subdued and his thrusts weakened, she brought him low.

Then it began.

She took him up and took him there, listening to his words—angry, pleading, challenging, threatening, desperate. She did this touching him, stroking him, gripping him, squeezing him, his tail jacking his ass low and high, Amélie watching the entire show, glorying in all that was Olivier.

On his third orgasm, less powerful than the first two, she set the plug to low, took her toy from the pocket of her robe, lifted the robe up to her waist and moved to straddle his back, facing his lower half. She dropped the robe and felt his whole body twitch powerfully and magnificently as the silk slithered over his skin.

Rubbing herself against him, pressing her toy to her clit, Olivier emitted low frustrated snarls, yanking at his lashes feebly, and Amélie loved every fucking second, eyes to his beautiful, filled ass as she made herself come against the small of his back.

He'd been so marvelous, this didn't take long.

And her orgasm was not as glorious as watching him have his, but it wasn't far from it.

When she caught her breath, she swung off him, turned off and carefully extricated his tail, and set it aside.

Only then did she turn to his head, doing this shifting astride him again, this time facing his upper half. She lowered her body to his.

She got close and smoothed his hair away from his temple, bent deep, and touched her lips there.

"You please me," she shared gently.

"Next time I fuck you, gonna split you in two," he muttered, his deep voice drowsy and muffled by the pillow.

"Something to look forward to," she whispered as she stroked his hair and watched his eyelids flutter.

He was fighting sleep.

Amélie had a lot of patience so she saw it when he lost.

OLIVIER

Olly woke up and the first thing he saw was the glass of ice water on the nightstand.

Then he realized he was no longer tied to the bed or lying in his own cum.

He was on his side and under the covers.

Fuck, she jacked it all out of him, he didn't even feel her take care of him afterward.

He pushed up, reached for the water, downed it and knew he needed food.

Seriously.

He rolled out of bed, went to the bathroom, saw his duffel and looked back to the nightstand.

He didn't hear her or see a note.

This meant, he assumed, he was at ease so he grabbed a quick shower, got out, toweled off and bent over his duffel, pawing through it. He nabbed underwear, clean jeans, a tee and tossed them to the counter, starting to get dressed when he saw his shaved cock and balls and stopped dead.

It wasn't like he checked his brothers out but it still was not lost on him God saw fit to grant him a great dick.

But fuck, he liked it shaved and he could not fucking *believe* after she worked him over and good, he felt himself start to get hard, remembering the feel of Amélie gliding the razor there, more of her dragging her tongue there, and her whispered "pretty."

His Mistress knocked it out of the park every time and he hoped her imagination never dried up because she rocked his world each time she did it.

He stopped staring at his dick, dressed, and went in search of two things in a specific order.

Amélie and food.

Fortunately, he found her in the kitchen.

As she'd once said, two birds . . .

Her eyes came to him as she watched him walk her way.

She was in another pair of jeans, hair down, no jewelry, but a sexy, slouchy green top that looked like it had wings under the arms and it also fell off her shoulder, exposing a white tank under it.

Hot.

She was facing him and he moved right into her. Lifting a hand to scoop her hair to hold it in a tail behind her neck, he slid his other hand from waist to the small of her back, drew her to him and bent, kissing her bare shoulder.

"How are you, darling?" she asked.

He lifted his head but held on to her. "Hungry."

Her mouth quirked. "I'll bet."

"Looked like you had enough to make ten sandwiches. You do that, I'll eat 'em all."

She gave him a full grin. "I've got the Foreman heated up, waiting for you, so in but a few minutes, I could give you a burger."

"Better," he grunted.

"Pull a stool around to the side of the island and I'll get cracking," she ordered.

"Got only about that in me to do, sweetheart, until you feed me."

"Then I best get cracking."

Even saying that, she rolled up on her toes and he took his cue.

He bent and gave her his mouth.

She took it and Olly took hers too. Even starving, he took his time to explore it with his tongue before he ended it and lifted away.

"Burger," he muttered.

"Right away," she replied.

He let her go and got his stool.

She shifted to the Foreman and got cracking.

Cleopatra came out and wove around the foot he had on the floor, tilting her kitty head to sniff the one he had on the rung.

"Water, beer, Coke, Sprite, something else?" Leigh asked and he looked from her cat to her.

"Water, babe. And a Coke."

She nodded and brought both to him.

"Cheese selection, Olly," she said after he'd downed half the bottle of water she gave him.

"You got American?"

"Alas, no."

He grinned at her. "Cheddar."

She nodded and he decided to buy a Foreman because she wasn't wrong. She had a double burger with double cheese in front of him in no time.

He didn't hesitate to lift it up and dig in.

"No condiments?"

He saw her at the opened fridge. "I'm good," he replied with his mouth full.

"Onion? Tomato? Pickle?"

"Good, Leigh."

She nodded again then asked, "Chips?"

"Whatever your hand grabs."

She brought him whatever her hand grabbed, sour cream and chive. He broke the bag open and dug in.

"I'm seeing I should feed my beast before I test him," she noted.

He shook his head, swallowing a huge bite. "No, baby. You go your own way. You got your shit *tight*. I can recuperate when you're ready."

She leaned a hip into the counter and remarked smugly, "I take it you enjoyed your morning."

He lifted eyes from burger to her, saw Leigh was cute when she looked smug, but when he spoke Olly dropped his voice to a rumble.

"Next time I'm inside you, gonna drill you and keep doin' it until you come for me . . . *repeatedly,* beggin' me for more until you beg me to stop."

Her lips parted and her eyes went half-mast.

His tone changed when he finished, "That said, how you worked me was staggering. And I mean that in a good way."

Her grin came back. "I'm pleased, Olly."

"Leigh," he called even though she was looking at him. But she got his tone and he knew it when her body locked and her gaze riveted to his. "Disappeared," he whispered. "That thing fuckin' with my head. Gone. Thank you for that freedom, sweetheart. If you didn't struggle with it, I'm seriously fuckin' glad, but if you didn't, you can't know what it means. And it means too much to say, Leigh-Leigh. So I hope you get how deep I'm givin' that gratitude because it's really fuckin' appreciated."

She got close and put a hand to his thigh. "So nothing fucking with your head as I took care of you this morning?"

"Outside wishin' I could get free to spank your ass, not knowin' if I wanted to do that before or after I fucked it, that is whenever I wasn't totally focused on what was happening up my own ass . . . no."

Her smile came back. It was softer, but happier.

"Good." She slid her hand up nearly to his dick. "But no one spanks me, Olly."

"Mm-hmm," he mumbled, tossing a chip into his mouth.

Her eyes sparkled at him before she bent in and touched her mouth to his cheek that was working the chip.

She moved away, doing things, tidying things, but Olly focused on eating.

He was downing the Coke when she came to whisk his empty plate away.

He put the Coke on the counter as she told him, "Dinner needs simmering so even though you just had lunch, I'm starting it now."

"You had lunch?" he asked.

She looked to him, having grabbed a yellow onion. "Yes."

He grinned at her. "So one meal this weekend we'll eat together."

She grinned back. "Perhaps. I do hope to have a few with you tomorrow, though."

What Olly hoped was that she worked him in the morning. Even if she did the same exact thing, he didn't care.

Though if it was up to him, he'd change one nuance of it.

He didn't share that. He looked to the onion she'd put on a cutting board.

"You need help?" he offered.

She turned to him and tipped her head to the side. "What I need right now, my sweet beast, is for you to stand up, pull your jeans down to your thighs, rest again on your stool, and let me see my pretty groomed cock while I work."

Her "pretty groomed cock" jumped at her words.

"Amélie."

"Now, Olivier, if you please."

"This servin' you all day?" he asked.

"Absolutely," she answered.

He held her eyes, not struggling against that thing that fucked with his brain.

Now battling the man he was who wanted to take control. Spread her on the counter and eat her until she begged him to fuck her and then fuck her hard until she came, crying out his name, rather than stand at command and give her what she ordered.

But this was the game and she knew how to play it, how to take him there at the same time keep the man he was intact. So he won the battle, accepted the challenge, stood up, and carried out her instructions then sat back down, bare cock semi-hard but not there yet.

"Gonna drill you 'til you beg me to stop," he whispered, his gaze still locked to hers.

"Stroke yourself leisurely, please," she replied.

He did.

She went about her business with the onion.

He kept stroking as she cooked. Filling the air of the room with good scents. Sautéed onions. Seared steak she cut up into cubes. Spices she dashed into the lot.

He watched her while she did it, liking seeing Amélie in a space like that, doing normal shit.

Getting off on seeing her do that while he was exposed for her, stroking his dick.

But his Amélie, she was hands-on. She didn't leave him be, ignore him, make him feel like a piece of furniture.

She looked to him a lot while she cooked. And his cock. Her face getting hungry. She'd often come to him and touch his jaw. Kiss the side of his lips. Run her finger along his that were fisted around his dick.

Oh yeah.

She knew how to play the game.

It occurred to him vaguely—because jacking himself, even leisurely, exposed to her eyes and touch, he was getting hotter as the minutes wore on—she was making steak chili.

"Chili?" he asked.

"Nachos," she answered.

She was making him her nachos.

Fuck, even that felt good.

"Baby," he murmured.

She looked to him.

"Will you come here?" he requested.

She came to him, getting close and putting her hands to either side of his neck.

He didn't know how to share this with her.

He just knew after that morning he needed to share it with her.

And she was his Mistress, his Amélie, his Leigh, she'd listen.

"You got a cock?" he asked.

Her brows drew together and her hands gave him a squeeze. "I'm sorry?"

"What we saw, in the hall, that Mistress—"

She swayed even closer, her movement cutting off his words, her face dipping to his, her eyes showing she was surprised and intrigued.

"Would you like me to fuck you, Olivier?"

"Was alone today, Leigh."

Something washed over her face, understanding, maybe regret, and through her lips, she breathed, "Sweetheart."

"You're up my ass, you take me there while you're there and my guess is, that'll take you there."

"Did you not like being alone?"

He couldn't say that. Not with the way she'd worked him.

Olly did not lie, it was staggering in a good way. Torture, pure and sweet, and in the end, she'd made every second worth it. He'd never come so hard as that first time she'd made him come that morning.

Which was what he felt in every new scene she gave him.

So he explained what he was feeling by sharing, "No one has spent that much time on me."

She nodded. "Just to say, what we did today is not unusual in play."

"Never had it."

"Did you not like it?"

"Didn't say that."

"You prefer me close," she stated.

That was where he was at.

"Yeah."

"I know that but I thought here, in my house, the two of us alone, you'd know I wasn't far."

"I knew that but—"

"We'll have prolonged play again, Olivier. But I'll have more of a care. You've always shown you don't like me far. When it happens again, we'll work up to it and see where you are."

"Thanks, baby, but just to say, where I am right now is needin' not to jack my junk leisurely."

She looked down then up and before he knew it, her hand was in the back of his hair, tugging it so she could drop her mouth to his and kiss him hard.

When she was done she ordered, "Up, *mon chou*, jeans where they are, hands to the counter."

His dick jerked in his hand, he felt it.

And he got up and did as she said.

His head turned to her, he saw her assessing his position before she looked to his eyes.

"Legs wider apart, my steed, and feet farther from the counter, please."

He felt his balls get heavier thinking she was in the mood to knock it out of the park again.

And Olly was always in the mood to let her.

He did as told and the second he was done, she ordered, "Tip your ass."

Fuck yes.

He tipped his ass.

She studied him again before she purred, "Perfect, *mon chou*. Now stay in that position, don't move or alter it until I give you leave."

He not only heard but felt the rough in his voice when he replied, "Yes, Mistress."

She gave him a small smile, hooded eyes, and he felt his balls grow even heavier.

Then she went back about her business, finishing with her chili.

But she was much more hands-on with Olly this time.

She came often to cup his balls, gently massage them, reach through and stroke his cock.

But after she tended him, she'd go back to what she was doing.

Through it, Olly didn't know if it was better, holding position, knowing she was acutely aware he was there, available for her to tend to, take from, give to, or if he preferred when she was actually there tending to him, taking from him, giving to him.

His cock was aching, his legs trembling, his ass clenching, his balls hanging heavy by the time she had the chili simmering and the kitchen wiped down and tidy.

She seemed to be set to start something else and he couldn't stop the words from rumbling out of his mouth.

"Need you, Mistress."

Amélie turned to him.

"Please," he whispered.

"So good," she whispered back, thank fuck, doing it moving to him.

She positioned behind him and he felt her press her tits in his back.

Fucking fuck, fuck, fuck.

"Amélie," he groaned.

She reached around with both hands, gripping his cock and cupping his balls.

"You do not move. You do not thrust. You take what I give you," she commanded.

"Right, baby," he grunted, amazed he could say words now that she was clearly getting down to business, his mind this time having a singular focus, her hands on his dick and balls.

She stroked, and fuck him, she did it like she had all fucking afternoon.

"Amélie," he forced out.

"You take what I give you."

"Need more."

"Patience."

Fuck.

He took what she gave him until his whole body was trembling, he felt a sheen of sweat break out, and he was grinding his teeth with the effort not to thrust.

Or come.

She released him and moved away.

"Jesus, fuck," he panted, his eyes slicing to her. "Baby, fuckin' *please.*"

She said nothing but Olly watched her walk to her purse on the counter and come back with a condom.

Thank Christ.

Standing behind him she slid it on.

"Up on your toes, Olivier, press your ass into me."

He instantly gave her what she wanted.

And staying behind him, pressed to his back, she reached around and wrapped his cock with her hand. She also slid a hand flat down his back, through his crevice, shoved her finger only to the first knuckle up his ass, and she started to jerk him off with a purpose.

"I wish to hear your pleasure, beast," she ordered.

"More up the ass, Mistress."

She slid her finger deeper.

Outstanding.

His head dropped back.

"I need to thrust, Amélie."

"No."

"Then jack me harder, baby."

She gripped him tight and stopped stroking.

Shit.

"Ask nice."

He turned his head and caught her eyes.

She looked into them and the hunger took over her features.

"Please."

"Hold still, Olivier."

He locked his body the best he could against the trembling.

And she jacked him harder.

"Fuck," he grunted. "Fuck. *Fuck*, baby. *Beautiful*."

"Come at will, *mon amour*."

"Faster," he grunted.

She went faster.

"Harder, Mistress."

She gripped him tighter, tugging deep.

And she gave it to him. His head flew back and he exploded, shooting hard into the condom.

When he was spent, head now bent, hips juddering with the aftershocks of a fantastic fucking handjob, and she was just milking him, she pulled out of the back, rimming his hole gently and pressing her tits into him.

"Clean up and when you get back, my Olivier, we'll be going to the stables."

He felt his body get tight.

She did too.

"Olivier?" she called.

"Those stables, that guy you had when you were younger—"

She pressed close with everything, her hand sliding up his cock to the base, her other hand flattening at the back so she was holding him through the cleft of his ass.

"The ranch we had back then was much bigger, *mon amour*. When my father passed, I downsized. In nothing we've done here do you come after another. Your place everywhere we go and everything I use on you is just yours."

Olly felt his body relax.

Then it hit him they were heading to the stables.

Jesus.

Fuck.

Serving her all day.

She'd laid down the challenge.

He'd accepted it.

It just might kill him.

But he was loving every minute of it.

His tail up his ass again, vibrating, Amélie and Olly were alone in one of her empty stalls.

She'd let the horses out to pasture.

She'd also restrained him at his ankles, legs spread wide, and his arms, also spread wide, not much slack.

She'd further strapped his ass open and harnessed his balls.

And she'd kept the vibrations low up his ass while she cropped it as well as the backs and insides of his thighs.

And last, she'd paddled his balls with that biting sweet sting he liked so goddamned much.

Sweet agony.

All of it.

Yeah, this just might kill him.

And it was going to be a fucking astounding way to go.

She'd taken her time with it all. Each step. Lavishing him with attention to the point Olly did not feel he was in a stall in a stable.

It was Amélie and Olivier, what she was doing, what he was feeling, that was his whole world.

The crop went away and he felt the vibrations increase even as he felt his hole stretched.

That fucking tail not only twitched, it lifted.

Olly shuddered.

"Beautiful," she whispered, and he felt the slide of the crop through his legs from behind, shafting up, stroking his balls and dick.

Olly rode it.

"*Beautiful,*" she breathed, taking more, watching him give her what she wanted.

Finally, she glided it away and, drifting a hand over his hip, she moved to his front.

He did his best to catch her eyes.

"Your ass red from my crop, your tail seated so pretty, your cock heavy." She gripped his dick and her grip shot from cock to balls to ass right up his spine, radiating over his scalp then spiking down over every inch of his skin.

Agony.

So damned sweet.

He gritted his teeth.

"Are you enjoying serving your Mistress, my beast?"

"Yes," he bit out.

"You have so much to give, all of it pleasing," she shared.

"Thrilled, Amélie," he grunted, because she'd said that while she stroked him deep.

"One last thing I ask of you, *mon chou*, and I'll be releasing you so you can give it to me."

"Anything."

He said it. He meant it. In a stall. In her barn at the club. In her bed. Balls paddled. Ass strapped. Bent over a table in the social room. On his back, his legs in the air, stretched wide, her pussy shoved in his face. Naked and on hands and knees before her, her pretty feet resting on his back while she read a goddamned book.

Fuck, he'd take her fucking him up the ass if she was behind the cock.

Olly would take anything from his Amélie.

So he could give everything to his Amélie.

"Do you remember the second time I had you?" she asked.

He tried to focus on her when he had so much to focus on. The air on his tanned ass and thighs was burning into his skin, up his hole, into his balls. Those balls were straining. His tail was still thumping up his ass. And if she didn't stroke him again, he was afraid he'd lose it and thrust.

She tugged him, it shot up and back, and he grunted at the beauty.

"Olivier?" she called.

"I remember," he pushed out.

"Assume that position."

"Yes, Mistress."

"So good," she murmured, let his cock go and moved to the restraints.

She released him and Olly dropped. He turned his calves in at the back, arched into them with his hands at his ankles, back bowed, this shoving his tail deeper up his ass, and that felt so fucking phenomenal, he felt a drop of pre-cum drip from his dick.

"And what caused that, I wonder," she purred.

She could take her pick.

Amélie smoothed her finger over the head of his cock, whisking away the cum, and he watched her touch that finger to her tongue.

Fuck, he needed this done.

"*Mistress.*"

She turned her eyes to him, on his knees, arched proudly, offering his cock to her.

The hunger took over her face and Olly nearly exploded at the look of it before she bent to him, latched on and jacked him brutally, just as he needed it. Using his dick to yank his whole body into a deeper arc, shoving his tail farther up his ass, blanking his mind to everything but her and him and that moment they had together of trust and giving and understanding and sheer fucking beauty.

"Take my cum," he grunted.

"Give it," she ordered.

And he shot, hearing his uncontrollable snarls, his cum jetting up his belly as she milked him dry.

When his load slowed, she drew down the vibrations and stroked him gently, gliding a hand over his cock head as he shuddered through the last spurts, and when she released him, he slumped, ass to calves, arms falling forward, head bowed.

He felt her get close and she stroked the back of his hair. So it took effort, but he gave his Mistress what she wanted.

He tipped his head back.

She moved and kissed him, deep and soft.

When she lifted away, she whispered, "You're like a dream come true, my Olivier."

He seriously fucking liked it that she thought that way, said it like she meant it more than he could imagine, and did it looking at him like it was the straight-up truth.

He also knew what she meant.

"Right back atcha, baby," he mumbled.

With his words, Olly watched his Amélie's eyes smile.

"Serving is done," she said softly. "I'm unsurprised but still feel the need to share that you've performed magnificently. I'll take care of you now, but for the rest of the night, it's just Olly and Leigh."

The good part about that was that he wanted that, was looking forward to having Leigh and nachos and probably college football (and some recuperation time) at her kick-ass ranch in the Arizona mountains.

At the same time he was disappointed it was over.

He'd get it back.

And if he worked it right—and he was going to fucking work it right—he'd have them both.

For a very long time.

It was the early hours of the morning when Olly woke her.

The cats vacating the premises immediately, he didn't delay.

He worked her until he had her excited and under him.

Then he hauled her up to her knees and he drilled her.

He'd come five times that day. He was primed.

So he mounted her, curving over her, mouth working every inch of her neck, up behind her ears, shifting her hair out of the way when he needed to, tugging it out of the way when he felt like it.

And he fucked her, powering into her, hard and deep, alternating fingers to clit and each tit like he could take her until dawn and beyond.

And her harsh breaths, her whimpers, her soft cries, her hot, drenched pussy spasming around him driving him on, her lips begging him not to stop, Olly took Leigh there.

And again.

And again.

And again.

Until her knees gave out from under her and she was held up only by his dick.

Olly caught her at the top insides of her thighs, pulling them apart, feeling the contraction of her cunt around his dick when he did, hearing her sharp gasp hit him right in his balls.

And he continued to pound into her.

Until she came again.

And after, finally she twisted her neck to catch his eyes and begged faintly, "Please, baby, I can't take more."

Only then did he drive deep, filling her and watching her head jerk back convulsively, her hair dark in the shadows flying down her back, her sweet ass arched to him, and his grunt scored through the room as he shot deep inside his Leigh.

Still recovering, he took her down to her belly, covering her and only pulled out when he heard her breath even.

He was a lot easier on his Leigh. One "please, baby," and he gave her what she wanted.

He thought this, doing it smiling, as he went to the bathroom, cleaned up, took a warm cloth out and cleaned her as she purred sleepily.

Leigh-Leigh purring sleepily, barely able to move her beautiful body.

Fucking cute.

Olly returned the cloth and climbed back into bed with Leigh, tucking her under him and yanking up the covers.

"Too much weight?" he asked.

"No," she mumbled.

Good to know.

He liked Leigh right there, trapped under him.

"You're right, Leigh-Leigh, the correct blend of sour cream and guacamole, a delicacy."

"Shut up, Olly," she ordered, her pretty voice drowsy and adorable.

He grinned into her hair.

She snuggled under his body.

But Olly lay in the dark thinking that this was having it all.

And like his dad with his mom, he finally understood that, when you had it all, you never let it go.

Even if it goes away from you.

seventeen

Remained Standing

AMÉLIE

The stroking of fingers on the small of her back penetrated the languid oblivion Amélie was experiencing and her eyes opened to see a strong collarbone proudly jutting along a set of wide shoulders.

She tilted her head back, and as she did, she watched Olly dip his chin.

"Hey," he whispered when their gazes caught.

Dream come true.

"Good morning, darling," she whispered back.

Something beautiful passed through his eyes before he bent to her and touched his mouth to hers.

It wasn't enough before he pulled away.

Oh, but she could wake up like this every day and she didn't even need the kiss. The words. The stroking.

Just Olly.

"You gonna work me, baby, or feed me?" he asked, still speaking softly, like the cocoon of bed and bedclothes would break wide open exposing them to the cold reality of life if he used a normal voice and he didn't want that.

Not at all.

Amélie loved that, *adored* it, felt the same way.

Even so, at the same time she felt something prick that cocoon, nagging at her, attempting to draw her attention.

She ignored it.

Instead Amélie thought that she'd tried him greatly the day before. Not further than where she would have taken a rookie sub with his experience (that experience mostly given by her so she had an excellent understanding of where she could take him), but she'd still tested him.

He'd bested her challenge magnificently (unsurprisingly).

But with their activities instigated by Olly earlier that morning, activities she still felt throbbing delicately in her pussy, she felt it was time they both had a break.

"I think it's best I feed you. We'll have a lazy morning."

Olly showed no disappointment, but not in a way that was disappointing to Amélie. He was simply relaxing into her flow.

"Works for me."

She gave him a soft smile before she gave him his choices. "I have everything, Olly. Eggs and bacon. Sausage. Pancake mix. And those cinnamon rolls you pop out of a tube."

His smile was not soft but wide and white.

"My Leigh bought cinnamon rolls you can pop out of a tube?"

He sounded like this was something he couldn't fathom. Not something he didn't like, but it was still something he couldn't fathom.

"Yes," she confirmed.

"Then definitely cinnamon rolls," he decided.

She drifted a hand up his spine. "Have I been remiss in not making you dessert?"

"Babe, you made enough nachos to fell an elephant. I'm not going hungry." He gathered her closer, his eyes saying more than his next words did. "But yeah, I like sweet."

She'd give him sweet. She'd bake him cinnamon rolls from a tube every day of his life if she had that opportunity.

That something again stabbed at their peaceful-togetherness cocoon.

"Then we'll have cinnamon rolls," she decided, again ignoring the sensation.

"And bacon," he added.

"And bacon," she agreed.

"You see to that, it'd be cool I could go out for a short run. You've been putting me through my paces, Leigh-Leigh, but not sure how many calories I'm burning. I won't be long."

She nodded against the pillow.

Olly's eyes dropped to her mouth then he rolled into her, pinning her to the bed under his warm, solid weight, and he gave her a kiss that was a good deal more than a touch of their mouths.

When he broke it, he ordered, "Wait for me for a shower."

She snuggled closer. "If I wait for you to return to have a shower, you eat breakfast sweaty or I can't bake the rolls until after we're done. I only have one tube. It'd be a shame they burned while we shower, or we ate them cold. They're best when they're all gooey and melty."

His lips quirked before he said, "You're right. They're best when they're all *gooey* and *melty*." He emphasized those two words in a tone trembling with barely held back laughter. He finished with, "Then hang. I can wait until I get back and get showered to eat. You?"

She gave him his words, "Works for me."

Olly then gave her another touch of his lips but this time, he came right back in and nipped her lower one.

That was new.

That was nice.

She could have that every day too.

God.

She felt that slither down her chest into her belly and below at the same time her arms tightened and she fought them doing that in a way she'd never let go.

"Run. Shower. Food," he muttered, his gaze losing focus as his eyes again drifted to her mouth.

"Run. Shower. Food," she repeated.

Clearly, before he could change his mind, he rolled, not losing hold on her as he did, and they were both on their feet.

Run. Shower. Food.

And eventually their chat.

That something pricked at her again but Amélie continued to ignore it as she reached for her robe at the same time watching Olly walk naked to the bathroom.

It was an excellent strategy, for watching Olly walk naked to the bathroom put everything else out of her mind.

Amélie sat in her robe on a stool at her island, cup of coffee held in both hands in front of her, eyes staring unseeing at the countertop, but her mind was not idle.

Olly was off on his run, and without him and his teasing and his good mood and his sweetness as a distraction, she should have turned on music. Stripped the bed and put the sheets and towels they'd used in the laundry to start getting things sorted to shut down the house to prepare for her to load her cats back up and return to the city.

Anything but sitting there letting her mind go to places that were ridiculous.

She thought (or more accurately, hoped) that they were ridiculous because, except for a strange tone in his voice over the phone during their week apart, Olly hadn't given her any indication whatsoever that the talk they'd be having that day was one with a conclusion she wouldn't want it to have.

Especially all through last week.

And most especially during their weekend.

It had been far better than she expected and she'd been anticipating wonderful things.

Playing with Olly. Making love with Olly. Getting fucked by Olly. Talking to Olly about her pets, the time she spent at Dr. Hill's, the nagging concerns she had about the emptiness that had been creeping into her life. Understanding, finally, the niggling thoughts she'd had about his apparent inexperience. Him giving that to her belatedly, but openly, sharing deeper things while doing it, offering her a different kind of trust and vulnerability that she held even more dear than the manipulation of his body.

No man, alpha or no, indeed no woman would give such gifts to someone they simply wanted to bind them and paddle them and make them orgasm.

But there still was that tone in his voice that she'd heard over the phone. There was disquiet in it that wasn't hidden. It had not been not dripping from every word, but it was there.

This was, however, contradictory to him calling at all, not to mention the frankness he'd always given her (outside his inexperience, which she could understand why he did what he did, even before he'd explained it—she could not condone it, of course, but she understood it), it had been there.

That said, the time they were apart, he'd called and made it clear *why* he'd called. That being he'd wanted her to "jack his shit."

He had, of course, called to ask about her parents, dig deeper into what he sensed she wasn't giving him.

But other than that, outside the club, he only minimally texted, and he did not call, doing this to connect to her or to invite her to do the same. Unless it was to request her to bring him under her command, he didn't connect except in a marginal way.

She'd asked him for this weekend.

He had not asked her out for a drink or to dinner or to come to his house to watch a game. Even before or after they met at the club, their togetherness was *at the club*.

Except this weekend, which, again, *she* had instigated.

Now, understanding his inexperience, it was easy for her mind to trick itself into believing that he didn't get it. He didn't get certain boundaries. He didn't know all he was giving and how it could be read.

He was no fool but it was the plain truth that he might perform with the instincts of a natural sub, one who had a great deal more time in that world. But Olly did not have that.

And Amélie had been in the "game" far too long.

She'd been burned twice.

What was assailing her with doubt and nerves was partially due to that.

Mostly, it was the fact that this time, with Olly, if where they were heading was not where she thought they were heading, she knew it would unravel her.

She couldn't imagine having another toy.

But more.

She couldn't imagine wanting to try to build something, with the hopes of that being building a life together, with any other man.

Just the thought of going back to the club without Olly made the back of her jaw tingle unpleasantly against sick sliding up her throat.

She was falling in love with him. Even though she'd never been that deep in that feeling, Amélie knew precisely what it was.

And to have all of Olly and to want more of all that was him and find he did not want the same . . .

It was unthinkable.

And now Amélie was sitting at her island, fighting back her disposition twisting into a tight bundle of nerves as the time for their chat drew nearer.

She was taking a sip of coffee, attempting to pull up the strength to shake these thoughts off and get herself together before Olly returned, when Olly returned.

Opening the front door, she saw him from her place all the way down the hall.

Cotton, loose-fitting tee. Also loose-fitting shorts that hung low down his thighs. Running shoes and socks.

Dripping in sweat.

He moved down the hall her way, a paradox of lumbering grace, and she watched, lowering her mug as he came right to her.

Careful of his sweat, he still bent to her with a, "Hey, babe," before he brushed his lips to hers.

He moved away and went right to the fridge to get water.

Amélie watched as he opened it and she watched even more avidly as he tipped his head back and guzzled half the large bottle.

And Amélie was no longer a bundle of nerves.

Something was tightening and a variety of nerve endings were involved but it had nothing to do with anxiety.

She watched Olly stop drinking and continued watching as he dropped his head, lifting the bottom of his shirt, exposing stomach and some chest as he rubbed the sweat away from his face with the damp material.

She allowed him to right this position and guzzle more water before she ordered, "Olivier, come here."

His head snapped to the right, his gaze slicing to her, and he stood still.

Amélie held her breath.

They'd locked eyes and they continued to do so as she watched with some satisfaction his start to heat.

She dropped her attention to his shorts and had evidence something else was reacting as well.

Amélie looked back to his face.

"I'm not fond of repeating myself," she warned quietly.

Olivier took another moment before he kept her gaze as he moved her way, setting his bottle of water on the counter as he walked around the island.

When he was where she wanted him, about three feet from her, she commanded, "Stop."

He stopped.

She took him in.

His shorts exposed his increasing stimulation.

But she didn't need to look to his growing erection.

His eyes were telling her everything she needed to know.

"Take off your shirt," she ordered.

His hands went to the hem and he pulled it up, slouching forward, curling his powerful shoulders in to tug it over his head.

"Toss it aside," she went on.

He did as told.

"Now, remove your socks and shoes."

He bent to do this without delay and was again standing before her.

She allowed her eyes to roam everywhere and this took time because there was a vast area to cover.

All of it, as ever, divine.

"Mistress," he whispered.

Her gaze cut back to his face. "Pull your shorts down to your thighs."

"Amélie," he growled, his eyes darkening, for some reason suddenly feeling in the mood to resist.

It was not lost on her that this particular order took Olivier back to his beast. For some reason exposing himself to her at her command brought up rebellion.

Rebellion that was luscious.

Rebellion she knew she could guide him through.

"What did I say about repeating myself?" she asked

Olivier took another moment, this one much longer, forcing Amélie to consider an additional element to their scenario that would require her to leave the area and find a paddle (unless she spanked him with her bare hand, a thought too luscious by half to have in her current state, so she banished it), before, with another growl, this one unintelligible, he pulled his shorts to his thighs.

His cock sprung free, fully hard and hanging low, so beautiful nude to her grooming.

She fought shifting her legs against the sensations gathering between them, drawing away her focus.

God, he never failed to entice her.

Watching his cock, she put her mug down to counter and turned her stool fully his way.

She then flicked one side of her robe open, exposing a leg, but nothing else.

She looked to his face and saw his gaze fastened between her legs.

"One step closer," she commanded.

No hesitation, he took that step.

"On your knees," she ordered.

He dropped down, heated gaze locked to the material covering her pussy.

She flicked the other side of her robe open and another growl sheared through the room when she gave him part of what he was wanting.

Time for more.

Amélie darted a hand out, caught Olivier at the back of his head, and his hands automatically shot to her thighs as she opened them for him, pulling his face into her sex.

Her next instruction was husky. "Do not eat."

"Baby," he groaned between her legs.

"Not until told, *chevalier*, understood?"

Another hesitation before, "Yes, Mistress."

Her eyes fell to his ass, and when they did, she shifted forward on her stool, feeling her pussy hit his mouth. She gripped his hair and rubbed his face in her.

His fingers clenched into the flesh of her thighs so powerfully, they caused a hint of pain.

Enchanting.

"Push your Mistress's legs open wider," she demanded.

His hands moved from the tops of her thighs to the insides and he opened her wider, which naturally slid her bottom down the seat of the stool and shoved her deeper into his face.

The growl that rolled out of him into her nearly signaled she was done.

She had to hold out just a little longer.

"Tongue out, Olivier."

She felt his tongue immediately and used her hand in his hair to position him, tongue right at her opening.

She settled her gaze to his ass again and whispered, "Eat, my beast."

Pure Olivier, he did as asked and did it magnificently. Pushing her thighs even wider, he buried his face deeper into her pussy, fucking her with his tongue, laving from near to the rim of her anus to her clit, drawing that hard nub in deep.

Amazing.

When she'd had enough, her head having fallen back, she yanked his hair so his was back, too, and then dropped hers forward, vaguely caught his eyes and breathed, "Fuck me, baby."

Again, no hesitation, Olivier tore open the belt of her robe and before she understood his intent, he'd swept her hips in the curve of his arm and she was off the stool. It seemed she was flying through the air but she was in his hold the whole time he stalked to the couch that had its back to the kitchen. Then she was face-and belly-down on it, her arms forced back as Olivier ripped her opened robe off.

Then her legs were forced wide and she was taking him.

Apparently, she'd pushed him further through his rebellion then she'd been aware.

Delightfully.

She knew this as his grunts of effort exploded through the savage beauty of his thrusts, one hand in the couch beside her, body arched away for leverage and power.

And she knew it when he buried his thumb up her ass.

"*Olivier,*" she breathed.

"Ride that, Leigh."

She didn't have much room to move with him powering her into the couch but she did what she could, unable to stop herself (not that she wished to do that), shifting a knee slightly into the cushion to ride his cock up her cunt and his thumb up her ass.

The thumb disappeared but only for a second before he shoved two wet fingers deep.

Amélie's head jerked back as a throb instantly gathered and grew between ass and pussy, and she cried out, *"Olly."*

"Gonna fuck that sweet ass, Leigh. Gonna take it, baby, and you're gonna beg me not to stop."

"Don't stop now," she panted, desperate—facedown beneath him taking only what he was giving—to get more things *Olly*.

"You gonna let me fuck your ass, Leigh?" he grunted, fucking it already with his fingers while his cock drove deep.

Take that big brute up her ass?

"Yes," she pushed out.

"You gonna beg me?" he clipped.

"Yes, Olly. I'm going to beg you to fuck my ass. Fuck it now with your fingers, baby. Please. God." Her frame started shaking as the power of that throb grew and grew. "Oh my God." Her hands clenched into the couch as her body started uncontrollably bucking when that throb exploded. *"Olly."*

He drove his fingers deep, pumping into her pussy, encouraging gruffly, "That's it, Leigh-Leigh. Fuck yeah, baby, take what I'm givin' you."

She took it, and gave it, shuddering violently as her mind scrambled and she continued to take Olly's pummeling.

And she kept giving it to him, pulsing around him with her pussy, her body trembling on the couch, when he orgasmed through his final, brutal thrusts, slipping his fingers out of her ass to grasp her hips to hold her to him as he shot his seed.

Finally, he went still, filling her completely in a way that seemed to her like he was straining, and she imagined him arching into his climax in that glorious way of his, before he relaxed. She felt the warmth of his body drop to hers, held up by a forearm in the couch, his forehead on her shoulder.

"Fuck, baby, *fuck*, you do it for me."

She closed her eyes as relief poured through her.

There it was. Just what Amélie needed to release the things that were now fucking with *her* head.

She felt him kiss her shoulder.

"Don't ever lose your imagination, sweetheart," he said, the relief vanished and she tensed. "Every time, every *fucking* time," he pressed his hips into hers, his cock pushing deeper, giving unmistakable meaning to what he was saying, "you knock it outta the park."

And there it was.

Indication that for Olly, it was all about her knocking it out of the park.

With a shocked gasp, she felt him pull out and abruptly she was teetering in front of him beside the couch, both of them on their feet.

Before she could even tip her head back to gauge the look on his face, he had the fingers of both of his hands tangled in her hair at the sides of her head, his lips declaring, "Time for our shower."

And then with a quiet cry, his hands were gone from her hair, she was naked, up over his shoulder, and a naked Olly was prowling through her house toward her bedroom.

In an odd twist she'd never allowed in *any* relationship, Amélie found herself powerless.

And what made that odder was she did not dislike this at all.

So she supposed it was time for their shower.

Then it was time to chat.

And that she didn't like.

They were in her front courtyard, plate of bacon consumed, three-quarters of the cinnamon rolls gone (and Amélie had had no bacon and only one roll).

She'd been right, her Olly needed a great deal of fuel.

After their shower, they'd both put on jeans and T-shirts. While accomplishing this, for some reason she didn't understand, Olly looked at her tee the second she'd pulled it on and then had given her a big, satisfied grin that had the added charming component of being vastly amused.

He didn't offer a reason as to why he had this reaction.

And Amélie was so deep in her head, she didn't ask for one.

They'd sorted the food, shuffling around the kitchen together (something Amélie had never had with a man in her life and she liked it immensely). Olly also had situated the chairs outside so that they were side to side while they ate, eyes to the road at the front of the house, the fountain flowing comfortingly behind them.

Amélie was not comforted.

No, Amélie felt that cinnamon roll sitting in her stomach like an anvil, weighing her down.

"How much of this land is yours?" Olly asked and she looked from her preoccupied perusal of a road no car had come down since they took their seats to Olly.

"Fifty-five acres," she answered.

"Mm," he mumbled, lifting a cup of coffee he'd told her while they were preparing breakfast he could "take or leave, usually only drink a cup with something sweet."

This was good to know for she hadn't caffeinated him as well as not feeding him before she'd played with him the morning before.

If things went as she hoped, in future, she'd make a note to provide him fuel.

But it was nice to know she didn't have to offer him caffeine.

"Olly," she called but it was more a blurt.

She wanted to relax. Spend time with him. Have one of their non-taxing, enjoyable conversations that still led to her learning more about him, every morsel she was hungry for. Have the lazy morning she said they were going to have. Push it into a lazy day. Maybe take him riding. Avoid the chat altogether and just continue the beauty they had, ride it wherever it was going.

She most assuredly wanted all that.

But she couldn't wait a second longer to know where they stood.

He looked to her, face relaxed, in a good place, and God, please God, she hoped it stayed that way.

"Yeah?" he answered her call.

"I'd like to see you," she began.

A big, white smile spread on his handsome face making him breathtaking.

Yes, please, God, she wanted him to stay just that way for as long as she was breathing.

"I go somewhere?" he teased.

She wasn't in the mood for teasing, even though she loved it when he did that.

What she was, was in a state.

And even her, Amélie Hélène Strand, Mistress of pretty much everything, she couldn't pull herself out of that state.

This was too important.

Olivier Hawkes was *way too important.*

"See you, as in, out on a date," she explained.

She watched his relaxed look melt into confusion before it changed to something else and it felt like a slap in the face when he tipped his head back and burst into loud laughter.

His uncontrolled laughter was always lovely to hear. In fact, it was beautiful.

Or it was on any other occasion but that.

She didn't see what was funny.

"Is something amusing?" she asked.

He did not read her tone.

But he did turn his attention to her, doing it still laughing, and also laughing, he asked, "Wasn't it you I fucked on the couch?"

"It was," she confirmed.

He looked away, now only chuckling, through which he said, "You wanna date, Leigh, I'll date." Before he muttered into the coffee cup he'd raised to his lips and unfortunately didn't stop speaking. "Lookin' forward to what you come up with on a date."

At that, Amélie experienced the intensely painful feeling of all her innards compressing into a hard, fiery-hot ball.

What you come up with on a date.

He was not talking about interesting conversation and getting to know her better.

She turned her attention to the road.

"Leigh?" he called.

"Yes," she said to the road.

"Baby." His tone had changed considerably but Amélie was too busy feeling that hard ball burning in the pit of her stomach and wondering how long it would take for the flame to go out.

She also wondered if it ever would.

"I miss something?" he finished on a query.

"No," she answered and then looked at him. "I believe it was me who missed something."

"Sorry?" he asked.

"Nothing," she mumbled. Leaning forward in her chair, she started to tidy their plates, going on, "We should tidy up and then perhaps you'd like to go with me to take the horses out for a ride before you—"

Both of her hands stopped moving even though he only caught one of her wrists.

He did this saying, "Hey, whoa. What just happened?"

She looked over her shoulder at him. "Release my wrist, if you would, please, Olivier."

He didn't release her wrist.

His eyes narrowed and he said in a strangely dangerous voice, "Olivier?"

"That's your name," Amélie remarked.

"You bein' my Mistress now?" he asked.

"No, I'm asking you to let me go."

"And I'll let you go when you tell me why you just completely shut down on me."

"How about we make a deal and you release me then I'll share where things are with us and after that, you can decide if you'd like to stay or if you'd like to go."

The danger she'd heard in his voice filled his face and Amélie felt a bizarre hint of fear.

"Where things are with us?" he queried softly.

She ignored the fear and inquired, "Are you going to repeat everything I say?"

He let go of her wrist but leaned into her aggressively, invading her space. "Are you gonna stop actin' like a bitch all of a sudden and tell me what the fuck just happened?"

The pain subsided but only because his words snagged at her temper.

"Do not call me a bitch," she hissed.

His narrowed eyes sparked fury she should have taken note of.

She very, very much should have taken note of it.

For she knew intimately how Olly allowed his temper to blow.

But she didn't take note of it before he threw up a hand and exploded, "Jesus Christ, *talk to me.*"

She turned more fully to him and he shifted back but an inch while she did it.

Other than that, he didn't move.

"All right, Olivier, you've been very forthcoming this weekend so I'll share a few things with you too," she said to begin and didn't hesitate to continue. "Unfortunately, I read certain things wrong and I had hoped that this weekend, we'd discuss where this is going."

"This?" he bit out.

"*Us,*" she snapped, doing so watching him lift his brows, his chin jerking back slightly, doing a slow blink. "You've just given me indication what *this* is to you and, as I said, I read certain things wrong and I'll share I find that disappointing. I had hoped to discuss having more with you, outside the club and . . ."

She shook her head vaguely, using her anger to fight that ball of fire that had seemed tiny but felt like it was growing.

She allowed her eyes to slide to the house to make her point before they moved back to him and she went on.

"Other places. You've just made it clear where we stand, and although I'd hoped for something different, something more, at least I now know where we stand."

As she spoke, the anger dissolved from his features as understanding set in but that ball was growing far too swiftly for Amélie to care.

It was imperative she fight back the pain before it consumed her.

"Now," she turned again to the table, beginning to reach out to plates, "as that's where we stand—"

"Baby," he called in a low, soothing, sweet tone that could beat back any blaze if a woman was open to hearing it.

Unfortunately, Amélie felt new things sparking from that ball of pain. Not just anger and despair but humiliation.

She didn't grab on to that first plate before she had his hand curled around the back of her neck and he used it to force her attention to him.

"Olivier—"

"Okay, Leigh-Leigh, seems a little bit ago, I didn't get where you were comin' from and reacted wrong. I'm sorry, sweetheart." His hand at her neck gave her a squeeze. "But in my defense, you were talkin' about wantin' to go out on a date and, Leigh," he shifted closer, "I just spent the weekend at your house. I know every inch of you and you know the same about me. A date was not what I was thinkin' our chat was about. Hell, I didn't even know we'd *started* our chat. I thought it was you bein' cute, as you can be, and I've told you that. And it *is* cute, you wantin' to go on a date."

All the first was good.

The last was not the same.

"I'm sorry, I don't understand how it's cute," she noted sharply.

His lips tipped up in a careful grin. "It's cute because we're beyond dating, Leigh. You wanna go out, I'll take you out. We'll eat. We'll drink. We'll go to your place in the city, or mine, make love." His smile deepened. "And if we're at your place, I'll try to survive the night 'cause I've seen that urchin lurking in there once, but she's got a death wish for me if her trying to suffocate me while I'm asleep is any indication. So, I'm happy to take you out, but we're beyond dating."

"I wasn't being cute, Olivier," she retorted.

"I'm getting that," he muttered.

She needed distance from him. She needed to gather her wits. She needed to think.

And she needed all that before they continued talking.

But even as she put pressure on her neck, indicating quite clearly she wished him to let her go, he held her secure.

Amélie did not like that.

Therefore, she requested tartly, "Could you please take your hand off me?"

His eyes narrowed again even as his fingers curled in deeper.

"Are you hearing me?" he asked.

"I heard you, I'd still like you to release me."

He didn't let her go.

He growled, "I got a feeling you're listening but you're not hearing me."

"I said I heard you," she retorted.

"And I can see just lookin' at your face you fuckin' did not."

She pulled at his hand harder and snapped, "I won't ask again, Olivier, take your damned hand off me."

He tugged her an inch forward. It wasn't gentle, it didn't hurt, what it did was make her go alert as the anger again flared in his gaze.

"So Mistress Amélie's got a bite," he clipped. "Good to know."

"I don't want you touching me," she clipped back.

He let her go so abruptly, her torso shot back half a foot.

"Yeah," he stated, not just anger in his blue eyes that had gone midnight. Now it was fury. "Good to know."

"What?" she bit out.

"This whole gig." He swept up a hand between them to indicate her. "The jeans. The tee. The courtyard facing a dusty road. Cinnamon rolls from a tube. All that's a big fake. Mistress Amélie in jeans or in heels with her horses and her ranch in the mountains and her shit ton of money is right up on that pedestal, not about to climb down. And you best be on your knees, preferably with your pants pulled down, looking up, gagging for it, because that's the only way she wants you."

On that, her torso swung back another half a foot.

"That's an incredibly insulting thing to say," she hissed.

"Yeah? Truth hurts?"

What he said hurt but it was far from the truth.

"If you think that of me, then—"

"I didn't, baby, you had me fooled." He shook his head but didn't stop talking. "Came up here, rarin' to go. Ready to set whatever I had to set aside to look to the future with you, even put my tail between my legs, figuratively and, it would turn out, literally," he sniped, "willin' to do whatever to give it a go with you."

Suddenly, that ball in her belly grew spikes and twisted, tearing through flesh.

"To give it a go with me?" she asked, her voice sounding choked.

He ignored her and continued on his bent.

"But sometimes, shit comes out early, even if it's still too late. That said, good to know you get pissed, you hold on, close down, get uppity, showin' your true nature and that would be you not letting anything fuckin' in because this is Amélie's world, we all just live in it with her, including me."

Another blow and the ball tore the other way.

"Olly—"

"I'm a firefighter," he ground out.

Amélie blinked in surprise, not only at receiving this astonishing information but also his swift declaration of it at this juncture in their discussion.

He mistook her response.

"Yeah, baby, you've been slummin', jackin' the shit of a scholarship. Still cut deep, what Weathers made me pay to join that club, but it was a fraction of what you pay. What the others pay. I'd never get in the door if he didn't give me a discount. Works in his favor to do that, though. I see that. New meat for his Mistresses to play with. So even if it didn't come out early, good for you it's not too late." He jerked his head to her house. "Don't got some shit-hot job that pays me a fortune to get you another house, another Mercedes. Fuck, I probably couldn't even afford to buy you one of your pairs of shoes. Definitely not take care of you in any way you couldn't do it yourself if we had a future that went the distance and we made a life together. Kids. College tuition?" He shrugged. "Leigh's got it covered. We have a daughter and she wants a big wedding?" Another shrug. "Not a problem. You'll fly her to Paris to have her gown custom made."

Kids.

A daughter?

Her torso caught fire.

"Please, Olly—" she tried.

But failed.

As he had when he lost his temper before, he didn't let her get but two words in and he didn't hear either of them, even though he was angry, it seemed, because he thought she hadn't heard his.

He kept seething.

"My guess, you got my face shoved in that sweet pussy of yours, pants around my thighs, it's all the same to you. But heads-up, I'm not a keeper for a woman like you. Depending on where you'd wanna go for our date, babe, not sure who'd be payin' for it, but it might be somethin' I'd have to cut back on gas for a month so I could afford it."

"You really need to stop talking," she whispered, anger, but mostly hurt scoring her soft tone.

"Yeah." He stood. "Actually, I do."

On that, he turned on his boot and stormed into the house.

Amélie took in one deep breath and followed it with another.

Yes, she thought, *I really should have taken note when Olly started to get angry.*

On that thought, she got up and hurried after him.

She found him in her bedroom, his bag on the bed, him shoving in clothes.

"Olly—"

"Olly, now," he muttered to his bag. "No more Olivier she can bring to heel. Her toy's ready to leave early, taking away her fun, she turns on the sweet."

And that ball of pain scored another path of agony through the inferno it had already created.

"You've said a number of hurtful things, sweetheart, please take a moment to take a breath so you don't say anything further that will cause more damage."

He didn't say anything, just shoved a pair of jeans into his bag.

She kept going.

"You've got an explosive temper and—"

His head shot up. "And yours?" He gave a fake shudder that was actually quite impressive. "Ice-cold."

Although this was true and he had a point, his response to her shutting down, in her opinion, was not deserved.

That said, she didn't think it was wise in that moment to get into debating their different reactions.

She had to get through to him, calm him down, at the very least to civility so they could discuss things that were crucial, it seemed, to *both* of their future happiness.

Amélie kept trying.

"What I'm saying is that we got started out on the wrong foot. We should collect ourselves and—"

He hefted up the bag and again interrupted her, "I've collected all I need."

Panic set in and Amélie shifted positions to bar the door and she did that quickly talking.

"I think there's a great deal at play here, for both of us, especially you. You have some—"

He was making his way toward her as she spoke but he stopped in front of her and cut her off.

"What I got is a desire to get the fuck out of here, Leigh. So get out of my way."

She looked up into his angry face. "I'd like you to stay and calm down so we can talk."

"Tried that," he bit off. "Didn't know where you were leading when you started, fucked up. I apologized, you didn't let it go. Got your *Olivier* thrown at me like you could bring me to heel. Yeah, you get me off with that shit and I don't gotta tell you that. You know. But that's not all there is to me, that wouldn't be all I want to *us*, and straight up, Leigh, it's not a future I'd dig having. Livin' in your nice houses, you buyin' me cars for my birthday, horses in your stable, only thing I got to give is lettin' you tie me to the bed, ass in the air so you can jack it. You get pissed, it's *Olivier* and I'm on my knees with my face shoved in your pussy."

"That's not what I meant when I called you that, Olly," she whispered.

"So it's me who fucked up again and you weren't closing down on me?"

"I was but I'd like to explain and then maybe we can explore all you're saying because it seems there's a good deal you're struggling with and I'd like—"

"No, actually, this scene, not strugglin' with dick. Again, you've made it crystal."

Amélie closed her mouth.

He stared down at her and she saw something in the backs of his eyes but there was no chance she had to read it since her focus was on beating back the pain.

"You gonna get out of my way?" he ground out.

She stepped aside.

He stalked out of her room.

Amélie stood looking for a moment at the mussed bed they'd woken up in in their warm, lovely cocoon before she turned and followed him.

Not to the door.

To a window that faced the drive.

She stood in it and stared out it, watching him round the drive, his truck kicking up gravel and dust and it kept doing that all the way down the lane.

She felt Stasia winding around her ankles but Amélie didn't tear her gaze away from the window.

Olly's truck still left a trail of dust once he hit the road and drove away.

And Amélie stood there even after he was long gone because she was unable to move.

That thing inside her exploded, obliterating everything it could reach.

But she was Amélie Hélène Strand so she remained standing.

Still, it took some time.

But eventually she felt the wetness as it coursed down her cheeks.

eighteen

Bitch of a Mistress

AMÉLIE

Two days later, Amélie moved through the front doors of the Honey, having done this too many times to count but doing it then feeling strange for two reasons.

The first, she didn't expect she'd come there again.

Perhaps it was melodramatic to think that "again" was forever. But at least for some time.

A long time.

Years.

Decades.

The second, she'd never been there at that time of day.

It was ten-thirty in the morning.

Unless a member made a special request, they weren't normally open for business at that time. But Aryas had phoned and asked her to come in and talk about something "important."

Although Amélie had shared just the day before with Mirabelle that things had not gone well with Olly during their weekend and that she would likely not be going to the club for some time, Aryas wouldn't know that. This was because, at her request, Mira had sworn she'd not breathe a word and Amélie trusted to her soul her friend wouldn't.

So she couldn't imagine anything "important" Aryas would have to talk to her about.

And he'd sounded short, and irate, though not being in his presence she could not know if these were aimed at her.

She couldn't imagine why that would be, unless Olivier had made some bizarre complaint (though she could not imagine that either, he was not the type).

Even so, as she made her way to the Honey to meet with Aryas, Amélie gave little thought to this idea as any complaint Olivier might make in his inexperience, Aryas would give no credence to for Amélie had done not one thing to complain about.

And further, in doing this, Olivier would expose himself to her sharing with Aryas he'd lied on his application, something that would get Olivier's membership revoked most assuredly.

She had no idea if Olivier intended to come back to the club to find another Mistress. She couldn't even think of it without that ball of pain re-forming in the pit of her belly, so she didn't allow herself to think of it.

But as she and Olivier shared a common nature, albeit either side of that coin, she knew he would again go looking at some point.

And the best could be found at the Honey.

Regardless of all of this, she knew a great deal about Olivier, including the fact he had an uncontrollable and exceptionally foul temper, but also the fact that it was highly unlikely he would expose any vulnerability to Aryas. Including coming forward to make some kind of complaint about their play.

So she seriously doubted it was that.

What it could be, Amélie couldn't fathom.

But she was about to find out.

Aryas had asked her to come directly back to his office, a room she hadn't been in since her interview prior to joining the club years before.

The club hadn't moved so it was doubtful Aryas's office had. Therefore, as she walked into what she felt was eerily-lit-by-sunlight foyer of the club behind the front desk to the hall at the back of it, she moved past doors that were open and occupied by office workers who likely managed membership, accounting, playroom reservations, and the like. She also moved past doors that were closed where she knew the security and monitoring stations were, as well as the controls and equipment of other technological components of Aryas's business.

Finally, she reached the door at the very back, which was also opened to the hall.

She stood in the frame and saw Aryas on his feet behind his handsome, large desk in his also handsome, large office, turned to the side, this putting his back to her, talking to a man that was standing there.

She gave a tap on the door even though, upon raising her hand, both men turned to look at her.

"Come in, Leigh, close the door if you don't mind, my sweet," Aryas invited and his tone was much more his normal self.

Amélie relaxed, moved in, closed the door, and entered the room with her eyes to the man with Aryas.

He was not as big as Aryas (or Olly), but he was much taller than her. His untucked, casual button-up shirt and jeans did not hide from her experienced eyes that his tall body was made up of lean, compacted muscle. His skin was quite tan and he had black hair with a pair of startling ice-blue eyes rimmed with exceptionally long, curling lashes.

In another time, she would be salivating at the sight of him, at the same time frustrated that a man like him most assuredly would not have a nature that would fulfill hers.

But as she moved in, those frosty-blue eyes shifted in a way that gave an impression they were not taking her in but *climbing* the length of her, from her red platform pumps, up her gray slacks, black blouse, all the way to her hair.

And Amélie was experienced. Experienced enough to know the way he was looking at her, regardless of the fact that his expression was carefully blank, with where he was standing and what happened in that building, he was attempting to understand which way she swung.

And with her experience, she was shocked to sense that this man swung the other way.

Of course it would occur that after years of going hungry, she'd be in the presence of another scrumptious specimen at a time when she had absolutely no interest because she was in love with another man.

"This is Branch Dillinger, Leigh. He's my PI," Aryas introduced.

She turned startled eyes to Aryas, wondering uneasily if Mr. Dillinger had done some checking and found Olivier had lied on his application, before she forced herself to move calmly to Branch Dillinger and put out her hand.

"Mr. Dillinger," she said. He took her hand in a firm grip, his own hand veined, tanned, square palm, long, square fingers, visibly capable. Lovely. "Amélie Strand," she introduced herself.

He let her go, murmuring, "Aryas mentioned your name."

She nodded.

"Sit, would you, Leigh?" Aryas requested.

She looked to him and then moved to one of the black suede chairs in front of his desk.

She sat. Aryas sat.

Branch Dillinger remained standing but crossed his arms on his impressive chest.

"Right, since you were concerned about it, gonna explain what went down. Also gotta ask something of you, Leigh," Aryas began.

Amélie was confused at this opening.

Not to mention she was still alarmed at the possibility she'd been called in to be informed Olly had lied on his application and therefore be involved in whatever repercussions there were to that. This necessitating she share that she knew it (albeit, discovering this fact only recently) and trying to explain why she didn't report that to Aryas at her first opportunity.

That said, she'd never mentioned to Aryas she was concerned about Olivier's inexperience. She felt it but didn't mention it to anybody.

Even with all that filtering through her mind, she replied, "If I can do it, I'll do anything you need."

Aryas gave her a warm look that made her (again) understand the devotion of his subs before he went on.

"After you and I had our chat about Delia and Tiffany, the first one," he gave her a humorless grin that did nothing to improve her disposition, "as I told you I'd do, we monitored the situation closely. Unfortunately, what we saw was all good. Nothing off. Nothing outside club policy. And every step she made when she was on club premises was watched. Further, she flipped her occupancy switch any time she entered a playroom and Tiffany usually left the room before Delia did."

Amélie nodded but said nothing, relieved that this wasn't about Olly, at the same time not, because it was about Delia and she knew there was more.

She was correct. There was more.

"Though, looked more like Tiffany was escaping," Aryas remarked.

"Oh no," Amélie said softly. Though this was not surprising, she was beginning to understand why there was a private investigator in the room.

"So, not having a good feeling about it, I set Branch on her," Aryas explained.

Amélie looked to Dillinger but only for a second before she returned her attention to Aryas.

"And?" she prompted hesitantly.

"Took her off premises, Leigh. Played with her in a private dungeon. And not only took pictures, but also video."

Anger set Amélie's body automatically sliding to the edge of her seat.

"She blackmailed her," Amélie spat.

Aryas nodded. "Not thinking Tiffany shares her inclinations with her folks who, even though Tiffany has a job, still hold the control over a trust fund that allows her to live the life she's used to. Delia found that out, knew Tiffany had resources, and forced Tiffany to pay for her services."

That *bitch*.

"Did Delia harm her?" she bit out.

Aryas shook his head but said, "Took play in a way Tiffany didn't like it all that much, probably mostly because she was subbing for a woman who held unacceptable power over her, but there was no physical harm. When we talked to her, not sure Tiffany even gave a shit about the money. She's tight with her family, the whole family is close, including her brother and sister, and she was terrified they'd cut her out if they knew how she was. So she played and she paid."

Amélie knew Tiffany was right to be terrified. Although Amélie had noted the closeness of the siblings in that family, the "tight" Aryas was talking about in regards to her father and mother (particularly her father) was that Tiffany was held tightly under their thumb.

Not to mention, her mother and father were both very conservative and ridiculously concerned about their reputations.

If they knew, they wouldn't only cut Tiffany off financially, they'd cut her out emotionally.

"This is . . . it's . . . unspeakable," Amélie hissed.

Aryas's expression showed he agreed as he carried on.

"When Branch cracked this, he found a shit ton of the same. Four subs she was working who frequented public and private parties or the Bolt. Some of them didn't have the money to spare, but they found it and that stung. Not to mention, she's got a history of this. She had the same on the Dominants and subs she needed to write recommendation letters for her to have membership here at the Honey."

Yes.

Unspeakable.

"Has she been neutralized?" Amélie rapped out her question.

Aryas grinned at her but didn't answer.

So she looked up to Dillinger to see he didn't find anything funny.

In fact, she wondered if he was thinking anything at all.

His face she had not noted due to her concentration on his startling eyes (and his lovely body) was quite rugged, but it was also an impenetrable mask.

"Well, has she been neutralized?" she pushed.

"She has," he confirmed shortly.

"How?" she clipped.

Dillinger looked to Aryas and so did Amélie.

"Branch is thorough, babe," Aryas shared. "Before we even confronted her, he dug deep, got it all and all of it is destroyed, as is her equipment, and her membership has been revoked. I've made a few calls and not just around town. Shared everything. She's now been blacklisted at every club in five countries. Also Branch tracked down the people she targeted. They know they aren't under her thumb anymore and they *were* pissed. Now they're *liberated* and pissed. They're also being vocal about it. And you can imagine they're not just gonna share she's a blackmailing cunt, but she might get more. That's not our business. I've done what I'm going to do because vengeance is for them, not us. At the very least I'm not thinking she's gonna find her kink anytime soon. And I would not be surprised that news comes fast she's been neutralized in other ways."

"Good," Amélie bit out, having no problem wishing the worst on Mistress Delia. She then promptly asked, "Now, what do you require of me?"

Aryas gave her another warm smile, this one also concerned, and he did it while replying without delay.

"We've talked to Tiffany, my sweet, and she's not in a good place. Delia was her first real Mistress outside training and it didn't leave a good taste in her mouth." His deep voice dropped low. "I'm worried she's not gonna come back for more. Give up the life. She's

terrified, Leigh. And you know her, her family. I was hoping you'd
have a chat with her. Try to settle her. Bring her back into the fold.
Talk with one of the Dommes who play with females who'd take
care of her and see if you can set something up so she can see Delia
is an anomaly and Tiffany's safe here. Or take her back to the playrooms and be with her while she observes so she can see there's good
out there for her if she can set all this shit behind her."

"I'll find time to do that as soon as I can," Amélie stated swiftly.

She had considered going to Paris and spending some time with
her family. Getting away from the club, her home, her recent memo-
ries in an attempt (though she knew in her heart it was in vain) to
alleviate the heartsick feeling that plagued her even in sleep.

She would delay this to sit down with Tiffany.

"Leigh, take that 'soon as you can' seriously," Aryas advised.
"The more time she has to get stuck in her head, the deeper that
shit's gonna burn in and scars like that last a lifetime."

At his words, Amélie suddenly worried for Olly, who had worked
past what was fucking with his head but in his anger showed that
might not be entirely true.

That said, it was obvious there were other factors. These being
he was the man he was with the tendencies he had who was with a
woman who had a great deal more money than he did (or would ever
have, really).

She could absolutely see how his nature would deepen his concerns about all the other.

And Amélie had no answers to his concerns. She was not a man
who had considerably less money than the woman he was considering making a part of his life.

She would just have liked to discuss it with him in a com-
posed way.

As she'd been doing for two days, Amélie shoved this out of her
head and assured Aryas, "I'll speak with her today."

"That would be appreciated, Leigh," Aryas replied.

She nodded and looked to Dillinger.

"Thank you for your assistance with this."

He said nothing. Just jerked up his chin.

She nodded to him as well and looked back to Aryas. "Is that all you need?"

"Yeah, Leigh." He stood and started to make his way around the desk. "Grateful for you comin' in. Grateful for anything you can do with Tiffany."

He made it to her and touched her cheek to cheek.

When that was done, she gave him a small smile that made his brows draw slightly together as his focus on her became more acute.

Amélie couldn't brighten her smile to save her life. So to save herself from any more of Aryas's attention, which might later require explanation, she turned from him, bid farewell to Dillinger, then Aryas, and she walked out of his office.

The next evening, after arriving together through an alternate entrance that Aryas provided for members who wished added privacy, Amélie sat next to Tiffany in the red room with the blinds drawn and the candles burning.

It had taken some coaxing to get her to come, but now they sat close in comfortable chairs, Amélie holding Tiffany's clutching hand, as they watched Mistress Belle work a female slave on the big bed.

The slave was bound naked, curled into a ball, arms tied to calves, no movement allowed through her binding. A vibrator was switched on and working inside her.

All of this as Mistress Belle lay reclined on the pillows wearing a man-tailored silk robe opened for her slave to feed from her pussy. Only Belle's legs were naked, spread wide and in view; her slave hid the rest of her as she ate voraciously.

But Belle's enjoyment of this was not the least hidden.

Although Amélie saw the beauty in the vision before her, it did nothing for her. Even if this was her penchant (same-sex play between females), it without a doubt still wouldn't be so soon after losing Olivier.

That was to say it did nothing for her except build an ache inside for she would much enjoy having Olly in this same position with a different toy working inside him, giving this to her as she gave it to him.

Something that would never happen.

Her heart-sore thoughts were interrupted when suddenly, Mistress Belle reached out a graceful hand, and with indolent eyes on Tiffany, invited, "Would you like to join us, my beauty?"

Tiffany's hand clutched Amélie's tighter.

Amélie held that hand and looked to Belle, giving her a short shake of her head, not wishing to interrupt the scene to remind Belle this wasn't the agreement.

Observation only.

Belle, who'd been a member for some time, coming to the Honey in Phoenix after having a membership at Aryas's other club in Seattle, read the situation a different way.

"Come to me," she cooed to Tiffany. "You're wet, I know it. Allow me the honor of cleaning such a sweet baby with my mouth."

Tiffany's voice was so timid it was nearly lost in the room. "Thank you, Mistress, but I—"

"Come, sweet," Mistress Belle cajoled. "Let me take care of you."

Amélie felt panic edge off Tiffany and she again shook her head at Belle, her grip tightening on the girl.

Belle didn't even look at Amélie.

"I'll take care of you," she whispered. "I vow it, sweet beauty. Come to your Mistress."

Amélie tightened her jaw in annoyance, about ready to stand and remove Tiffany from the room before she felt Tiffany's hand relaxing in hers.

She looked to the girl.

She saw the effort it took Tiffany to tear her eyes away from a scene that Amélie, in her distracted thoughts, had not noted she was quite enjoying.

She turned them to Amélie.

"I think . . . do you—?"

Yes. Mistress Belle knew what she was doing. Amélie should not have doubted.

Amélie didn't allow her to finish. "I do, Tiffany."

Through the candlelight, Tiffany stared into Amélie's eyes.

Amélie gave her hand a reassuring squeeze.

Feeling it, Tiffany cast a quick glance at the scene as did Amélie. She needed to decide, and soon, before things culminated.

Tiffany must have sensed this for, with a reciprocating squeeze, she let Amélie's hand go.

She rose from her chair and Amélie watched as she cautiously moved to the bed.

Belle, having been informed of the situation when Aryas contacted her to ask if she'd be willing to perform for observers in a special scene (for Belle often liked multiple partners, but she also liked her privacy), acted instantly.

And appropriately.

"You can keep your clothes on if you wish, lovely baby, but take off your panties and come offer your wetness to your Mistress."

Amélie then watched as Tiffany did as told, keeping her clothes on but shimmying up her tight skirt to take off her panties before she climbed into bed and, slowly, hesitantly, climbed on Belle's face.

Belle didn't hurry her but when Tiffany relaxed into her, she took over.

Her pretty head falling back, Tiffany gave herself over to experienced, gentle hands.

Even though she would like to have left, for Tiffany, Amélie felt it important to wait and watch until things culminated for them both.

And she continued to watch while Mistress Belle guided Tiffany into helping her pleasure her other slave.

Only when Belle caught Amélie's eyes before she cast hers to the door did Amélie focus entirely on Tiffany.

The girl nodded, mouthed, "Thank you, Mistress Amélie," and then turned her gaze to her Mistress.

Belle had it in hand, so Amélie silently left the room.

One worry done, Delia hadn't wrought lasting damage on Tiffany.

At least there was that.

She went to the Dom lounge where she'd stowed her purse in her locker, as she didn't come in the front not only for Tiffany, but also because she wanted no attention on her on a night with no Olly.

She also didn't want to confront the possibility it *was* a night with Olly.

If he wished to end their separation, he did not have to come to the club to find her.

He had her number to call.

Hell, on the courier parcel, he had her address.

So if he was there, he'd be there for something else.

That something else not being her.

In the lounge, she retrieved her purse and pulled out her phone, quickly texting Aryas that Belle was taking care of Tiffany before she looked into her locker to see a scattering of toys that she rarely used.

She stared at them, having the depressing urge to collect them as well as all her things from the Honey and take them home. There was no point to them staying there for they wouldn't be used.

And an even more melancholy thought, they would not be used at her home either.

"Leigh."

She turned, closing her locker as she did, when she heard Stellan say her name.

Anger spiked, an emotion she'd felt frequently since Olly walked out on her because it was an emotion she could handle far better than all the others.

She had it now because she absolutely did not need this.

"Stellan, now's not the time," she declared, barely looking at him and moving to leave him, the room and the club.

He blocked her progress and she came to a stuttering halt and snapped her head back to glare at him.

"Please get out of my way," she requested briskly.

"We need——" he began but stopped himself as he regarded her closely. Then he whispered, "Oh fuck. *Leigh*."

She really needed to learn to hide her heartbreak. It wasn't good everyone could read it in a glance.

She gathered her irritation around her and snapped, "I asked you to get out of my way."

"He chewed you up and spit you out, didn't he, honey?" Stellan asked gently.

He had.

That was none of Stellan's business.

"I won't ask again," she warned.

But he didn't move out of her way.

He lifted a hand and curled it around the side of her neck, dropping closer so his face was but an inch away.

He wore very nice cologne. It smelled expensive but it wasn't obtrusive and this was not the first time she'd had that thought.

Though it was the first time she'd had that thought with it causing annoyance that he was detaining her rather than frustration that he smelled so lovely and would do so while she played with him if things were different.

"It's a hard lesson to learn, I know, Leigh. It's painful," he said quietly, taking her out of her thoughts. "But there are those of us who understand the life and there are those of us who wish to live outside of it even if they need what they can get in the times they allow themselves in." His body also moved closer. "When we go searching for what we ultimately need, honey, we have to be sure we find the ones who understand that."

Although she was angry with him, and frustrated with this encounter, she wondered how Stellan knew about that pain.

She didn't ask.

"Are you done?" she queried acidly.

"I know you're pissed because of what you're feeling, Leigh. I'm just telling you I get it and I'm here for you."

"Thank you for that offer, Stellan, and I hope you take no offense when I decline."

His hand at her neck curled deeper and Amélie was feeling quite tired of men not adhering to her wishes of not . . . being . . . *touched*.

"Then I'll be very clear with what I'm offering, Leigh," he ground out, suddenly impatient, his new tone and look snapping her alert. "You want to go out there for a drink and talk, I'll be right beside you. You want to leave here and go somewhere else for a drink so you can talk, I'll be right beside you there too. You want to go to my place so I can make you a drink and then we can talk, I'm there too. After that, you want me to fuck his memory right out of you, I'm *really* there for you. But," he came even closer and something changed in his eyes she was shocked to her core to see, "if you need to take me to a playroom, bind me, paddle me, plug my ass, and make me eat you until you come and I can't breathe, I'm buried so deep in your pussy, I'm there for that too."

"Stellan—"

"You know I've been waiting for you and do not deny that," he bit out.

She had no idea—outside Olly determinedly sharing that without Amélie ever quite accepting it—and she could not believe she'd read him so wrongly.

"Honestly, I didn't," she shared.

She saw the hurt flicker in his eyes before he dropped his hand and stepped back.

Amélie understood that hurt in an instant.

If what he said was true, he'd been watching, waiting, and thinking she'd been doing the same and intended to approach when the time was right.

That time being when she was through with playing with others and wanted a toy who truly understood the game to call her own, in and out of the club.

"Stellan, my sweet friend—" she began.

His handsome face turned hard.

"Don't," he clipped.

She lifted a hand to his chest but he stepped back so swiftly, it was like he was avoiding the touch of a flame.

She understood that, too, and dropped her hand.

"Games anyone should be smart enough not to play," he said and her gaze cut to his. "You wanted me."

She had.

"You're a Dom," she pointed out.

"For everyone but you."

"I couldn't know that," she told him, something he had to know, because there were many switches but he'd *never* given that indication.

"You're right. Unfortunately, you couldn't, except I've been giving it to you openly since you found your stallion. But I played a game, Leigh, one that was fucking stupid. But I did it because I knew you were looking for a challenge. Not looking, it was a *need* and that challenge had to be significant. And I waited for you to take up my challenge, but I was too good at giving it to you because you didn't even fucking see it was a challenge. Then you found what you wanted, and instead of me giving you that myself, since I had my head up my ass I thought you'd see what I was giving and eventually turn to me."

So Olly had been right.

And she'd missed it totally.

"As lovely as your offer is, and as much as it means to me, which is a great deal, I'm afraid now is not the time for us to go there, my handsome Stellan," she said softly.

"Right," he bit off and started to turn.

She caught his arm and he turned back, anger hiding the other emotion flaring in his eyes.

"Are you a Dom?" she asked.

"For everyone but you," he whispered.

Then he pulled free of her hold and prowled out after giving her a bewildering statement that just months ago she would have loved to explore its meaning.

She stared across the plush lounge Aryas provided his Doms and thought of Stellan.

She also thought of Branch Dillinger.

She further thought about Olly and the three days that had passed since their argument.

And last, she thought that life was a bitch of a Mistress.

And she didn't care one whit about the pain.

nineteen

Make It All Okay

OLIVIER

"Boy, you gonna give me what's messed up in your head or what?"

Olly, sitting in a recliner next to his dad, turned his attention from the football game they were watching to his father.

"Come again?" he asked, trying to fake like he didn't know what his dad was talking about.

But he knew.

"Son, known you since you were born, had a hand in makin' you, you don't think I know when something's up with my boy?" Teddy Hawkes asked.

Olly stared at him, trying to decide if it was worth the hassle of attempting to convince his father that nothing was wrong.

Having over three decades of experience knowing this was an impossible task, his hands moved before he told them to, right to his face, where they rubbed, then he swept them back over his hair to his neck, which he squeezed with them both.

His neck was tight as a bow and had been for a week.

Fuck.

He dropped his arms and looked back to his dad.

"You know how Mom used to say that if I didn't get hold of my temper it'd get me in hot water?" Olly asked.

His dad whispered, "Shit," lifted the remote, took the volume on the game down low, and turned in his recliner to face Olly. "What kinda hot water did you get yourself in, Olly?"

"There's a woman."

He said it like she was still there.

But she wasn't.

Lost to him.

No, fuck him, she wasn't.

He'd thrown her away.

"You've had your fair share of those and none of them had you starin' at my plasma like you wanted to rip it off the wall and throw it out the window, so I'm guessin' this one actually means something to you," his dad observed.

"She did," Olly replied quietly.

Teddy Hawkes's brows shot up. "Did?"

"Does," Olly corrected then shook his head. "She does, Dad. She's classy and sweet and can be cute and she has a beautiful voice and an even more beautiful face."

"And?" Teddy prompted.

"And we got into it and I spewed some ugly shit that crossed a serious line, none of it I can take back. Doing that, I broke us."

"So what's got you starin' at my plasma like you mean it harm is that you're tryin' to figure out how to fix what that hot head of yours broke," his father guessed.

Olly shook his head again, knowing he just ate a ton of hot wings and still having an empty feeling in his gut.

He also knew this feeling was because of the next words he said. "No fixing it."

"Boy, I know you and I know you got it in your head to do something, you can do it, especially if it means somethin' to you. So don't give me that malarkey."

Olly turned more fully in his recliner toward his father. "What I'm saying is, even if I could fix it ... and she's Leigh, I lost it with her before, that time I had reason, and she got it and got over it fast, this time it really was not good. It started with me having a reason but I lost that and took it too far. But saying all that, I'm not sure even if I *could* fix it that I could actually fix *us*."

"I think you know I'm not following."

"We don't fit," Olly shared.

"And how's that?" Teddy asked.

"She's rich, Dad," Olly stated. "Her family bought into Xerox when it was time to buy into Xerox and they had money before that kind of rich."

"So?"

Olly stared at his father a beat before he pointed out, "I'm not."

"So?" Teddy repeated.

Olly was losing his temper, not a good thing, as he'd been living with for the last week, so he clamped it down.

"So, Dad, I'm not rich in a way I'm never gonna give her more than she already has."

"What's your point?"

Olly blinked.

Teddy studied his son for a while before he kept talking.

"Olly, you should thank your lucky stars I didn't feel that way about your mother or we'd both be screwed."

"It's not the same when it's the man," Olly told him something he knew.

"Damn, seems I hit the twenty-first century and left my boy behind," Teddy remarked impatiently.

Olly kept a grip on his anger and started, "Dad—"

"Your momma didn't work, my boys would have the second-best cleats when they played football, rather than top of the line."

"It's not—"

"She didn't work, your sister would have some crappy, shiny, cheap fabric when your mother made her prom dress instead of the finest silk."

"With Leigh, it isn't—"

"She didn't work, we woulda had an inside cabin on that family cruise we took when you were sixteen, rather than the nice one with the balcony."

"I get what you're saying, Dad, but—"

Teddy leaned over the arm of his chair toward his son. "No, I'm thinkin' I gotta give you about a million more examples of what your mother offered this family before you get that your mom didn't bring in much, but what she did bring in gave us all a better life."

"You are not a millionaire," Olly clipped.

"Nope, but I bet my boy who's got a brain in his head and knows how to use it . . . most of the time," Teddy started irritably, "knows well enough to pick himself a good one when it's the one who means something to him. So I'll also bet this girl you're talkin' about could be sitting on a mile-high pile of money and if her man came home with a bouquet of flowers he worked for the money to buy them just to let her know she was on his mind, that'd mean something to her and not a little something. A lot."

Olly said nothing.

Teddy didn't do the same.

"And I bet if he took her out for wings and a beer, she wouldn't care, just as long as she was with him."

That, uncomfortably and more than a little painfully, Olly suspected was the truth.

Teddy kept at his son.

"And I bet if you saved and worked overtime to buy her a diamond bracelet, even if she had twenty others, none of them would mean more to her than that one."

Olly turned his head to look at the TV because he suspected his father wasn't wrong about that either.

When he did, Teddy whispered, "Damn, I'm right."

Olly looked back to him but didn't confirm.

He didn't need to.

His father knew.

"Boy, when it matters most, that's the time to use that brain I know you know how to use," his father advised.

Christ, his throat was burning in a way Olly knew even taking a tug of his beer wouldn't help.

He knew it because he'd had that feeling a lot the last week.

"Just to say, we're talkin' about money," Teddy went on. "Could spend five years explainin' to you what your mother brought to our home, our family, and our marriage that had not one thing to do with money. And to push that point home, I mighta made the lion's share of what we had in the bank, but I was no slouch in bringin' what this family needed, what she needed, to the table too. And none of that had anything to do with how much money I made. This life, money means somethin', absolutely. But it doesn't mean everything and the bottom line truth of it is, when you rack up what's important, it isn't even close to the top."

Olly knew that. He even suspected that with Leigh, the conversation they had about her not liking following in her father's footsteps, he gave her something far more important than a mile-high pile of money.

He knew he had something to give.

He just did what he always did. Lost his temper and lost sight of everything but that.

"Okay, Dad. I heard you. You've pushed that point home," Olly shared.

"You give her the good parts of you too?" his father asked, his tone more calm.

Olly looked to him. "Our fight happened when we started to talk about where what we had was going."

"So you gave her the good in you, and boy, you got so much. So much of your mom in you. Your sense of humor. Your smart mouth that's smart in a way it's hilarious. The way you look at things and understand where people are a lot faster than anyone I know. The way you give a crap. So much, you have a job where you're on call and puttin' yourself on the line to help a city full of folks you don't even know. But you two started talkin' about where you were going and your girl's got the scales all hanging to one side, no doubt knowin' exactly where she wants to take it, and you give her the only bad part of you and the other side goes crashing down."

"That's about it," Olly stated roughly.

"Then fix it," Teddy returned quietly.

"I get what you're saying about Mom, Dad, but you did not face what I'm gonna be facing if I can fix things with Leigh, and that's a big 'if,' I messed that up so bad. So you can't say it's that easy."

His father nodded. "You're right. I can't. I'm a man. A man who had a wife and made a family. The man who raised you to be the man you are. I hear you. And I get you. And I get that I'm lookin' at it from an entirely different perspective than you. Because I had the love of my life and she died in my arms. So I can look back to the life we had and twist it with a variety of scenarios. I could make your mother a millionaire and me a quarry foreman. And with what she gave me in the life we had, I'd know down to the pit of my gut that I would not care, Olly. I'd find a way to be all right with it because the alternative wouldn't bear thinking."

Teddy leaned farther across the arm of his chair and locked eyes with his son.

"I get it, too, that you aren't there with this girl. You can't see that because you don't have that experience. You can't know where you're sitting if it's gonna be worth it. What you gotta decide, boy, is if *the risk* is worth it. And I know you, Olly. With the pain you got in your eyes at losing her, you've already made the decision. So stop messin' around and sort it out."

With all his father's words, that burning in his throat had a different meaning.

Through it, he shared that with his dad by saying, "I got midnights tonight."

Teddy grinned. "Then do it tomorrow." He sat back in his chair and grabbed his beer, doing this continuing on a mutter, "And I want her at my table as soon as. Been a while since I had a beautiful woman with a beautiful voice at my table who wasn't my daughter." He glanced at Olly. "No offense to your brother's girl. She ain't hard to look at but the woman's got a voice like nails on a chalkboard."

That was, unfortunately for Luc, true.

For the first time in a week, Olly felt his lips curving.

He turned back to the TV and his smile died.

Fuck, he'd said some seriously stupid shit and she'd even told him he'd done damage.

I had hoped to discuss having more with you . . .

They didn't know each other well enough . . .

No.

Olly didn't know her well enough to know she needed space to ratchet down her temper when it flared. Not knowing that, he hadn't given her that, hadn't even tried to read it from her. Instead he tried to force it low himself and took her calling him Olivier wrong. Made an assumption about that where he jumped to conclusions, let the shit he was worried about that came between them rear up and he lost his mind.

I had hoped to discuss having more with you . . .

She wanted more with him.

And I bet if you saved and worked overtime to buy her a diamond bracelet, even if she had twenty others, none of them would mean more to her than that one.

Olly had no idea if this was true.

But that didn't mean he didn't sense, like his dad said, right down to the pit of his gut, that it was.

And more, if he never gave her a diamond bracelet, if all he had to give was a bouquet of flowers every once in a while that said she was on his mind and she meant something to him, she'd take that.

She'd take anything.

Leigh just wanted Olly.

Fuck, he'd fucked up.

His Leigh.

His Leigh-Leigh.

Fuck.

He had to fix it.

And he sat for the rest of the afternoon, watching football with his dad, knowing no matter what he had to do, he needed to find a fucking way.

And he was damn well going to.

AMÉLIE

Late that evening, Amélie moved out to her garage, wondering if her present course was the right one, giving one last lingering look to her poor Cleopatra, who was trying to follow.

But she had an excellent cat sitter who she paid not only to come and feed them and take care of their litter but also to stay, play, and keep them company.

They'd miss their mummy, but they'd be all right.

Now, her bags were already in her car and she was off to France for three weeks.

A break. Time away. Time to heal. Time to be with people who loved her mother and loved her.

And maybe she'd learn more French this time.

She had her phone in her hand, looking at four texts that had just come in.

The first was from Mira asking (for the hundredth time) if she was okay and telling her to connect when she was safe in France.

The second was from Felicia, inviting her to a movie the next night.

Amélie suspected Mirabelle hadn't said anything but Felicia would have definitely noted that Amélie had not been to the club all week and it was not a secret that she and Olly had had a weekend together outside the club.

Her friend was worried.

The third was from Romy, saying she needed to get drunk and laid, go on the prowl vanilla-style and give an unsuspecting gentleman the time of his life, and she wanted Amélie to go with her.

This, too, was Romy's way of saying she'd noted Amélie's (and Olly's) absence from the club, suspected the reasons behind it, and wanted to help Amélie move past it.

She had good friends.

Alas, this did not make her feel any better.

The last text she saw was from Aryas informing her that Tiffany was again with Belle that night and all was good.

She smiled to herself, knowing this was the third time Belle had played with Tiffany.

The young.

Quick recoveries.

On this thought, without sound or warning, she was struck on the side of the head by what she would realize much later was a fist.

But the blow was forceful, the pain immense, and it took her by such surprise, before she could even consider launching a defense, she fell to her hands and knees.

Then, in her very own garage, she took more, much more, including several vicious kicks to her mid-section that had her coughing up the metallic taste of blood.

And finally, a hand in her hair yanking it back to her feeble, whimpering cry.

"Delia says to mind your own business next time, you cunt," a man spat in her ear and then he pushed her head from him. It cracked against the cement, stars shone in Amélie's eyes, which she could fortunately focus on rather than feeling the spittle he landed on her temple.

Blinking slowly, pain coursing with intent through her body, she watched him walk out the side door it was clear needed a much better lock.

He slammed the door behind him.

Phone.

Phone.

What had happened to her phone?

Crawling in a way that was more like dragging, Amélie saw the phone under her car, gratefully collapsed to her belly, and reached under.

She grasped it.

And blinked again, slower still.

She was losing consciousness.

A boon. It would take away the pain pounding through her midsection and throbbing sharply in her face.

No.

She had to make the call first.

She pressed her finger to the phone and tried to lift her head, the effort mammoth. It felt woozy, stuffed full, way too heavy.

Wetness dribbled down her face.

Taking more effort she could ill afford to lose as she felt herself fading fast, Amélie forced her eyes wide and engaged the phone function, unfortunately not hitting the icon for the keypad but for contacts.

She kept blinking, trying to keep focus, her brain fighting back, shifting concentration to her pain, her finger senselessly scrolling like she could find the keypad in her contacts.

And there was Olly's name.

He was a firefighter. Even if they were done, he would be able to activate emergency. And she was beginning to realize she'd taken too much time fumbling with her screen. She no longer had it in her to find the keypad and dial the three digits she needed.

Further, he was Olly. Her Olly. Even if that was now buried somewhere deep inside him.

He'd take care of her.

She touched his beautiful name and put the phone to her ear.

OLIVIER

Olly sat at head of the table in the kitchen at the firehouse, surrounded by the guys.

"We get a call, I'm gonna be dragging," Emilio said.

"Scored last night?" Chad asked on a grin.

"No. Total tease." Emilio grinned back. "But I put effort in trying."

Olly, his mind on things not the inane conversation about pussy that seemed the priority discussion at the firehouse, looked down when his phone on the table in front of him went off. The second he did, he felt his gut tightening and his heart squeeze.

The display said LEIGH.

It was late. Really late.

But she was calling.

Maybe she'd had a few and got up the nerve, though that was unlikely.

More likely, she was just Leigh. A class act, strong enough to make the first move because it was important enough to do that.

It sucked she beat him by a few hours but he didn't dwell on that. She'd called.

Olly focused on that.

He snatched up the phone and pushed back his chair just as Chad asked, "Leigh. Who's Leigh?"

Jesus, the guys were nosy. No woman had anything on a man who wanted to be up in your shit.

Olly didn't answer Chad.

He took the call, moving from the room, muttering, "Gotta take this."

He put it to his ear and didn't say anything until he was out of the room.

Then he did.

It was, "Leigh-Leigh?"

"Olly."

She sounded funny, tentative.

Probably worried he'd be a dick.

Fuck.

"Baby," he said gently. "So fuckin' glad you called. So fuckin' glad. Love it. Though you beat me. Was gonna call you tomorrow morning. Minute I was off. But I'm at work. Midnights. Won't be done until morning. I can't talk now."

"Olly—"

"Call you the minute I'm off," he semi-repeated. "I'll come over. We'll talk."

"Ol—"

"Fucks me to say this because I wanna talk, I just can't. But I wanna talk, baby. Fucked up again and I wanna work that through with you. Right now, the guys close, they'll get up in my shit and we can't say the things we need to say and anyway, the things I need to say to you, gotta say to your face."

She didn't reply.

"I fucked up, Leigh-Leigh, but we're gonna fix this. I'm gonna fix it. Promise that, baby."

Leigh said nothing.

"Leigh?" he called.

Silence.

"Leigh," he bit out.

Nothing.

"Fuck," he hissed, disconnected, and called her back.

It rang and he got voicemail.

"Fuck," he repeated, disconnecting again, calling again, getting voicemail a-fucking-gain, then disconnecting and staring at his phone.

Why'd she call and hang up?

If she didn't answer, he couldn't find out.

And he was working, he couldn't leave. He was working, so he also couldn't talk even if he did get through to her.

Shit, he had to wait it out, call her in the morning, and if she didn't answer, go home, find the packaging the stuff she'd sent him came in that he hoped like fuck he didn't throw out (and he wasn't into cleaning so this was luckily a good probability), get her address and go to her place.

If she didn't answer the door, he was going to break the god-damned thing down.

He looked to his watch.

Six hours he had to wait.

Fuck.

He turned back toward the kitchen to see Chad standing there.

Terrific.

"Who's Leigh?"

Olly looked in his friend's eyes and gave it to him.

"Woman I'm seein'."

"You're seeing someone?"

Olly nodded. "A while." Suddenly he shook his head. "Fucked shit up, lost my temper, but we're gonna work it out."

"You lost your temper?"

Olly felt some tension slide out of his shoulders at hearing Chad's tone, a tone he knew well since it was his giving-shit tone.

"As crazy as that sounds, considering I'm such a laid-back guy, yeah, I lost my temper," Olly returned, moving his way.

This time, Chad shook his head.

Olly made to move by him but, Chad's hand landing on his shoulder, he stopped, turned, and looked down at him.

"You puttin' in the effort to work shit out, this Leigh must be something," Chad noted, dropping his hand.

Olly even felt his shoulders straightening with pride as he replied, "She is, brother."

"Am I gonna meet her?" Chad asked.

"Yes," Olly answered.

"Is Annie gonna like her?" Chad went on.

"She's good for me and Annie's gonna sense that, so yeah, she's gonna like her."

"Please, bro, tell me she's into football."

All good with Chad after too long of it not being quite right because Olly never got a lock on his temper, he just let loose (except what still wasn't good with Leigh, but it would be), Olly smiled. "Men tackling each other, she's got different reasons, man, but she's totally into it."

Chad started chuckling, doing this muttering through it, "That's why Annie likes it," and moved into the kitchen.

Olly took one last look at his phone, thought, *Just six hours,* and he followed his friend.

In his truck on his way home from work, Olly decided not to call Leigh.

When they talked, he didn't need to be driving.

He needed to be all about Leigh, talking her into letting him come over and straightening out what he'd fucked up between them.

But Olly had a bad feeling when he saw a black Cayenne parked in front of his house with a big black man outside leaning against it, watching Olly's truck approach through wraparound shades.

Olly didn't hit his garage door opener. He parked in the drive of his fake adobe house that was in a neighborhood of fake adobe houses, all of them looking the same even if they were all one of five different façades that could be picked when they were built fifteen years ago.

He figured Leigh lived in a vastly different neighborhood.

He also figured, she was at his house with him, lazing in the back by the pool, snuggled into him watching football and eating nachos, she'd wouldn't give a shit how different it was.

He got out and moved to the bed of his truck to see Aryas Weathers was on his way there.

Leigh would not out his lie to Weathers.

No way.

But there was no reason for the man to be there, so that meant some way he'd found out.

That way wasn't Leigh. Olly was no spy laying down cover. It could be anything.

This still was a surprise, getting a personal visit. He couldn't imagine something like this would merit more than a phone call.

He just had to sort this, not so it was good for Olly, so Weathers wouldn't get in Barclay's face about something his friend never really wanted to do.

"Help you with something?" he asked then stopped abruptly when he noticed Weathers's gait was aggressive.

Olly went on alert and straightened with all his muscles tightening when Weathers didn't stop until he was smack in Olly's space and his face.

He lifted a hand with a phone in it to their sides.

"You wanna tell me why Leigh called you and talked to you for three minutes right after she was attacked and she was still on the floor of her garage, beat to shit, five cracked ribs, when the police and ambulance arrived twenty minutes after you disconnected, called back, *repeatedly*, but it wasn't you who called emergency? It was Leigh who regained consciousness and did it her-fuckin'-self."

Olly heard his words but didn't reply because he was suddenly not confronting Aryas Weathers in his space and face.

His mind had blanked to nothing but a violent sheen of red.

"You better answer me, man."

Olly's mouth moved. "Where is she?"

"That's not answering—"

Olly's vision cleared, he bumped chests and noses with the man as he roared, *"Where is she?"*

Weathers stared into his eyes before he noted, "Did she black out after she dialed you?"

Olly bumped chests with him again, taking the man back a foot, and watched Weathers's eyes go alert and pissed.

"Ask this one last time, where the fuck is she?"

"She took a few to the face, spent the night in the hospital for observation to watch for concussion. She's gonna be fine, is being released today and Mira's taking her to her ranch."

"Which hospital?"

"What happened during that call, Hawkes?"

Olly could see Leigh meant something to the guy so he expended some needed but quickly waning patience to say, "We had a thing. I thought she was callin' to work it out. I was on the job and couldn't talk. I had no fuckin' clue and thought she hung up on me."

"Fuck, brother," Weathers whispered.

"Jesus, man, tell me where she fuckin' is."

"Going there now. You're in a state, Hawkes, so you're not behind a wheel. You're coming with me."

Olly was not going to waste time arguing.

He jogged to the Cayenne.

He didn't know if Weathers was the type of man to jog to anything but he sensed Olly's tension so Olly was grateful when he followed him in the same way.

They were in and on the road when Olly asked confirmation by saying, "So she's good."

"She doesn't look all that great but when the swelling goes down, her ribs heal, she'll be good as new."

Olly felt his hands form fists on his knees and ground out, "Burglary? What?"

Weathers didn't answer.

Olly looked his way. "How the fuck she get jumped in her goddamned garage?"

"Well, thinkin' you're seriously wound up and as big as a house in a vehicle I kinda like, so even though I know it's piss-poor judgment to share this with you right now, you gotta hear it, deal with it, and be about her when you see her."

"Give it to me," Olly grunted.

"We had a situation with a Domme at the club. She was taken care of, though apparently the message wasn't made as clear as I thought. She's a cunt and from what Leigh shared, she somehow found out Leigh was concerned and voiced that to me. We'll be findin' out how that happened. But bottom line, she acted on that and sent someone to work Leigh over."

Olly was again looking at him. "Delia."

Weathers glanced his way. "She share her concern with you?"

"I shared mine with her and she told me she had the same thoughts."

Weathers nodded.

"Police been called?" Olly asked.

"He got the drop on her. She knows he's a guy, he's white, he's bigger than her and he beat the shit out of her. Other than that, she didn't get anything. He did something stupid, spit in her face . . ."

Olly's focus on the road disappeared as it shifted to stopping himself from punching through the windshield or roaring like an animal.

"Lock it down, brother," Aryas said quietly, not surprisingly feeling Olly's rage. "Deep breath. Then another one. Keep doin' that."

Olly took his advice.

On breath five when Olly's vibe stopped choking the air in the cab, Weathers went on.

"Means he left DNA at the scene. Don't know if he left prints or got seen. If they don't have that to try and track him, and he's not in the system with his DNA, which is unlikely, they're not gonna find him. They don't find him, they can't trace him to Delia. But yeah, to answer your question, Leigh's given a statement to the police."

"Are you gonna leave it at that?" Olly pushed.

Weathers's glance was longer before he looked at the road.

"No."

"I'm on that," Olly stated.

"Man, I get you and Leigh are tight but you let my man work. He knows what he's doing."

"I wasn't asking."

Weathers waited until he'd stopped at a stoplight before he looked to Olly and spoke.

"You gonna do something stupid if I don't partner you up with Branch?"

Olly had no idea who Branch was.

And he wasn't going to do anything stupid.

He was going to do what needed to be done.

He said none of this and didn't need to.

Weathers read it.

"I'll partner you up with Branch," he murmured.

Olly faced forward.

The light changed and Weathers drove.

She was asleep when he arrived.

Olly didn't go anywhere, not even to get coffee to stay awake after being up all night.

Didn't matter. He didn't need caffeine.

He wouldn't fall asleep.

But her friend Mira, giving him close looks he decided to ignore, brought him some anyway.

Olly drank some of it but only to be nice.

Mostly, he sat in the chair beside her bed, exploring new boundaries of controlling his hot head.

She'd had a number done on her, a small cut under her eye that was taped together being the worst of it, if you didn't count her ribs, which Olly was absolutely not allowing himself even to consider.

He actually didn't let himself think of anything but what he'd say when she woke up or he knew he'd lose it.

Right then he didn't need to lose it.

He needed to keep his shit so he could do what needed to be done.

He'd been there twenty minutes before the halls getting noisier with the day's activities woke her.

The second he saw her eyes fluttering, Olly stood and leaned over the bed.

She saw him; her one eye not swollen shut widened then she shut it and turned her face away.

He gently pushed his hand under the healthy cheek she was pressing against the pillow but he didn't force her to look at him.

He bent to her ear.

"Fucked up again. Fucked up, you called me when you needed me and I didn't—"

"Please don't," she whispered. "Just go."

His gut twisted.

"Leigh-Leigh."

Even with her swollen eye he could see her squeezing it shut.

"Go."

"Can't, baby, you know that. I'm a jackass with a bad temper but you gotta know no way I can leave this room with you in that bed."

She pressed her face into his hand but did it to get away when she whispered, "I don't want you to see me like this."

Olly relaxed.

"Leigh, you got jumped. It's not your—"

She turned and opened her good eye. "I didn't fight back. I couldn't. He was suddenly there and on me and I didn't even get a single—"

"Please, baby, I wanna hear this if you wanna give it to me, but for right now, you gotta stop talking."

She closed her mouth and stared into his eyes.

Then she whispered, "I'll stop talking."

She was learning.

He bent closer. "Last night, I shoulda shut my trap and listened to you."

"Well, all you were saying was quite lovely and I did fully intend to tell you why I called once you shut up but I'm afraid I blacked out in the middle of it."

He felt a muscle jump up his jaw right to his temple.

And she watched it, stating hurriedly, "I'll stop talking again."

"Good call."

She pressed chapped lips together.

Olly watched and felt another muscle jump.

He turned his thoughts and asked, "You goin' to the ranch?"

She nodded.

"I'm gonna be doin' something with some guy named Branch."

She clearly knew who Branch was because her one eye got wide again and she opened her mouth. "Olly—"

Olly cut her off. "Your girl, can she stay with you?"

She nodded. "She's taking time off."

So was he.

He was also going to talk to Weathers about what they could do to cover her. Two women at that remote ranch, they needed more protection until shit was seen to.

That was for him and Weathers. Leigh didn't need to worry about that.

"Get to you when I can," he told her.

"I wouldn't possibly be able to talk you out of doing something foolish with Aryas and his private investigator, would I?"

So this Branch dude was a PI.

That'd be useful.

"No," he answered.

Her good eye rolled to the head of the bed.

"Leigh-Leigh," he called.

Her eye rolled back to him.

Olly bent even closer.

"We're gonna work it out, all of it, Leigh," he promised. "I'm gonna apologize for bein' a dick to you again and I'm gonna do it in a way I make you believe how fuckin' sorry I am that I was. But I'm gonna state right now that all that shit I spewed was shit. I was feelin' down deep a load of crap I should have talked out with you. It was huge, I couldn't see my way past it, I really fuckin' wanted to get past it because beyond that was you, and I took all of that out on you. My mom warned me if I didn't check my temper, it'd land me in hot water. And I cannot say after her givin' me that for years and me not takin' good advice that I can turn that on a dime. What I can say is actin' like that and nearly losin' you is a lesson I'm not gonna forget. Not ever, Leigh. So we'll work things out, we'll figure out where we're goin', that bein' somewhere together, and along the way, I'll do my fuckin' all to check it."

When he was done talking, she asked, "How do you do that?"

He didn't understand the question. "Do what?"

"Make it all okay just like that."

Olly's relief was so great he dropped his head and nearly didn't stop it before he hit hers.

Instead, when he got close enough to touch his mouth to hers, he did it.

"You've a very foul temper, darling," she whispered when he'd moved away half an inch.

"I'll do my fuckin' all to check it."

She looked him in the eyes.

Then she nodded and said softly, "We'll talk more later."

That was when he nodded.

"Please be careful with Aryas and his PI."

"It'll all be good."

She studied him dubiously, mumbling, "Mm-hmm."

"You do what the doctors say you can and no more," he ordered.

"I have no desire at the present juncture to tiptoe through any tulips, Olly, so don't worry about me."

He grinned at her, bent in, and touched his mouth to hers again.

This time, she touched hers back.

Thank fuck.

"I'll call," he promised as he pulled away.

"I'll answer and not black out this time."

"Right," he grunted. "Time to joke about that will be around two, three decades from now."

Something shifted in her eyes, he caught it and he got it.

What he said indicated they might have decades.

And it further indicated he wanted that.

He'd said it and he'd meant it so he just stared into her face that was still beautiful, even with half of it mottled and swollen.

"So noted," she murmured.

"Be in touch."

She nodded again.

"Mean the world to me, Leigh-Leigh," he whispered.

Her face got soft, her good eye got wet and she lifted a hand to cup his jaw.

"I know how that feels," she whispered back.

Christ, he wanted to kiss her.

But Olly couldn't kiss her the way he wanted to.

So he kissed her nose, her forehead, her good eye and her bad one before he touched his lips to hers again.

"Later, Leigh."

"Later, Olly."

He ran his thumb along her jaw, straightened, gave her a grin, and then turned around and walked out of her hospital room.

twenty

I May Already Have Landed

OLIVIER

"Yo!"

At the sound, Olly quit beating the absolute shit out of the man who was barely conscious, held up by one of Olly's hands fisted in his shirt, the left side of his face, just like Leigh's, having taken a pummeling.

His was not swollen and mottled.

It was annihilated.

"Think that does it, man," Branch called out.

Olly looked from the man he held to the guy leaning casually against a wall, eyes on Olly.

He lifted his chin, dropped the man, delivered two kicks from his boot into his ribs then bent over him.

"Some cunt wants you to deliver a message again, brother, think twice," he advised.

The guy replied with nothing but a noise of pain.

"You with me?" Olly pushed.

He barely heard the mumbled, "With you."

"Be happy to do this again, you think twice," Olly shared.

"Won't," the guy forced out.

"Smart," Olly muttered.

Then he hocked as much phlegm as he could get up his throat and spat it in the man's face.

He straightened, looked back to Branch, and as he moved to the door, said, "Let's roll."

They left the apartment building, swung up in Branch's GMC SUV, and Branch set them rolling.

It had been two days since it happened. Aryas put Branch on it the minute he'd been called by Mira and told Leigh had been attacked.

Before and after Weathers shared with Branch that he had a partner, something the other man made no comment to and just worked with it, Branch did not fuck around.

He wasn't a big talker. He was also the most focused guy Olly had ever met. He saw to the job, shared what needed to be done, was so diligent, intent, and intuitive it was uncanny, so he never lost a lead, and Olly went with his flow.

This all meant now, in a short expanse of time, they'd dealt with the first issue and Olly knew not to hash it out with Branch. Not that he'd want to.

It was done.

He pulled out his phone, engaged it, saw the time was late and still called Leigh.

"Darling," she answered, sounding sleepy.

He had not been keeping her up to date with what they were doing.

But he had been calling her frequently, not to have long chats, just to check in to make sure she was okay.

"Did I wake you?" he asked.

"It doesn't matter."

It did. She needed to rest. He shouldn't have called.

"Let you sleep. Just wanted you to know, things are on course and I'll be at the ranch, latest, tomorrow night."

"That's good, Olly," she replied then asked, "Are you good?"

"I'm fine. It's all gonna be fine, Leigh-Leigh. Just go back to sleep."

"All right," she murmured. "Talk to you tomorrow."

He grinned at the phone. "Yeah, you will."

"You get some sleep too."

That, he probably wouldn't do until this was done.

"I will, baby," he lied. "Call you tomorrow."

"Okay, Olly. Tomorrow, sweetheart."

"Later, Leigh."

He hung up and shoved the phone back in his pocket.

There was silence in the cab until Branch told him, "You need ice on your hands."

"They'll be fine."

Branch was silent again before he asked quietly, "She good?"

"Woke her. Sleepy, but she sounds stronger."

Branch had nothing to say to that for long beats until he amended, "No, brother, what I mean is, *is she good?*"

Olly turned his head to look at the guy.

"Sorry?"

"You're hers."

Fuck.

He knew. The way he stated that, he knew *exactly.*

He had to know Weathers's business since he worked for the dude but somehow he also knew what Olly and Leigh had.

"Not sure that's your business, Dillinger," he returned, forcing back his irritation and looking again through the windshield.

There were more moments of silence, now loaded, before Branch spoke again.

"You got it all, Hawkes, don't fuck it up."

Although his comment was surprising, including the fact he even made one, the guy was so taciturn, Olly turned his way impatiently.

"Thanks for the advice," he said tersely. "And no offense, but it isn't needed."

"She gives it to you like you like it *and* gives you what you both got that I keep hearing when you talk on the phone, I'm meaning no offense either. Just sayin' that's hard to find. You got it and you can get lost in the easy and not work to keep the good."

"Nothin' about what we got has been easy," Olly told him.

"Reckon that's the fuckin' truth," Branch muttered.

Olly stared at him closely.

Fuck.

Fuck.

What he was thinking couldn't be right.

But Branch's words, he was right.

"You're a brother," he noted carefully.

Branch didn't confirm verbally and it took some time for him to confirm at all. When he did, it was an almost-not-there lift of his chin.

Christ, Olly felt that. Looking at the man, he felt it, sitting next to someone like Branch Dillinger who was a brother in a lot of ways.

And it was then he understood precisely why Barclay took Olly's back and made time for him, even when he was being a dick.

"It was hard to find, Branch, but I found it, which means it's out there," Olly shared.

"You're a good man, Hawkes, know it the way you're doin' what needs to be done for your woman. Glad you got that. But that shit's not gonna happen for me."

Olly guessed where he was at.

"You go lookin'?" he asked.

"No."

Shit.

"The Honey's got goods on offer, brother," he gave him something the man had to know.

"Aryas sets me up. Private. I get what I need. That doesn't mean I'll get what you have. But I get what I need."

There was something awesome about this, an open conversation about shit that was real that was hidden day to day but out there in the dark cab of an SUV, two men cut from the same cloth in a number of ways were connecting.

And the way Branch introduced it, it was clear he needed that connection.

Olly would never have thought he'd be on the Barclay side of things, offering advice to a brother who needed it.

But being right there, it felt fucking good.

That said, what was coming from Branch was all bad.

"Leigh and me found our way. While doin' that, another Domme at the Honey, friend of Leigh's, gorgeous, works her man sweet, they found it too. So Leigh and me are no glitch."

"No good woman deserves the shit I got festering inside of me."

"I know that shit, Branch," Olly said quietly. "And it isn't shit. It's who you are and you are far from alone in that. Any woman you find worth the effort to look toward a future is gonna know that shit, too, and help you through it."

"No, you don't, Olly. You don't know my brand of shit. I get you think you do but I'm totally cool with what I like to get off. Take that, walk away. It's going the distance that isn't going to happen for me and I'm down with that too. My point here is, glad to know good men like you find what you need, but it's not gonna happen for me."

"Not sure what that's about, but what I am sure is that I always got cold beer in my fridge so if you wanna talk it out, door's open."

"Gratitude, and not throwin' that offer in your face 'cause it means something. Just sharing that that's not gonna happen," Branch replied.

"Door's still always open and not just for that chat."

There was again silence before Branch murmured, "Gratitude, Olly."

Olly got that Branch needed to let it go.

So he let it go.

But for a man he'd learned to respect in about five minutes, the man who was marking the course for Olly to do what needed to be done for his Leigh, he wanted something more for him.

Aryas set him up privately?

Olly was going to have a word with Leigh.

Then they'd see what Branch would get next.

The next evening, Olly stood with his shoulders against the window in Barclay's office, his arms on his chest, his eyes not on the TV screen playing the video, but on the bitch sitting, looking just as ridiculous as she just fucking was (by the mere fact she was breathing) as she was trying (and failing) to do it with dignity in one of Barclay's absurd chairs.

Barclay was in that office with him, standing close to the door.

Branch was there too.

Delia had her focus on the TV, her face pointy with anger, her body held tight as a bow.

Olly turned his attention from the woman to the TV but he didn't keep it there long because it turned his stomach, what he was seeing.

Multiple partner play, all at Delia's command, her all done up in Dominatrix gear, though her bodysuit was crotchless so her subs had access when she ordered it.

None of it was extreme. No blood play, torture, mutilation, anything like that.

That didn't matter.

When Dillinger switched it off and got Delia's and Olly's attention, he gave to her what mattered.

"Turnabout is fair play," he said quietly.

Delia didn't reply.

"Courier waiting," he announced. "DVD of that ready to be dispatched to your boss's home. He's got an open mind, another one ready to be dispatched to *his* boss's home. To be thorough, two more, one to the president of your company and one to your ex-husband. You lost your kids to him and the divorce wasn't a walk in the park for you, but you ever want anything or to get your kids back, he's got evidence of your kink, it ain't gonna happen."

Olly glanced at Barclay, who was staring at Delia with a look of unhidden digust on his face.

Barclay had arranged the whole thing with subs who were totally okay with having their video disbursed if Delia called their bluff. Something Aryas was not good to do even if he had a ton of tape starring Delia, seeing as he'd have to ask his members to out themselves for him to do it.

Enter Barclay and he'd delivered.

The subs on that video lived the life and were open about it. Hell, one was the kitten Olly met who worked for the Bolt.

All the participants knew Delia's thing, not only the blackmail but also what she did to Leigh. So they were all down with crippling her.

"First, the name of the person who gave you intel about what was heard at the Honey," Branch demanded.

"Julie," she bit out, obviously not giving a shit whoever Julie was was next going to get it because Aryas was going to lose his fucking mind he had an employee who fucked any of his members over.

Especially Leigh.

Branch didn't even nod before he kept at her.

"Now, tomorrow, you go into your office and tender your resignation," he continued. "You also contact a real estate agent and put your house on the market. It sells or not, I don't give a shit. You're out of Phoenix by the end of the month and I'll throw in here, by out of Phoenix I mean you land nowhere in the south-fucking-west."

"I can hardly—" she began.

"Shut up, I'm not done talking," Branch barked.

Olly straightened from the window and turned watchful eyes to his partner, because he'd never seen the guy show much emotion at all and it sounded like he was losing it.

At the burning fury suddenly blazing out of Branch's usually emotionless light-blue eyes, Delia wisely shut her trap.

"You will be watched," Branch told her, snapping right back to calm in a way that was completely focused, straight-up badass, and totally fucking eerie.

Delia didn't miss it. She got visibly wired.

Branch kept going.

"You will be watched in the short time you'll remain in Phoenix and you'll be watched wherever you go. You try to fuck with anyone who has anything to do with the Bee's Honey, the consequences you'll face . . . advice, and I suggest you listen carefully . . . they'll be consequences you do not want to face. You think this retaliation is a pain in your ass, trust me, you don't demonstrate with every move you make from the minute you leave this room that you get the message I'm right now sending, you will know pain."

Olly looked from Branch to the bitch and saw that her bravado was cracking. She wasn't reeking of fear but she sure the fuck was leaking it.

Dillinger wasn't done.

"And just so you know, there will never be a time when you'll be safe. Someone will be checking in randomly. Not for months, but for as long as Aryas feels necessary to make sure you don't fuck with anybody in the life. Not just associated with the Honey, but *in the life*. You're not a bitch. You're not a cunt. You're a fuckin' waste of space. And the reason I know that is because you're so goddamned stupid, it's mind-boggling. And the reason I know *that* is you are what you are and you didn't take care of the beauty that was handed to you. But the bigger reason I know that is you fucked with Aryas Weathers and it is known wide he *does* take care of the beauty that's under his protection and he does not fuck around in doing that."

Olly watched her swallow but she didn't say anything.

So Branch prompted, "Now, confirm you've heard me."

"I heard you," she spat.

"Resignation tomorrow," Branch returned on a sharp nod. "Trailing your slimy path to whatever unfortunate destination you choose by the end of the month. And please, don't be any more fuckin' stupid. We nailed your messenger and we nailed you in three days. I report to Aryas you're not bein' smart, look in my eyes, woman, and see I'll enjoy every fuckin' second of the next message I get to deliver."

She didn't spend a lot of time looking into his eyes.

She read his eyes. She couldn't miss it.

"Are we done?" she snapped.

"We are," Branch replied.

She glanced to the TV. "Is there a time when I'll get those DVDs?"

Olly felt a shiver feather up his spine when Branch whispered, "You're bein' stupid."

At that, on a glare that was meant to save face and a hilariously graceless ascent from her chair, she took her feet, lifted her nose, and stomped to the door.

It opened and one of Barclay's bouncers was standing in the narrow space outside it.

Undoubtedly told by Barclay to make her exit as unpleasant as it could be, the bouncer grabbed her upper arm, and with a controlled push, shoved her down the stairs with him as her escort and her leash.

Barclay slammed the door and shouted at it, *"Boo-yah!"*

Olly started chuckling.

Barclay looked to Branch. "You're the fuckin' shit, man."

"I'm somethin'," Branch muttered and the words were not only bizarre, the way he voiced them was the same, so Olly felt his brows draw together as he studied the man. Branch looked to Olly. "Julie gets the Aryas treatment. You and me are done."

"Yeah, we are, brother, and you got my thanks," Olly replied. "Any time, beer's on me."

Branch nodded. "Now that, Ol, I might take you up on."

Olly gave him a grin and jerked up his chin.

"Dealing with that trash, letting me have a hand in it, same's on offer from me, Dillinger," Barclay put in, moving from the door into the room.

"Thanks," Branch murmured, looked to both men but said to Olly, "Later."

"Later," Olly replied.

"Later, man," Barclay called after him as he was going down the stairs. When Branch disappeared, he turned his attention to Olly. "Dude's got it going on."

He did.

Olly only nodded.

Barclay gave him a huge smile. "Offer you a beer but I'm thinking you're *this close* to sprinting to your truck."

Olly smiled back. "You'd be right."

"Go to her, brother," Barclay urged quietly.

He didn't go to Leigh. Not immediately.

He went to Barclay and they grasped forearms before they let go, moved in and lifted them, bumping them up the length.

"Means a lot, all you've done, buddy," Olly said low as they moved apart.

"I know it, Olly, so you don't have to say it."

Olly kept giving his friend a look before he muttered, "Later," and turned away.

"Later," Barclay called to his back.

Then Olly was gone.

He'd called to tell her he was coming so Olly wasn't surprised, even though it was late, when the door to her ranch opened as Olly was shifting his truck into park next to a BMW SUV.

He also wasn't surprised it was Leigh's girl Mira who was standing in the lit doorway.

He grabbed his bag, hauled his body out of the truck and was again unsurprised she didn't offer him a greeting or get out of his way when he made it to her.

He stopped and looked down at her.

She looked up at him.

Women talked, Leigh and Mira were tight, so he knew his woman's friend knew. Probably everything.

Or mostly everything.

"There won't be a strike three," he assured her quietly.

She continued to study him for a beat, two, before she stepped aside, murmuring, "There better not be."

Olly fought back his grin, moved in, and dropped his bag by the door Mira closed behind him.

Cleopatra came calling, slinking with her slightly hitched feline grace down the hall.

"She's in the living room," Mira told his back.

He glanced over his shoulder at her, gave her a nod, and then moved that way, bending to scoop up Leigh's cat as he went.

He saw Leigh wrapped in a throw on the couch in the great room, firelight dancing on her, as Mira called down the hall, "I'm going to bed!"

"All right, *chérie*," Leigh called back, her eyes on Olly. "Sleep well."

"You too," Mira yelled back, her voice retreating.

Olly kept moving through this, taking Leigh in.

The swelling was down but the bruising had come up, dark and angry.

As much as that burned through him, he focused on doing the only thing left now to do.

He approached, dropped her cat in her lap, and then entered the couch with her, carefully pulling her in his arms so they were side to side, turned slightly into each other.

Cleopatra split the scene, apparently not feeling like cuddling.

Olly took one arm from around Leigh, lifted a hand, and with fingers curled, he moved them to within an inch of her battered, beautiful face.

He thought better of touching her but as he was dropping his hand, she caught it.

She inspected his scabbed knuckles and looked to him.

"Do I want to know?" she asked.

"No," he answered.

"So I know," she whispered.

He figured she did, but he didn't confirm it.

Instead he sat, his body still, his mind filled with good things, as he watched her kiss his knuckles one by one.

Done with that, she laced her hand with his and rested them in her lap.

"How you feeling?" he asked.

"Every day it gets better," she told him.

He searched her face for a lie but he couldn't see that anywhere.

"Good," he muttered.

"You look tired, darling," she observed.

He was. He'd been amped for days but suddenly, in her space, sitting in front of her fireplace, with Leigh in his arms, he was exhausted.

"I am."

She made a move to get them up, saying, "Let's get you to bed."

He didn't move with her. Instead, he gently gave her a squeeze with his arms telling her he didn't want them to go anywhere.

She looked to him, saw something in his face, and cuddled closer, whispering, "We can talk tomorrow, Olly."

"Dad knows what happened to you," he announced. "He also knows I'm takin' time off but he thinks it's so I can look after you in a way that's not how I've spent the last three days lookin' after you. And he knows I got two more days off before I gotta go back to work. And he knows that I'm bringin' you back to the city when I go back and you'll be stayin' at my place until you're all good. He's givin' us that. After that, though, he wants you at his table and, babe, he says he's makin' his brisket so, trust me, serious as shit, you'll wanna be sittin' there."

He'd kept talking even as her face changed, churning through alarm, surprise, astonishment, marvel, and finally it melted, her eyes getting wet, as she stared up at him with lips parted.

When he was done talking, she asked immediately, "You talked with your father about me?"

Olly nodded but didn't get further into that.

He gave her more.

"Chad, my best bud at the firehouse, says that his wife says that if you're not ass to their couch watchin' a game first Sunday you're up for it, she's gonna get pissy. *At me.* And Annie's a good woman but she's hell on wheels when she's riled so I'd appreciate you savin' me from that."

While he gave her that, it wasn't her face that melted but her body into his.

"Olly," she said, and that was all she said, but his name in that sweet tone was all she needed to give him.

She didn't need to say more.

His name was weighty, there was so much feeling dripping from it, and it might have been the prettiest thing he ever heard.

"In between all that, you're takin' me out for beer and wings," he declared. "But once you're all good and you can get dressed up for me, I'm takin' my woman out for a fat, juicy steak at an uppity place where they know how to make her cocktail. Donovan's, maybe. But I'm thinkin' Durant's is more your style."

She let his hand go to rest hers on the side of his neck when she replied, "I love all this, Olly. I really do. You can't . . ." She swallowed, he let her work at it, find it and when she did, he was quiet as she kept going. "You can't know how much. But the things you said, they need to be discussed."

He fought his mouth getting tight, angry at himself at the reminder of his own stupidity, while he told her, "Dad set me straight."

She did a slow blink.

"You . . . you . . . you talked to your father about—"

"About what was really fuckin' with my head," he cut her off to say. "What we got between us, Leigh-Leigh, it is what it is or it was vanilla, none of his business. That wasn't what was holding me back. You took that from me and I told you that was all good and I didn't lie. You gave me that freedom. That was all good. I gave him what was holding me back when I'd think about our future. And he set me straight." He grinned at her. "Made me feel like a moron doing it, but that's his way."

Her hand gave him a squeeze. "You aren't a moron."

And that was Leigh. Even when he *was* a moron, she didn't make him feel that way.

In return his arms gave her a squeeze, but cautiously. "My dad's the shit, Leigh, and fortunately for him, he's got a daughter who has her shit together and can do no wrong, no joke, which is annoying." She gave him a slight grin and he kept going. "But he's got two boys who have no problem shoving their heads up their own asses on more than the rare occasion. So when he has to pull one out, he doesn't fuck around."

"It's as easy as that?" she asked skeptically.

"I don't figure it will be," he answered truthfully. "I figure I'm gonna hit roadblocks but that isn't this. Us. That's life. Life always has roadblocks. Just can't keep bein' the dick who doesn't negotiate them the right way. You get blocked, eventually you gotta learn to get smart and figure out how to navigate past it. Bein' an asshole and blowing my stack clearly isn't the way to do that. So I'm aware of that, of the consequences that might bring, it's better than rammin' my head against the obstacle until I've hammered my own self senseless. So I'm aware, I work like fuck not to do that again and make you watch me do it, slammin' you right along with me while I do."

"It's good you have a handle on that, darling, but there was a great deal more to what you said."

"Yeah, there was," he agreed readily. "And Dad made it crystal just how deep my head was up my ass about that too."

"He seems to have significant powers," she noted hesitantly.

Olly gave her another grin but that grin faded and his next was said softly.

"Yeah, baby, 'cause, see I told you he had it all with Mom. And he did. He had it all. Just what he needed."

Her lips parted again, she got what he was saying, which was exactly what he was saying, and Olly gave the rest to her.

"But there was a time when he didn't know. He didn't know if she was the one who would give him everything. He had to take that risk. And I don't know what obstacles they faced but they're human. They didn't live in a magical world where everything was glitter dust and carefree. He just had a gut feeling, went with it, and had the woman by his side who could help him clear those obstacles. A woman he felt everything for so he busted his ass helping her clear hers. And in the end and all along the way, he was proved right, listening to his gut and taking that risk."

"Are you saying you want to take that risk with me?" she asked, more wet in her eyes, hope there, too, and fuck him, banged-up face, she was never more beautiful.

"Where I'm at right now is *knowing* I want that and hoping like fuck you want to take that risk with me."

She slid up his chest, her hand sliding into the back of his hair, and she whispered, "I do, Olly. I very much do."

That.

Felt.

Great.

He closed his eyes and dropped his forehead to hers.

"Olly?" she called.

He opened his eyes but didn't lift his head from hers.

She kept talking.

"My part in that . . ." She paused before she went on, "I was wanting, *very much*, what we're discussing now. And I'd allowed myself to . . ." She paused again and seemed unable to figure out how to get back to it.

"Lay it on me, gorgeous," he urged gently.

"There were . . . I . . ." More hesitation before she rushed it out. "It never got very far because I learned in ways that were more than a little unpleasant precisely what I was, what my use was, the place I had in their lives with two other men that I'd hoped . . ."

She trailed off then she got it together and finished it.

"I want a man in my life, sweetheart. Not a sub. A man to shuffle around the kitchen with and argue with about whiskers in the sink and," her hand at his neck tightened, "make babies with. I'd allowed myself to hope before and got burned. I mistakenly assumed that you . . . all you wanted from me was what I'd been giving you in the playrooms and you're correct, I *do* have an ice-cold temper, as you said. I need space and I think deliberately and—"

"Leigh-Leigh, it's okay," he cut her off, getting where she was coming from now, too, hating that happened to her with those other guys (at the same time, in a way, glad it did because it meant she was free for him) and hating more he did one fucking thing to put her in that place in her head.

But now that was over. They both had to let it go and move on.

To get her there, he reminded her, "We're learning about each other and just as long as we actually pay attention and *learn*, we'll get there."

"All right, Olly."

He smiled into her eyes. "But, just sayin', I'm not real good with rinsing my whiskers out of the sink."

Her eyes smiled back. "It may take time, darling, but I have a feeling I'll learn to live with that."

They stared at each other up close and Olly watched it happen for her as it happened for him. The shadows clearing in her eyes, the backs becoming brighter because the shit was done and what they had to look forward to was not shadows.

It was light.

And when they were both there, Leigh felt it, tilted her head, and pressed her lips to his.

He opened his over hers and kissed her.

When he'd had enough (for now), he lifted a breath away and whispered, "Thank you for giving me that."

"Thank you for giving me what you gave me," she replied, also whispering.

Her words struck something that made him study her face and the look in her eyes even more closely.

Olly appreciated her gratitude but he also found it miraculous. *She* had a lot to forgive.

He just had to hope he could explain it so she'd find it in herself to do that.

He'd explained it, she'd done that, but he got the sense she'd already done that days ago in the hospital.

And with what he'd done to them, it was too easy.

"I want you to get, for certain, baby," he whispered fiercely, "that I mean all I'm sayin'."

"I get that, Olly."

"I love the mercy you're showin', but I fucked up, said shit, hurt you, caused damage and—"

She cut him off. "It seems you've gone to a lot of trouble to find ways to sort that, not only with me, but for your own sake."

"I did. But what I'm tryin' to say now is, I actually *did*. And since I did, I don't want you livin' in fear I'm gonna blow again," Olly admitted.

She gave him a sweet smile and pressed closer. "Darling, with all you've explained, with the way you've always been to me, except for one lapse," even smiling, her lips started twitching, "you've also always been open with me. So if you promise you'll do everything you can not to allow it to happen again, I believe you. And you've promised. So I believe you."

"You're making this very easy when I don't deserve that, Leigh-Leigh," he pointed out cautiously.

"And I made it very hard for my mother to find her way in through doors I'd closed against her in my heart," she returned and Olly felt his breath suspend. "I took too long opening those doors. I loved her. I lost her before I allowed her back in. So I've learned the *very* hard way not to make that mistake again."

Now *that* he got so he said no more.

Leigh didn't either.

Olly kept the quiet going, then he finally gave it all to his Leigh.

"Okay, gorgeous, what we got is young but right here, right now, I want you to go into that risk we were talkin' about, the one you're takin' on me, knowin' right where I'm at. So you go in knowin' I'm fallin' in love with you and the way that feels, I don't think that fall is gonna last very long."

She stared at him, her pretty tawny eyes watery.

Then a tear slid out of her good eye.

He adjusted his hand so he could catch it with his thumb.

And he was still whispering when he said, "Shit, baby, no crying."

She continued to stare into his eyes.

And fuck him, just like Leigh, she gave him back exactly what he needed.

"I think I may already have landed."

And that . . .

Felt . . .

Phenomenal.

Olly wanted to be gentle but when he took her mouth after she gave him that, he couldn't accomplish that feat.

She burrowed into him and totally didn't seem to mind.

It was Leigh who pulled away and shared with obvious regret, "We should go to bed, and Olly, I'm afraid my ribs mean—"

"We'll wait," he assured her.

She nodded.

"Bed," he said.

"Bed," she agreed.

With that, Olly angled up, carefully lifting her in his arms when he did it.

He then carried Leigh to bed.

He came back to turn out the lights, make sure the doors were locked, the windows secured, the fire banked, and the cats had enough water to get through until morning.

After he was assured all was set, he returned to his Leigh.

epilogue

The Tangle That Was Them

AMÉLIE

Months later, Amélie drifted through the maze of playrooms at the Honey carrying her champagne glass, the drink inside mostly finished, noting it was a busy night.

She did not pause, not even to watch Trey taking a cat from Mira.

Amélie had no idea if Trey had done something for which to be punished. Mira and she spoke of a great deal, but they didn't speak of those things. It was between Mirabelle and her boyfriend.

As was the same between Olivier and Amélie.

Amélie did know that things were still going strong between those two with no hint that wouldn't keep coming. To this end, they were discussing moving in together and had only not done so because Trey wanted to keep his house, Mirabelle wanted to keep hers, and no compromise had yet been reached.

At their last book club, Romy had suggested they both sell and find something together that was not his or hers, but theirs.

When Mira shared this with Trey, he'd thought that was an excellent suggestion.

Mira, however, was digging in.

Amélie was all set to intervene when Olly stopped her.

"Trey'll get his way," he'd said.

She'd found this assertion dubious.

He'd grinned at her look, hooked her with an arm around her shoulders, pulling her so their chests were touching, and dropped his face close.

"Your girl will give her guy anything. Just keep your pretty nose to yourself and let it play out."

She suspected he might be right (if Mirabelle felt anything like what Amélie felt for Olly and it was clear she did).

She also liked that Olly had called her nose pretty.

So Amélie was doing as he advised and would continue to do so until the time, as Olly would say, Mirabelle needed her head pulled out of her ass.

She smiled to herself, delighting in her thoughts as well as the news she'd just learned from Marisol while they lingered, sipping their cocktails in a booth, news that was drifting through the hunting ground.

This being Penn and Shane had finally become engaged.

Still smiling at this thought, her attention was taken with the scene to her left, and for some reason, when she turned her head, she stopped.

Stellan was in a room with a sub, the female sub positioned just as Amélie had once done to Olly, naked on her back with her body strapped to the table, but her ankles manacled and lifted straight and high, legs spread wide.

Stellan was standing between those legs, thrusting inside.

As if he felt her regard, his focus shifted from the sub in front of him to the window.

Right to Amélie.

The instant it did, she felt the inappropriate urge to lift her hand, touch the glass, communicate something, even though she had no idea of what that something would be.

As the months had passed since their discussion in the lounge, they had not moved back to what they had been. Stellan was avoiding her and she was giving him that because she sensed that was what he needed.

But in the interim, it felt like she'd lost a friend and that was never a pleasant feeling.

Before she could do anything at that present moment, however, Stellan dipped his chin, reached out, and pulled on the chain that was between the clamps tightened on his sub's nipples. He pulled hard, Amélie could see, the sub's nipples and breasts dragging down. He also moved his mouth in a command she instantly acquiesced to, for her neck arched and it was clear she was coming.

Stellan released the chain and bent over her then, his face in her neck, mouth close to her ear and Amélie wondered briefly if he was the kind of Master who whispered loving words to his sub after she'd performed well for him or if he was someone else.

She would never know, and although the loss of his friendship did, this in particular didn't trouble her in the slightest.

She continued through the halls and again stopped, taken with a scene now to her right.

Mistress Sixx was back in town for an unknown period of time, brought there by her work.

And as she had the same kind of membership Amélie did, allowing her to visit any of Aryas's clubs, she was also back at the Honey.

She was seated in a comfortable armchair, long legs crossed, a glass of wine in one hand held up and just to the side, elbow to the arm of the chair.

A male sub was standing in front of her, several light chains with weights on the end draped at intervals along his very hard cock, his arms raised, fingers linked behind his head.

Kneeling behind him was another male sub who had the cheeks of the standing toy's ass spread open, his face buried there, eating.

It was clear the sub being eaten was challenged with keeping the chains on his dick. He seemed to be doing this quite well, even if it was taking so much effort, his entire body was covered in a sheen of sweat and his face was a vision of pleasure at what was happening at his ass, mixed with pain that was the fight to control the need to come.

Amélie also knew of this sub, though she'd never had him, regardless that he had a very nice physique and an exceptionally handsome face.

She further knew he was hetero only.

But even so, perfectly happy, it appeared, to have his ass eaten by another man if it got him in a playroom with Sixx.

As it always was, and with Sixx's talents, as Amélie expected it always would be.

Sixx was not looking for what Amélie had with Olivier. She made that clear. She'd always be seeking variation and choice, as well as challenge.

And she'd find it.

Amélie watched and saw this performance was being taken in by Mistress Sixx, who looked happy enough watching it, but she also looked as if she might suddenly get bored and reach for a magazine.

And right before Amélie was going to continue on her way, it appeared Sixx did get bored for her mouth opened and instantly the man eating got to his feet and used his hard, already oiled cock to start fucking.

The chains with their weights swung precariously with the force of the thrusts the performing sub was taking up his ass.

And not surprisingly, under his Mistress's regard, it didn't take long for pre-cum to glisten the tip of his cock, his handsome face twisting to become even more handsome as it filled with need.

Suddenly, Amélie felt Sixx's regard and she looked to her fellow Domme.

Amélie lifted her chin.

Sixx sent her the cat's-getting-her-cream smile she was famous for before she looked back to her toys.

Amélie turned away and continued moving through the halls, now keen to get where she was going.

But when she heard voices raised, she was so surprised, before she could stop herself from doing it, she ducked behind a dark playroom and did something highly inappropriate.

With the darkened glass hiding her, she peeked around it and saw Aryas and Talia down the hall close to the door to the red room, clearly in a heated discussion.

"Keep your voice down," Aryas growled, but even with his command, he did this loudly.

"Right. Fine. You want that, you got it," Talia returned, but did so not actually giving it to him as her voice was also quite loud. Her beautiful face was also filled with ire. "And when you sort out your head and understand what you *really* want, you know where to find me, baby."

With that, it looked like she was going to flounce away, and feeling ludicrous and inelegant, both feelings Amélie *never* felt and didn't much like, she ducked back and turned swiftly, moving much more hurriedly to her and Olly's room.

Although it was safe to say she was curious about what she'd just witnessed, Amélie moved resolutely focusing on what was ahead, not all she'd noted behind.

In that world, whatever happened was the business of who it was happening to, not Amélie's.

But mostly, she had something delicious to turn her attention to.

So she put it out of her mind (even though, in doing so, she hoped Stellan came around and Talia and Aryas worked something out because she missed Stellan, and regardless of what she knew of them both, she sensed Talia was perfect for her handsome friend).

When she arrived at her destination she saw, as usual, her beast had an audience. Not many. The novelty of Olivier and Amélie had worn off.

This happened. Especially when the game had been well played and the players were enjoying the fruits of victory.

For Amélie and Olly, this meant he'd moved in a month previously.

In truth, they hadn't been together very long.

But it was time. They fit. They worked splendidly in all ways that could be. When the explosion settled, it ended with Amélie and Olly tangled together magnificently.

And anyway, her house was closer to his work.

And the very first time he'd stepped foot in it, he'd only just glanced up to the glass art on her ceiling before he'd swung her in his arms, burst out laughing, and declared it, "So you, Leigh-Leigh." Then he'd kissed her.

When he was done kissing her, he'd looked around while telling her loved it.

He hadn't even moved out of the foyer.

Then again, from there you could see the living room with the view so he could easily see there was a lot to love.

Not to mention, he liked her cats.

Another grin played at her mouth as she opened the door and entered.

She stopped, leaning against the door she'd closed behind her and taking the last sip of her drink as she drew him in with all her senses.

He was strapped to a sawhorse that had a five-inch-wide padded beam on which to rest his considerable bulk. The straps that were attached to the horse and now binding Olivier were many. His arms stretched down the front legs of the beam, his legs the same at the back; there was one strap every few inches up his arms, along his shoulders, back, waist and hips and down his legs.

His bottom half was pointed toward the door, his buttocks strapped open, his tail seated up his ass, tipped high and obviously vibrating.

His balls and cock were both harnessed, the latter thick, swollen, and chained with some slack to the floor at a forward angle.

She moved to the table to her left, set her empty glass on it, and made her way to her steed.

She wisped a light touch along the indent of his ass cheek.

"Baby," he growled.

Another smile while Amélie bent to him and touched her lips to the opposite cheek. She then ran her tongue along the outside of his ass strap.

His body gave a powerful buck, taking the horse with him.

"Fuck, *baby.*"

She kissed the small of his back and ran her fingers through his tail.

"Amélie," he bit off.

It was time to take care of her sweet beast.

Pausing only to drag the nails of both hands hard down both the cheeks of his ass, she smiled at the fierce growl he emitted that ended in a groan, all this through another powerful buck, moving the horse at least half a foot; she walked to his front, pulling the remote out from where she'd tucked it in her bra.

She arrived at her destination and crouched down so they were face-to-face.

And there she saw it, that magnificent need.

She turned his tail to high.

His beautiful face saturated with pleasure.

"Come at will, my beast," she whispered.

And she watched with great satisfaction as he did.

"Yes, God, don't stop, Olly."

Amélie was on her knees at the side of her couch in their living room, hands planted in the arm of the couch, her Olly's big brute planted (mostly) up her ass.

He had one strong arm wrapped around her chest to hold her steady, one arm slanted down, thumb at her clit, long finger buried in her pussy.

"Think I can stop, Leigh-Leigh, you're fuckin' crazy," he grunted.

She almost smiled but he gave her more and her head snapped back.

"Good?" he ground out.

"Yes, baby," she whispered.

"So fuckin' hot," he growled, gliding in and out, not hard but strong and *deep*. "Goddamned tight. Leigh, you're gonna need to come for me."

"More."

"Christ, baby."

"More, Olly. Please."

He drove in.

And that was all she needed.

Her head dropped forward as her body shuddered its climax violently in his hold and he murmured, "My Leigh. Always so fuckin' pretty."

And her body trembled more at his words.

Through her orgasm, she took him up her ass and then she took his cum up her ass, his groans in her ear as his finger automatically fucked her pussy, those of his other hand finding, squeezing, and pulling hard on her nipple.

So, it wasn't as intense, but Amélie came again, this time doing it with Olly.

Olly carefully pulled out almost before his own tremors ceased and she bit her lip as he removed his hand but slid his still-hard cock along the wet, sensitive area between her legs, the hand he had at her breast going to hold his own weight at the arm of the couch (though he pressed a good deal of it into her), the other one holding her tight to him under her breasts.

His forehead, though, he rested on her shoulder.

"Are you good, darling?" she asked.

"So warm and tight up there, baby. Beautiful. Fuckin' love takin' your ass."

She loved it too.

"Mm," she purred.

He turned his head and kissed her neck. "You're starting to drip. Gotta clean you and let Cleo free."

"Mm," she purred again.

She felt him smile in her neck and then she felt him move away. But he moved her with him, up into his arms, taking her to the master bath off their bedroom.

He cleaned her up and himself. She pulled on a robe. He pulled on a pair of low-slung, soft-knit pajama bottoms she'd given to him for Christmas after she'd discovered all the ones he owned he'd had since college and they were falling apart.

She had not thrown them away.

But she had noted, if they were clean, he wore the ones she gave him.

"Bath for you later, make sure you're all good before we hit the sack," he told her after he shifted her loosely, front to front, in his arms. "First, make sure the kids are okay."

He called their pets "the kids."

It was cute.

It was Olly.

He gave her a squeeze and a light kiss before he let her go and wandered out of their room to go get Cleo, the taking care of the animals portion of their living arrangement falling on him as he got up earlier than she did.

This was also because he was a pushover. Even bigger than her.

Thus Cleopatra had given him her undying love.

Stasia still slept on his pillow by his head. But other than that, as with Amélie, she was choosy with how much and when she gave her attention.

Still, when she slunk close, Amélie noted she did it closer to Olly than her mummy.

This did not bother Amélie. Whatever love Stasia wanted to get after the life she'd lived before she came to her true home, Amélie was happy to give her.

And Amélie well knew love from Olly was the best there could be.

She wandered out of their room back to where Olly had just fucked her on the couch.

As she did, she didn't miss the vase of perfect red roses that sat proudly at the edge of the island that delineated the kitchen from the vast great room.

Olly bought her flowers every week. They were not always red roses, but they were always roses and they were always perfect.

She had no idea why he did this. In other ways he was not romantically inclined (at least not like that).

And he didn't make a big deal about it. It was just that one day the last ones he'd given her were there, and before the bloom went off those roses, the next day new ones were in their place with a note that always said the same:

> *Leigh-Leigh,*
> *You're it for me.*
> *Olly*

In the dozens of roses he'd bought her, knowing countless others were to come, same type, same note, just different colors, Amélie knew she'd never take them for granted.

Because a man like Olly was not romantically inclined like that.

He gave that to her because she was *it* for him and he wanted to be certain she never forgot it.

He could win the lottery. Be discovered by an agent and become an action hero movie star making tens of millions of dollars a movie. Buy her diamonds and yachts.

But the best thing she'd ever get from him was his roses.

That was, the best thing she'd ever get from him, outside of everything that was just her Olly, was his beautiful roses.

A smile tinkering at her mouth, Amélie collapsed on the sofa and drew a throw up her body.

The fire was lit in the gas fireplace that stood between the couch and the floor-to-ceiling windows that had that amazing view off Camelback Mountain.

It soon gave her a view of her Olly in his pajama pants, who had not only released Cleopatra but also released Chevy (short for *chevalier*), their new dog. A mutt that it took Amélie precisely five point seven seconds to talk Olly into adopting when she'd made him come to Dr. Hill's to have a look at the poor baby.

Olly was playing fetch with Chevy in expensive pajama bottoms by a negative-edge pool in a pricey house on an exclusive lot on a beautiful mountain.

He did not look like he didn't fit.

He looked like he was right where he was supposed to be.

This, Amélie knew, was because he was.

Olly got tired of fetch before Chevy (as usual) and since he had opposable thumbs and access to treats, it was his decision that they both come in, something they did, Chevy far more exuberantly.

The dog bounded to her. She gave him cuddles, got kisses, and finally Olly wrestled his mutt away but he only could do this successfully because he tossed some treats into the room that Chevy dashed to retrieve.

All so he could lay claim to Amélie.

This he did, pulling the throw from her and exchanging it with his body, trapping her under him on the couch and nuzzling her neck with his nose and chin.

"Dad's house, babe," he said there, reminding her. "Dinner Saturday."

"It's on the calendar, Olly."

He lifted his head and looked down at her. "And got a call from Barclay today. This new chick he has he's liking. He wants to know if we can set up dinner, go on a double date."

She was glad of this for Barclay. He was a lovely man. He needed to find someone to make him happy.

However, she was skeptical about this dinner.

"By that meaning he wants you to suss her out and give your stamp of approval," she returned. "And because he thinks the world of you, even if they work in ways you can't see, if you say one word, he'll dump her, possibly exceptionally foolishly."

Olly grinned. "Doesn't work that way, babe. He wants *you* to suss her out and give your stamp of approval. So if you say one word, he'll totally dump her because he thinks you're the shit."

"Ah," she murmured.

Olly kept grinning but did it ordering, "You get a bad vibe, you save my brother from headache."

"Is that my job as your woman?" she asked. "To cast judgment on all your friends' girlfriends and possibly fuck up their lives?"

"Yep," he answered casually. "Least one of 'em."

She rolled her eyes to the arm of the couch over her head.

He dropped his head and kissed her jaw but did it chuckling.

When he lifted it again, she rolled her eyes back and saw he was serious.

"You know if Aryas took care of Branch?" he asked.

What she knew was that for some time, this had been preying on Olly's mind.

"I know you know that I shared your concerns with him and I told you Aryas shared the same concerns. He said he'd handle it. I know it's been some time but he's Aryas. If he says that, he handles it."

"Ask, babe, because Branch isn't returning calls."

At this news, Amélie began to feel troubled.

Branch Dillinger was not the kind of man who showed at Chad and Annie's for beer, lots of food that was really bad for you, and football (like Amélie and Olly did).

But Olly and he met out for a few beers on a somewhat regular occasion and Branch had been to either Olly's house (sometimes when Amélie was there before he put his place on the market and moved in with her) and her place (when Olly was with her, even before they were living together).

Branch was not overtly friendly. He was definitely not talkative.

But he was courteous and when he spoke, he was interesting. It was clear he was respectful of women because he was very much that with Amélie and not because she was a Domme and he was submissive (this, Olly did not share outright, but did confirm nonverbally with a slight jerk of his chin when she'd mentioned it—though he didn't need to confirm; with time spent together, she'd read it all over Branch). That was just his manner.

It was also clear he liked Olly a good deal, even if it was mostly intuition and his being somewhat a fixture in their lives that shared that.

"I'll ask Aryas," she offered.

"Don't bother. Take it direct. I'll ask him," Olly replied.

And he could. For Amélie, delightfully, with Olly came his dad, brother, sister, Barclay, Chad, Annie, and his many other friends.

For Olly, with Amélie came Mira, Trey, Felicia, Romy, Talia, her many other friends . . . and Aryas.

They'd had a moving-in party. Everyone came.

And they got along well.

She'd been right.

In every way he could be, even some she hadn't anticipated, Olivier Hawkes was a dream come true.

And obviously getting to that had been well proven, over and over (and over many more times), as worth the risk.

Her thoughts returned to the man happily trapping her to her own couch when he cupped her cheek in his big hand.

"What's on your mind, baby?" he asked, his lovely, deep voice that was lovely just in idle life conversation was even lovelier, sounding low, trembling through her belly and chest because he spoke while both were pressed to her.

Dream come true.

She slid a hand up his chest and rounded his back, arching her own to share with him she wanted more of his weight. He got the message and gave it to her.

"Babe," he prompted.

"I was just thinking you were worth the risk."

He'd clearly read her mood but still hadn't considered that was where her thoughts lay because his head twitched before his face warmed and he dropped it closer.

"Dream come true," she whispered, taking in all that was Olly right there in front of her face and weighing her warmly into their couch.

"Shut up," he growled.

She saw the feeling burning in his eyes but she still snapped, "That's not nice."

"Shut up," he repeated, still growling.

"Olly—"

"Love you so damned much, I let myself think about it, honest to Christ, it makes me dizzy."

Amélie shut up.

Olly did not.

"Nothin' better, not in this world, nothin' and I know that in a way I'll know it until I die, nothin' better than knowin' you feel that too."

She melted under him.

"Olly—"

"Shut up," he said yet again.

She felt her eyes narrow and opened her mouth.

But she said nothing.

Her magnificent Olly's mouth crashed down on hers and he kissed her quiet.

When he was done doing that, he lifted his head and said, "Time for our bath."

Our bath.

Lovely.

And it clearly was because with no further ado, Olly knifed off of her, took her up with him, and they had their bath.

Then, tangled up in a way that was the best part of the tangle that was them, after their bath, they went to bed and Amélie fell asleep trapped under her sweet beast.

Read on for a preview of the next book in
Kristen Ashley's The Honey Series

The Farthest Edge

Available June 2017 from St. Martin's Griffin

Prologue

Of Course I'm Going to Kill You

Gerald Raines turned the corner into his bedroom and flipped the switch just inside the door that would illuminate the lights on the nightstand.

They didn't turn on.

His first thought was always his first thought when something went wrong.

To blame whatever wasn't working on his wife.

His second thought was always his second thought, or at least the one he'd had the last two years.

That being the reminder the bitch had moved out and divorced him.

He flipped the switch repeatedly, and when nothing happened, he stomped into the dark room, grousing, "I do not need this shit today."

"Not another move."

The voice came from the dark, rough, male, deep, quiet, calm.

Gerald's entire body froze solid.

He knew that voice.

Impossible. Totally impossible, he thought.

But what he knew was that if anyone could come back from the dead, it would be a member of that team.

That *damned* team.

Gerald didn't move even when the shadow formed in front of him, tall, lean. Healthy.

Impossible.

It got close, lifted its arm, and Gerald felt a circle of cold steel pressed tight to his forehead.

Not a ghost.

Real.

It couldn't be.

But it was.

"John," he whispered.

"I'd say you got nothin' to worry about," the shadow replied. "They're all dead. But you do got somethin' to worry about because, contrary to officially unofficial reports, I'm not."

"How did you—"

Gerald stopped speaking when the cold hardness pressed deeper into his forehead, forcing him to arch back several inches.

In that moment, it took grave effort not to foul himself.

But when the voice came again, it was still eerily calm.

"You set us up."

"It was the mission," Gerald returned swiftly, raising his hands to the side, showing he was unarmed, not a threat.

The shadow kept the gun to his forehead.

"You set us up."

"It's always the mission, John," he reminded him. "In the briefing notes, the estimates of success are communicated and they're never good." His tone turned from desperate to desperately flattering. "That's why we'd send your team. You had the skills to beat the odds. And you did. You always did."

Until they didn't because the mission had been designed that way.

"You set us up."

"It was the job, John. You know that."

"It was a goddamned," he pressed Gerald's head back with the gun as his shadowed face got closer, "*suicide mission.* With my team's corpses right now rotting in that fucking jungle, except Benetta and Lex, who were blown to fuckin' bits right in front of Rob and me, Rob dyin' in my goddamned fuckin' arms not two hours later. Do not stand there lying to me, telling me it was *the job.* You . . . *set us up.*"

Gerald tried for bravado, straightening his shoulders. "You understood the work we do, John. You signed up for it."

He took off the pressure of the gun and moved back inches but he didn't leave Gerald's space nor did he drop the weapon.

"What I understand is that you had a shot at a deal with Castillo, he had a beef with the team because *you* sent us to take out his brother, somethin' we did, and Lex almost bit it during *that* mission, so you offered us up, ducks in a barrel so you could use Castillo's network to get your arms where you needed them."

Jesus, how did he know that much?

Goddamn.

That team.

They could do anything.

And they did.

Even one of them surviving a mission that was designed to kill them all.

"Those fighters needed weapons and they're the only hope our government has to keep peace in that region without us engaging our own soldiers to do it at great cost of money and lives," Gerald shot back in his defense.

"So you set up your own fucking team to go down?"

"Castillo was an important asset," Gerald returned. "The only shot we had. Every mission, every move, we weigh the gains and losses, John, and you know how we reach those scores."

"We were your soldiers. *Our country's* soldiers. And you sacrificed us for shot at a deal with a sleazy arms dealer? Who, by the

way, fucked you the minute he could and didn't deliver one goddamned gun where you needed it."

Damn, he knew everything.

Gerald changed tactics.

"As far as your country's concerned, John, you don't exist. You
gave up your lives. You kept your dog tags but gave up your identities.
All seven of you did. You were ghosts before you became *this* ghost."

"We were," he pushed the gun back to Gerald's forehead, "*your*
soldiers."

That was true.

But in that game, it didn't matter in the slightest.

There were no soldiers.

In that game, everyone was a pawn.

"I have to make tough decisions every day," Gerald spat, losing
patience so he wouldn't lose control of his fear. "You can't imagine,
you can't even——"

The shadow cut him off, stating, "I got a tough decision to
make too."

Gerald felt his bowels loosening.

God, he was going to die at the hands of a man he'd personally
handpicked to be trained as a killing machine.

"Are you going to kill me?"

"Of course I'm going to kill you," the shadow replied calmly.

The bowels didn't go but Gerald felt the wet trickle down his leg.

There was the barest sneer in his voice when the shadow whispered, "Jesus, did you spend even a minute in the field?"

He smelled the urine.

Humiliated, terrified, Gerald stood there, staring into the dark,
featureless face of a man who'd been trained to do a great many
things, do them in a variety of ways, do them exceptionally well, and
one of those things was to kill, and he said nothing.

"You didn't," the shadow kept whispering. "You sent us to
dirty, rotten, stinking places, dealing with filth, doing shit that
marked our souls, bought us each a ticket straight to hell, and you

haven't spent a minute in the field. In your bedroom, you got one shot to be a real man, to die with dignity, and you wet yourself. Fuck me."

"Just get it over with," Gerald whispered back.

"One each," the shadow returned.

Gerald's head shook reflexively with confusion but when the gun pressed deeper, he stopped it.

"One?" he asked.

The shadow didn't answer.

"One what?" he pushed.

"One whatever I want," the shadow replied. "One day. One week. One month. One year. One for each. Five of them. Maybe a year for Rob. A day for Benetta. A week for Piz. A month for Lex. Another for Di. However I want it. You could have five years. You could have five days. Whatever I want. That's all you got. Then it's over for you."

And with that and not another word, the cold metal left his head, the shadow left his vision, and without a sound, he felt the presence leave the room.

And Gerald Raines stood beside his bed, his shoes sinking into the carpet in a puddle of his own hot piss.

One

Set Up a Meet

BRANCH

Two years, three months later . . .

The man dropped to his feet.

Without hesitation, even though his jaw was hanging loose from its hinge, Branch kicked the man's face with his boot.

The head shot back, the body moving with it, but no noise was made, no movement outside what came with the kick.

The guy was out.

And Branch didn't give that first fuck if he ever checked back in.

Without another glance, he turned and walked away, pulling his phone from his back pocket.

He kept walking, out of the building, right to his truck while engaging.

"Branch," Aryas said as greeting.

"It's done," Branch replied, beeping the locks on his truck.

"Message conveyed?" Aryas asked for confirmation.

"Absolutely."

"Good. Send me a bill."

"Will do. Later."

"Later."

Branch disconnected, swung up in his truck and drove away.

Eleven months later . . .

Branch parked directly in front of her house.

It had just gone two thirty in the morning.

He got out of his truck, his eyes to the home in front of him, not for the first time noting that the Willo Historic District of Phoenix was the shit.

Especially her place.

Second house from a dead end that led to a thick, tall hedge beyond which was a parking lot off Central. The location gave the property an odd sense of quiet, even right in the city close to a busy street like Central, and also a definite sense of privacy on that dead end.

He kept his gaze on her place, the abundant tall trees and full shrubs around her house making it look like something not out of Phoenix, but from the East Coast.

Her water bill had to be off the charts.

She had a ton of planters bursting with flowers decorating the front steps of her bungalow.

Yup.

Definitely off the charts.

His eyes turned right.

She didn't have a garage, just a carport, but she didn't need one with those trees shading the house and her lot. When summer hit Phoenix and temperatures hit 115, her place would be thirty degrees cooler, a little oasis in a vast desert valley.

He walked up the front walk but took the path that led along her front porch to the side. Her drop-top white Fiat was parked under the carport, Branch headed by it, seeing the interior was red and white, sporty, cute, such a girl car, it was a wonder it didn't reach out and smear lipstick on his jeans when he walked past it.

Two side doors to the house, one from the floorplan he'd downloaded he knew led to a laundry room, the one closer to the back of her house let you into her kitchen.

He saw the moon gleam off the pool beyond the house, but just barely due to the foliage and plant-covered pergolas that acted as covered pathways between house, carport and the small studio that stood at the back side of her property.

He stopped at the door to the kitchen and made a decision.

He'd inspect the studio later.

He picked the lock to her house.

He moved in and turned immediately to disable the alarm at the panel, feeling his mouth get tight when it didn't buzz.

She hadn't set it.

She didn't even have a badge in the window that said she had an alarm.

She also didn't have a dog.

And further, she didn't have motion sensor lights outside.

But she did have a fucking car that sat under an open carport that screamed a girl lived there.

He drew in breath, turned to face the kitchen, and went completely still.

The floorplan showed the house had three sections of rooms, each section running the length of the house. One side office, laundry room, kitchen. Down the middle, living room opening directly into dining room opening directly into a family room. Other side, guest room, bathroom, small study, Arizona room jutting off the back. The bottom-level ceilings had been lowered so a master bedroom, with a walk-in closet and master bath, could be set in the attic.

None of the rooms was big except the master.

But in that day of great rooms where kitchens were open, large and part of the house, Branch hadn't been prepared for this room to be so small, downright snug, filled everywhere, even if he was seeing it by moonlight, with shit that declared boldly a person who liked cooking lived there.

There was a small breakfast nook beyond the counter with the sink that faced the big picture window at the back of the house. There was a little table there, only space for two ladder-back chairs on each side. Plants hung from hooks in the ceiling and sat on high stands, making gazing out the window seem as if it were done through a jungle of leaves.

This was not a kitchen.

This was a kitchen in a house that someone had made a *home*.

Branch turned and exited immediately, pulling in oxygen when it seemed his breath might turn shallow, and his eyes hit on the studio.

A better place to start.

He moved there, noting the plantation shutters on the windows had been carefully closed. No one could see inside. Not from any angle.

He picked the lock, went in, pulled his small Maglite from his pocket and shined it around the space.

He knew this was her playroom before he'd entered but right then he saw that she didn't hide it under sheets and tarps, just behind shutters.

Branch shifted the light around, seeing a horse, a bench, a table, all of them good quality. It cost a mint to outfit a good playroom and she didn't make do. She'd been investing. Making smart purchases that would look good, stand strong during play and last a while.

Fashionable sink in the corner set in an attractive wood vanity, two matching tall, slim cupboards on each side.

He moved there, looked through the vanity and cupboards. Thick towels. Washcloths. Wet wipes. Soap. Bottles of anti-bacterial foam. Cleaning supplies. A large box of condoms. A little basket filled with some cosmetics—powder, lipsticks, gloss. Another filled with first-aid supplies—Band-Aids, bottles of antiseptic, tubes of ointment, gauze, cotton.

He closed the door to the cupboard, turned and shined the light around the room. Moving across the space, he noted hooks on the walls, in the ceiling, eyes in the floor, all looking sturdy. Whoever put them in might have wondered why or he'd been hers. But whoever that was knew what they were doing.

There was a tall cabinet and a large dresser across the room, both in the wood that made up the vanity and the cupboards. It all matched, was heavy and dark but attractive, giving the space the definite feel of a playroom, not a dungeon. It was stylish and handsome, even warm, somewhere you'd want to stay awhile.

He didn't think as he opened the top cupboard doors of the cabinet and shined the light in, feeling what he found there in his dick.

Cats. Whips. Switches. Flogs. Paddles. Some straps. Some harnesses. All hanging from hooks. All well organized and well maintained. All also excellent quality. Not many, but again, quality, not quantity, was what she was clearly going for.

He closed the doors and crouched down to the two drawers at the bottom of the cabinet, opening them. The top one had silk ropes, some chains, shackles, cuffs. The bottom drawer was full of leather straps with cinches attached.

Branch straightened, moved to the dresser. Nothing littered the top, so he opened the first drawer.

What he found there made his balls draw up.

Carefully placed in what looked like purple silk-lined, custommade grooves were her toys. Plugs. Cocks. Vibrators. The first two in an impressive range of lengths, girths, and shapes. If they had them, remotes were placed at the side of the toy they controlled. There was also a complicated cock ring, rabbit ears at the front for clit stimulation, and a strap that would lead between the balls to a bullet that could be inserted in the anus, all of it obviously vibrated—triple the fun.

She liked ass.

Not many of her kind didn't.

He didn't think on that either.

He closed the drawer, opened the next, and found baskets,

carefully organized and containing a large variety of necessary items. Lubes. Oils. Gels. Lotions.

Next drawer down he found scarves and eye masks, no sensory deprivation, no ball gags, no hoods.

Putting a hand in and touching the fabric, Branch noted she had a fondness for silk and all of them were either dark purple, deep blue, or black.

He also noted in an intense way that almost made him feel something, not only in his dick and balls, but somewhere else, that she had her shit tight.

She knew who she was. She knew what she liked. And what she liked wasn't common or vulgar, as many people might see it (but he didn't, he still couldn't deny he liked the way she obviously played it).

There was an elegance to her style.

It wasn't about ball gags and he didn't find a single strap on.

She got the life.

But she did it her way.

Yeah, that definitely almost made him feel something.

Almost.

The next drawer down, he found more harnesses, these for smaller uses, balls, cock, jaw. There were also two carved boxes he pulled out and opened, their original use was for rings or jewelry but she'd put four cock rings in the purple velvet in one and a number of gleaming nipple clamps with and without chains tangled against the blue silk lining in the other.

He put the boxes back, closed the drawer, straightened and took one last look around.

It was a well-equipped playroom. She could get creative and be clean and safe doing it.

He cast his eyes down to the top of the dresser, lifted his hand and swiped it along the top, shining his flashlight on his fingers when he was done.

Dust.

She hadn't been in there in months.

He drew a breath in through his nose, switched off the light, and turned his attention across the studio toward the wall beyond which was her house.

Aryas had made him an offer.

He needed to make a decision.

So he needed to go there.

He went there.

The inspection he made of her house was cursory. She liked furniture. A lot of it. She liked it to be comfortable. She liked knickknacks, all of which, if he'd paid much attention, something he didn't do, likely had a story or meant something to her.

The Willo district might have been set with land purchases made in the Victorian era, but homes hadn't been added until the '20s and '30s. Her bungalow, his research had told him, had gone up in the late '20s.

Still, she decorated like that particular queen was going to rise up, make a visit and cast her judgment.

The heavy, cluttered, busy, flowery, frilly, fringy shit was not Branch's style.

Then again, he didn't have a style and he wasn't moving in.

He was just deciding if he wanted the woman who lived there to fuck him.

So how she decorated didn't factor.

On this thought, he moved from the living room up the narrow, steep-angled stairs that had been added at the front of the house when the attic had been converted.

The stairs led to a landing that had one of those plush lounge chairs women liked, a marble-topped table and standing lamp, all illuminated in that moment by the only window to the space that was original; the others were two sunlights set in the ceiling. Those sun lights would let in light, but with her trees, they wouldn't bake the room.

He turned to take the last short flight of steps that went from a right angle to the other stairs and saw her four-poster bed.

It was colossal.

Definitely made for the space, not something you got in a store.

Branch wondered if she'd had it made.

Then he wondered why he wondered.

With that, he stopped wondering and walked to the bed.

She was sleeping, smack in the middle of it.

Her huge mass of dark curls were easily visible against the light sheets and her small body barely took up any of the large mattress.

He looked away immediately and did the checks he needed to do.

Silk ropes hidden under the bed, tied securely to the feet of the footboard and headboard. Nothing but a vibrator for her in the left nightstand (also excellent quality and a premier brand).

The bathroom off the left side of the room was sunken, the ceilings in the eaves of the house, so the large, oval tub with jets at the end was recessed even further, in the floor and down two steps. The shower at the top, though, was big enough for two (or three).

And the room was pale green and baby pink and also decorated busy, frilly, flowery, so over the top, it nearly made Branch smile.

Nearly.

The walk-in closet to the other side of the room was close quarters, nowhere near as big as the bathroom (but still large), two steps down and stuffed full of clothes.

In fact, he'd never seen so many clothes. And shoes. Shelves and shelves of them. And handbags.

She kept her playroom neat and organized.

Her closet, however, was a disaster.

He found what he was looking for, silently slid it out, made sure the closet door was tightly shut and again engaged his flashlight to look into her toy chest.

He almost didn't bite back the low whistle when he saw how she liked to play in the intimacy of her bedroom.

Picking up a huge, black plastic phallus, he stared at it, his teeth in his lip to bite back his reaction.

"She likes to test a man's manhood, that's for fuckin' sure," he muttered.

Unbidden, thoughts of that cock shoved up his ass while he was in her massive frilly bed in her frilly room in her frilly house, maybe with his face stuffed in her wet pussy, Branch dropped the toy, closed the chest and pushed it back where it was meant to be.

Without delay, not looking at her sleeping in bed or making a sound, he exited the house, locked up behind him and walked to his truck.

He got in, fired his baby up, turned around in her drive without switching on his headlights, and he was all the way down her street before he turned them on.

He drove to his condo, parked in the underground parking and took the stairs at a jog up to the fifth floor.

He let himself into his place.

He had a TV. A DVD player. A sectional. A coffee table. Two stools at the bar (even if he was the only one who'd sat on either of them). And a bed in the one bedroom with a single nightstand and one lamp.

He had blinds.

He further had dishes. One pot. One skillet. One pint glass. And a set of four forks and spoons but only three knives he bought at Goodwill. He also had a bread knife, a butcher knife, and a toaster.

These, and some clothes, belts, and shoes in his closet, his truck and his gear that was stored somewhere else were all his worldly possessions.

He could move in with Evangeline Brooks in her frilly house in an hour, not needing his furniture, not having any problem at all with leaving it behind.

On that thought, he went to the packet on his coffee table and upended it.

One DVD fell out.

Aryas's handwriting in red marker was across the clear front.

Watch this, it said, *and call me.*